Date Due

SEP 1 2 1955		
DEC 20 1962		
Dec 21 '64		
DEC 2 8 1967		
DEC 3 1974		
ⓖ	PRINTED IN U. S. A.	

A NEW
CHRISTMAS
TREASURY

*With More Stories for
Reading Aloud*

Edited by
ROBERT and MARIA LOHAN

STEPHEN DAYE PRESS
NEW YORK

COPYRIGHTS AND ACKNOWLEDGMENTS

The editors and the publishers express their appreciation to the authors and publishers listed below for permission to reprint various selections, including copyrighted material. Every effort has been made to trace all copyright owners; if any acknowledgment has been inadvertently omitted, the publishers will gladly make the necessary correction in the next printing.

Appleton-Century-Crofts, Inc.: for "Bid the Tapers Twinkle" from *The Man Who Caught the Weather* by Bess Streeter Aldrich. Copyright, 1936, D. Appleton-Century Co., Inc. Reprinted by permission of the publishers. Two stories — Hezekiah Butterworth's "My Grandmother's Grandmother's Christmas Candle" and W. D. Howells' "Christmas Every Day" — are reprinted from the same publishers' *St. Nicholas Magazine*.

Brandt & Brandt: for "Christmas Eve's Day" by Barry Benefield, originally published in *Woman's Home Companion* and copyright 1926 by Barry Benefield.

Kenneth Irving Brown: for his story "The Christmas Guest," copyright 1924 by The Atlantic Monthly Company, Boston 16, Mass.

The Cresset Press, Ltd.: for "A Christmas Gift" by T. F. Powys from *An Anthology of Christmas Prose and Verse*, published by Cresset.

Doubleday & Company, Inc.: for "A Day of Pleasant Bread" from *Adventures in Friendship* by David Grayson, copyright 1910 by Doubleday & Company, Inc.; for "White Kid Gloves" from *Christmas Gift* by Margaret Cousins, copyright 1952 by Margaret Cousins, reprinted by permission of the publishers.

Zona Gale (Breese) Estate: for "Human" by Zona Gale.

Harcourt, Brace and Company, Inc. for "As Ye Sow" copyright 1947, 1949 by Dorothy Canfield Fisher, reprinted from her volume *Four-Square* by permission of Harcourt, Brace and Company, Inc.; for "The Donkey of God" from *The Donkey of God and Other Stories* by Louis Untermeyer, copyright 1932 by Harcourt, Brace and Company, Inc.

Walter Hard: for "Holy Night" from his book *A Mountain Township*, published by Stephen Daye Press.

James Hilton: for "Twilight of the Wise."

Alfred A. Knopf, Inc.: for "Christmas Eve," the first section of *Christmas Eve* by Alistair Cooke, copyright 1952 by Alistair Cooke; for "Song from Heaven." reprinted, in the Reader's Digest condensation, from *Silent Night* by Hertha Pauli, copyright 1943 by Alfred A. Knopf, Inc. Both selections used by permission of the publishers.

Copyrights and Acknowledgments

Manuel Komroff and Esquire, Inc.: for their permission to reprint Mr. Komroff's "What Is a Miracle?"

Little, Brown & Co.: for "The Boy Who Laughed at Santa Claus" from *Good Intentions* by Ogden Nash, copyright 1942 by Ogden Nash, by permission of the publishers.

William Morris Agency: for "Signor Santa" by Jo Pagano, copyright 1935 by The Atlantic Monthly Company.

Quickborn-Verlag: for "Homesickness Night," especially translated for this volume and taken from *Mien bunte Tüller* by Rudolf Kinau, a book of stories in low German dialect, by permission of the publishers, Quickborn-Verlag, Hamburg, Germany.

Reader's Digest: for permission to use their condensation of Hertha Pauli's *Silent Night*, published by Alfred A. Knopf, Inc.

Rinehart & Company, Inc.: for "Eminence" from *Children and Older People*, copyright 1931 by Ruth Suckow, reprinted by permission of the publishers.

Dorothy Thompson: for "Once on Christmas."

Ann Watkins, Inc.: for "Mr. Huffam," copyright 1933 by Hugh Walpole; for "Midnight in the Stable," copyright 1938 by Elizabeth Goudge.

Contents

Contents

"GREAT TIDINGS, STRANGE AND TRUE"

CHRISTMAS EVERYWHERE

Introduction

LIKE CHRISTMAS itself, the Christmas story renews its magic every year. That is as true for those who lovingly put together a book of stories as it is for the reader, which, in its own way, explains this book. This volume of Christmas reading is both a companion piece to the earlier *Christmas Tales for Reading Aloud* and a separate and different book. More than half of the selections are eminently adapted to reading aloud—at Christmas parties, before club members and friends, at school— with the vivid, lively action, the bold characterization and entertaining or suspenseful incidents that make them wonderful instruments for the art of the interpreter. But there are also several longer stories that the reader may prefer to enjoy in silent reading. All selections except one appear complete, without abridgment.

At least three of the longer stories and several of the others appear in a Christmas anthology for the first time, to the editors' knowledge. But "firsts" were not primarily important in the selection of the stories and poems. The ultimate consideration was, simply, enjoyment heightened by variety—good stories of genuine literary merit and of widely diversified backgrounds and styles. Here the reader will find realism and fantasy, disarming humor and gentle touches of sadness, religious sentiment, adventure, and the exhilarating tingle of the unexpected. There are stories of Christmas in the warmth of the family hearth, and, of course, several stories about children, for children—especially the grown-up children of holiday time. There are stories about Christmases celebrated in many faraway places and in other times, and there are stories that reveal the Christmas touch in surprising ways throughout the year. Not to be forgotten are the half dozen or so poems and carols, true treasures of Christmas literature, which echo and re-echo the enduring spirit of this most joyful of seasons.

While the uncontested favorites of storytelling have not been forgotten—indeed, what would Christmas be without the familiar classics we all of us love?—the editors are particularly happy to include so much that is new and little known. Hugh Walpole's fascinating story of the mysterious Mr. Huffam is a memorable example of brilliant storytelling and is hardly known to most readers of Walpole's many books; despite its length, many readers will be unable to resist reading all of it aloud. That it will take the place, in this volume, of the undisputed Christmas classic, "A Christmas Carol"—already included in *Christmas Tales for Reading Aloud*—is a fairly certain guess.

Especially translated for this collection is the charming portrait of the famous musical family of Johann Sebastian Bach, taken from one of the most widely read novels of the nineteenth century by A. E. Brachvogel, popular German novelist, dramatist, and short story writer; apparently this is the first time any of his works has appeared in English. Rudolf Kinau's laconic account of a typical seaman's holiday ashore is also translated here for the first time; although it loses something of the vigor of the original, which is in almost untranslatable dialect, it is an interesting example of the work of one of the newer contemporary German writers.

We take an especial pride in having the moving "Holy Night" by Walter Hard, an outstanding contemporary New England poet who excels in the characteristic rhythm of Vermont speech. Again, here is an irresistible invitation to read aloud.

Laughter is one of the precious gifts of a joyous Christmas festival. To children it is exemplified in the image of a fat and jolly Santa. There are three particularly entertaining pieces on the Old Gentleman, ranging from Ogden Nash's impudent rhymes—"*All you who sneer at Santa Claus / Beware the fate of Jabez Dawes*"—to a delightful "report" of a modern-day Santa by the urbane Alistair Cooke. Jo Pagano, who has written several fine novels and stories about the Italian-Americans of California, has never done a more delightful story than "Signor Santa," which is unqualifiedly recommended to every family that has ever harbored a wearer of the red suit and the white whiskers. Adult readers will relish this trio.

For mothers and fathers especially, the juxtaposition of Ruth Suckow's sharply drawn picture of a sheltered child and Dorothy Canfield Fisher's discerning and heartwarming "As Ye Sow . . . " will strike a responsive chord. Both of these stories by noted American writers, one a Midwesterner, the other a New Englander, deal with the Christmas entertainments that parents attend, with so much love and trepidation, each year.

The recollections of Christmas Everywhere boast, if it may be said, several unusual selections by writers of half a dozen nations. Karin Michaelis was an extremely prolific Danish writer, author of scores of novels and popular children's books until her death after the Second World War. Her story of a strange Christmas celebration has the dark overtones of a typically European legend. Of the eternally popular "Silent Night" little need be said, but Hertha Pauli's lovely account gives the true story of the beginnings, high in the Austrian Alps, of this most famous of Christmas carols. This one selection is a condensation of the author's longer story about her two little-known compatriots, who gave the world this beloved song. All readers— and this surely includes everyone who has ever read a Christmas story—all readers who once smiled affectionately at the gallant young lovers of O. Henry's inimitable classic, "The Gift of the Magi," will be intrigued by the somewhat more sophisticated variation in Hans Fallada's lighthearted picture of a charming young German couple. This story, like Fallada's best-selling novel *Little Man, What Now?*, recreates the atmosphere of the Europe of the early 1930's.

Of the other well-known writers, British and American, who complete this section, two who wrote in the last half of the nineteenth century stand apart as representatives of very different streams of writing. The tale of two brothers, one gentle and honorable, the other cold and selfishly ambitious, is an anonymous gem of Victorian prose that modern readers will read with a smile for its old-fashioned melodramatics, while at the same time they find themselves unexpectedly absorbed in its unfolding. At the other end of the scale stands the author of "A Journey into Christmas," in his time a breaker of forms and something of a revolutionary in American writing, who set a bold new style of Western fiction. Owen Wister is the author of one of the most famous of American books, *The Virginian,* in which he created the prototype of the fearless, gentlemanly, resourceful hero so familiar to all devotees of the "Western"—movie or literary variety. It was Wister who wrote for *The Virginian* perhaps the most famous single line of dialogue in all American fiction: "When you call me that, *smile!*" His long story of the Colorado of the 90's and one cowboy's lonely search for companionship makes unusual Christmas reading.

These are some of the highlights; the reader will have the satisfaction of discovering others for himself.

One final word about the selections. Robert Lohan, who compiled *Christmas Tales for Reading Aloud,* started to gather new stories for this volume not long afterward. His enthusiasm for this project, for which he determinedly made time from the numerous others which claimed his attention as teacher and writer, soon enlisted the interest and support of his wife. I drew up the final table of contents, a task to which my husband had looked forward with customary eagerness and which, through the onset of a final illness, he could not himself undertake. I could not have completed the book alone if so much of the foundation had not already been set in place by a devoted editor.

Now, we shall let the stories take over. A very Merry Christmas, and good reading all the year 'round!

MARIA LOHAN

A Prayer for Christmas Morning

HENRY VAN DYKE

The day of joy returns, Father in Heaven,
and crowns another year with peace and good will.

Help us rightly to remember the birth of Jesus
that we may share in the song of the angels,
the gladness of the shepherds,
and the worship of the wise men.

Close the doors of hate and open the doors of love
all over the world.
Let kindness come with every gift,
and good wishes with every greeting.

Deliver us from evil by the blessing that Christ brings,
and teach us to be merry with clean hearts.

May the Christmas morning make us happy to be Thy children,
and the Christmas evening bring us to our beds
with grateful thoughts,
forgiving and forgiven,
     for Jesus' sake.

                                         Amen

☆

ON
THE
EVE

☆

The Donkey of God

LOUIS UNTERMEYER

YOU MUST know that, at the time of this story, Italy was not one country as she is today. Italy was divided into many provinces, each of them jealous of the other. There was not even a united feeling within the provinces themselves. In the Middle Ages every city had its own government, and every city hated its neighbor. Milan fought with Mantua; Florence despised Siena and spoke of its citizens as "the treacherous Sienese"; Pisa sneered at Florence, there being continual conflict between the proud Pisans "already powerful when the ancient Greeks struggled beneath the walls of Troy" and "the upstart Florentines"; Assisi and Perugia always had been at war with each other.

Assisi claimed to be the oldest of the hill-towns. It boasted of tombs that were even older than the temple-ruins; its vine-terraced slopes grew the richest grapes and the juiciest olives. More important from the point of view of the generals of Assisi, those slopes commanded a view of the Umbrian valley and no enemy could approach without being seen from a great distance. Thus prepared and fortified, Assisi was a happy place. It was even a merry one. Its merchants were wealthy, its churches were richly decorated, its young people were dressed as though life were one long carnival.

Of all the gay youths none was as richly costumed as Francis. His father was a cloth-merchant and Francis was his favorite son. No wonder his horse was the swiftest, his cap-feather the longest, his armor the handsomest, and his eyes the most impudent in Assisi. No one danced more wildly in the festival masquerades; no one swung a lute so gallantly or composed a

5

livelier serenade; no one shook his fist more patriotically than Francis at the towers of Perugia. When, after an uncomfortable peace, the neighboring cities threatened a new war, no one was quicker to call for action than the bold son of the cloth-merchant.

"Let us not wait until Perugia comes out against us," cried Francis. "Let us carry the war into her own fields, against her own gates. Let our swords break down her pride; let torches lay waste the old enemy. On to Perugia!"

A little past midnight, after the moon had gone down, the army from Assisi set out to surprise the foe. But the Perugians must have had the same idea, for that night the Umbrian plain held two armies marching against each other. It was still dark when they met. The surprise was complete and all plans of orderly battle vanished with the first blow. They fought recklessly in a blackness lit only by torches suddenly lifted, suddenly dashed out. The quiet plain was shocked from its nightly peace to a hideous awaking. Arrows and spear-throwing machines were useless; it was short range fighting. Shield and sword, mace and dagger rang against each other in utter confusion.

With the first streak of dawn the fight came to an end. The scene was horrible beyond description. Each army had killed more of its own men than the enemy's. What was left of the Perugians was a battered remnant of soldiers; the champions of Assisi were too worn to continue. Without another blow, without a word of hate, the remainder of the two armies turned towards their towns. No one had a boast left to utter. It was a broken army that returned to Assisi in a dull, red dawn. The stoutest of the old horsemen felt sick.

None felt sicker than Francis. He had seen things that turned his ideas upside down. He had seen a man lying dead—not beautifully dead like an image on a stone-coffin, but deformedly, unspeakably dead—dead at his feet. His encrusted armor was foul with blood—blood that, a few hours ago, had flowed in veins as happy as his—there was blood on his hands. His heart felt as though an unseen dagger had run through it. With the dawn something new had dawned in Francis, something that would not die.

For weeks he lay tossing in a high fever. The doctors could do nothing to make him rest. Francis would start from a short sleep, call out, and lie awake the rest of the night, crying things that no one could understand. He was wasting away; his condition seemed hopeless. On the fortieth day, after the doctors had shaken their heads and gone, Francis got up. No one saw him go. He walked out of the house at dawn as softly as the light that showed him the way. Assisi was just awaking as he passed through the crooked streets and out of town.

It was a different Francis that wandered, silently and alone, past the Umbrian plain. The rich suit had been exchanged for a coarse brown frock; instead of a sword he carried a wooden staff; there were no ornaments on his sleeves, no feathers on his hat—even the hat was gone. The impudent look had vanished from his eyes, the lines of boastfulness had left his lips. The face of Francis had grown long and finely cut; the eyes looked *through* things, not merely at them; a light seemed to be upon his brow.

Forty more days Francis wandered. He crossed valleys and climbed mountains; now in shaded woods, now in sun-baked marshes, making his way without a chart. He journeyed through Orvieto and Rome as in a dream. At the end of the fortieth day he came to the sea. Still following some inner guide, he took passage on a boat and landed on the island of Sardinia. He had no plan, but somehow he knew that he must work out his cure in this primitive place.

Here, far from the frivolous life of his past, he learned to live. Poorer than the poorest peasant, he was grateful for the common *frue*, or sour milk, and he who had been used to the rarest and most delicate dishes considered an occasional bowl of fresh cheese, which the natives called *ricotta*, a great treat. He did not indulge himself often in this, nor, for that matter, in anything

7

else; his little hut was the humblest on an island where everything was scanty.

Little by little Francis' health returned; his step grew more vigorous, and he became himself again. But it was another self that now saw grandeur in the lowly and good in everything. He preferred the simple customs and dignity of the poor Sardinians to the hot carelessness of his one-time companions. But, though he visited the peasants every evening, he spent most of his time alone. He learned to know the animals of the island and was trusted by them. He became so familiar a sight that even the shy mouflon, a sort of wild sheep, let him walk among them, stroking their long coats. He understood their ways; he began to understand their speech.

One day as he was walking among the ruins of monuments as old as the stone-age, he noticed he had gone farther than usual and was straying in a circle of queer structures that the natives called "Fairy Houses." He smiled as he thought of the fear the peasants had of these stone-chambers and the superstition that any one resting within the circle would "dream true." He noticed a donkey standing in the shade of a stunted tree, but it did not appear in the least astonished to see him. Now that he observed it closer, he could not remember ever having seen a donkey so small. It was no larger than a large dog, a sheep-dog with unusually long ears. Its ankles were more delicate than a deer's and the eyes had a speaking softness. But the most peculiar feature was revealed to Francis only when he stood close. The color was a soft pigeon-gray without a spot except for one distinguishing mark: a pattern made by two intersecting lines of black, one line running down the back from head to tail, the other line running across the shoulders. Presently, Francis noticed that the animal was speaking to him and he was aware that he understood it.

"Tell me, my good man," it was saying, "for I can see you are good, is there no justice in creation? Isn't it bad enough that we donkeys have to carry every sort of burden—twice as much as the much larger horse—without also being a joke among men and animals? Is that just? And if that were not enough, why should we be made still more foolish by having to wear such a disfiguring pattern on our back? Can you answer that?"

To his surprise, Francis heard himself replying to the little donkey as if he were a priest and it were one of his flock.

"Yes, my daughter, I think I can. There is a justice in all things, though we cannot see it at once. We must wait until the pattern is completed before we judge any of its parts. In your case the answer is easier than most, for you are the donkey of God."

"The donkey of God?" asked the little animal.

"Surely," replied Francis, amazed at the way he was talking, but keeping on in an even voice. "If you do not know your own story, I will tell it to you."

And Francis, who had never seen the creature before, and who certainly had never thought of its origin, heard himself telling this strange legend:

It was morning of the Sixth Day. God had spent the First Day inventing Light. Then, seeing that continued light would be too cruel on the eyes, He made Darkness for relief. On the Second Day God had designed the seas and had put a clear border of sky about them to prevent the waters from overflowing. On the Third Day, being dissatisfied with the emptiness of a world of water, He had gathered the waters in one place and had put dry land carefully among the seas. He called the dry land Earth and liked it much better, especially after he had caused green things to grow and had planned fruit to come after the flower. He had told himself it was good. On the Fourth Day God had looked at the widespread Heaven and realized it needed something. So He had put lights in it: a great gold light to rule the day, and a soft silver one to rule the night, and a lot of lesser lights to decorate the evening. And once more He had been pleased. On the Fifth Day He decided He wanted more motion and sound in the universe. So He had filled the waters with whales and minnows and the air with insects and eagles. He had smiled when the first whale, that island afloat, had blown his first spout, and His great heart had tightened when the lark, hoping to reach heaven, sang his first song.

And now it was the Sixth Day. The earth, God saw, needed life no less than sea and sky. So early in the morning He began making animals. First He made small simple ones: the snake and the the snail, the mouse and the mole, rat and rabbit, cat and dog, lamb and wolf, goat, mink, fox, hedge-hog, beaver, woodchuck and a hundred others, each after his kind. Then, watching them leap or crawl or dig or prowl, He tried the same design on an ever-growing scale. It was then He made donkey and deer, horse and cattle, lion and tiger, bear, buffalo, elk, the great apes, the giant lizards, the mammoths like mountains on the move. Then God, out of the humor of His heart, indulged Himself in a few experiments. He made the giraffe with his feet in the mud, his long neck lost in the leaves, and his silly head trying to scrape the stars. He tied a bird and a snake together and made the ostrich. He took a lump of clay, shaped it, unshaped it, dug His thumb twice into it and threw it away—and that was the camel. He thought of a hill-side with a tiny tail and nose-arm-fingers in one long trunk—and thus the elephant was made. He took some river-mud, breathed on it, changed His mind, saying, "No animal that looked like that would want to live"— and it was the hippopotamus. When He saw these absurd shapes strut about. He laughed so long that the stars began to fall from their places— some of them are still so loose that they tremble in the sky—and for a while. He did nothing at all.

But since He was God, He could not stop creating. So in the afternoon He looked at everything and said, "It is good." After a little while He added, "But it could be better. It lacks something."

All afternoon He sat pondering among the clouds. At last toward evening, He said, "It is not enough like Me. I will take the very best soil from the earth, for this will be an earth-creature. I will mix it with water so he need not be afraid of the sea. I will knead it with air so he can trust himself in any element and even fly if he wishes. I will then put a spark of Myself deep in him so he may be God-like. And it will be Man."

When the animals heard this they began arguing with God.

"Consider, O Lord," said the lion in his gentlest, most persuasive roar. He was already known as the king of beasts, so he spoke first. "Consider, O Lord, before You breathe life into the creature. If You make him of the elements, he will be master not only of them, but of us all."

"Yes," said the elephant with gruff simplicity, "such an animal as Man will do no labor at all. He'll say he's not made for it, and we'll have to do his work for him."

"Not that we mind, Lord," hissed the serpent with false meekness. "But if You put Your spark in him, he'll think he's divine. And after he's mastered us—not that *we* mind—he'll try to master what created him. And then—"

"And then," said God in the still small voice which was more terrible than thunder, "he will be part of Me again. Meanwhile I have no need of advice from my own creations."

And so he made Man.

You are wondering, I see, what had become of the donkey. Up to now he had done nothing but listen and mind his own affairs. While the others were arguing with God or grumbling among themselves, the donkey calmly went on eating rose-leaves and lettuces and growing lovelier every minute. Perhaps I should have told you that he had been born the most perfect of four-footed creatures. He was very much like the donkeys of today except that his color was softer, his eyes more tender, his ankles even more graceful—and, at that time, the long ears of his great-great-grandchildren did not disguise his head. Instead of the grotesque flapping sails of the donkey of today, the original donkey had two of the finest, most perfectly shaped ears you can imagine. They were like those of a dainty fox, only smaller, and so wax-like that you could half see through them. Everything satisfied him; he feared nothing; the world was good. So he continued to munch lettuce and rose-leaves.

The donkey was so busy eating—it was at the beautiful beginning of things when there were no worms in the lettuces nor thorns on the roses—that he did not see God make the first man. Nor did he see Him, late in the night, creating the first woman. The next morning—it was Sunday—the other animals told him about it and said the man-animal was called Adam and the woman-animal was called Eve. A little tired of doing nothing but eating, the donkey joined the other beasts and peered into the garden where the two newest-born creatures were sitting. When he saw them he burst into the loudest and most ridiculous laugh on earth. It was like no sound that had ever been made; it was the first wild, weird, astonishing bray. Today only the smallest echoes are in the throat of all the donkeys, but then it rang so fiercely against the skies that it almost threw the fixed stars out of their courses.

"Ho-hee-haw!" screamed the donkey. "It was *too* funny! *Such* animals! They're made all wrong! No hide! No hoofs! Not even a tail! And so pink—so *naked!* God must have meant to put a coat of fleece on them and forgot it! Ho-hee-*haw!*"

Eve, frightened by the screaming and screeching, ran into the woods. Adam sprang to his feet.

"And look!" the donkey brayed in a still ruder laugh, while the other beasts roared and cackled and barked. "Look! The she-man runs on her hind legs! She doesn't even know how to walk! Ho-ho—hee—haw—hee—HAW!"

This was too much for Adam. He ran over to the donkey and grasped him by the ears. The donkey tried to pull himself free, but Adam held fast. As he tugged and Adam tightened, his ears began to stretch, grow longer. . . . And while they were pulling, God suddenly appeared.

Said the Lord, "Because you have spoiled My day of rest and because you have made fun of My creation you shall be punished. Because you saw fit to laugh at your betters, you shall never cease from laughing. But no one will listen with joy; your voice will be a mockery by day and a horror by night. The louder you laugh, the longer will you be despised. You shall serve man and be subject to him all the days of your life. Other animals shall serve him, also: the horse, the cow, the elephant and the dog. But unlike them, you shall work for man without winning his love. Unlike them, you shall resist him foolishly, and he shall beat you for it. You who are the most comely of My creatures shall be the most comic. Instead of roses you shall feed on thorns and thistles. You shall have a rope for a tail. And your ears shall remain long."

So it was decreed. And so it turned out. When Adam and Eve were forced to leave the Garden and go to work, the donkey went with them. Adam rode on the horse, the dog trotted at Eve's side, but it was the donkey who carried the tools, the spinning-wheel and all the household machinery. Throughout Adam's life the donkey was reminded of the saying about laugh-last instead of first. Sometimes he was ashamed and dropped his long ears like a lop-eared rabbit; sometimes his pride came back and he refused to take another step. At such times Adam beat him and the donkey remembered the Lord's prophecy. He wondered how long the burdens would be piled upon him.

After Adam died the donkey thought things would go easier, but he soon realized his hardships were only beginning. He belonged, he discovered not to one man but to all men. Cain, the brutal son of Adam, broke him to harness and made him drag a heavy plow. When Noah built the ark the donkey carried more timber than the elephant, but no one praised him for it. Forty days and forty nights the floating menagerie breasted the flood, and every day and most of the nights the other animals jeered and mocked him. He knew now what it was to be laughed at. And when the windows of heaven were closed and the fountains of the flood went back into the heart of the sea, the donkey walked the earth again with meek eyes and bowed head. From that time on he swore to serve man faithfully and ask no reward.

At the building of Babel, the donkey was there, working willingly, although he knew no tower built by hands would ever reach Heaven. After the city was deserted, the donkey helped Abraham with his flocks, and carried for Isaac, and wandered with Jacob. So, through Bible times, the donkey remained loyal to his masters. He brought Joseph and his twelve brothers together; he dragged bricks for the Hebrews during their long slavery in Egypt; he crossed the Red Sea with Moses; he was beaten for trying to save the wizard Balaam; he entered Canaan with Joshua.

He worked; he wandered; he did not die.

Years passed; centuries vanished. The donkey was in Palestine. His master was a carpenter in the little town of Nazareth, a good master by the name of Joseph, though far different from the Joseph who had become ruler in the land of Egypt. He had worked for him a long time, and he had served his owner well. A few years ago, when Joseph and his wife Mary were on their wanderings, the little donkey carried them everywhere without complaining. They were terribly poor and the innkeepers had no room for them. The donkey trudged on, carrying his load that seemed to grow heavier with each step. For a long day and longer night he plodded toward the distant haven, never stopping or stumbling till he brought them to the little town of Bethlehem. That night, in a cattle-stall, Mary's child had been born.

The donkey obeyed his master, but he worshipped his master's small son. The child was not only beautiful, but even as perfect as he seemed to his mother. Goodness shone from his eyes; miracles, they said, flowed from his hands. The donkey believed it, for he had seen one performed.

Once, when playing with some other children in the streets of Nazareth, the carpenter's son picked up some clay from the gutter and kneaded it into a shape. His companions gathered around to watch him.

"Good," said Simon, "let's all do it. What shall we model?"

"Let's make horses," cried Zadoc, the son of the priest. "When I grow up I'm going to have six horses of my own—two white ones, two black ones and two horses with many-colored coats."

"Stupid!" said Azor, the broom-maker's child. "There are no horses with many-colored coats. Besides, horses are too hard to model. Let's make pigeons."

So they started to make pigeons out of clay. After a while Zadoc called out. "I've made seven. How many have the rest of you?"

"Five," said Zithri, the beggar's boy.

"Four," said Simon.

"Three," said Azor.

"Two," said Jesus, who was the carpenter's son.

"Only two!" sneered Zadoc. "And not even good ones. Mine look much more like pigeons than yours!"

"You are right," said Jesus and he tossed his aside. But though the clay pigeons were thrown, they did not fall to the ground. Instead, they hung in the air, spread wings and flew away.

The other children stared for a moment and then grew angry. "He's playing tricks on us!" cried Zadoc, son of the priest. "Let's play a trick on him!" The others joined Zadoc and soon they had tied the little Jesus tightly. The cord bit deep into his wrists but he did not cry.

"He's just making believe he's brave," said Zadoc. "He acts as if he were a king."

"All right," jeered Azor. "Let him be king."

"I'll get him a crown," shouted Zithri.

They pulled part of a withered rose-tree and twisted two small branches into a crown. They pressed this upon his forehead and cried, "King Jesus! Hail to King Jesus!" Then they ran away laughing, while tears stood in the eyes of the carpenter's son.

The donkey had seen it all, had seen that the hands of Jesus were still tied and that the child could not remove the crown of thorns. Then he nuzzled his soft nose along the child's shoulder, raised his head and, though the thorns stabbed his lips, lifted the piercing weight from Jesus' forehead. He tugged at the cords till he freed the child's hands; then he carried him home.

More years passed. Jesus had gone away. Though the donkey did not know it, the carpenter's son had grown from childhood to manhood, had traveled and studied, had healed the sick, restored eyesight to the blind, cast out devils, had suffered untold hardships. But now the moment had come; Jesus was to enter Jerusalem in triumph.

It was a tremendous moment; one that must be celebrated in the proper manner. Naturally, Jesus could not enter the queen-city of Palestine on foot; he must ride, they said, on a charger worthy of the event. So the Archangel Michael called all the animals before Jesus that they might plead their case.

"Choose me," said the lion. "I am the king of beasts; you are a king among men. Men respect royalty—but only when they recognize it! When the people of Jerusalem see you riding on my back, they will know you are of noble blood and they will bow down and fear you. With me as your mascot, they will never dare oppose, but follow you in terror."

"Choose me," said the eagle. "I am lord of the upper air. Choose me and you will have power to leave the earth and fly on the very back of the wind. I will take you to borders of the sky; there, from heights unknown to man, you shall see everything that happens below. When you enter Jerusalem flying between my strong wings, the people will believe you are a god and they will worship."

"Choose me," said the mole. "I go where the eagle is helpless and the lion cannot follow. Choose me and I will give you the keys of earth. I will guide you to the roots of power, to secrets buried beneath the stones. I know where every vein of gold is hidden; my home is among caves of rubies, hills of emerald, ledges of pure diamond. Choose me and you will be greater than the greatest; you will be able to buy empires; you will not only be a king, but King of kings."

"The great ones laugh at treasures," whispered the fox. "Who but a fool desires gold and glittering pebbles that turn men against each other with greed and jealousy. Choose me and I will give you cunning. I will show you how to outwit all men and overcome your enemies with shrewdness. Choose me and I will teach you cleverness that is better than wealth and craft that is stronger than strength."

"Craft!" trumpeted the elephant. "Craft and cunning are for knaves who will never be wise. Choose me and I will give you true wisdom. I am the oldest of living creatures; my years span a century and I have watched the comings and goings of all the races. Choose me and you will rule the changing mind of the unchanging world."

"Choose me," lowed the cow. "I am sacred. India and Egypt worship me. I feed the world."

"Choose me," bellowed the dragon. "I will spread fire before you and magic wherever you go."

"Choose me," neighed the horse. "I am swift as rage. The glory of my nostrils is terrible to the enemy. I swallow the ground; I laugh at fear."

"Choose me!" screamed the camel. "Choose me! Choose me!" cried the animals separately and in chorus. Only the donkey was silent.

"And what can you give?" asked Jesus, speaking for the first time and turning to the dusty little fellow. "What have you to promise?"

"Nothing," murmured the donkey. "Nothing. I am the lowest of all God's creature's and the least."

17

But Jesus remembered. "The lowest shall be lifted up," he said, "And the last shall be first."

And so the meekest of men chose the meekest of animals. And they entered Jerusalem together.

But the great moment passed. Proud Jerusalem sneered at the carpenter's son even as it had stoned the prophets before him, and only a handful of poor folk listened to his words. He was despised and rejected. The people turned against him. He was imprisoned on a false charge and condemned to death. They put a crown of thorns upon his head, mocked him and made him carry his own cross.

It was while Jesus was struggling up the hill that the donkey saw him for the last time. Their sad eyes met.

"No," said Jesus. "You cannot help me now. Yet, since you have done more for me than have most men, you shall be rewarded. I cannot undo what God has done; what He has ordained must be carried out. But I can soften his decree. True, you will have to fetch and carry and feed on thorns. Yet these things will never again be hard for you. Because you carried me three times, so shall you be able to carry three times as much as animals thrice your size—and your load will seem lighter than theirs. You suffered thorns for my sake; so shall you be nourished when others can find nothing to feed on. You shall eat the thorns and nettles of the field—and they shall taste like sweet salads. You bore me when I grew to manhood, when I was a child, and even my mother before I was born. So shall you bear my cross but you shall bear it without pain. Here —!" And as Jesus touched the shoulders of the donkey, a velvet-black cross appeared on the back of the kneeling animal.

And Jesus shouldering his burden, climbed up Calvary . . .

Francis heard the last syllable leave his lips in a kind of wonder. His tiredness had gone: everything in him was full of strength. He was surprised to see that the sun had set and that a little horned moon had come into the sky, one horn pointing to Assisi. He thought he understood the sign. When he turned back, the donkey had disappeared. The field was dark. But a light greater than the moon's was on Francis' face.

A Hymn on the Nativity of My Saviour

BEN JOHNSON

I sing the birth was born tonight,
The author both of life and light;
   The angels so did sound it.
And like the ravished shepherds said,
Who saw the light and were afraid,
   Yet searched, and true they found it.

The Son of God, the eternal king,
That did us all salvation bring,
   And freed the soul from danger:
He whom the whole world could not take,
The Word, which heaven and earth did make,
   Was now laid in a manger.

The Father's wisdom willed it so,
The Son's obedience knew no No,
   Both wills were in one stature;
And as that wisdom had decreed,
The Word was now made flesh indeed,
   And took on Him our Nature.

What comfort by Him do we win,
Who made Himself the price of sin,
   To make us heirs of glory!
To see this babe all innocence,
A martyr born in our defence—
   Can man forget the story?

A Christmas Gift

T. F. POWYS

I T IS a harmless wish to like a little notice to be taken of one's
name, and a number of people, besides Mr. Balliboy, the
Dodder carrier, like attention to be paid to their names when
they are written down. Children will write their names upon a
fair stretch of yellow sand, young men will carve their names
upon an old oak in the forest, and even the most simple peasant
will like to see his name printed in a newspaper.

For most of his life Mr. Balliboy was satisfied with having his
name written upon the side of his van, and he was always
pleased and interested when anyone paused in the street to
read his name.

But Mr. Balliboy's pride in his name made him do more than
one foolish thing.

Once he cut "Mr. Balliboy, Carrier," with his market knife
upon one of the doors of Mr. Told's old barn, and again upon
the right-hand post of the village pound. But, on his going to
see how the names looked the next Sunday,—and perhaps hoping that a stranger might be found regarding them,—he discovered, to his sorrow, that the rude village boys had changed
the first letters of his name into an unpleasant and ill-sounding
word.

Mr. Balliboy was a lonely man, and a bachelor—for no young
woman would ever look at his name twice and none had ever
wished to have his name written beside hers in a church register.

One Christmas Mr. Balliboy journeyed, as was his wont, to
Weyminster. His van was full of country women, each one of
whom thought herself to be of the highest quality, for each had

21

put on the finest airs with her market clothes and, so dressed, could talk in a superior manner.

Mr. Balliboy had certainly one reason for happiness—other than the ordinary joyfulness of the merry season—which was that his rival, John Hawkins, had passed by with his van empty of customers,—yet Mr. Balliboy was sad. His sadness came, strangely enough, only because he wished, for the first time in his life, to give a Christmas present.

It might have been only to give himslf pleasure that he wished to do this.—For whatever the present was that he should buy, he determined that a label should be tied on it, with his name clearly upon it—"From Mr. Balliboy."

What the present would be, and to whom it should be given, Mr. Balliboy did not know. He decided to buy something that he fancied, and then allow destiny to decide to whom the gift should go.

When Mr. Balliboy reached the town he walked about the streets in order to see what could be bought for money. Many a shop window did he look into and many a time did he stand and scratch his head, wondering what he should buy.

There was one oddity that he fancied in a toy-shop,—a demon holding a fork in his hand, upon which he was raising a naked young woman. Mr. Balliboy thought the demon might do, but over the young woman he shook his head.

Mr. Balliboy moved to another window. Here at once, he saw what pleased him,—a little cross, made of cardboard and covered with tinsel, that shone and glistened before Mr. Balliboy's admiring eyes.

Mr. Balliboy purchased the cross for a shilling and attached a label to it, with his name written large. . . .

Sometimes a change comes over a scene, now so happy and gay but in one moment altered into a frown. As soon as Mr. Balliboy had buttoned the cross into his pocket the streets of Weyminster showed this changed look. The shoppers' merriment and joyful surprise at what they saw in the windows gave place to a sad and tired look. The great church that so many hurried by in order to reach their favorite tavern, appeared more dark and sombre than a winter's day should ever have made it.

Even the warm drinks served out by black-haired Mabel at the "Rod and Lion" could not make the drinkers forget that care and trouble could cut a Christmas cake and sing a Christmas carol as well as they.

The general gloom of the town touched Mr. Balliboy, and had he not had the present hid in his coat, he might have entered an Inn, in order to drown the troubled feelings that moved about him, in a deep mug.

But, having bought the Christmas present, he had now the amusement of seeking the right person to give it to. And so, instead of walking along the street with downcast eyes, he walked along smiling.

While he was yet some way off his van, he could see that a figure was standing beside it, who seemed to be reading his name. And, whoever this was, Mr. Balliboy determined as he walked, that it should be the one to receive his Christmas gift.

As he drew near he saw that the figure was that of a young woman—wrapped in a thin cloak—who showed by her wan look and by her shape that she expected soon to be a mother.

At a little distance from his van Mr. Balliboy waited, pretending to admire a row of bottles in a wine-merchant's shop-window, but, at the same time, keeping an eye upon the woman.

"Was she a thief,—was she come there to steal?" A passing policeman, with a fine military strut, evidently thought so.

"Don't stand about here," he shouted. "Go along home with you!"

The policeman seized her roughly.

"I am doing no harm," the woman said, looking at the name again, "I am only waiting for Mr. Balliboy."

"Go along, you lying drab," grumbled the policeman.

He would have pushed her along, only Mr. Balliboy, who had heard his name mentioned, came nearer.

"Baint 'ee poor Mary," he asked, "who was to have married the carpenter at Shelton?"

The policeman winked twice at Mr. Balliboy, smiled and walked on.

"What was it," asked Mr. Balliboy, kindly, as soon as the policeman was out of hearing, "that made 'ee wish to study and remember the name of a poor carrier?"

"I wished to ask you," said the young woman, "whether you would take me as far as the 'Norbury Arms.' Here is my fare," and she handed Mr. Balliboy a shilling—the price of the cross.

Mr. Balliboy put the shilling into his pocket.

"Get up into van," he said, "and 'tis to be hoped they t'others won't mind 'ee."

That day the most respectable of the people of the village had come to town in Mr. Balliboy's van. There was even rich Mrs. Told, clad in warm furs, whose own motor-car had met with an accident the day before. There were others too, as comfortably off,—Mrs. Potten and Mrs. Biggs—and none of these, or even his lesser customers, did Mr. Balliboy wish to offend. He looked anxiously up the street and then into the van.

The young woman's clothes were rags, her toes peeped from her shoes, and she sighed woefully.

Mr. Balliboy gave her a rug to cover her. "Keep tight hold of 'en," he said, "for t'other women be grabbers."

The change in the town from joy to trouble had caused the women who had journeyed with Mr. Balliboy that day to arrive at the van a little late, and in no very good tempers. And, when they did come, they were not best pleased to see a poor woman —worse clothed than a tramp—sitting in the best seat in the van, with her knees covered by Mr. Balliboy's rug.

" 'Tis only Mary," said Mr. Balliboy, hoping to put them at their ease. " 'Tis only thik poor toad."

"Mary, is it?" cried Mrs. Biggs angrily, "who did deceive Joseph with her wickedness. What lady would ride with her? Turn her out at once, Mr. Balliboy,—the horrid wretch."

"Out with her!" cried Mrs. Told. "Just look at her," and she whispered unpleasant words to Mrs. Potten.

Mr. Balliboy hesitated. He hardly knew what to do. He had more than once borrowed a little straw from Mrs. Told's stack-yard and now he did not want to offend her.

He had a mind to order Mary out, only—putting his hand under his coat to look at his watch—he felt the Christmas present that he had purchased—the cardboard cross.

"Thee needn't sit beside her," he said coaxingly to Mrs. Told, "though she's skin as white and clean as any lamb's."

"We won't have no lousy breeding beggar with we," shouted Mrs. Biggs, who had taken a little too much to drink at the tavern.

"Let she alone," said Mr. Balliboy, scratching his head and wondering what he had better do.

"Thrust her out," cried Mrs. Potten, and, climbing into the van, she spat at the woman.

"Out with her," screamed Mrs. Told. "Away with her, away with her!" cried all the women.

Now, had it not been that Mr. Balliboy had taken Mary's shilling and so made her free of his van, with the right to be carried as far as the "Norbury Arms," he might have performed the commands of the drunken woman and thrown Mary into the street. But, as he had taken her shilling, Mr. Balliboy bethought him of what was his own.

The woman had read his name; he had taken her fare.

"Let she alone," said Mr. Balliboy gruffly to Mrs. Biggs, who had laid hands upon the woman.

"We'll go to John Hawkins; he'll take us home," said Mrs. Told angrily.

Mr. Balliboy winced. He knew how glad his rival would be to welcome all his company.

"Why, what evil has she done?" Mr. Balliboy asked in a milder tone.

With one accord the women shouted out Mary's sorrow.

25

"Away with her, away with her!" they called.

Mr. Balliboy put his hand into his coat, but it was not his watch that he felt for this time,—it was his Christmas gift.

"Away with your own selves," he said stoutly. "Thik maiden be going wi' I, for 'tis me own van."

Mr. Balliboy took his seat angrily and the women left him. He knew that what had happened that afternoon was likely to have a lasting effect upon his future. Everyone in the village would side with the women with whom he had quarrelled, and the story of his kindness to Mary would not lose in the telling.

But, before very long, an accident happened that troubled Mr. Balliboy even more than the loss of his customers.—In the middle of a long and lonely road his van broke down.

Mr. Balliboy tried to start the car, but with no success. Other carriers passed by, amongst whom was John Hawkins, and many were the taunts and unseemly jests shouted at him by the Christmas revellers who sat therein.—But soon all was silence, and the road was utterly deserted, for the time was near midnight.

For some while Mr. Balliboy busied himself with the aid of the car lamps, trying to start the engine. But, all at once and without any warning, the lamps went out.

Mr. Balliboy shivered. The weather was changed, a sharp frost had set in and the stars shone brightly. Someone groaned. Mary's pains had come upon her.

"I be going," said Mr. Balliboy, "to get some help for 'ee."

Mr. Balliboy had noticed a little cottage across the moor, with a light in the window. He hurried there, but before he reached the cottage the light had vanished, and, knock as he would at the door, no one replied.

"What be I to do?" cried Mr. Balliboy anxiously, and looked up at the sky.—A large and brightly-shining star appeared exactly above his van.

Mr. Balliboy looked at his van and rubbed his eyes. The van was lit up and beams of strange light seemed to emanate from it.

A *Christmas Gift*

" 'Tain't on fire, I do hope," said Mr. Balliboy. He began to run and came quickly to the car.

Mary was now resting comfortably, while two shining creatures with white wings leaned over her. Upon her lap was her new-born babe, smiling happily.

Mr. Balliboy fumbled in his coat for his Christmas gift. He stepped into the van and held out the cross to the babe.

Mary looked proudly at her infant, and the babe, delighted with the shining toy, took hold of the cross.

The angels wept.

Holy Night

WALTER HARD

As Doctor Stevens came into the village
He let his horse slow down to a walk.
The moon broke through the clouds.
There was not a track on the new-fallen snow.
He was thinking how nice it was
That the Judson baby had come on Christmas eve.
He smiled his pleasant smile
As he passed lighted houses with trimmed trees inside.

What could Ellen Hicks be doing up at this late hour?
She didn't have anyone to be filling stockings for.
Poor thing! She didn't have anything to fill a stocking with.
A shadow moved regularly across the drawn shade.
She was sitting there rocking—rocking.

The village clock struck eleven.
From the south came the faint tinkle of sleighbells.

The snow creaked as he went up the steps.
The rocking stopped.
The light moved through the door into the hall.
Ellen unlocked the door.
She held the light up to see who her late caller was.
She had a worn patchwork quilt around her shoulders.

The Doctor went over to the chunk stove to warm his hands.
It gave out no heat. He touched it. It was barely warm.
No, of course there wasn't anything the matter with her.

Holy Night

She always sat up until midnight on Christmas eve.
She'd got to thinking about that Stebbins family,
And sat there rocking and forgot her fire.
How they could get along with all those young ones,
And him all crippled, she couldn't see.
They didn't even have wood to keep them warm.

"Ellen, have you been giving wood to the Stebbinses?"
She admitted she had called the boy in and loaded his sled.
Well, maybe she had sent some food.

Little by little the truth came out.
Her nephew did look after her; he always had.
But he'd told her she'd got to stop this sharing.
She'd promised.
But she couldn't bear to think of those Stebbinses.
She could get along. She still had wood in the shed.
The Doctor's scolding stuck in his throat.
He went to the shed and brought in the last armful of wood.

He shut the stable door.
He stopped to look down on the sleeping village.
So Ellen had to share.
He recalled the look on her face.
Sharing. That was what Christmas meant.

The clock in the village struck twelve.
Down in the valley a rooster crowed.
Overhead the moon moved slowly across the winter sky.
Holy night. Peaceful night.

☆

CHRISTMAS
IN THE
FAMILY

☆

Once on Christmas

DOROTHY THOMPSON

IT IS Christmas Eve—the festival that belongs to mothers and fathers and children, all over the so-called western world. It's not a time to talk about situations, or conditions, or reactions, or people who emerge briefly into the news. My seven-year-old son asked me this evening to tell him what Christmas was like when I was a little girl, before people came home for Christmas in airplanes, thirty odd years ago. And so I told him this:

A long, long time ago, when your mother was your age, and not nearly as tall as you, she lived with her mother, and father, and younger brother, and little sister, in a Methodist parsonage, in Hamburg, New York. It was a tall wooden house, with a narrow verandah on the side, edged with curley-cues of woodwork at the top, and it looked across a lawn at the church where father preached every Sunday morning and evening. In the backyard there were old Baldwin and Greening apple trees, and a wonderful, wonderful barn. But that is another story. The village now has turned into a suburb of the neighboring city of Buffalo, and fathers who work there go in and out every day on the trains and buses, but then it was just a little country town, supported by the surrounding farms.

Father preached in his main church there on Sunday mornings but in the afternoons he had to drive out to the neighboring village of Armor where there was just a little box of church in the middle of the farming country. For serving both parishes, he received his house and one thousand dollars a year. But he didn't always get the thousand dollars. Sometimes the crops were bad, and the farmers had no money, and when the farmers

33

had no money the village people didn't have any either. Then the farmers would come to us with quarters of beef, or halves of pigs, or baskets of potatoes, and make what they call a donation. My mother hated the word, and sometimes would protest, but my father would laugh, and say, "Let them pay in what they can! We are all in the same boat together."

For weeks before Christmas we were very, very busy. Mother was busy in the kitchen, cutting up citron and sorting out raisins and clarifying suet for the Christmas pudding—and shooing all of us out of the room, when we crept in to snatch a raisin, or a bit of kernel from the butternuts that my little brother was set to cracking on the woodshed floor, with an old-fashioned flat-iron.

I would lock myself into my little bedroom, to bend over a handkerchief that I was hemstitching for my mother. It is very hard to hemstitch when you are seven years old, and the thread would knot, and break, and then one would have to begin again, with a little rough place, where one had started over. I'm afraid the border of that handkerchief was just one succession of knots and starts.

The home-made presents were only a tiny part of the work. There was the Christmas tree! Mr. Heist, from my father's Armor parish, had brought it in from his farm, a magnificent hemlock, that touched the ceiling. We were transported with admiration, but what a tree to trim! For there was no money to buy miles of tinsel and boxes of colored glass balls.

But in the pantry was a huge stone jar of popcorn. When school was over, in the afternoons, we all gathered in the back parlor, which was the family sitting room. The front parlor was a cold place, where portraits of John Wesley and Frances Willard hung on the walls, and their eyes, I remember, would follow a naughty child accusingly around the room. The sofas in that room were of walnut, with roses and grapes carved on their backs, just where they'd stick into your back, if you fidgeted in them, and were covered with horsehair which was slippery when it was new, and tickly when it was old. But that room was given over to visits from the local tycoons who sometimes contributed to the church funds, and couples who came to be married.

The back parlor was quite, quite, different. It had an ingrain carpet on the floor, with patterns of maple leaves, and white muslin curtains at the windows, and an assortment of chairs contributed by the Parsonage Committee. A Morris chair, I remember, and some rockers, and a fascinating cabinet which was a desk and a bookcase, and a chest of drawers, and a mirror, all in one.

In this room there was a round iron stove, a very jolly stove, a cozy stove that winked at you with its red isin-glass eyes. On top of this stove was a round iron plate; it was flat, and a wonderful place to pop corn. There was a great copper kettle, used for making maple syrup, and we shook the popper on the top of the stove—first I shook, until my arm was tired, and then Willard shook, until he was tired, and even the baby shook. The corn popped, and we poured it into the kettle and emptied the kettle, and poured it full again, until there was a whole barrelfull of popcorn, as white and fluffy as the snow that carpeted the lawn between the parsonage and the church.

Then we got a darning needle, a big one, and a ball of string. We strung the popcorn into long, long ropes, to hang upon the tree. But that was only half of it! There were stars to be cut out of kindergarten paper, red, and green, and silver, and gold, and walnuts to be wrapped in gold paper, or painted with gold paint out of the paintbox that I had been given for my birthday. One got the paint into one's fingernails, and it smelled like bananas. And red apples to be polished, because a shiny apple makes a brave show on a tree. And when it was all finished, it was Christmas Eve.

For Christmas Eve we all wore our best clothes. Baby in a litle challis dress as blue as her eyes, and I had a new pinafore of Swiss lawn that my Aunt Margaret had sent me from England. We waited, breathless, in the front parlor while the candles were lit.

Then my mother sat at the upright piano in a rose-red cashmere dress and played, and my father sang, in his lovely, pure, gay, tenor voice:

> It came upon the midnight clear
> That glorious song of old,
> From angels bending near the earth
> To touch their harps of gold.

And then we all marched in. It is true that we had decorated the tree ourselves, and knew intimately everything on it, but it shone in the dark room like an angel, and I could see the angels bending down, and it was so beautiful that one could hardly bear it. We all cried, "Merry Christmas!" and kissed each other.

There were bundles under the tree, most alluring bundles! But they didn't belong to Christmas Eve. They were for the morning. Before the morning came three little children would sit sleepily in the pews of their father's church and hear words drowsily, and shift impatiently, and want to go to sleep in order to wake up very, very, early!

And wake up early we did! The windows were still gray, and, oh, how cold the room was! The church janitor had come over at dawn to stoke the hot air furnace in the parsonage, but at its best it only heated the rooms directly above it, and the upstairs depended on grates in the floor, and the theory that heat rises. We shuddered out of our beds, trembling with cold and excitement, and into our clothes, which, when I was a little girl were very complicated affairs indeed. First, a long fleecelined union suit, and then a ferris waist dripping with buttons, then the cambric edged drawers edged with embroidery, and a flannel petticoat handsome with scallops, and another petticoat of cambric and embroidery, just for show, and over that a gay plaid dress, and a dainty pinafore. What polishing of cheeks, and what brushing of hair and then a grand tumble down into the warm, cozy back parlor.

Presents! There was my beloved Miss Jam-up with a brand new head! Miss Jam-up was once a sweet little doll, dears, who had become badly battered about the face in the course of too affectionate ministrations, and here she was again, with a new head altogether and new clothes, and eyes that open and shut. Scarfs and mittens from my mother's lively fingers. A doll house made from a wooden cracker box and odds and ends of wall paper, with furniture cut from stiff cardboard—and that was mother's work, too. And a new woolen dress, and new pinafores!

Under the tree there was a book: *The Water Babies*, by Charles Kingsley. To my beloved daughter Dorothy.

Books meant sheer magic. There were no automobiles—none for Methodist ministers, in those days. No moving pictures. No radio. But inside the covers of books was everything, everything that exists outside in the world today. Lovely, lovely words of poetry, that slipped like colored beads along a string; tales of rose-red cities, half as old as time. All that men can imagine, and construct, and make others imagine.

One couldn't read the book now. But there it lay, the promise of a perfect afternoon. Before one could get at it, one would go into the dining room. And what a dinner! This Christmas there was Turkey—with best wishes from one of my father's parishioners. And the pudding, steaming, and with two kinds of sauce. And no one to say, "No, dear, I think one helping is enough."

We glutted ourselves, we distended ourselves, we ate ourselves into a coma, so that we all had to lie down and have a nap.

Then, lying before the stove, propped on my elbows, I opened the covers of my Christmas book.

"Once upon a time there was a little chimney sweep, and his name was Tom. He lived in a great town of the North Country . . . in England."

How well I knew that North Country, with its rows on rows of dark stone houses, its mine pits, its poor workmen. From such a town my father had come, across the ocean, to this village in up-state New York. I forgot Christmas, forgot everything, except the fate of little Tom. What a book! It wasn't just a story. There was poetry in it. The words of the poems sang in my head, so that after all these years I can remember them:

> When all the world is young, lad,
> And all the trees are green,
> And every goose, a swan, lad,
> And every lass a Queen;
> Then hey for boot and spur, lad,
> And 'round the world away;
> Young blood must have its course, lad,
> And every dog his day.

The little girl lay and dreamed that all the world was wide and beautiful, filled only with hearts as warm and hands as tender, and spirits as generous as the only ones she had ever known . . . when she was seven years old.

I wish you all a Merry Christmas! I wish us all a world as kind as a child can imagine it!

The White Kid Gloves

MARGARET COUSINS

THE dictionary defines happiness as good luck, prosperity, a state of well-being, and whenever I read this accepted description, it interests me to remember that the moment of utter happiness I cherish out of a lifetime was attended by no one of these things. On the contrary, luck had been so long absent as to become a total stranger, prosperity was not even around the most distant corner, and I was running a low fever.

The winter that I was sixteen, my father suffered a series of paralyzing business reverses owing to circumstances he could not control. He was the owner of a small, independent organization which he had founded and built into a comfortable position, and he loved it with the devotion of a man who understands responsibility and appreciates work. A series of misadventures, which began in the middle of the year, culminated in October with the default of a note he had signed for a friend in cheerful confidence, and he was forced to pay out of his working capital the sum of $25,000, which was about the total of it. He found that he was literally penniless and that eventual recovery lay months, even years, in the future, if at all. The times were inflationary, and almost the bitterest pill to swallow was the fact that prosperity flourished on all sides but eschewed his path. He had established a standard of living commensurate with his prospects, which included a pleasant house with a sizable mortgage, a wife he loved to indulge, and two expensive and slightly spoiled children, Stanley and me.

My father was not a man to burden his family with business worries, and during the early days of his travail he brooded in silence on the downward path of his fortunes. As the number of his employees diminished and then vanished altogether and his working hours increased, he was forced to take my mother into his confidence. I do not know to what extent she was frightened by his revelations, for she never gave an overt sign, past dispensing with the maid of all work, the yard man, and the assumption of the full role of cook and houseworker, with my brother and me as her assistants, positions which did not fill us with enthusiasm. While I fretted at the ironing board and my brother grumbled as he stoked the furnace and raked the autumn leaves, my mother sang at her work, and my father summoned a kind of haunted cheer in our presence. It was only after we had been driven abovestairs to attack our homework that the burden of unease seeped through the house. I would lean over the banister in the dark and observe my parents clinging together on the sofa as if they occupied a bit of driftwood in a raging ocean, and pick up bits and pieces of their conversation . . . the low, murmurous undertones of distress.

"But, Whit, could you sell the business?"

"I don't know. I suppose so—at a loss."

"It would relieve you of a burden. You could always get a job."

"That might solve things. Gebhardt would take me on. Or I think so."

"But you don't really want to sell it, do you?"

"No, I believe in it—if we can weather this spell."

"I believe in it too," my mother would cry loyally. "We'll find a way. Now, you're not to worry about it another minute!"

My father would smile wanly.

The dominion of money over human beings is a devastating thing. It is, as everybody knows, inedible and of no use in building a fire, and in any elemental situation it is worse than useless, but in the limits of our society too much can be a dagger and too little a bludgeon. I do not suppose that my father and mother ever thought we should actually go hungry or cold, but they knew that the quarterly note on the house mortgage would roll around inevitably, along with the insurance premiums and the taxes and the fuel bills and the grocery accounts, and that credit and honor are inseparable. I had not the experience at the time to know how their minds ran around in tortured circles, like frightened squirrels caught in a maze, but I have since had reason to discover.

"I don't know how to tell you this, Eloise," my father said one night, as he stood before the fireplace, drumming his whitened knuckles on the mantel and looking away from her. "I've taken a job."

"You've decided to give up the business," she said, her voice gray with defeat.

"No," he said. "I'm on the night shift at the Eldorado Hotel —night clerk. Would you like a room, lady, single bed?"

"But, Whit," my mother cried, "you can't work day and night!"

"You underestimate me," he answered. "And I expected a more passionate protest."

"Oh, Whit," moaned my mother, "how can you joke about it!" and began to cry.

My father enfolded her in his arms and nuzzled her hair. "Now don't blubber," he ordered. "You know I can't stand a crying woman."

She continued to cry.

"Your eyes are beginning to look like shrimps," he told her, "and your nose is swelling. I should think you would consider your looks on our last evening together."

She moaned afresh. "You'll wake the children, sweetheart," he chided. "And anyway, it's only temporary. Just think, they're going to pay me regularly."

My mother took a dim view of a regular stipend. "It's too lonely," she wailed.

"I'm here," he reminded her. "And time's wasting."

I scuttled up from the landing as they began to turn out the light. My cheeks were hot with shame. My father—working in a cheap hotel. I didn't know anybody whose father was a night clerk. It was mean and horrid, something I could not admit to my friends. I felt very rebellious.

If life had been uneasy heretofore, after my father began his double duty, it became more so. He used to stumble home at 6 A.M. and fall into bed until noon, then eat lunch and set out for his empty office. He did not come home at dinnertime, and my brother and I rarely saw him except on Saturday and Sunday mornings, when we were not in school. He looked very tired and cross, and we missed his joking and his teasing. We missed him, but my mother was as one bereft. She pursued a program of the stiff upper lip when we were in earshot, and most of the time she was certainly too busy to mope, but during the long winter evenings I can remember her attacking the darning as if each raveled sock were a bitter enemy, staring out the window into the night, or looking around our pleasant living room with its mellow chintzes and books, deep sofa and rosy fire, as if she might never see it again.

Christmas had always been a halcyon time for us. My father loved it as he loved all bright and charming things— the flowing eggnog bowl and the people who came to call, the red satin ribbons and the mystery of packages, the turkey to be carved and the salad mixed, surprise and affection and gestures. They were part of his nature. He set store by tradition, and his Christmas trees were a marvel of taste and originality, though he was very bad in the electrical province, and the strings of lights were always going off and reducing him to profanity. My mother had a warm heart for Christmas, too, and in that season her bustling hostess-ship reached its finest flower. From my earliest childhood I could remember the rows of cakes—the fresh coconut and the children's cake, a tower of splendid white icing bristling with little colored candies, the plummy dark fruitcakes and the chocolate layer; the mince and apple pies; the homemade fudge and divinity candy; the popcorn balls and the candy apples. The house was always rife with delicious smells—baking fowl and spice and the scent of drying spruce. The doorbell never stopped ringing. But the doorbell gets less busy in troubled times.

As Christmas came on, general nervousness around the house increased. Nobody mentioned it, and Stanley and I waited in vain for some cheering word.

"I want a bike," Stan said. "Ed Miller's got a bike. Garry's going to get a bike. I've got to have a bike."

"I don't think we can afford it," I said, from the store of intelligence I had harvested eavesdropping. "I think we're poor."

"Are we?" my brother asked anxiously. "Who told you?"

"Nobody, I just think so."

"We still go to the movies," he pointed out.

"But *they* don't," I said meaningfully. "They don't want us to be deprived."

"What's that?"

"Well—not to have things."

"Then they must want me to have a bike," Stanley said. "If I had one I could get a paper route. Then I could make money." Stan was always ready with a rationalization.

"I want something pretty," I said. "Something not practical."

"Like what?"

"Like a party dress with a long skirt and a pair of white kid gloves."

"Aaah. You're not going to any party."

"I am too. I'm going to Ruthie's Christmas dance, but I won't go in a short dress without gloves."

"Who wants an old pair of gloves?" said Stan. "I want a bike. But don't tell anybody."

We had long solemn conferences about how we could dispel the pall from the household. I thought of marrying a rich old man and lifting the mortgage, since I had been busy reading trashy novels. Stan saw himself winning an air race and bringing home a bag of gold and presenting it to my father. None of these schemes seemed to lead to any practical solution of the problem of getting money for Christmas shopping. We had one enthusiastic notion which devolved upon selling our school books to the secondhand store, an idea which seemed to have everything except that we should certainly be found out.

Time flowed into December. The busy merchandising season, replete with emerald and scarlet trappings, department-store chimes, draggled wreaths, and pseudo Santa Clauses, broke over us, and still nobody said anything. My mother had a haunted look, as if she were waiting for my father to speak, and he seemed impervious to the brash advance guard of the Yule. We began to feel both betrayed and dogged. The bicycle and the white kid gloves ceased to be desires and became causes with us. We whined aloud, though it made my mother cringe. We complained at our housework.

"Maybe it isn't coming this year," I said at last, banging the pots and pans about after dinner.

"What isn't coming?" my mother asked.

"Christmas," I cried.

"Christmas always comes for people who have the right spirit."

"Not to us!"

"Christmas comes in your heart."

"But not like last year," I wailed. "Nothing's the same any more. Nothing." I began to sniffle, and rushed up to my room, where I sobbed on the bed, luxuriating in self-pity.

She followed me and voiced the immemorial platitudes. "The real joy of life is giving—not getting," my mother said. "You probably won't believe me now, but you'll find out."

"But that's just it," I wept. "I want to give too, but I haven't anything to buy it with. I haven't any money!"

"Darling, I haven't either," my mother said sadly. "You're a grown girl. You'll have to find your own way. Please don't mention this to your father."

"I never see him, anyway."

"No more do I. And I'm afraid it's harder on me than on you. Now wash your face."

"I'll show them," I muttered after she had left me.

Thereafter I was sullen and fierce, and my pride was draggled. Surreptitiously I had applied for a job in the school cafeteria, not as a waitress but as a dishwasher, since I could not bear the thought of moving among my schoolmates collecting their soiled trays. I made my way to the steamy kitchen after my last class by various subterfuges and lied out of after-school strolls and sodas with uncompromising duplicity. I did not much mind the job, though it was tiresome work, but with youthful snobbery despised the thought of stigma. Only my ability to weave any incident into the fantasies of an overactive imagination made it bearable. To myself, during this period, I was all the heroines of history, but I still smelled to myself of steam and suds. For my munificent effort I was paid two dollars per week, and since Christmas was three weeks away I could not hope for more than six dollars. Nobody knew about this venture. I could not bring myself to tell even Stan.

I didn't see much of Stan, anyway. I got home late and Stan was usually gone. Sometimes my mother was gone. The whole close-knit structure of our household seemed to have fallen apart. We were all silent and secretive, and when we were together we did not find anything to talk about. My mother's eyes pleaded with me, but I held myself stiffly away from her. My father made wistful little jokes at Sunday-morning breakfast, but I would frown instead of laugh. It did not occur to me that night clerking was as hard for him as dishwashing for me. Inside me there was a dark bruise engendered by what seemed his neglect.

Only Stan was normal.

"I'm making *him* a pipe rack," Stan said to me. "In manual training."

45

"But he doesn't smoke a pipe," I objected.

"I guess he would if he had one," said Stan. "I figure to get one to go with it."

"How?"

"I'm going to trade my knife," he said. "I know a guy who's got a pipe that's nearly new."

"What about *her?*"

"I'm making her a little box," Stan said, looking proud. "I'm carving her initials on it. She can put her beads and stuff in it. It's a real strong box."

I thought warmly of my four dollars buried in the bureau drawer among my pictures of movie stars. I had spent it a hundred times and stretched it a thousand ways until it had become a fortune.

Christmas came on Wednesday that year. The Sunday before, my father came downstairs haggard but cheerful. His step was full of bounce, and his eyes were bright. I did not know until years later that he had finally scraped enough cash together to pay the interest and the installments on the house and we were sheltered for another six months.

"Well, I'm taking the day off," he announced. "To gather the Christmas greens. Who would like to accompany me on a search for a Christmas tree?"

"They're so expensive this year," my mother protested. "Don't you think we're all old enough to get along without?"

"Nonsense," said my father with his old authority. "Never too old for a Christmas tree. Besides, we have received a gift. Mr. Feeneman, an elderly guest at the Eldorado Hotel, has given me permission to raid his wood lot. In the spirit of our ancestors, we will obtain a tree by dint of the ringing ax."

I loved to hear my father talk when he was in his historical mood, and the thought of a Christmas tree broke up the ice in my bosom. My heart lightened and Stan squirmed with excitement. As an added boon, my mother said she would remain behind and put the house to rights so that we could get an early start. Dishwashing by now had become anathema, and to be spared any session of it was more to be desired than rubies.

We set off through a light snow, already coating the earth, for Mr. Feeneman's wood lot, which turned out to be four miles in the country. My father made hearty comments upon the wholesome value of winter exercise, though I think this was to camouflage our lack of carfare. As we trudged, he pointed out the various trees to us and told us their Latin names. Awed by his unfailing erudition, I panted after his long steps, though I was tired enough to faint and the snow was running down my collar.

The cold wind began to blow more bitterly. Stan's teeth chattered, and my father's face began to look pinched. When we at last arrived at Feeneman's wood lot it was the most unprepossessing acre of scraggy, leafless trees and brambles, without a deciduous shrub in sight. Just like the wood lot of any guest of the Eldorado Hotel, I thought in rage. We went over it microscopically, and when we were just giving up Stan raised a shout from the farthest corner, and we rushed there to find a lopsided little cedar, ravaged by wind and weather, gnarled, frazzled, and old before its time. I thought it looked awful, but my father pronounced it prime. He unsheathed Stan's Boy Scout hatchet and began to chop.

The tree was very tough and my father was an inept woodsman. About halfway through the proceedings, a chip flew off the trunk and smacked Stanley in the eye. He yelled like an Indian and began to dance in pain. My father was sick with self-disgust and misery, and I was soundly frightened. The blood ran down Stan's cheek and he bent himself double to stop his own outcry.

"We must get him to the doctor," my father said.

"No, no," Stan wailed. "We have to finish chopping."

"It doesn't matter about the tree," my father quavered. "Your eyes are the most important thing!"

"It doesn't hurt," Stanley bellowed, mopping at the gore

with his sleeve. "I can see out of it. And it *does* matter about the Christmas tree. I want a Christmas tree," he babbled, like a baby.

My father was in a frenzy of indecision, and while he traveled in circles, Stan seized the hatchet and finished chopping down the cedar—the blood from the cut above his eye staining the snow.

"Oh, my God," Father croaked. "Come here, boy. I must bandage up that thing."

He examined the eye, which was swelling and turning plum color, and bound up Stanley's head in his white linen handkerchief. This turned out to be a minor blessing, as a farmer in an old car, witnessing the miserable tableau, drew up by the side of the road and took us in, Stanley still clutching the pathetic cedar as we huddled together on the back seat, the cedar needles prickling through our clothing. I began to sneeze and my father divided worried glances between Stanley and me. His face was long, and I suppose he was thinking that nothing would ever turn out right again.

We hurtled up to our door and staggered out. Stanley was shaken but cheerful. I was having trouble with my nose, and my father looked as if a feather would knock him flat. While he paused to give his thanks to our samaritan and wish him the compliments of the season, Stan and I dragged the cedar to the door.

My mother came out and stared speechless at our woebegone looks.

"Madame," said my father, "I have given your son a mouse."

"Stanley," she shrieked, and Stan began to cry for the first time.

That evening we trimmed the Christmas tree. Nothing could disguise the fact that it was a dingy little cedar, not shaped to bear the lovely loot of Christmas, but it was the finest tree I ever saw. Stan was so proud of it, and as he bent his abrasions, contusions, and bruises above it, while he and my father affixed the stand, the light of happiness gleamed from his good eye. Through some inexplicable stroke on my father's part the lights all burned brightly, and as I sat stringing the garlands of pop-corn and cranberries, and my mother tied on the cherished old baubles of a dozen childhood Christmases, it seemed to me that our mutual estrangement had vanished and we were a family again, safe from the world's alarms. This enabled me to ignore partially the fact that my throat was getting more sore by the minute.

By morning, my tonsils seemed to have closed off my wind-pipe almost entirely, but I did not mention it. It was my last day in the cafeteria, and I had to have the other two dollars. I took my accumulated wealth with me and after school I went shopping. The stores were crowded and I felt very warm and light-headed. As I began to hunt for the things I had imagined buying, I soon discovered the inadequacy of six dollars. One by one I discarded my dreams, but I could not quite give up the thirst for luxury, and instead of the warm woolen socks my father needed I came home with a pair of fine black silk ones, embroidered with a clock. Though my mother could have done with a pair of stout gloves, I chose a ruffly nightgown of some sleazy pink stuff, since it was what I would have wanted. For Stanley, I got a bicycle bell, knowing full well he hadn't got a bicycle, but it seemed to me that if you could not have what your heart desired, a bit of its music would be better than nothing. As I say, I was light-headed.

On Christmas Eve, I felt really dreadful. My throat ached, along with my head and all the other bones in my body, and my stomach kept turning over to add to the general dismay, so that I could not share in the frenzied celebration which marked the arrival of a twenty-pound turkey from Uncle Robert's farm. The very presence of the traditional meat seemed to buoy Mother and to make her feel that the times were back in joint, while Stanley and my father responded to the thought of something beside chopped meat; but I was not hungry.

I wished for nothing so much as to lie still in bed and not even think, but this was out of the question, as the bubble and squeak of Christmas now rose to crescendo. I alternated between chills and burning and resorted often to the bathroom for gargle and first aid, to retch or douse my aching head with cold water from the tap. Between chores I repaired to my bedroom to admire my offerings and try to persuade myself to wrap them up. When I had time I thought of Ruth's party, which I still had some hope of attending, having assured myself if worst came to worst, I would wear my mother's old black dress. In my fevered state this possibility seemed quite likely to me, though it never could have happened.

The day passed in a wave of hysteria, puncuated with nausea inspired by the delicious smells which came from the kitchen— the old smells of Christmas. In spite of my indisposition I felt cheerful. The house had come to life again and was full of happy secrets, bustle, and normalcy, and if the Christmas tree bore no tangible fruit, still it was there, setting its seal upon the season. My mother's moodiness had vanished and her voice had its ring of maternal authority. Stan, his face piebald in the yellow and mauve of bruise, bore his scars like a soldier and seemed to have turned overnight from a nagging little brother into a man. My father had been whistling when he left the house.

According to our custom, the Christmas tree was scheduled for the night of Christmas Eve. My father had got the night off from the Eldorado. When I came into the room in the late afternoon Stan was laying the fire on the hearth. Three forlorn little packages, wrapped up by Stanley in scraps of ribbon and string, were disposed under its scrubby branches. I arranged my three around them.

"I guess that's all," I said hoarsely.

"I guess so," Stan mused. "I hope you like what I got you."

"I will."

"You want me to tell you what it is?" he asked eagerly.

"No, no! I want to be surprised. I *have* to be surprised!" I cried out with passion.

"I wasn't going to tell you, anyway," he said, grinning on the unbruised side of his face.

At dinner I could not eat.

"She's too excited," my mother said. "She can't take anything calmly. Look at that flush. She looks as if she had a fever."

I shrank from the tentative hand she put out to explore my brow.

My father leaned over and, putting his forefinger under my chin, he tipped up my hot face and looked into my burning eyes.

"My little girl," he said, "is turning into a beauty."

The effect of his almost forgotten tenderness was to send a shiver down me, and I had to rush out of the room to stop the blinding tears. My love for him ached like a tooth. The lump of anxiety and worry and fear of the months past got mixed up in my sore throat and everything hurt terribly, all at the same time. I could not keep from wishing I were dead, a natural emotion at sixteen, when the possibility is remote.

By the time I had regained composure the inevitable dishes had to be washed, but I was almost grateful to have something to occupy me until eight o'clock. I offered to let Stan off from drying to be alone, for I was afraid another word would send me flying into little pieces, but gallantly he insisted, not to be outdone in generosity.

Embarrassment fell on Stan and me in the kitchen. Our friendship was deep and lasting, but neither of us could talk about it, so we did not talk. We hung about in the kitchen after we had finished, not knowing what to do with ourselves. Then we heard my mother at the piano and my father's sweet, true voice, singing snatches of "Silent Night." The year before we had raced like little children, but now we walked sedately, and Stan stood back and let me go in first.

The fire blazed and the room was soft with candlelight from the stubby storm candles set in the old brass candelabra. The little red and green bulbs glowed like jeweled fruit on the cedar tree. A snowfall of packages piled around the base, and to one side, refracting the firelight, stood the gleaming bicycle. Stan's mouth dropped and I thought, with almost my first pure unselfishness, that I would rather he had got it than to have anything myself.

It is impossible to say more about the intimacy of the scene which ensued. It happens multiplied millions of times in this season, and you had best remember your own time. The happy cry which leaps from a young girl's lips when she draws from its tissue wrappings her first long party dress, even if it be fashioned from her mother's last taffeta negligee, is an old story. Surely you too have unwrapped your first pair of long white kid gloves with the dear little buttons at the wrist—the beautiful, delicate, white kid gloves which mean that you are a grown woman, forever above the soil of childhood. And if they were the product of sacrifice, you cannot escape my intention.

It was late when we settled back from charged emotions of exchange of regard to sip the mulled cider. Stan was in a stupor of pleasure, swathed in his new sweater my mother had knitted up in the school colors, and assaulting our ears with the brassy twang of the bicycle bell. My father was already wearing his new shoes (my mother's present), and his old ones, lined with the gray soles cut from old laundry boards to keep the damp from the holes, stood grotesquely under the Christmas tree. He was smoking the pipe that had been smoked only a time or two before and coughing, while he fondled his silk socks, his face alive with awareness that they were the best money could buy. My mother had put on her pink nightgown over her dress, and it became her. She sat tracing the initials of her name, which Stan had carved into the box top, with gentle pride. I stroked my treasure alternately. I could not keep from touching what I loved. Stan had made me a fan and it was the crowning fillip of frivolity.

"Why, it's midnight," my mother said, aghast. "It's been a long day. Run along to bed."

A slight contretemps followed, which could be solved only by permitting Stanley to take his bicycle upstairs with him. He swore he could not be parted from it overnight. I then persisted that I must try on my dress and gloves and show them off. A strange leniency had descended upon our parents. These things were permitted.

I stood before the mirror in my room, slipping the amethyst taffeta over my head, which continued to feel dizzy. It had a low neck which showed the smooth curve of my shoulder, and the live color reflected in my eyes. I swished the skirt and I caught up my long white gloves and swept out of the room in an exaggerated copy of my favorite movie heroine. I touched the hair at the back of the neck tentatively and smiled an enigmatic smile. I paused on the landing in my made-over finery, drawing on a glove. All my senses responded to the sibilance of silk and the satiny softness of the glove against my bare arm. As I peered in the dark, enjoying the rash décolletage of the dress and the unaccustomed flow of skirt around my ankles, I leaned over the banister in a last excess of childish eavesdropping.

My father and mother were standing before the hearth. I saw how stooped his shoulders were and the new frost on his dark hair.

"Whitney," my mother said in a voice of happy puzzlement, "however did you do it—the bicycle, the gloves . . . "

"I don't blame you, Ellie, for thinking I've been at the Eldorado's till. It looks too foolish for our busted economy. But it was luck, honey, the Barton luck!" He summoned a grin. "So help me, I won the bike on a punchboard at the Rexall Drug-store. I went in there the other night to get a cup of coffee and a doughnut, and there was one hole left in the board. What did I have to lose but a cup of coffee?"

"Oh, Whit!" she cried. "You went hungry."

"Just a tinhorn gambler," my father said. "But you've got to take a chance now and then!"

"But the gloves——"

"Well, I saved five dollars. I've been walking home from the hotel. Need a breath of air after an all-night stetch, you know."

My mother didn't speak.

"I had luck again," he said. "There were a bunch of measly-looking gloves on a table marked 'clearance,' and right down in one corner was this pair—just what the doctor ordered—and dirt cheap!"

"They're beautiful! You've made them both so happy."

"When you're sixteen," my father said, "or just twelve, you deserve to be happy. And when you're an old man, you can't bear it if now and then—at Christmas, say—you can't make wishes come true. You can't bear it, Ellie, being a failure to your children!"

"Don't say a thing like that. They've never wanted for anything in their lives!"

"But it's not enough—food and shelter and advice. You've got to give them something else, some kind of symbol of what the world can hold—something to reach for. Anyway," said my father, his voice trailing off into a whisper, "my luck didn't last."

"You can only have so much luck, Whit," my mother said.

He faced her, and his face was broken up and he swallowed painfully. "I haven't got anything for you, Ellie," he said. "I bought you a bottle of that stuff you like—that lilac stuff, whatchamacallit? But I got tangled up in that damn bicycle chain and fell down. Lord help me, I broke it!"

His despair was comic, and the picture of my debonair father entwined in the chain of Stan's new bike was funny enough to

54

tickle anybody. I wanted to giggle and I waited for my mother's laughter.

But she didn't laugh. She turned toward him so that her full face was to me, and such radiance burned on it, such an indescribable expression of pride and fulfillment, of faith and hope and love, that I was forced to drop my eyes.

"I love you," she said. "I'd rather be married to you than any man alive!"

They were motionless, two figures in a frieze, immobilized by the force of mutual feeling. They moved at the same time, without volition, melted together, entwined, touching—man and woman, but one entity.

It was then that my moment of happiness broke over me in brilliant, prismatic splendor. All finite things dissolved, the horizons of the earth rolled back, the firmament immeasurably deepened, and I could hear that strange music which falls upon the inner ear only a few times in a life. All the voices of all the angels sang in my head, and every beat of every heart. I knew that the secret of life was almost in my grasp. I looked up the long arches of the years, and they beckoned. I leaned toward the future, abandoning fear. I was dizzy with my untrammeled ability to see what cannot be seen with the physical eye, to see beyond the little limitations of the human orb into the extensions of the spirit. I turned upon my infinite pinnacle and saw them far below—the two loving figures who had given me the secret. How small they were and far away, and how my heart surged toward them. My father had straightened up and was standing tall, and my mother's laughter now spilled out. From my eminence I knew that they were invincible as long as they had breath, and even after. I did not doubt it for a moment.

In this eternity which occupied only a second in time, I had continued to tug at my other glove without knowing it. Now I drew it off and looked at it and pulled at the fingers to smooth them. Then I turned and went back upstairs. I could not intrude further on what I had witnessed, and I did not want to see anybody. I wanted to be alone and remember what I was waiting for.

On Christmas morning I had a high fever, and thickly over my swollen face the rash had materialized. The doctor, summoned from his own Christmas, sniffed at the door, and almost before he had looked at me he made the diagnosis. "Measles," he said. "Fine thing for a great strapping girl! And a fine time to have the measles!"

But nothing could touch me. I could not even regret too deeply the loss of the Christmas party. I was quite happy to lie in the dark and ponder my thoughts.

There was compensation in the measles, for if I had had to go to the Christmas party, my father would have discovered what he never in all his life knew. Both of the white kid gloves he had struggled to buy were for the left hand.

A Day of Pleasant Bread

DAVID GRAYSON

THEY have all gone now, and the house is very still. For the first time this evening I can hear the familiar sound of the December wind blustering about the house, complaining at closed doorways, asking questions at the shutters; but here in my room, under the green reading lamp, it is warm and still. Although Harriet has closed the doors, covered the coals in the fireplace, and said good-night, the atmosphere still seems to tingle with the electricity of genial humanity.

The parting voice of the Scotch Preacher still booms in my ears:

"This," said he, as he was going out of our door, wrapped like an Arctic highlander in cloaks and tippets, "has been a day of pleasant bread."

One of the very pleasantest I can remember!

I sometimes think we expect too much of Christmas Day. We try to crowd into it the long arrears of kindliness and humanity of the whole year. As for me, I like to take my Christmas a little at a time, all through the year. And thus I drift along into the holidays—let them overtake me unexpectedly—waking up some fine morning and suddenly saying to myself:

"Why, this is Christmas Day!"

How the discovery makes one bound out of his bed! What a new sense of life and adventure it imparts! Almost anything may happen on a day like this—one thinks. I may meet friends I have not seen before in years. Who knows? I may discover that this is a far better and kindlier world than I had ever dreamed it could be.

So I sing out to Harriet as I go down:

"Merry Christmas, Harriet"—and not waiting for her sleepy reply I go down and build the biggest, warmest, friendliest fire of the year. Then I get into my thick coat and mittens and open the back door. All around the sill, deep on the step, and all about the yard lies the drifted snow: it has transformed my wood pile into a grotesque Indian mound, and it frosts the roof of my barn like a wedding cake. I go at it lustily with my wooden shovel, clearing out a pathway to the gate.

Cold, too; one of the coldest mornings we've had—but clear and very still. The sun is just coming up over the hill near Horace's farm. From Horace's chimney the white wood-smoke of an early fire rises straight upward, all golden with sunshine, into the measureless blue of the sky—on its way to heaven, for aught I know. When I reach the gate my blood is racing warmly in my veins. I straighten my back, thrust my shovel into the snow pile, and shout at the top of my voice, for I can no longer contain myself:

"Merry Christmas, Harriet."

Harriet opens the door—just a crack.

"Merry Christmas yourself, you Arctic explorer! Oo—but it's cold!"

And she closes the door.

Upon hearing these riotous sounds the barnyard suddenly awakens. I hear my horse whinnying from the barn, the chickens begin to crow and cackle, and such a grunting and squealing as the pigs set up from behind the straw stack, it would do a man's heart good to hear!

"It's a friendly world," I say to myself, "and full of business."

I plow through the snow to the stable door. I scuff and stamp the snow away and pull it open with difficulty. A cloud of steam arises out of the warmth within. I step inside. My horse raises his head above the stanchion, looks around at me, and strikes his forefoot on the stable floor—the best greeting he has at his command for a fine Christmas morning. My cow, until now silent, begins to bawl.

I lay my hand on the horse's flank and he steps over in his stall to let me go by. I slap his neck and he lays back his ears playfully. Thus I go out into the passageway and give my horse his oats, throw corn and stalks to the pigs and a handful of grain to Harriet's chickens (it's the only way to stop the cackling!). And thus presently the barnyard is quiet again except for the sound of contented feeding.

Take my word for it, this is one of the pleasant moments of life. I stand and look long at my barnyard family. I observe with satisfaction how plump they are and how well they are bearing the winter. Then I look up at my mountainous straw stack with its capping of snow, and my corn crib with the yellow ears visible through the slats, and my barn with its mow full of hay —all the gatherings of the year, now being expended in growth. I cannot at all explain it, but at such moments the circuit of that dim spiritual battery which each of us conceals within seems to close, and the full current of contentment flows through our lives.

All the morning as I went about my chores I had a peculiar sense of expected pleasure. It seemed certain to me that something unusual and adventurous was about to happen—and if it did not happen offhand, why I was there to make it happen! When I went in to breakfast (do you know the fragrance of broiling bacon when you have worked for an hour before breakfast on a morning of zero weather? If you do not, consider that heaven still has gifts in store for you!)—when I went into breakfast, I fancied that Harriet looked preoccupied, but I was too busy just then (hot corn muffins) to make an inquiry, and I knew by experience that the best solvent of secrecy is patience.

"David," said Harriet, presently, "the cousins can't come!"

"Can't come!" I exclaimed.

"Why, you act as if you were delighted."

"No—well, yes," I said, "I knew that some extraordinary adventure was about to happen!"

"Adventure! It's a cruel disappointment—I was all ready for them."

"Harriet," I said, "adventure is just what we make it. And aren't we to have the Scotch Preacher and his wife?"

"But I've got such a good dinner."

"Well," I said, "there are no two ways about it: it must be eaten! You may depend upon me to do my duty."

"We'll have to send out into the highways and compel them to come in," said Harriet ruefully.

I had several choice observations I should have liked to make upon this problem, but Harriet was plainly not listening; she sat with her eyes fixed reflectively on the coffeepot. I watched her for a moment, then I remarked:

"There aren't any."

"David," she exclaimed, "how did you know what I was thinking about?"

"I merely wanted to show you," I said, "that my genius is not properly appreciated in my own household. You thought of highways, didn't you? Then you thought of the poor; especially the poor on Christmas Day; then of Mrs. Heney, who isn't poor any more, having married John Daniels; and then I said, 'There aren't any.'"

Harriet laughed.

"It has come to a pretty pass," she said, "when there are no poor people to invite to dinner on Christmas Day."

"It's a tragedy, I'll admit," I said, "but let's be logical about it."

"I am willing," said Harriet, "to be as logical as you like."

"Then," I said, "having no poor to invite to dinner we must necessarily try the rich. That's logical, isn't it?"

"Who?" asked Harriet, which is just like a woman. Whenever you get a good healthy argument started with her, she will suddenly shortcircuit it, and want to know if you mean Mr. Smith, or Joe Perkins's boys, which I maintain is not logical.

"Well, there are the Starkweathers," I said.

"David!"

"They're rich, aren't they?"

"Yes, but you know how they live—what dinners they have—and besides, they probably have a houseful of company."

"Weren't you telling me the other day how many people who were really suffering were too proud to let anyone know about it? Weren't you advising the necessity of getting acquainted with people and finding out—tactfully, of course—you made a point of tact—what the trouble was?"

"But I was talking of poor people."

"Why shouldn't a rule that is good for poor people be equally good for rich people? Aren't they proud?"

"Oh, you can argue," observed Harriet.

"And I can act, too," I said. "I am now going over to invite the Starkweathers. I heard a rumor that their cook has left them and I expect to find them starving in their parlor. Of course they'll be very haughty and proud, but I'll be tactful, and when I go away I'll casually leave a diamond tiara in the front hall."

"What is the matter with you this morning?"

"Christmas," I said.

I can't tell how pleased I was with the enterprise I had in mind: it suggested all sorts of amusing and surprising developments. Moreover, I left Harriet, finally, in the breeziest of spirits, having quite forgotten her disappointment over the non-arrival of the cousins.

"If you should get the Starkweathers——"

" 'In the bright lexicon of youth,' " I observed, " 'there is no such word as fail.' "

So I set off up the town road. A team or two had already been that way and had broken a track through the snow. The sun was now fully up, but the air still tingled with the electricity of zero weather. And the fields! I have seen the fields of June and the fields of October, but I think I never saw our countryside, hills and valleys, tree spaces and brook bottoms, more enchantingly beautiful than it was this morning. Snow everywhere—the

61

fences half hidden, the bridges clogged, the trees laden: where the road was hard it squeaked under my feet, and where it was soft I strode through the drifts. And the air went to one's head like wine!

So I tramped past the Pattersons'. The old man, a grumpy old fellow, was going to the barn with a pail on his arm.

"Merry Christmas," I shouted.

He looked around at me wonderingly and did not reply. At the corners I met the Newton boys so wrapped in tippets that I could see only their eyes and the red ends of their small noses. I passed the Williams's house, where there was a cheerful smoke in the chimney and in the window a green wreath with a lively red bow. And I thought how happy everyone must be on a Christmas morning like this! At the hill bridge who should I meet but the Scotch Preacher himself, God bless him!

"Well, well, David," he exclaimed heartily, "Merry Christmas."

I drew my face down and said solemnly:

"Dr. McAlway, I am on a most serious errand."

"Why, now, what's the matter?" He was all sympathy at once.

"I am out in the highways trying to compel the poor of this neighborhood to come to our feast."

The Scotch Preacher observed me with a twinkle in his eye.

"David," he said, putting his hand to his mouth as if to speak in my ear, "here is a poor man you will na' have to compel."

"Oh, you don't count," I said. "You're coming anyhow."

Then I told him of the errand with our millionaire friends, into the spirit of which he entered with the greatest zest. He was full of advice and much excited lest I fail to do a thoroughly competent job. For a moment I think he wanted to take the whole thing out of my hands.

"Man, man, it's a lovely thing to do," he exclaimed, "but I ha' me doots—I ha' me doots."

At parting he hesitated a moment, and with a serious face inquired:

"Is it by any chance a goose?"

"It is," I said, "a goose—a big one."

He heaved a sigh of complete satisfaction. "You have comforted my mind," he said, "with the joys of anticipation—a goose, a big goose."

So I left him and went onward toward the Starkweathers'. Presently I saw the great house standing among its wintry trees. There was smoke in the chimney but no other evidence of life. At the gate my spirits, which had been of the best all the morning, began to fail me. Though Harriet and I were well enough acquainted with the Starkweathers, yet at this late moment on Christmas morning it did seem rather a hairbrained scheme to think of inviting them to dinner.

"Never mind," I said, "they'll not be displeased to see me anyway."

I waited in the reception-room, which was cold and felt damp. In the parlor beyond I could see the innumerable things of beauty—furniture, pictures, books, so very, very much of everything—with which the room was filled. I saw it now, as I had often seen it before, with a peculiar sense of weariness. How all these things, though beautiful enough in themselves, must clutter up a man's life!

Do you know, the more I look into life, the more things it seems to me I can successfully lack—and continue to grow happier. How many kinds of food I do not need, nor cooks to cook them, how much curious clothing nor tailors to make it, how many books that I never read, and pictures that are not worth while! The farther I run, the more I feel like casting aside all such impedimenta—lest I fail to arrive at the far goal of my endeavor.

I like to think of an old Japanese nobleman I once read about, who ornamented his house with a single vase at a time, living with it, absorbing its message of beauty, and when he tired of it, replacing it with another. I wonder if he had the right way, and we, with so many objects to hang on our walls, place on our shelves, drape on our chairs, and spread on our floors, have mistaken our course and placed our hearts upon the multiplicity rather than the quality of our possessions!

Presently Mr. Starkweather appeared in the doorway. He wore a velvet smoking-jacket and slippers; and somehow, for a bright morning like this, he seemed old, and worn, and cold.

"Well, well, friend," he said, "I'm glad to see you."

He said it as though he meant it.

"Come into the library; it's the only room in the whole house that is comfortably warm. You've no idea what a task it is to heat a place like this in really cold weather. No sooner do I find a man who can run my furnace than he goes off and leaves me."

"I can sympathize with you," I said, "we often have trouble at our house with the man who builds the fires."

He looked around at me quizzically.

"He lies too long in bed in the morning," I said.

By this time we had arrived at the library, where a bright fire was burning in the grate. It was a fine big room, with dark oak furnishings and books in cases along one wall, but this morning it had a disheveled and untidy look. On a little table at one side of the fireplace were the remains of a breakfast; at the other a number of wraps were thrown carelessly upon a chair. As I came in Mrs. Starkweather rose from her place, drawing a silk scarf round her shoulders. She is a robust, rather handsome woman, with many rings on her fingers, and a pair of glasses hanging to a little gold hook on her ample bosom; but this morning she, too, looked worried and old.

"Oh, yes," she said with a rueful laugh, "we're beginning a merry Christmas, as you see. Think of Christmas with no cook in the house!"

I felt as if I had discovered a gold mine. Poor starving millionaires!

But Mrs. Starkweather had not told the whole of her sorrowful story.

"We had a company of friends invited for dinner today," she said, "and our cook was ill—or said she was—and had to go. One of the maids went with her. The man who looks after the furnace disappeared on Friday, and the stableman has been drinking. We can't very well leave the place without someone who is responsible in charge of it—and so here we are. Merry Christmas!"

I couldn't help laughing. Poor people!

"You might," I said, "apply for Mrs. Heney's place."

"Who is Mrs. Heney?" asked Mrs. Starkweather.

"You don't mean to say that you never heard of Mrs. Heney!" I exclaimed. "Mrs. Heney, who is now Mrs. 'Penny' Daniels? You've missed one of our greatest celebrities."

With that, of course, I had to tell them about Mrs. Heney, who has for years performed a most important function in this community. Alone and unaided she has been the poor whom we are supposed to have always with us. If it had not been for the devoted faithfulness of Mrs. Heney at Thanksgiving, Christmas and other times of the year, I suppose our Woman's Aid Society and the King's Daughters would have perished miserably of undistributed turkeys and tufted comforters. For years Mrs. Heney filled the place most acceptably. Curbing the natural outpourings of a rather jovial soul she could upon occasion look as deserving of charity as any person that ever I met. But I pitied the little Heneys: it always comes hard on the children. For weeks after every Thanksgiving and Christmas they always wore a painfully stuffed and suffocated look. I only came to appreciate fully what a self-sacrificing public servant Mrs. Heney really was when I learned that she had taken the desperate alternative of marrying "Penny" Daniels.

"So you think we might possibly aspire to the position?" laughed Mrs. Starkweather.

Upon this I told them of the trouble in our household and asked them to come down and help us enjoy Dr. McAlway and the goose.

When I left, after much more pleasant talk, they both came with me to the door seeming greatly improved in spirits.

"You've given us something to live for, Mr. Grayson," said Mrs. Starkweather.

So I walked homeward in the highest spirits, and an hour or more later who should we see in the top of our upper field but Mr. Starkweather and his wife floundering in the snow. They reached the lane literally covered from top to toe with snow and both of them ruddy with cold.

"We walked over," said Mrs. Starkweather breathlessly, "and I haven't had so much fun in years."

Mr. Starkweather helped her over the fence. The Scotch Preacher stood on the steps to receive them, and we all went in together.

I can't pretend to describe Harriet's dinner: the gorgeous brown goose, and the apple sauce, and all the other things that best go with it, and the pumpkin pie at the end—the finest, thickest, most delicious pumpkin pie I ever ate in all my life. It melted in one's mouth and brought visions of celestial bliss. And I wish I could have a picture of Harriet presiding. I have never seen her happier, or more in her element. Every time she brought in a new dish or took off a cover it was a sort of miracle. And her coffee—— But I must not and dare not elaborate.

And what great talk we had afterward!

I've known the Scotch Preacher for a long time, but I never saw him in quite such a mood of hilarity. He and Mr. Starkweather told stories of their boyhood—and we laughed, and laughed—Mrs. Starkweather the most of all. Seeing her so often in her carriage, or in the dignity of her home, I didn't think she had so much jollity in her. Finally she discovered Harriet's cabinet organ and nothing would do but she must sing for one.

"None of the new-fangled ones, Clara," cried her husband: "Some of the old ones we used to know."

So she sat herself down at the organ and threw her head back and began to sing:

"Believe me, if all those endearing young charms,
   Which I gaze on so fondly to-day——,"

Mr. Starkweather jumped up and ran over to the organ and joined in with his deep voice. Harriet and I followed. The Scotch Preacher's wife nodded in time with the music, and presently I saw the tears in her eyes. As for Dr. McAlway, he sat on the edge of his chair with his hands on his knees and wagged his shaggy head, and before we got through he, too, joined in with his big sonorous voice:

"Thou wouldst still be adored as this moment thou art——,"

Oh, I can't tell here—it grows late and there's work tomorrow —all the things we did and said. They stayed until it was dark, and when Mrs. Starkweather was ready to go, she took both of Harriet's hands in hers and said with great earnestness:

"I haven't had such a good time at Christmas since I was a little girl. I shall never forget it."

And the dear old Scotch Preacher, when Harriet and I had wrapped him up, went out, saying:

"This has been a day of pleasant bread."

It has; it has. I shall not soon forget it. What a lot of kindness and common human nature, childlike simplicity—if you will— there is in people once you get them down together and persuade them that the things they think serious are not serious at all.

Christmas at the Bachs'

A. E. BRACHVOGEL

IT WAS the morning of Christmas Eve. The days are then astonishingly short. One can hardly get down to a job before it's dark again, and yet father and son need the daylight so badly for their work! In the living room Friedemann and Sebastian are sitting at a table, which has been pulled up in front of the window. Each has a shining copperplate in front of him, set upon an old windowseat cushion for pad, upon which the copperplate rotates while the gleaming metal stylus etches deep, restlessly moving back and forth, and digging out measures, intervals and cadenzas on the already marked staves of the original MSS. Sebastian Bach, too poor to have the work done by an engraver, too little a follower of the modern trend in music fashion to find a publisher—this same Sebastian Bach painfully engraves the whole *Art of the Fugue* with his son, so that his life's masterpiece shall not be lost.

The old man's mouth is twisted bitterly. Yes, yes, he is no Hasse, no Rameau, no Couperin or Chiabran. He does not write operas or dear little Canzonettas! Who the devil would buy church music today, or even listen to it? Gradually, the century prepares to erase the Lord God from His universe, so who would have a taste for His hymns?

The old man is wearing green glasses. Can't you see how rheumy his eyes are? The blinding brightness of the copper burns them, and he may go blind before he has succeeded in casting the ephemeral tones he creates into permanence for posterity. Quiet Anna Magdalena decorates the Christmas tree in the schoolroom, Friedrich and Christian are still at school, and David is sitting on the floor, playing with scraps of paper

68

which he throws high up into the air. He is making "pigeons fly."

"I wonder how Old Nicolas and Fredericka are faring in Naumburg?" says the father, who had to interrupt his work to sharpen his instrument and wipe his glasses. "They haven't written for quite some time. I thought perhaps they would have come to Leipzig for Christmas."

"How can they be anything but well?" replies Friedemann without looking up. "They have their own home, a good job— oh, indeed, everything must go well with them."

His father looks at Friedemann, and then the conversation was already at an end. Every time their talk got onto any subject other than their work, the evil spirits of envy and anguish, which raged within the son, closed his father's lips. Even the most innocent banter was thus poisoned. Finally, the father put down his stylus with an authoritative air.

"Friedemann," he said, "it's just no good. Your misfortunes make you wicked and envious. You cling far too stubbornly to your melancholy, and you will isolate yourself more and more from your fellow men. If you were truly religious, you would know that in the end God works everything out well, and that faith would give you the strength to lift yourself above your sorrow, and hope, in its turn, would give you the strength to work cheerfully."

"But, dear father, am I not doing all I possibly can? What else is there I can do?"

"Just making such an effort, Friedemann, will not help you. You are only torturing yourself by trying to force yourself. That's why you don't succeed. Without joy, without hope, any work of art is stillborn. It becomes more and more clear to me that you don't have the basic essentials of religious faith. You are lacking in the spirit of service, which finds creative strength in its very humility. Today our Lord is born, the Saviour of our poor human race. Oh, if only God would give me the joy of knowing that a Saviour was born in you, too, who would set you free from yourself, and would give you new heart, new courage! For then, my dear son, everything would work out, believe me. All of us, and you yourself, would together find our happiness in you."

In spite of himself he had begun to cry, and he silently embraced his son. It was a last cry wrung from his paternal heart. Friedemann could hardly bear it. Gently he pushed his father aside. "Wait just one moment, dear Father, I'll be right back." He rushed out of the room in order to hide his emotion. Sebastian was left to his sad thoughts, while David played quietly at his feet. The old man put his hands together as though in a despairing prayer, and turned his burning eyes toward the window, and out, up to the gray sky full of swirling snowflakes.

Shortly after Friedemann entered the room quietly. He was very pale, and in his hand he was holding a sheet with music on it.

"Here, father, I have made one last attempt. I was going to give it to you tonight, but since you and I are so sad I thought perhaps that this is the best moment."

Sebastian pressed his hand. He was trembling as he took the composition and spread it out suspiciously. Dear God, how the fear of false hope showed in his face! His son watched him closely, as though his father were about to pass a sentence of death upon him. Sebastian's face was flushed a deep red. He looked now at Friedemann, now at the paper, as though he were in a dream.

"Oh, father, it is bad, isn't it?"

"Bad? Are you crazy? No, my dearest, it's good, so good and so beautiful, that if you will forgive me for saying so, I can't really quite believe that it is yours." As he spoke a blissful joy, all his old pride in his Friedemann, came back into Sebastian's heart with heady jubilation. Sobbing and laughing at the same time, like a child, he embraced his son and rushed out to the boy's mother, waving the music high in the air in front of him.

Friedemann felt reborn. The sun of his old self-confidence be-

gan to warm his sick heart, and rosy hope softly opened the
doors of its temple, through which his trembling soul advanced
furtively. He followed his father. There, in the schoolroom, the
old man was already at the piano, and he played the introduction, while Mother Magdalena in her dear voice was singing
the hymn which rose up to our Lord like a prayer.

> On earth grows no small blade,
> But heaven has dew besprint
> Each small flower in the shade.
> Still the sun's gold does glint,
> And when your self finds you
> Alone in forest night,
> Your dew and sunshine, too,
> Will pour upon you bright.
> Then shoots shall blossom green
> From out your deepest heart,
> For no live thing is seen
> But flowering is its part.

His mother was beside herself with joy. She laughed and
cried, and the father played and hummed the hymn again and
again, and could not get his fill of it. Finally he jumped up.
"Tell me, dear son, wherever in all the world did you find the
beautiful poem? And how glorious the music is!"

"I wrote the poem, too, father."

"Oh, you see, mother, how the old strength is still in him!
This came straight from his very soul, it is part of his very self,
and that is why it is so magnificent and mighty! Take courage,
dearest Friedemann, and don't be moody any more, because the
old Lord is still alive, and today he has sent you the genuine,
most beautiful Christ child, Who is your own Saviour, and
without Whom we cannot exist in this our life."

And that is how it was. Friedemann smiled again, and the
old blessed spirit of love, rosy self-confidence with its shy smile,
dwelt with him again. Today is the Christ feast, and it was

71

caroled throughout the house as of old. Familiar voices called "Christ's feast," and there, standing on the threshold, was dear Fredericka holding two blond children and there was cheerful Old Nicolas.

"Come in, come in," said Sebastian happily, "that my house may be filled." And greetings and kisses and joy and tears were all mixed up, because once again it was like in the old days. The days of sorrow were forgotten, or melted away into the hours of joy, into the hope of happy days. And once again the door opened, and in came Mietzler, with a deputation from the society of the musical sciences, and presented Sebastian with an honorary membership in the name of all the musicians.

"You know, Mother, when heaven sends you joy, it does so thoroughly, and I must thank God and praise this day, when I can be truly happy, from the bottom of my heart, after the long days of sorrow. And Friedemann, you, too, must help me. Come, put your thinking cap on! We will write a Christmas song, and the society shall have it right away, so that they may learn what kind of new member they are getting. Come, dear boy."

Evening came. The Christmas tree shone in fairy splendor, the lovely legend of the Love that descended from heaven for the salvation and freedom and brotherhood of the divided world wove its golden web once more around the mourning hearts of a sorrowful mankind. There, at the instrument, in the magical twinkling light of the Christmas tree, sat the old bard, in a frenzy of enthusiasm, with his wife, his child, and his child's child. And all were singing the Christmas song:

> Be not afraid; look ye,
> for I bring unto you joyful tidings
> which shall be to all people.
> For unto you there is born this day
> in the city of David a Saviour which is
> **Christ the Lord.**

Christmas at the Bachs'

The old carol singer has long been sleeping in the kingdom of peace, but his immortal song still clarions forth in our hearts, and they become young and new, when the organ plays on Christmas night:

For I bring unto you joyful tidings.

FROM *Friedemann Bach*
TRANSLATED BY ANNE FREMANTLE

Bid the Tapers Twinkle

BESS STREETER ALDRICH

THE ATKIN house sat well back in a tree-filled yard on a busy corner of town, its wide frame porch running around two sides, thirty feet of it facing Churchill Avenue, thirty feet facing Seventh Street, its long brick walk sloping across the lot to an iron gateway in the exact corner, as though with impartial deference to both streets.

The arrangement might have been almost symbolic of the character of old Mrs. Atkin, who had lived there for many years, so impartially gracious to her well-to-do Churchill Avenue callers and her hired help from Seventh Street.

Old Sara Atkin had known the town longer than any one now living in it. Indeed, she had arrived as a bride only a few weeks after the first timbers were laid for the sawmill which became the nucleus of a village. She had seen a store go up near the sawmill, a single pine room with a porch across the front, onto which a man threw a sack of mail from the back of a pony twice a week. She had seen the first house built—a queer little box of a cottonwood house; had seen another follow, and others; then a one-roomed school-house and a stout frame church with a thick spire like a work-worn hand pointing a clumsy finger to the blue sky. She had seen whips of cottonwood trees set out at the edge of the grassy streets, had watched them grow to giants, live out their lives and fall to the ground under the axes of the third generation. She had seen a shining roadway of steel laid through the village and the first iron horse snort its way into the sunset. All these things and many others had old Sara Atkin seen.

John Atkin had gone back to Ohio for her and brought her by

wagon and ferry to his bachelor sod house on land he had purchased from the railroad company for two dollars an acre. She had been nineteen then, her cheeks as pink as the wild roses that sprang up in the prairie grass, her eyes as blue as the wild gentians that grew near them.

A few years later they had moved into a new three-room house with a lean-to and turned the soddie over to the stock. John Atkin had possessed the knack of making money where some of his neighbors had not. He had started a general store and a sorghum mill, had shipped in coal and lumber, had prospered to such an extent in a short time, that they were able to build the present residence, a castle of a house for the raw prairie town—so unusual, with its parlor and back parlor and its two fireplaces, that people had driven for miles in their top buggies or buckboards to see its capacious framework and the mottled marble of its mantels.

When it was completed, new furniture had come for it too —walnut bedsteads and center tables and a tall hall rack with a beveled-glass mirror. But the house which had once been such a source of pride to the whole community was merely a fussy and rather shabby old place now, with its furniture outmoded. John Atkin had been dead for many years, and Sara, whose cheeks had once been like wild roses, was a great-grandmother.

In the passing years the town had taken on an unbelievable size, and even a bit of sophistication, with its fine homes and university, its business blocks and country clubs. It had grown noisily around Sara Atkin; the tide of traffic now banged and clanged on the paved corner that had once been rutty and grass-grown.

But even though a filling station had gone up across the alley on the Seventh Street side and rather high-priced apartments on the Churchill Avenue side, old Sara would not leave, but stayed on in the fussy house with the walnut hall rack and the marble mantels.

She lived there all alone, too, except for the daily presence of one Jennie Williams, who came ploddingly down Seventh Street each day to work. Once, in Jennie's high-school days, Sara had taken her on temporarily until she could find someone else to help. But Jennie had grown fat and forty waiting for Mrs. Atkin to find another girl.

This morning she came puffingly through the kitchen door in time to see Sara Atkin turning the page of the drug-store calendar on the kitchen wall and pinning back the flapping leaf so that the word "December" stood out boldly.

Old Sara greeted Jennie with a subtle, "Do you know what date this is, Jennie?"

She asked the same darkly mysterious question every year, and, as always, Jennie feigned surprise: "Don't tell me it's December a'ready, Mis' Atkin?"

Yes, it was December; old Sara Atkin's own special month— the one for which she lived, the one toward which all the other months led like steps to some shining Taj Mahal. It was the month in which all the children came home.

"It's true, Jennie. Time again to bid the tapers twinkle fair. Did I ever tell you how our family came to use that expression, Jennie?"

Jennie had heard the explanation every year for a quarter of a century, but she obligingly assumed ignorance.

"How's that, Mis' Atkin?" As a stooge Jennie Williams could not have been surpassed.

Sara Atkin's white old face took on a glow. "Well, it was years ago. My goodness, I don't know how many—maybe forty-one or two; I could figure it out if I took time. But our Dickie was just a little chap—that's Mr. Richard Atkin, you know, my lawyer son—and he was going to speak his first piece in the new schoolhouse on Christmas Eve. The piece he was to give began:

"We hang up garlands everywhere
And bid the tapers twinkle fair.

76

"When you stop to think about it, Jennie, that's a hard line for anybody to say, let alone a little codger with his first piece. I can just see him—he had on a little brown suit I'd made him and was so round and roly-poly, and he stood up so bravely in front of all those folks and began so cute:

> " 'We hang up garlands everywhere
> And bid the twapers tinkle tair.'

"He knew something was wrong—every one was grinning—and he stopped and tried again, but this time he got it:

> " 'And bid the taters pinkle tair.'

"Every one laughed out loud and he said, 'I mean:

> " 'And tid the bapers finkle fair.' "

Sara Atkin laughed at the little memory so dear to her old heart, and Jennie politely followed suit with as extensive a show of hilarity as one could muster after hearing the anecdote for twenty-five years.

"Richard never heard the last of it. And after that whenever Christmas was coming we'd always say it was time to bid the tapers twinkle fair. I guess all big families have jokes that way, Jennie."

"I guess yours more than most folks, Mis' Atkin. My, I never knew anybody to make such a hullabaloo over Christmas as you Atkinses do."

It was just faintly possible that a bit of acidity had crept into Jennie's voice. The coming month was not going to be exactly a period of inertia for fat, slow Jennie. But to old Sara it was merely an invitation to indulge in a line of reminiscences, so that it was almost a half hour before Jennie needed to start working.

Jennie Williams was right. The Atkins made much of Christmas festivities.

There are those to whom Christmas means little or nothing; those whose liking for it is more or less superficial; those who worship it with a love that cannot be told. Sara Atkin had always been one of these last. Christmas to her meant the climax of the year, the day for which one lived. It meant vast preparation, the coming together of the clan. She had never been able to understand women to whom it was merely half interesting, sometimes even a cause for complaint. From the first Christmas in the sod house with a makeshift tree for the baby to the previous year with twenty-one coming, she had sunk herself in loving preparation for the day. No matter what experiences had preceded it—drought, blizzards, crop failures, financial losses, illness—she had approached The Day with a warmth of gladness, an uplift of the spirit which no other season could bring forth.

In those old pioneer days she had neighbors who possessed no initiative by which to make Christmas gifts out of their meager supplies. She herself had known that it took only love and energy to make them.

There had been two sons and two daughters born to her. They were middle-aged now, but by some strange magic she had transmitted to them this vital love for the Christmastime, so that they, too, held the same intense ardor for the day. In the years that were gone sons and grandsons had wrangled with wives that they must go to Grandma Atkin's for Christmas. As for the daughters and granddaughters, they had made it clear from the times of their engagements that it was not even a subject for debate whether they should attend the family reunion. To the Atkin descendants at large old Sara Atkin *was* Christmas.

So now the annual preparations began. Life took on a rose-colored hue for old Sara, and a dark blue one for Jennie. Rugs came out to be beaten and curtains down to be washed. Permanent beds were made immaculate and temporary ones installed. A dozen cook-books were consulted and the tree ordered. Jennie in her obesity and obstinacy was urged gently to try to make more effective motions. Once in her happiness old Sara said chucklingly:

"Jennie, Doctor Pitkin was wrong. Life begins at eighty."

To which Jennie made acrid reply, "Good land, don't tell me you've took up with a new doctor at your age, Mis' Atkin."

Eva, dropping in from a bridge afternoon, found her mother on the couch at the close of a day's preparations, a pan of strung pop corn at her side. The daughter was perturbed, scolded a little.

"Mother, what is there about you that makes you attack Christmas this hard way? You'll make yourself sick. Why don't we all go to the University Club? We can get a private room if we get in our bid right away."

"What—a club? On Christmas? Not while I have a roof over my head."

"But you do so many unnecessary things. No one strings pop corn any more for a tree. That was in the days when there weren't so many decorations."

"There's no law against it," said old Sara. "Or is there," she twinkled, "since the government has so much to say?"

In a few days Eva dropped in again. She had something on her mind, was hesitant in getting it out, averted her eyes a bit when she told it. "Mother, I hope I'm not going to disappoint you too much, but Fred and I think our family will have to go to Josephine's for Christmas. She's the farthest away . . . and can't come . . . and would like to have us . . . and . . ." Her voice trailed off apologetically.

Old Sara was sorry. But, "You do what's best," she said cheerily. She must not be selfish. It was not always possible for all of them to be with her, so she would not let it disturb her.

She told Jennie about it next morning. "There will be five less than we thought, Jennie. My daughter, Mrs. Fleming, and Professor Fleming and their daughter's family won't be here."

Jennie was not thrown into a state which one might term

brokenhearted, interpreting the guests' attendance as she did in terms of food and dishes.

The next evening Sara Atkin had a long-distance call from Arnold. He visited with his mother with alarming lack of toll economy—in fact, it was some little time before he led up to the news that they were not coming. He and Mame and the boys were going to Marian's. Marian's baby was only nine months old and Marian thought it better for them all to come there.

When she assured him it was all right old Sara tried her best to keep a quaver out of her voice. In her disappointment she did not sleep well. In the morning she broke the news to Jennie with some slight manipulating of the truth, inasmuch as she told her there was a faint possibility that not all of Arnold's family might get there.

When the letter from Helen arrived next day she had almost a premonition, so that her eyes went immediately down the page to the distressing statement. They were not coming. They couldn't afford it this year, Helen said—not after the drought. It hurt Sara worse than the others. It wasn't a reason. It was an excuse. That wasn't true about not affording it. It had been a bad year of drought, but Carl had his corn loan. If she had died they could have afforded to come to the funeral. And she could not bring herself to tell Jennie they, too, were not coming. She had too much pride to let Jennie know that Helen and Carl, who had no children to provide for or educate, thought they were too poor to come home for Christmas.

She had scarcely laid the letter and her glasses aside when the phone rang. It was Mr. Schloss telling her that the turkeys were in. "I'll save you two as always, Mis' Atkin?"

"Yes," said old Sara. Two turkeys for no one but herself and Richard and Clarice and their son Jimmie, who was sixteen. But she would not admit that the Atkin reunion was to be composed of only four people.

Bid the Tapers Twinkle

Before breakfast the next morning the night letter came in:

SORRY CAN'T COME MOTHER STOP JIMMIE HAS HARD COLD
CAUGHT IT PLAYING BASKETBALL STOP HOPE MESSAGE DOESN'T
FRIGHTEN YOU STOP THOUGHT LET YOU KNOW RIGHT AWAY STOP
SENDING PACKAGES STOP WILL BE THINKING OF YOU ALL DAY
CHRISTMAS

RICHARD

Old Sara got up and shut the door between herself and the
kitchen, for fear that Jennie would come in and see her before
she had gained control of herself. Twenty-one of them. *And not
one was coming.* It was unbelievable. She sat stunned, the tele-
gram still in her hand. She tried to reason with herself, but she
seemed to have no reasoning powers; tried to comfort herself,
but the heart had gone out of her. All her life she had held to a
philosophy of helpfulness, but she knew now she was seeing herself as she really was. A great many people who had no relatives
for Christmas gatherings made it a point to invite those who
were lonely. They went out into the highways and hedges and
brought them in. The Bible said to do so. Old Sara didn't want
to. Tears filled her old eyes. She didn't want lonely people
from the highways and hedges. She wanted her own folks. *She
wanted all the Atkins.*

Jennie was at work in the kitchen now. She seemed slower
than ever this morning, trudging about heavily in her flat-heeled
slippers. Sara did not care, did not hurry her, gave her no extra
duties.

The morning half over, the phone rang, and it was Mr.
Schloss again. "Ve got de trees dis mornin', Mis' Atkin. Fine
nice vons. I tell you first so you can get your choice same as always. Can you come over?"

Jennie was listening, craning her head to hear. Something
made old Sara do it. "Yes, I'll come over."

81

Mr. Schloss led her mysteriously through the store to the back. "I like you to get the pick. Folks all comin', I suppose? I never saw such relations as you got to have dose goot Christmases. Like when I'm a boy in Germany. Most folks now, it ain't so much to dem any more."

He sent the tree right over by a boy. Sara and Jennie had the big pail ready with the wet gravel in it. The boy told them Mr. Schloss said he was to stay and put it up. They placed it in the front parlor by the mottled marble fireplace, its slender green tip reaching nearly to the ceiling. Jennie got down the boxes of ornaments and tinsels and placed them invitingly on the mantel. Old Sara started to decorate. She draped and festooned and stood back mechanically to get the effect, her old eyes not seeing anything but silence louder than ever noise had been.

For the next two days she went on mechanically with preparations. Before Christmas Eve she would rouse herself and ask in some people—the food and decorations must not be wasted. She would probably have Grandma Bremmer and her old-maid daughters. They would be glad to get the home cooking, but Christmas had never meant very much to them. It was just another day at the hotel. Not a vital thing. Not a warm, living experience. Not a fundamental necessity, as it was to the Atkins.

In the meantime her pride would not allow her to tell Jennie or the merchants or the occasional caller who dropped in. "Our family reunion is to be cut down quite a bit this year," she would say casually. "Some of them aren't coming."

Some? Not one was coming.

In the late afternoon before Christmas Eve snowflakes began falling, as lazily as though fat Jennie was scattering them. The house was immaculate, everything prepared.

"Shall I put all the table leaves in, Mis' Atkin?" Jennie was asking.

"No," said Old Sara. "You needn't stay to set the table at all. The—the ones that get here will be in time to help."

"I've got a package I'm bringing you in the morning," Jennie informed her.

"So have I one for you, Jennie. Come early . . . we . . . we'll open them by the tree."

"Well, good night then, Mis' Atkin, and Merry Christmas."

"Good night, Jennie—and Merry Christmas."

Jennie was gone and the house was quiet. The snowflakes were falling faster. The house was shining from front to back. Beds were ready. The tree was sparkling with colored lights, packages from all the children under its tinseled branches. The cupboards were filled with good food. So far as preparations were concerned, everything was ready for the family reunion. And no one but herself knew that there was to be no reunion.

Later in the evening she would call up the Bremmers. But in the meantime she would lie down in the back parlor and rest. Strange how very tired she felt, when there had been so little confusion. She pulled a shawl about her and lay down on the old leather couch.

Through the archway she could see the tree, shining in all its bravery, as though trying to be gay and gallant. Then she nodded and it looked far away and small. She dozed, awakened, dozed again. The tiny tree out there now had tufts of cotton from a quilt on it, bits of tinfoil from a package of tea, homemade candles of mutton tallow. It was a queer little cottonwood tree trying to look like an evergreen—a tree such as she had in the pioneer days.

She could not have told the exact moment in which she began to hear them, could not have named the precise time in which she first saw them vaguely through the shadows. But somewhere on the borderland of her consciousness she suddenly realized they were out there under the crude little tree. Arnold was examining a homemade sled, his face alight with boyish eagerness. Eva and Helen were excitedly taking the brown paper wrappings from rag dolls. Dickie was on the floor spinning a top made from empty spools. Every little face was clear, every little figure plain. For a long time she watched them playing under the makeshift tree, a warm glow of happiness suffusing her whole being. Some vague previous hurt she had experienced was healed. Everything was all right. The children were here.

Then she roused, swept her hand over her eyes in the perplexity of her bewilderment, felt herself grow cold and numb with the disappointment of it. The children were not here. When you grew old you must face the fact that you could have them only in dreams.

It was almost dusk outside now, with the falling of the early December twilight. Christmas Eve was descending—the magic hour before the coming of the Child. It was the enchanted time in which all children should seek their homes—the family time. So under the spell of the magic moment was she that when the bell rang and she realized it was not the children, she thought at first that she would not pay any attention to the noisy summons. It would be some kind friend or neighbor whose very kindness would unnerve her. But the habit of years was strong. When one's bell rang, one went to the door.

So she rose, brushed back a straying lock, pulled her wool shawl about her shoulders and went into the hallway, holding her head gallantly.

"Merry Christmas, mother. . . . Merry Christmas, grandma." It came from countless throats, lustily, joyfully.

"Bid the tapers twinkle fair, mother."

"He means bid the taters finkle tair, grandma." Laughter rose noisily.

She could not believe it. Her brain was addled. The vision of the children under the tree had been bright, also. This was another illusion.

But if the figures on the porch were wraiths from some hinterland they were very substantial ones. If they were apparitions they were then phantoms which wore fur coats and tweeds and knitted sport suits, shadows whose frosty breath came forth in a most unghostly fashion in the cold air of the December twilight.

They were bursting through the doorway now, bringing mingled odors of frost, holly, faint perfumes, food, mistletoe, evergreens; stamping snow from shoes, carrying packages to the chins—Eva and Fred, Arnold and Mame, Dick and Clarice, Helen and Carl, Josephine and her family, Marian with her husband and baby, Richard's Jimmie, and Arnold's boys. They noisily filled the old hall, oozed out into the dining-room, backed up the stairway, fell over the tall old walnut hatrack. They did not once cease their loud and merry talking.

"Aren't we the rabble?"

"Did you ever know there were so many Atkins?"

"We look like a movie mob scene."

"The President should give us a silver loving cup or something."

They surged around old Sara Atkin, who had her hand on her throat to stop the tumultuous beating of its pulse.

"But I don't understand. Why did—why did you say you weren't coming?" she was asking feebly to those nearest to her.

Several feminine voices answered simultaneously—Eva and Helen and Dick's wife. "To save you working your fingers to the bone, mother. The way you always slave—it's just ridiculous."

"We decided that the only way to keep you from it was just to say we weren't any of us coming, and then walk in the last minute and bring all the things."

"Carl and I couldn't think of an excuse." It was Helen. "So we laid it to the poor old drought. And we'd a perfectly dreadful time—writing and phoning around to get it planned, what every one should do. I brought the turkey all ready for the oven. . . . Carl, where's the turkey? Get it from the car."

"Fred and I have the tree outside and——" Eva broke off to say, "Why, mother, *you've* a tree?"

Clarice said, "Oh, look, folks, her packages are under it. And she thought she was going to open them all by herself. Why that makes me feel teary."

Old Sara Atkin sat down heavily in a hall chair. There were twenty-one of them—some of them flesh of her flesh. They had done this for her own good, they thought. Twenty-one of them—and not one had understood how much less painful it is to be tired in your body than to be weary in your mind—how much less distressing it is to have an ache in your bones than to have a hurt in your heart.

There was the oyster supper, gay and noisy. There were stockings hung up and additional Christmas wreaths. There was Christmas music from a radio and from a phonograph and from the more-or-less unmusical throats of a dozen Atkins. There were Christmas stories and Christmas jokes. There were wide-eyed children put to bed and a session of grown people around the tree. There were early lights on Christmas morning and a great crowd of Atkins piling out in the cold of their bedrooms and calling raucous Merry Christmases to one another. There was a hasty unwanted breakfast with many pert remarks about hurrying up. There was the great family circle about the fireplace and the tree with Arnold Atkin, Jr., calling out the names on the gifts, accompanied by a run of funny flippances. There were snow banks of tissue paper and entanglements of string. There was the turkey dinner. And through it all, after the manner of the Atkin clan, there was constant talk and laughter.

The noise beat against the contented mind of Sara Atkin all day, like the wash of breakers against the sturdy shore.

All of this transpired until the late Christmas afternoon, when the entire crowd went up to Eva's new home near the campus.

"Don't you feel like coming, too, mother?"

"No, I'm a little tired and I'll just rest awhile before you come back."

They were gone. The house was appallingly quiet after the din of the passing day. There was no sound but the pad-padding of Jennie Williams in the kitchen.

Old Sara lay down on the couch in the back parlor. Through the archway she could see a portion of the disheveled front room, over which a cyclone apparently had swept. The tree with its lights still shining gaily stood in the midst of the débris.

In her bodily weariness she nodded, dozed, awakened, dozed. Suddenly the tree blurred, then grew enormous; the green of its branches became other trees, a vast number of them springing from the shadows. They massed together in a huge cedar forest, some candle laden and some electric lighted, but all gallant with Christmas cheer. Under the branches were countless children and grown people. And then suddenly she almost laughed aloud, to see that they were all her own. There were a dozen Arnolds, a dozen Helens—all her boys and girls at all their ages playing under all the trees which had ever been trimmed for them. It was as though in one short moment she had seen together the entire Christmases of the sixty years.

She roused and smiled at the memory of having seen such a wondrous sight. "Well, I suppose there'll not be many more for me," she thought, "but I've passed on the tapers. They all love it as I do. They won't forget to light the tapers after—after I'm gone."

Then she sat up and threw off her shawl with vehement gesture. "Fiddlesticks! Imagine me talking that way about dying— as if I were an old woman. I'm only eighty-one. I'm good for a dozen more Christmases. My body isn't feeble—at least—only at times. As for my mind—my mind's just as clear as a bell."

She rose and went out to the dining-room. Jennie Williams was trudging about putting away the last of the dishes. Some of the women had helped her, but there were a dozen things she had been obliged to finish herself. She was tired and cross with the unnecessary work and the undue commotion. Her feet hurt her. She liked the peaceful, slow days better.

"Well, Jennie, it's all over," old Sara said happily. "We had a good time, same as always. We've had a grand day to bid the tapers twinkle fair. Jennie, did I ever tell you how we Atkins happened to start using that expression?"

Jennie jerked her heavy body about and opened her mouth to answer determinedly, for she felt her provocation was great. But she stopped suddenly at the sight of old Sara Atkin standing in the doorway. For old Sara's sweet white face glowed with an inner light, and the illumination from the tree behind her gave the appearance of a halo around her head. Suddenly Jennie Williams had a strange thought about old Sara. It was that Mary the Mother might have looked that way when she was old.

"No," said Jennie kindly. "I don't believe you ever have told me, Mis' Atkin. How *did* you?"

☆

THERE'S
ALWAYS
SANTA CLAUS

☆

The Boy Who Laughed at Santa Claus

OGDEN NASH

In Baltimore there lived a boy.
He wasn't anybody's joy.
Although his name was Jabez Dawes,
His character was full of flaws.
In school he never led the classes,
He hid old ladies' reading glasses,
His mouth was open while he chewed,
And elbows to the table glued.
He stole the milk of hungry kittens,
And walked through doors marked No Admittance.
He said he acted thus because
There wasn't any Santa Claus.
Another trick that tickled Jabez
Was crying "Boo!" at little babies.
He brushed his teeth, they said in town,
Sideways instead of up and down.
Yet people pardoned every sin
And viewed his antics with a grin
Till they were told by Jabez Dawes,
"There isn't any Santa Claus!"
Deploring how he did behave,
His parents quickly sought their grave.
They hurried through the portals pearly,
And Jabez left the funeral early.
Like whooping cough, from child to child,
He sped to spread the rumor wild:
"Sure as my name is Jabez Dawes
There isn't any Santa Claus!"

Slunk like a weasel or a marten
Through nursery and kindergarten,
Whispering low to every tot,
"There isn't any, no, there's not!
No beard, no pipe, no scarlet clothes,
No twinkling eyes, no cherry nose,
No sleigh, and furthermore, by Jiminy,
Nobody coming down the chimney!"
The children wept all Christmas Eve
And Jabez chortled up his sleeve.
No infant dared to hang up his stocking
For fear of Jabez' ribald mocking.
He sprawled on his untidy bed,
Fresh malice dancing in his head,
When presently with scalp a-tingling,
Jabez heard a distant jingling;
He heard the crunch of sleigh and hoof
Crisply alighting on the roof.
What good to rise and bar the door?
A shower of soot was on the floor.
Jabez beheld, oh, awe of awes,
The fireplace full of Santa Claus!
Then Jabez fell upon his knees
With cries of "Don't," and "Pretty please."
He howled, "I don't know where you read it.
I swear some other fellow said it!"
"Jabez," replied the angry saint,
"It isn't I, it's you that ain't.
Although there *is* a Santa Claus,
There isn't any Jabez Dawes!"
Said Jabez then with impudent vim,
"Oh, yes there is; and I am him!
Your language don't scare me, it doesn't—"
And suddenly he found he wasn't!
From grinning feet to unkempt locks

The Boy Who Laughed at Santa Claus

Jabez became a jack-in-the-box,
An ugly toy in Santa's sack,
Mounting the flue on Santa's back.
The neighbors heard his mournful squeal;
They searched for him, but not with zeal.
No trace was found of Jabez Dawes,
Which led to thunderous applause,
And people drank a loving cup
And went and hung their stockings up.
All you who sneer at Santa Claus,
Beware the fate of Jabez Dawes,
The saucy boy who told the saint off;
The child who got him, licked his paint off.

Signor Santa

JO PAGANO

I

THE WHOLE blame says my mother, lies on my father's *stubborn insistence* that he play Santa Claus. If he had taken her advice in the first place and minded his own business everything would have turned out differently; as it was . . .

"But what was I to do?" cries my father. "*Corpo di Bacco!* Why lay all the blame on me? It was not my idea in the beginning. Gianpaolo himself suggested it. With my stomach, said he, I would make an admirable Santa Claus—and I thought, for the sake of the occasion . . . "

And so on and so forth. Nevertheless, in all fairness, I do not think it just to lay the whole blame for what happened on my father. Certainly he acted from the best of motives—that much cannot be denied; but can the same be said of Signor Simone? In this there are those of us who are inclined to take my father's view of the matter; indeed, we are inclined to feel that if ever the last detail of all that bewildering tangle of cross-purposes which went to make up that fateful Christmas Eve were finally unearthed and laid fair and square before an impartial jury, Signor Simone would not have a leg left to stand on. On the other hand, there is also, without doubt, a certain amount of reasonableness in the position taken by my mother—that is, that my father would have been much better off if, in the first place, he had gracefully withdrawn and let Signor Simone go ahead and *be* Santa Claus, since his heart seemed so set on it; still, can one exactly blame my father? After all, why *should* he have given in? Who did Signor Simone think he was anyway? Simply because he was Gianpaolo's wife's second cousin.

But let us not anticipate. To begin at the beginning:

It was a couple of weeks before Christmas that we first learned of the great gathering which our *paesanos*, the Maccaluccis, were planning on having that Christmas Eve. (May God help us forget it, as my mother wailed afterwards.) The celebration was to have a dual function, for not only were we to gather in humble memory of the Holy One, we were also to give honor to Erminio, the Maccaluccis' second son, who was returning for his Christmas vacation from the seminary where he was studying to become a priest. They were going to have a great celebration—cards, music, dancing, as well as the traditional Christmas Eve supper, and they had invited all of their friends.

Gianpaolo grew very excited as he told us about it. Like all peasant-Italians, he had a devout respect for holidays and formal occasions of any description, especially those of a churchly origin, and if necessary he would have mortgaged his house in order to celebrate this Christmas in a fitting manner—but fortunately such a drastic measure was not necessary. As usual, it was my father who provided the necessary finances—fifty dollars, to be exact. ("He must think you really *are* Santa Claus," said my mother.) But to proceed:—

All, no doubt, would have gone without mishap, had it not been for the unexpected arrival, some ten days or so before Christmas, of Mrs. Maccalucci's second cousin, Silvestro Simone. (Accursed be his name!) He was an imposing individual, matching, in fleshly bulk, the two hundred odd pounds with which Heaven (and my mother's spaghetti) had adorned my father; he had a face like a beefsteak, a voice like a steam roller, and a huge belly which seemed almost too much for the rest of him to carry around. This man, this contemptible, loathsome scoundrel, had worked alongside my father and Gianpaolo in the Colorado coal mines of their youth, but it had been nearly thirty years since he and my father had seen each other. ("Could he not have made it thirty more?" wailed my mother.) During this time, much water, as the old saw has it, had flowed under

many bridges; the passing years had carried my father and Gianpaolo many miles from those dark tunnels beneath the earth in
which they had spent their first years in this country. These
same years had carried Signor Simone many miles from the coal
mines also, but in a different direction; for, while Gianpaolo
and my father, imitating the course of the sun, had traveled
westward, arriving, by successive stages, in California, Simone
had journeyed east. He had been married (as we were to hear
a dozen times from his own lips) three times; he had had six
children by his first wife, four by his second, and eight by his
last. ("By God, Luigi, I bet you can't beat *that* record!" he
roared to my father.) During these years he had been in one business after another—saloon keeper, restaurant owner, hotel proprietor; and he had wound up in Boston (where he had spent
the past six years) as the proprietor of a fancy Italian grocery.

I I

So much for a few brief facts about this reprehensible individual. Would any of us have resented him on the basis, so to
speak, of himself? In all fairness, I must say *I do not think so.*
We did not begrudge him his money, the diamond-studded elk's
tooth that dangled like a glittering eye from his stomach, the
fancy Italian grocery (which from his description must have
put to shame the Grand Central Terminal); certainly he could
have had a dozen wives and fifty children for all we cared
about it. What then? Just this—*we did not like his manner.* As
my father so succinctly put it, who did Simone think he was
anyway? He moved in on Gianpaolo, accompanied by his wife
and the four youngest of their eight children, without warning,
without apology, seeming to think that the mere fact of his
presence was sufficient to put the Maccaluccis in a very ecstasy of
appreciation; he ate their food, drank their wine, slept like a king
in the paternal bed (which, for want of another, Mr. and Mrs.
Maccalucci had had to give up to the Simones, themselves sleep-

ing on a mattress in the attic); and he did not offer to buy even an ice-cream cone for the children! And there is something more, too. In the morning, when the children were waiting in line, so to speak, to get to the bathroom, he—but let us not go into that; enough is enough; suffice it to say that never, in all of our collective experience, had we run across anyone with such a positive genius for making himself offensive.

Does this not make understandable, then, my father's attitude in the matter? Had it been anyone but Simone (as my father himself will vehemently tell you), he would have withdrawn courteously at the first indication of a misunderstanding as to who was to play Santa Claus. But for nearly a week—that is to say, ever since the Simones had popped in from Boston for their 'visit'—we had been hearing reports, from Gianpaolo and Mrs. Maccalucci, about his patronizing behavior; and therefore when, at dinner the Sunday before Christmas (to which the Maccaluccis had invited us in order to meet their house guests), Simone gave indication that he himself had intentions of playing Santa Claus at the celebration, we were more than prepared to resent his presumptuousness.

Long before he proclaimed his intention, however, my father had had more than enough of Signor Simone. He had never liked him, even back in the old days (as he later confessed), but in spite of this dislike, which he had almost forgotten, and which had been revived by the reports Gianpaolo had been relaying to us regarding his guest's behavior, he had looked forward to seeing Simone again, to reminisce about the days of their youth, to discuss old names, old friends, old experiences which they had had in common—this was the spirit in which, accompanied by my mother and me, he had gone to the Maccaluccis' for dinner, prepared, that is to say, to ignore all the ancient dislike and to meet Simone as an old friend, found again after many years of parting, with whom he could drink a glass or two of cordial wine for the sake of the old times. And did Simone

make such an agreeable reunion possible? Did he, indeed? *I will
present only the simple facts.* Would you like to know the first
remark he made to my father as we entered the house?

"Luigi Altieri!" he roared, pumping my father's hand and
nearly knocking him down with a terrific blow in the small of
his back. "You alive after all these years? By God, I thought
you'd be dead long before now!"

This, the greeting he gave to my father; and to my mother?

"Rosa, Rosa!" said he, as though reproachfully. "You still?
But how have you been able to endure each other?" And then he
laughed, and threw his massive arms about her. "But how fat
you've become!" he cried. *"Per Dio,* I should never have known
you!"

My father, trying to recover his breath, which had been
knocked out of his lungs by the pounding Simone had given
him, coughed, sputtered, wheezed; my mother extended one
cheek for the kiss which Simone straightaway implanted on it
through his mustache.

"And this young man?" said Simone, fixing a curious eye upon
me. "Your son, no doubt?"

"This is Robert, my youngest," said my mother coldly. "He is
an artist."

"But no!" he said, his features expanding; and suddenly he
clasped my hand in a grip that made my toes quiver. "An artist!
Well, don't worry, I won't tell anyone!" he cried, and opening
his mouth he let loose an extraordinary sound that seemed to
begin somewhere in the innermost depths of that remarkable
stomach and thence to billow up through his lungs and out of
his throat like the mounting roar of a flood-burst; he laughed,
chortled, groaned; the walls rocked, the diamond elk's tooth
quivered; tears came to his eyes, and he slapped his stomach
with his hands.

Was it then so humorous? We all stared; my mother coughed
discreetly behind her handkerchief; I drew myself up, and—
But no matter.

III

Such was our introduction to this monster, but unfortunately our acquaintance did not end there; we had come to the Maccaluccis' for dinner, and to dinner we stayed. Meanwhile, we met Mrs. Simone, a pale, ferret-eyed wisp of a woman, and the Simone children, two boys, two girls, the oldest ten, the youngest five; Mr. and Mrs. Maccalucci hovered around us anxiously, took our hats and coats, pulled out chairs, poured some wine; and at last we sat down to dinner.

In the meantime, Simone plied my father with questions: how had he fared during all these years?

"One thing is sure, you haven't starved!" he said, glancing jocularly at my father's stomach. "Do you have so many friends, then?"

My father laughed politely and muttered something behind his moustache; and at that moment the spaghetti arrived.

"Ah!" said Simone, tucking his napkin into his collar contentedly; and forthwith proceeded to heap a good half of the platter onto his own plate.

Midway through the meal the talk turned to the forthcoming Christmas celebration, and then it was that Simone made the remark which, like a lighted match tossed carelessly into a haystack, started everything.

"I have been told," said he to my father in Italian, "that you are planning to play Santa Claus for the children?" And, before my father could answer, "That will have to be changed," said he (precisely, as my father remarked afterward, as though he *owned* the place). "For the past five years I have played Santa Claus for my children, and," said he (waving his fork in the air), "they would not know you, they would think you were an impostor—"

"But, my good friend," began my father courteously, glancing timidly toward Gianpaolo, whose face had turned blood-red . . .

"And besides," Simone continued obliviously, "you have not

got the figure for it. Look!" he cried, pounding his stomach. "You should see what a Santa Claus *I* make—ain't that so?" he added in sudden English to his wife.

At this point Gianpaolo, who had been making an ill-concealed attempt to disguise his mounting anger, exploded into action.

"Eet'sa too late!" he said, so excited that he too lapsed into English, which language, for some reason, he invariably used when he wished to be emphatic. "Eet'sa too late!" he repeated, and then, finding he could not go on without resorting to his native tongue, he let forth a torrent of voluble Italian. The plans had all been made, he explained heatedly. It was impossible to change them now!

But why? Simone demanded. What difference did it make? It made lots of difference! said Gianpaolo. The plans had been made, and and made they must stay. *It was too late to change them!* At this point a gleam came into Simone's eyes. And what of his children? he demanded. How would they feel to see an unfamiliar Santa Claus? That could not be helped, said Gianpaolo, his own eyes glinting; Simone's were not the only children who would be present; *did Simone by any chance think the celebration was given for his special benefit?*

"*Sangue de la Madonna!*" bellowed Simone, crashing his fist against the table. "What do you mean by that?"

Gianpaolo leaped up from his chair, quivering with fury. Simone rose like a great shaggy bear to meet him.

"Stop!" cried my father, getting between them. What nonsense! he added. He would gladly withdraw in favor of Simone—

Not for one moment, said Gianpaolo, looking venomously at Simone. *The plans had been made, and made they must stay!*

Simone shrugged and sat down again; finally Gianpaolo resumed his seat, and we went on with the dinner as though nothing had happened.

The question of who was to play Santa Claus at the celebration was not mentioned again, but once or twice I caught Simone giving furtive glances both to Gianpaolo and to my father. Ah, had we but known what lay behind those glances!

But we did not know. The following afternoon my father (despite the warnings of my mother that he had better mind his own business) went downtown, as per arrangement, and rented himself a resplendent Santa Claus outfit; and so the great day arrived.

I V

It was not yet five o'clock when we approached the Maccaluccis' that fateful Christmas Eve, but already darkness had fallen. It had been drizzling all afternoon, and the streets were filled with puddles; long before we got to the house itself we heard the sounds of the gathering; the windows were ablaze with light, and we could hear singing and laughter, the lilting strains of an accordion, the strum of guitars. They had put holly wreaths and silver crosses in the windows, and through the panes we could see the shadowy forms of people moving about.

My father hid the box containing his Santa Claus outfit in the back of the car, and we went up the steps and into the house. There, in the small living room, dining room, and kitchen, upwards of fifty people were gathered. There was a huge fire roaring in the living-room fireplace, and underneath the Christmas tree stood a miniature manger, complete with the infant Christ, the Virgin Mother, and the Three Wise Men of Bethlehem, all in tiny figures of wax; the walls and ceiling were festooned with ribbons of colored paper and the tip of the tree was crowned with a gleaming star. As Gianpaolo proudly told us, no expense had been spared to make the celebration a magnificent one; he had invited all his friends and their children and the tables groaned beneath the pitchers of wine, and the house was filled with the tantalizing odors of the feast which the women were preparing.

In the midst of all this sat, in lordly fashion, Simone, ensconced in the most comfortable chair in the house, a goblet of wine in one huge hand; he nodded to us coolly as we entered, and I thought I saw a peculiar gleam, as though of calculation, come into his eyes as we went past him into the bedroom to dispose of our hats and coats.

Our arrival had interrupted the music and singing, but as soon as we had greeted the assembled guests and paid our respects to Erminio, who, since he was one day to be a priest, was treated with considerable awe by the rest, we found places and joined in the festivities. The accordionist and guitar players formed as it were a hub, from which all the other activity radiated; almost all joined in in the singing, and we heard again and again the familiar melodies of the land from which we had stemmed,—O *Sole Mio, Ciribiribin, Santa Lucia,*—folksongs, too, the songs of the field and the plough, deep in the memories of the oldest present; my father beamed and swayed and shouted; my mother nodded her head with a far-away look in her eyes. . . .

As it neared time to eat, the gathering became increasingly exuberant; the wine flowed more and more freely, faces became flushed, voices grew louder; the musicians perspired and struggled with their instruments and the house rocked to the sound of stamping feet and clapping hands. In the midst of all this, it was announced that the feast was ready, and in a few moments more great steaming platters were brought in and laid upon the tables set in the living and dining rooms.

In obedience to the Catholic custom, there was no meat. The main courses were of spaghetti with a savory sauce composed of olive oil flavored with garlic, parsley, and ground hot peppers; a dozen different kinds of fish, fried peppers in oil, olives, three or four kinds of salads, roasted chestnuts, a dozen varieties of Italian pastry drenched in honey, dates, dried figs, fresh grapes and apples and oranges. . . . For upwards of two hours we sat and gorged ourselves, while the flickering candles grew shorter and shorter, and the wind lashed the rain against the windows, and the logs crackled in the fireplace. Gallon after gallon of wine had been consumed, and by the time the feast was over there was not an adult present, at least among the men, who remained sober.

And what of Simone, during all this? He ate and drank as much as any four people present, making slanderous remarks, all the while, regarding the food: the spaghetti had not been salted enough, the fish was undercooked, the olives were dry. . . . Several times it looked as though Gianpaolo, who was seated opposite him across the table, were on the point of throwing some of the cutlery in his direction; but nothing, fortunately, happened, and the meal was concluded without mishap.

As soon as we had finished, the tables were cleared of everything save the fresh fruit, the nuts, and the wine, and the festivities recommenced. In obedience to the Italian custom, the plans were to eat, drink, and make merry all the night long, then go in a troop to early-morning Mass, then return for the Christmas Day dinner. Those who wished could catch an hour or two's sleep in the meantime, but usually there were few, aside from some of the oldest, who slept; the festivities by tradition usually continued without let-up from the afternoon of Christmas Eve on through Christmas Day.

V

It was now approaching ten o'clock, but the exuberance had not abated. At the tables the men played cards, shouting and slapping their hands on the table as they brought the cards down; the women busied themselves washing the dishes and cleaning up the kitchen; some of the younger couples danced. And through all this the children ran about playing games, shouting, crying, throwing candies and cookies at each other . . . frantic mothers scurried about, trying to control their offspring . . . an argument or two developed amongst the card players . . . someone spilled a pitcher of wine on the floor . . . yes, everything was progressing beautifully.

And then the fateful hour of midnight approached.

The plans, which my father and his *paesano* had gone over carefully a hundred times, were as follows: a few minutes before midnight my father was to take his Santa Claus outfit and go out in the back to the garage. Here a great sack had been hidden, filled with presents for the children. In the house, meanwhile, the children were to be herded into the living room, around the Christmas tree. Promptly at the stroke of midnight my father was to appear, dressed as Santa Claus, the sack of presents slung over his shoulder.

These, the plans; and what happened?

Fifteen minutes or so before midnight, my father and his *paesano* exchanged a knowing glance. My father coughed, glanced at the children blandly, then, motioning to me to follow him, he got up from the table and went out the front door. We got the box with the Santa Claus suit from the car, then went around the house and to the back, where Gianpaolo was waiting for us in the garage. In a few minutes we had helped my father change into the Santa Claus suit, with its red coat and pantaloons; he stood up proudly and stroked the white whiskers which enveloped his ruddy face like a cloud.

"Well, how do I look?" he demanded.

But he looked magnificent! Gianpaolo reassured him, in a very ecstasy of enthusiasm; he straightened the coat, patted my father's stomach, tucked one sagging corner of the trousers into the boots. Magnificent, magnificent! he repeated. And now for the presents, he added, turning to a canvas which had been laid over some jugs in one corner of the garage, where the sack of presents had been hidden. He lifted the canvas—and then it was that we gained our first inkling that all was not to happen, this fateful eve, as planned. *The sack with the presents had disappeared.*

"*Sangue de la Madonna!*" Gianpaolo ejaculated, wrinkling his forehead in agony, and staring at the blank space beneath the canvas. He tore the canvas off frantically and began to search among the jugs, throwing them this way and that wildly.

But what was the matter? asked my father courteously.

Matter! said Gianpaolo. The presents—*someone had stolen them!*

What? said my father. But that was impossible!

At that moment, from the direction of the house, we heard a familiar voice calling our *paesano's* name.

"Gianpaolo, Gianpaolo!"

We rushed out into the yard. Mrs. Maccalucci was running toward us, her hair flying wildly in the drizzling rain.

"What's-a-matter?" cried her husband.

"Simone!" she gasped, then began to wail some more and wring her hands. Gianpaolo grabbed her by the shoulders and shook her.

"*What's-a-matter?*" he repeated.

Simone had stolen the presents and, dressed in a Santa Claus suit of his own, was even now preparing to give them out to the children!

"*Corpo di Bacco!*" bellowed Gianpaolo, and, pushing her aside, he ran toward the house, followed by my father and me.

We rushed up the back steps, through the kitchen, through the dining room, into the living room—and sure enough, there he was, surrounded by the awe-struck children, dressed in a resplendent red Santa Claus suit, complete with whiskers and all.

"Simone!" screamed Gianpaolo.

And do you know what Simone did? *He turned and looked at us blandly!*

"*Che fai*, what are you doing?" stuttered Gianpaolo, so beside himself he could hardly talk.

"But can you not see?" retorted Simone suavely. "I am giving the children their presents!"

"You? You?" cried Gianpaolo; then, "Monster!" he cried, and, leaping forward on his short bandy legs, he swung his fist against Simone's jaw. Simone ducked, and with a push of one huge paw knocked Gianpaolo to the floor. My father stared at

105

his undersized friend, where he lay on the floor, then turned to Simone.

"So!" he said; and without another word he leaped upon his friend's assailant. The women screamed, the children whimpered and wailed, the other male guests began milling around excitedly; and in the middle of all this my father and Simone groaned, flailed, tugged. Suddenly my father dealt Simone a resounding smack that knocked him into the fireplace. He bellowed and struggled to regain his feet; suddenly the flames leaped over him and his whiskers caught fire.

.. "*Mamma mia!*" he screamed. "Help, help!"

From victorious antagonist my father turned abruptly to the rôle of rescuer; he reached forward and pulled Simone upright, slapping at the whiskers to put the fire out. Simone, however, apparently mistook these friendly blows as the signal of a new attack; he hit back; they began to wrestle; suddenly my father's own whiskers caught fire.

They released each other and began dancing around, pulling at their smouldering whiskers. Someone threw a pitcher of wine over them; then all at once there was a scream:—

"Fire! Fire!"

The paper festoons had caught flame; in a moment more the fire had swept to the curtains and the ceiling; pandemonium broke loose. Hysterical mothers grabbed for their children; the men rushed back and forth from the kitchen frantically, bearing buckets and pans of water; someone put in a call for the fire wagon.

From this point on so many things happened at once it is impossible to relate them with any pretense of order; the fire wagons arrived with much clanging of bells and screaming of sirens, and a great crowd of people collected in the street. We had already put out the fire, however, and presently the engines departed. Meanwhile a couple of police patrol cars arrived on the scene, and to these worthy guardians of the public morale much explanation had to be given before they could be persuaded not to herd "the whole damn bunch of us" down to the station. Simone, upon orders of his erstwhile host, packed his clothes (still maintaining stubbornly that it was all a misunderstanding, that his intentions had been the most honorable), and, accompanied by his wife and children, departed in a huff for a hotel; then the guests, one by one, began to leave. At the last, none were left save the Maccaluccis and their own children, my mother and father, and me. My mother and Mrs. Maccalucci were weeping; we sat desolately amidst, as it were, the ruins, and surveyed the charred walls and ceiling, the water-drenched furniture, the sorry remains of the magnificent Christmas tree.

"*Per l'amore di Dio!*" wailed Gianpaolo. "Cousin or no cousin—if I ever see him again I'll kill him!"

At that moment there was the sound of someone coming up the front steps, then entering the house.

"But who can that be?" muttered Gianpaolo, and, mumbling to himself, he started to rise.

At that moment—yes!—we saw the countenance and figure of Simone (carrying an umbrella archly) appear in the doorway.

He stood and looked at us all haughtily.

"Excuse me," he said coldly. "I forgot my shaving brush."

Gianpaolo stared at him; then suddenly he let out a scream, and, picking up a long knife from the table, he started after Simone. Simone stared at the knife, paled, dropped the umbrella, then, whirling around, started pellmell down the steps, with Gianpaolo hard after him.

V I

These, then, are the simple facts of the case. In conclusion it may be added that Gianpaolo received thirty days for attempted assault with a deadly weapon; Simone, on the other hand, went scot-free, and even now, no doubt, is back in that magnificent Italian grocery in Boston, safely barricaded behind his salami and cheese. Is this, then, justice? On top of all that, my father had to foot the bill for the damages—one hundred and six dollars and eighty cents, to be exact. It is such things that make my mother bitter. If my father had not been so *stubbornly insistent* in the first place, says she, all might have turned out differently; as it was—But enough of all that; we shall leave it for the reader to judge.

Christmas Eve

ALISTAIR COOKE

IN THE middle of Rockefeller Plaza, in the middle of New
York City, there is at Christmas time a great tree about
seventy feet high. It is said to be a Norway fir, but by the
time they have sprayed it with a fireproof silver paint it looks
like something between a redwood and a giant aspen. It is
fitted out with several thousand light bulbs and leads strangers
to America to complain about the "commercializing" of Christmas. But the practice of eating, drinking, and making merry
at Christmas time is an entirely pagan idea, and it was on that
ground that the early colonists of New England forbade their
flock to drink a mug of beer. They even resented the success of
blasphemers in monkeying around with the calendar so as to
make an unholy feast coincide with the birth of Jesus. One of
the good Yorkshiremen on the *Mayflower* who kept a diary
noted with some pride that the first day everybody was off the
boat, the first day of digging the foundations of the Plymouth
colony, was Christmas Day. He mentions that there was no
pause for any nonsense like carols or dancing and adds the comment: "because what day soever our Lord was born, most certainly it was not the twenty-fifth of December."

But the Puritans lost out, in this as in many other things.
Christmas has become a cheerful jumble of pious and heathen
customs. And in New York the big tree in Rockefeller Plaza is
the proper meeting-point of a pagan and a holy Christmas, for
it magnificently combines electricity with a Gothic spire.

It was at this tree, a year ago, that Santa Claus got into trouble.

The real name of Santa Claus, by the way, is Zebby Adams.

He lives in an old folks' home. I can't say for sure what the Zebby stands for. He may have been christened Zebah or Zebedee, but most likely it was Zebulun, one of those Biblical first names which are very common still in New England and the Midwest and which make so many unlikely-looking Americans sound like seventeenth-century bishops.

Zebby Adams entered the old folks' home up near Riverside Drive shortly after Pearl Harbor, because he lost a son in the First World War and got depressed at the prospect of another generation of lost sons. He had been a small-town banker in Massachusetts and was wiped out in the 1929 crash. He was a widower by then and had few relatives. He was also one of that strange breed of people—who will be with us, I fear, for a few years yet—who refuse charity and are too proud to seek out a helping hand. His house had been attached in January 1930 for debts he could not pay. And he took a bus a couple of hundred miles down to New York and lived anonymously for ten years or more doing odd and humble jobs. He lived in a little rented room and saved a few dollars whenever he could. Having lost his faith in the banking system, he kept his savings in a miniature mahogany desk, a Christmas present he had had as a child. He kept this money for the day when he would feel the first twinge of old age in the form of a sudden backache, an ominous stiff hand, or whatever it might be. He had a plan for this money.

One morning a few years ago he woke up and felt very tired. It was like no tiredness he had ever known and he knew in the instant of waking that he had passed over into old age. It was time to put his plan into action.

He went to the tiny desk and opened its drawers. There were bills of all denominations stuffed in there. He took them out and unfolded them and counted up to four hundred dollars. He put them in his pocket and went off to the old folks' home. He said it was a contribution. He said he could no longer keep up the rent of his room and wished to be taken in. They asked him for some credentials, and he pulled out a worn little card, a membership card in some forgotten club, which read: "Zebulun Adams, banker." The officials at the home took this badly. But after a day or two, and some discreet telephone calls to the rather surprised inhabitants of the small town in Massachusetts, they took him in. He is there today.

Now, Zebby, a gentle blue-eyed man with tiny hands and a portliness that failed to fill out a frail-looking body, had long had a secret ambition. It was to be Santa Claus. He did it at the old folks' home two years in a row. It satisfied the old folks, some of whom doubted there was any such person. But it didn't satisfy Zebby. It only whetted his appetite. Then one October he read in the paper about a school or college way up the Hudson, in upstate New York: a college for Santa Clauses. It offered a two-weeks course and guaranteed to train and qualify "Master Santa Clauses" for employment in the big city department stores. "A calling," the advertisement said, "that has for too long been left to the amateur and the well-meaning bum." Zebby Adams felt a wince of conscience on both scores and resolved to qualify as a professional, so that he might look people, no matter how young, clear in the eye. He told the treasurer of the home that he needed one hundred and fifty dollars, which was the fee for the course and bed and board, and offered to repay it from his earnings in Christmas week. After a little niggling and finagling he got it. He wrote off to the college, received an application blank, filled it out, registered, and on the first day of December was on a train whistling up the Hudson.

He had the time of his life. He had always loved children and he had a way with them. He took them for what they were—cobras or tigers, say—and it never occurred to him in all his life to try to influence them, or mold them, or show them what was what. But like many another man with a special skill he was troubled by what he didn't know, and was unaware of the glaring fact that he was already superior to most people around him.

111

He therefore applied himself with much zest and humility to learning what the college had to teach. He never missed a class. The first course was in "Greeting the Child," and he got an A for that in four days flat (on the third day he turned into the teacher). "Personal Cleanliness in the Role of Santa Claus" was something else he had no trouble with: his family had been Episcopalians and, having boasted of venerable connections with the carpenters and butchers who came over on the *Mayflower*, they had very genteel notions about personal appearance, combing the hair, and what coat ought to go with what pair of pants. To be precise, Zebby was a Harvard man, but in ordinary civilized intercourse he always kept a decent secret of it.

There was an afternoon class in "Problems of Denial" which puzzled him sorely. He discovered to his horror that department stores do not give away the gorgeous articles they bait the children with, and he shed a sneaking tear when he learned the correct answers to the quiz on this course. "Santa Claus: Father Substitute or Father Rival?" almost threw him, for it was his understanding that Santa Claus was a benefactor dropped from the skies who was practically honor-bound not to get mixed up with the female of the species. "That," said the instructor snappishly, "is not the point. It is what you mean to the little one that matters." That, said Zebby, was the way he'd always understood it. He got a B in this course, until he memorized a page from a psychology or geometry book— he can't now remember which—and passed up into the select company of the A's.

He did very well in everything and at the end he impatiently took the train back to the city, carrying his bag and the special comb, make-up kit, and beard-deodorizing spray the college gave you along with your certificate. He also bore a letter to the personnel manager of a big midtown department store. For ten days he was a sensation with the young and a cause of misgiving to the floor manager, for in spite of his professional training he tended in an emergency to trust his instincts. He more than earned his loan from the old folks' home, however, and on Christmas Eve he picked up his check and left the store. He was happy and he was sad. He was also, I forgot to say, dressed in his scarlet costume—a gift from the well-contented store. He wanted to prolong his role and he conveniently forgot to change into street clothes. Instead, he showered moth flakes on his ordinary suit and carefully packed it away in his bag.

He went to a restaurant near by and was such a warming sight that strangers bought him drinks. A waiter insisted on sneaking him a stein of "heeltaps," the leavings of orders of brandy, whisky, champagne, and beer, to which the kitchen help used to add a little spice and sugar and brew it into a powerful punch.

When Zebby Adams left the restaurant it was very late and I'm afraid he was not himself. He started to march uptown swinging his bag; all the tiredness of his new-found old age had magically disappeared. He suddenly thought of the tree in Rockefeller Plaza and hurried to bask in its genial blaze. He was going at a fine pace by the time he reached Forty-second Street, and seeing the lonely lions outside the Public Library he stopped and serenaded them with a favorite carol. "The Holly and the Ivy," he sang, "in Rocky-feller Plaza." By the time he came in sight of the British Empire Building he heard the three notes of the National Broadcasting Company pealing out on the midnight clear. They were sounding, in fact, the witching hour. And as they died on the air, the big tree suddenly went out. The only colored light in the Plaza came from the roof of a taxi waiting for a fare.

This was the fatal moment in the old age of Zebby Adams. For the little yellow light revived another long-buried ambition, which he was sure a reindeer now reminded him of. It was to drive a cab. He pattered over to the driver.

"My good fellow!" he cried.

"Listen," said the driver, "this is Christmas Eve. I ain't nobody's good fellow. I'm a Democrat."

The driver also wasn't himself, though it was true he was a Democrat. Zebby, however, leaned against the cab and put his head through the window. He told his secret to the driver.

"I couldn't do a thing like that," the driver said. "Liable to get my head broke, or a ticket or somepn."

"Only sit by my side," Zebby pleaded. "I will be a learner. You can be my sponsor, my guide. The traffic-bureau regulations permit it."

"Well—" said the driver, weakening.

Zebby saw his chance and almost lulled the driver to sleep with a flood of persuasive eloquence. He imagined the sheer sensual pleasure of flying past all the lighted trees of Park Avenue "without let or hindrance." He acknowledged the "enormous Christian favor" he was begging. More than that though, he argued, it would represent "a deep symbolic act." The driver bounced awake at the word "symbolic." He liked it.

"Is that what it would be, symbolic?" he asked.

"Nothing less," said Zebby, stroking his beard with one hand and pointing to the stars with the other.

"You sure?"

"Certain of it."

The driver jumped out on his side and came around the cab. He pulled the door wide open. He pointed to the steering wheel and bowed low. "Santa," he said, "it's all yours." (This was one of those historic sentences, like "I see no retreat" and "Don't shoot till you see the whites of their eyes.")

Santa hopped in and banged the door. He ground into first gear. He behaved like Zebby Adams on the crosstown street; but once he turned uptown and saw the splendid highway of Park Avenue ahead and its dancing lights, and not a human anywhere, he got the authentic high sign from the reindeer that had whispered to him in the Plaza. He put his foot way down, and as the lights winked from green to red, Santa flew on. A Cadillac screamed to a stop at Fifty-ninth Street as it slid across the avenue when the light changed. Through the Sixties the crosstown streets flashed by like the ribs of a fan. "Hot Diggety!" cried Santa. And they flew on.

They didn't fly very far before they heard behind them a sound of bells.

"Donner and Blitzen," shouted Santa, "they are with us still."

"You know them poissonally?" asked the driver with a little anxiety.

"Splendid fellows both," roared Santa.

It was not, however, the reindeer. It was a cop.

When they came into night court, the man on the bench looked stonily down at Zebby. Then he sighed and bent over a book with a pencil.

"Name?" he asked.

"Adams, Zebulun."

The judge wrote it down without a comma.

"Trade or profession?" he said, looking at his book.

"Santa Claus," said Zebby. "Master Santa Claus—M.S.C."

The judge scraped at his teeth with a fingernail.

"Five days in jail," he said. "Have you anything to say for yourself?"

"Merry Christmas, your Honor," Zebby said.

"—and five days for contempt of court," the judge added.

"And a happy New Year," said Santa.

The judge paused. He put his thumbnail to his teeth again and this time he rescued a shred of beef.

"Sentence suspended," said the judge.

The cabdriver took Zebby away uptown and drew up before an iron gate. He went round and opened the door on the passenger's side and led Zebby to the gate. He kissed him twice on both cheeks. "Bon sewer, mon general," he said, and opened up the gate and Zebby trotted up the path of the old folks' home. He stopped at the door and looked back.

"Au revoir, mon colonel," cried Zebby.

☆

CHRISTMAS
AND THE
CHILDREN

☆

Christmas Every Day

W. D. HOWELLS

THE LITTLE girl came into her papa's study, as she always did Saturday morning before breakfast, and asked for a story. He tried to beg off that morning, for he was very busy, but she would not let him. So he began:

"Well, once there was a little pig——"

She put her hand over his mouth and stopped him at the word. She said she had heard little pig stories till she was perfectly sick of them.

"Well, what kind of story *shall* I tell, then?"

"About Christmas. It's getting to be the season. It's past Thanksgiving already."

"It seems to me," argued her papa, "that I've told as often about Christmas as I have about little pigs."

"No difference! Christmas is more interesting."

"Well!" Her papa roused himself from his writing by a great effort. "Well, then, I'll tell you about the little girl that wanted it Christmas every day in the year. How would you like that?"

"First-rate!" said the little girl; and she nestled into comfortable shape in his lap, ready for listening.

"Very well, then, this little pig,——Oh, what are you pounding me for?"

"Because you said little pig instead of little girl."

"I should like to know what's the difference between a little pig and a little girl that wanted it Christmas every day!"

"Papa," said the little girl, warningly, "if you don't go on, I'll *give* it to you!" And at this her papa darted off like lightning, and began to tell the story as fast as he could.

Well, once there was a little girl who liked Christmas so much that she wanted it to be Christmas every day in the year; and as soon as Thanksgiving was over she began to send postal cards to the old Christmas Fairy to ask if she mightn't have it. But the old Fairy never answered any of the postals; and, after a while, the little girl found out that the Fairy was pretty particular, and wouldn't notice anything but letters, not even correspondence cards in envelopes; but real letters on sheets of paper, and sealed outside with a monogram,—or your initial, any way. So, then, she began to send her letters; and in about three weeks—or just the day before Christmas, it was—she got a letter from the Fairy, saying she might have it Christmas every day for a year, and then they would see about having it longer.

The little girl was a good deal excited already, preparing for the old-fashioned, once-a-year Christmas that was coming the next day, and perhaps the Fairy's promise didn't make such an impression on her as it would have made at some other time. She just resolved to keep it to herself, and surprise everybody with it as it kept coming true; and then it slipped out of her mind altogether.

She had a splendid Christmas. She went to bed early, so as to let Santa Claus have a chance at the stockings, and in the morning she was up the first of anybody and went and felt them, and found hers all lumpy with packages of candy, and oranges and grapes, and pocket-books and rubber balls and all kinds of small presents, and her big brother's with nothing but the tongs in them, and her young lady sister's with a new silk umbrella, and her papa's and mamma's with potatoes and pieces of coal wrapped up in tissue paper, just as they always had every Christmas. Then she waited around till the rest of the family were up, and she was the first to burst into the library, when the doors were opened, and look at the large presents laid out on the library-table—books, and portfolios, and boxes of stationery, and breast-pins, and dolls, and little stoves, and dozens of handkerchiefs, and ink-stands, and skates, and snow-shovels, and photograph-frames, and little easels, and boxes of water-colors, and Turkish paste, and nougat, and candied cherries, and dolls' houses, and water-proofs,—and the big Christmas-tree, lighted and standing in a waste-basket in the middle.

She had a splendid Christmas all day. She ate so much candy that she did not want any breakfast; and the whole forenoon the presents kept pouring in that the expressman had not had time to deliver the night before; and she went 'round giving the presents she had got for other people, and came home and ate turkey and cranberry for dinner, and plum-pudding and nuts and raisins and oranges and more candy, and then went out and coasted and came in with a stomach-ache, crying; and her papa said he would see if his house was turned into that sort of fool's paradise another year; and they had a light supper, and pretty early everybody went to bed cross.

Here the little girl pounded her papa in the back, again.

"Well, what now? Did I say pigs?"

"You made them *act* like pigs."

"Well, didn't they?"

"No matter; you oughtn't to put it into a story."

"Very well, then, I'll take it all out."

Her father went on:

The little girl slept very heavily, and she slept very late, but she was wakened at last by the other children dancing 'round her bed with their stockings full of presents in their hands.

"What is it?" said the little girl, and she rubbed her eyes and tried to rise up in bed.

"Christmas! Christmas! Christmas!" they all shouted, and waved their stockings.

"Nonsense! It was Christmas yesterday."

Her brothers and sisters just laughed. "We don't know about that. It's Christmas to-day, any way. You come into the library and see."

Then all at once it flashed on the little girl that the Fairy

121

was keeping her promise, and her year of Christmases was beginning. She was dreadfully sleepy, but she sprang up like a lark—a lark that had overeaten itself and gone to bed cross—and darted into the library. There it was again! Books, and portfolios, and boxes of stationery, and breast-pins——

You needn't go over it all, Papa; I guess I can remember just what was there," said the little girl.

Well, and there was the Christmas-tree blazing away, and the family picking out their presents, but looking pretty sleepy, and her father perfectly puzzled, and her mother ready to cry. "I'm sure I don't see how I'm to dispose of all these things," said her mother, and her father said it seemed to him they had had something just like it the day before, but he supposed he must have dreamed it. This struck the little girl as the best kind of a joke; and so she ate so much candy she didn't want any breakfast, and went 'round carrying presents, and had turkey and cranberry for dinner, and then went out and coasted, and came in with a——

"Papa!"

"Well, what now?"

"What did you promise, you forgetful thing?"

"Oh! oh, yes!"

Well, the next day it was just the same thing over again, but everybody getting crosser; and at the end of a week's time so many people had lost their tempers that you could pick up lost tempers anywhere; they perfectly strewed the ground. Even when people tried to recover their tempers they usually got somebody else's, and it made the most dreadful mix.

The little girl began to get frightened, keeping the secret all to herself; she wanted to tell her mother, but she didn't dare to; and she was ashamed to ask the Fairy to take back her gift, it

seemed ungrateful and ill-bred, and she thought she would try
to stand it, but she hardly knew how she could, for a whole
year. So it went on and on, and it was Christmas on St. Valen-
tine's Day, and Washington's Birthday just the same as any
day, and it didn't skip even the First of April, though everything was counterfeit that day, and that was some *little* relief.

After a while, coal and potatoes began to be awfully scarce,
so many had been wrapped up in tissue paper to fool papas and
mammas with. Turkeys got to be about a thousand dollars
apiece——

"Papa!"

"Well, what?"

"You're beginning to fib."

"Well, *two* thousand, then."

And they got to passing off almost anything for turkeys,—
half-grown hummingbirds, and even rocs out of the "Arabian
Nights,"—the real turkeys were so scarce. And cranberries—
well, they asked a diamond apiece for cranberries. All the woods
and orchards were cut down for Christmas-trees, and where the
woods and orchards used to be, it looked just like a stubble-field,
with the stumps. After a while they had to make Christmas-
trees out of rags, and stuff them with bran, like old-fashioned
dolls; but there were plenty of rags, because people got so poor,
buying presents for one another, that they couldn't get any
new clothes, and they just wore their old ones to tatters. They
got so poor that everybody had to go to the poor-house, except
the confectioners, and the fancy storekeepers, and the picture-
booksellers, and the expressmen; and *they* all got so rich and
proud that they would hardly wait upon a person when he came
to buy; it was perfectly shameful!

Well, after it had gone on about three or four months, the
little girl, whenever she came into the room in the morning

and saw those great ugly lumpy stockings dangling at the fireplace, and the disgusting presents around everywhere, used to just sit down and burst out crying. In six months she was perfectly exhausted; she couldn't even cry any more; she just lay on the lounge and rolled her eyes and panted. About the beginning of October she took to sitting down on dolls, wherever she found them,—French dolls, or any kind,— she hated the sight of them so; and by Thanksgiving she was crazy, and just slammed her presents across the room.

By that time people didn't carry presents around nicely any more. They flung them over the fence, or through the window, or anything; and, instead of running their tongues out and taking great pains to write "For dear Papa," or "Mamma," or "Brother," or "Sister," or "Susie," or "Sammie," or "Billie," or "Bobby," or "Jimmie," or "Jennie," or whoever it was, and troubling to get the spelling right, and then signing their names, and "Xmas, 188—," they used to write in the gift-books, "Take it, you horrid old thing!" and then go and bang it against the front door. Nearly everybody had built barns to hold their presents, but pretty soon the barns overflowed, and then they used to let them lie out in the rain, or anywhere. Sometimes the police used to come and tell them to shovel their presents off the sidewalks, or they would arrest them.

"I thought you said everybody had gone to the poor-house," interrupted the little girl.

"They did go, at first," said her papa; "but after a while the poor-houses got so full that they had to send the people back to their own houses. They tried to cry, when they got back, but they couldn't make the least sound."

"Why couldn't they?"

"Because they had lost their voices, saying 'Merry Christmas' so much. Did I tell you how it was on the Fourth of July?"

"No; how was it?" And the little girl nestled closer, in expectation of something uncommon.

Well, the night before, the boys staid up to celebrate, as they always do, and fell asleep to be wakened by the bells and cannon. But it was nearly eight o'clock before the first boy in the United States woke up, and then he found out what the trouble was. As soon as he could get his clothes on, he ran out of the house and smashed a big cannon-torpedo down on the pavement; but it didn't make any more noise than a damp wad of paper, and, after he tried about twenty or thirty more, he began to pick them up and look at them. Every single torpedo was a big raisin! Then he just streaked it upstairs, and examined his fire-crackers and toy-pistol and two-dollar collection of fireworks, and found that they were nothing but sugar and candy painted up to look like fireworks! Before ten o'clock, every boy in the United States found that his Fourth of July things had turned into Christmas things; and then they just sat down and cried,—they were so mad. There are about twenty million boys in the United States, and so you can imagine what noise they made. Some men got together before night, with a little powder that hadn't turned into purple sugar yet, and they said they would fire *one* cannon, anyway. But the cannon burst into a thousand pieces, for it was nothing but rock-candy, and some of the men nearly got killed. The Fourth of July orations all turned into Christmas carols, and when anybody tried to read the Declaration, instead of saying, "When in the course of human events it becomes necessary," he was sure to sing, "God rest you, merry gentlemen." It was perfectly awful.

The little girl drew a deep sigh of satisfaction.

"And how was it at Thanksgiving?" she asked.

Her papa hesitated. "Well, I'm almost afraid to tell you. I'm afraid you'll think it's wicked."

"Well, tell, any way," said the little girl.

Well, before it came Thanksgiving, it had leaked out who had caused all these Christmases. The little girl had suffered so

125

much that she had talked about it in her sleep; and after that, hardly anybody would play with her, because if it had not been for her greediness, it wouldn't have happened; and now, when it came Thanksgiving, and she wanted them to go to church, and have squash-pie and turkey, and show their gratitude, they said that all the turkeys had been eaten up for her old Christmases, they would see about the gratitude. Wasn't it dreadful? And the very next day the little girl began to send letters to the Christmas Fairy, and then telegrams, to stop it. But it didn't do any good; and then she got to calling at the Fairy's house, but the girl that came to the door always said "Not at home," or "Engaged," or "At dinner," or something like that; and so it went on till it came to the old once-a-year Christmas Eve. The little girl fell asleep, and when she woke up in the morning——

"She found it was all nothing but a dream," suggested the little girl.

"No, indeed!" said her papa. "It was all every bit true!"

"Well, what *did* she find out then?"

"Why, that it wasn't Christmas at last, and wasn't ever going to be, any more. Now it's time for breakfast."

The little girl held her papa fast around the neck.

"You sha'n't go if you're going to leave it *so!*"

"How do you want it left?"

"Christmas once a year."

"All right," said her papa; and he went on again.

Well, there was the greatest rejoicing all over the country, and it extended clear up into Canada. The people met together everywhere, and kissed and cried for joy. The city carts went around and gathered up all the candy and raisins and nuts, and dumped them into the river; and it made the fish perfectly sick; and the whole United States, as far out as Alaska, was one blaze of bonfires, where the children were burning up their gift-books and presents of all kinds. They had the greatest *time!*

The little girl went to thank the old Fairy because she had stopped its being Christmas, and she said she hoped she would keep her promise, and see that Christmas never, never came again. Then the Fairy frowned, and asked her if she was sure she knew what she meant; and the little girl asked her, why not? and the old Fairy said that now she was behaving just as greedily as ever, and she'd better look out. This made the little girl think it all over carefully again, and she said she would be willing to have it Christmas about once in a thousand years; and then she said a hundred, and then she said ten, and at last she got down to one. Then the Fairy said that was the good old way that had pleased people ever since Christmas began, and she was agreed. Then the little girl said, "What're your shoes made of?" And the Fairy said, "Leather." And the little girl said, "Bargain's done forever," and skipped off, and hippity-hopped the whole way home, she was so glad.

"How will that do?" asked the papa.

"First-rate!" said the little girl; but she hated to have the story stop, and was rather sober. However, her mamma put her head in at the door, and asked her papa:

"Are you never coming to breakfast? What have you been telling that child?"

"Oh, just a moral tale."

The little girl caught him around the neck again.

"*We* know! Don't you tell *what*, Papa! Don't you tell *what!*"

What Is a Miracle?

MANUEL KOMROFF

THE LITTLE tiny one had a Christmas card for old Rufus, who drove the school bus. She held it tightly in her hand as she hurried with her sister across the village square. The school bus was waiting, as it always did, in front of Doctor Wilson's house and beside the grocery. The beautiful great elms of the old sleepy village of Meadows spread their graceful black arms upward toward a bleak winter sky.

Four children with gay woolen caps and mufflers were already in the bus when the tiny one, Dolly, and her sister Alice mounted the step and climbed in. Old Rufus closed the door with the jointed lever handle beside the steering wheel and started the motor. The little tiny one held the card in her red mitten.

"What is it?" asked the old bus driver.

"For you, Uncle Rufus."

"Oh my. For me?"

She nodded her head as he took the card.

"Oh, that's a very nice Christmas card," said old Rufus. "Thank you very much. It's a pretty picture."

Her eyes were wide open and earnest as she nodded her head again.

Rufus placed the card over the windshield of the bus. The children crowded about to look at the colored picture which showed the Christ Child in the manger with a golden halo over the Child's head.

"Yes, it's a very nice picture," Rufus repeated.

"It's a picture of the miracle," one of the bright children mentioned.

128

"It's not," said Dolly. "It's the birth of our Lord."

And the children laughed for the little tiny one did not understand and she stood there and looked at them earnestly with wide open eyes. "It's not what you say. It's the birth of the Lord in the stable."

The children laughed again. The bus started and the tiny one began to cry. Great tears came to her eyes and rolled down her cheeks.

Alice mopped up the tears with her red mitten and consoled her sister by saying: "Now don't cry. 'Cause you don't understand. It is a miracle."

Dolly looked up at the little picture over Rufus's head and stopped crying. The bus rolled on.

For a whole long week the children had been making preparations for Christmas. They came to school in the morning with bright smiles, their faces glistening, their hair neat, shoes shined, and even their hands were clean. They sang their morning songs earnestly and loud. Arithmetic, geography, and spelling were neglected. The extra time was devoted to recitations, rehearsals for the play that was always given in the assembly hall on the last day before Christmas vacation, and art work in colored crayon. These masterpieces were hung on the classroom walls, and then when all was over the children would be allowed to take them home and present them to their parents.

And also, each class made bright paper chains that they strung from wall to wall just to make the whole school look gay and Christmasy. All worked very hard, but it was real fun. At three o'clock all hands were sticky with paste.

Most of the children lived close to the school, and only twenty-one came in the bus which was driven by old Rufus. For many years he had been chauffeur, nursemaid, smoother-down of youthful sorrows, arbiter of disputes, critic of homework, and trusted companion. For nineteen years this old bachelor watched over the children in his bus, and daily, in any kind of weather, his bus traveled the twelve miles of winding road up to Highridge and then back in the afternoon to Meadows. Some years there were more children to bring to school. Once he had as many as twenty-seven and one year only fourteen. But this year it was twenty-one. The oldest was a farmer's boy. Buzzie Clark, who was over fourteen and would soon be going to the county high school. And the youngest was Dolly Pierson, who was only four, but she came along with her sister Alice, who was six and a half.

The bus rolled on. About a mile down the road Buzzie Clark and two other children were waiting.

"Oh, look at the Christmas card!" exclaimed one who had just come in.

"She gave it to him," said another, pointing to the tiny one.

"I said it was a miracle picture and she began to cry," another called out.

"It is a miracle picture!" another shouted.

"Now quiet, children," spoke Rufus as the bus went up the country road.

The tiny one kept looking at the picture and after a while she turned and asked her sister: "What is a miracle?"

"You are too young to understand."

"Look," called one. "She don't even know what a miracle is."

And others joined in to make fun of the tiny one until tears again filled her eyes, and when the bus stopped to take on several more children Rufus took the tiny one and placed her on the driver's seat beside himself.

"You children need not be so smart," he remarked. "I bet none of you know what a miracle is."

"We do," several called out at once.

"Very well, but you need not tease the little one." And with this he started the bus again.

"Mamma's pet!" someone whispered. And the bus rolled on.

In this way, on the day before Christmas, all twenty-one children arrived safely, as they always did, at the schoolhouse in

Highridge. And here on this last day before the Christmas vacation everything was most happy and gay.

Rufus sat in a chair in the rear of the assembly hall and listened to the young voices singing old English songs. Then the story of the Three Wise Kings and the Star of Bethlehem was read aloud.

For nineteen years at Christmas time old Rufus had come into the assembly hall and listened to the singing and festival readings. They brought to his mind memories of events long long ago.

And now as they were reading about the Three Wise Kings, he thought of the time when he was a boy on the farm with his mother and father. And how large the farm seemed to him then. And how much snow they used to have in the old days and how clean and white it all seemed.

And while someone was reading this story of the Three Magi he saw the fragments of his whole life pass before him in quick vivid snatches like a jerky moving picture.

"*Come, Rufus. Get the axe, it is time.*" *His father's voice was clear and distinct and he stood in the yard with his old brown jacket and fur cap. His father had a short, bushy beard, as was the custom of men long ago. "No, son, not the little hatchet. Bring the big axe."*

The big long-handled axe seemed very heavy to him as they walked across the frozen field and the crust of the snow crunched beneath their boots. And then in the woods they saw the tracks of little animals and they heard the breaking of branches. But it was far off and they could not see the cause of this disturbance. "Must be a bear."

"*No son. Bears are all asleep at this season.*"

"*How can they sleep all winter, Daddy, without eating?*"

"*Yes, son. That is one of the wonderful mysteries of nature.*"

"*And do they dream, Daddy?*"

"*Perhaps.*"

131

"And do they know what Christmas is?"

"No, son. They are but animals and cannot understand such things."

"And all their lives they live without once having a single Christmas?"

"Without once."

Oh, this was so sad. To think that all the creatures of the fields and forests were born and lived and died without once knowing the full-flowing joy of Christmas. And why did the Lord in heaven deny them?

Soon they stood before a green spruce tree, Father and boy.

"Not this one, Daddy. It's too small."

"Well, stand up beside it, son, and we will measure it."

He stood beside the tree and his father stepped back a pace or two and eyed the boy and tree together. And he smiled. There was a hidden joy in that smile.

"Yes," he said. "It will do. A larger one would touch the ceiling. Your grandfather used to say that the tree should be twice the height of the boy. Here, give me the axe."

And when the tree was falling over, just toppling, he had a strange feeling in his heart because it made a low cracking sound as though it were someone crying . . . crying alone and secretly. Crying like a woman at night in bed . . .

The reader's voice was loud and clear.

"In the blue heaven a star shined brightly and this star was the fulfillment of a prophecy."

"Mother, is that you?" he called. "Mother!"

She did not answer. He came to the head of the stair. He heard her crying alone and secretly.

"Mother!"

"Yes, son," she finally replied. "Go to bed."

"I thought I heard . . . "

"It's nothing, son. Go to bed."

But the sound continued night after night, and the doctor came twice each day until she died.

What Is a Miracle?

In the school assembly hall the reader had just pronounced the words: "And the Three Kings with valuable gifts in their hands journeyed forth. And the star in heaven glistened brightly and guided them safely across the wide desert."

The children sat spellbound and the tiny one saw it all before her most clearly in jewel-like colors. It was so beautiful; and even if she did not understand what a miracle was, still, even then it was beautiful anyway. Her large eyes were open and she could see the deep blue of the sky and the star that shone to guide the kings. And they were dressed in gorgeous robes.

Rufus closed his eyes. He saw one star in a vast blue sky.

Alone on the farm. All alone. The tree is twice the size of the boy. The bears sleep all winter. Creatures are born and die without once feeling the thing that. . . . And seeds are frozen in the ground all winter long and in the spring they swell up and burst through the soft soil. They, they, they—hundreds of them—but not all. Here and there one is frozen and does not burst out into life. The shell rots away and soon it becomes part of the earth. And the whole world is earth and water. The ocean is filled with salt waves that are dark green, the color of the branches of the tree that is twice the height of the boy. And there are rocks cold and gray that form a mineral winter and pepper the surface of the vast world.

"And they did not know the meaning of stone that He gave them. For it meant that so firm as the stone should they hold the faith. And they threw the stone into a well in the desert and, lo behold! it burst into flames."

Rufus heard these words of the reader and closing his eyes he saw the great burst of flame against the heaven of a dark night. And the fire was also part of flesh and blood.

Oh, how different it might have been! She was the only one and there could be no other. And for two years the nights were lit by a magic flame. And the fresh wallpaper that we bought together had large red roses. And I wanted only what she wanted. And then it was on a cold night before Christmas. "No,

Rufus. It can never be. I know you love me, but try as I may, I am unable to return this love. The heart has reasons that reason itself cannot know."

"But perhaps later on. Perhaps in time."

And time brought the letter that was folded in the magazine that had a colored cover of a man on a horse high on a sunlit cliff. And when he read the letter the roses on the wall lost all meaning. And it took so many kettles of water to wash off that pulpy paper. And now even the ink in the letter is faded. *Twenty years. And what is it that makes things fade? Is it only the bright flow of time? Or is it more? Does not nature heal her wounds by a slow fading and does she not build up a new color before the old has been washed clean? Nineteen years of children—twice a day, counting them over in the bus—the small voices, the small hands and feet, the front teeth missing from all seven-year-olds, the clear eyes searching to understand a world slowly unfolding. Eyes seeking wonder. Yes, a new color arrives when the old begins to dim. Surely this is also a miracle that should be noted down in a book. And the colored picture of the man on the horse, that I hung in the kitchen, that too has faded and should be thrown away. It has lived out its life.*

When the reading was over and it was time for the children's play to begin Rufus looked out of the window at the dark slate sky and saw tiny flakes of wet snow falling. It was necessary to put the chains on the bus tires, for the winding road from Highridge to Meadows was a slippery one when wet. He left the assembly room just as the improvised curtain parted and he heard a small voice pipe: "The evil king has enchanted us and the white lovely princess is asleep."

The light snow was hardly more than a wet drizzle. He got out the chains and stretched them on the ground and as he bent down to clamp the links together a strange sensation came over him. He felt a quick thumping of his heart and his head seemed to feel queer. He stood up and leaned against the fender of the bus but soon finished the job of clasping on the chains. Then he climbed into his seat and started up the motor so that the car heater would warm up the bus before the children were out of school.

He sat there before the wheel and looked up at the colored card that the tiny one had given him that morning. His lips smiled and he closed his eyes.

How pretty it would be if it turned colder and a white blanket of snow covered the whole country as it so often did in the days of long ago. And then tonight I might take the long-handled axe and walk out on the hill—the same hill—and find a little tree. A small one would be big enough. And suddenly he saw himself walking across the soft, flaky snow and he stood before a small tree, but he could not raise the axe. *How strange to feel so powerless.* "Yes, I know, I know. You want to cry out when the wood cracks and I have no right to make anything cry like that because . . . But the tree is not for me. It is for the tiny one. The one who brought me the card. And you could not cry out like that because she is innocent . . . So innocent." But no. He could not raise the axe. "Yes, I know. It could not fall without crying, and nature is so full and so understanding she does not want me to hear that voice. Because . . . because we live by forgetting."

The night is so still and the air so gentle that you can walk without hardly breathing. And he let the axe fall in the snow and walked away between the trees on the soft white pathless carpet. And the strange and wonderful thing about it all was that his feet left no footprints in the snow. He marveled at this and he paused once or twice to reflect. He could not explain why his feet left no tracks in the snow. This was just another thing that was wonderful. Nature was filled with wonders. He walked on and on.

"Open the door, Uncle Rufus," called some of the children. "Open the door."

But Rufus did not move.

Soon quite a few of them were at the door and they banged

on the window-pane. The door opened and they piled in. Eighteen were in the bus and it waited. The other three were shouting: "Merry Christmas everybody!" and were soon skipping across the yard with their art work in their hands.

The door seemed to close without any motion from Rufus and the bus started out of the yard. It went through the village street and took the turn for Meadows. It rolled along a little slower than usual, but perhaps this was due to the wet road.

"Uncle Rufus is sleeping," said one of the children in the back.

"He is not," called Buzzie Clark.

"Does it always snow on Christmas?" the tiny one asked.

"No. Not always. Only when it wants to," replied her sister.

The bus stopped at a crossroad and several children got out. When it started again the door was open, but soon it closed by itself when the bus swung around a long curve. It went on and on a long down grade of many turns.

In this way, in about an hour, after three or more stops they arrived at the store in Meadows.

"Merry Christmas, Uncle Rufus," called the children.

Rufus did not turn his head and did not reply.

"Open the door for us!"

He did not move.

One of the children pulled on the handle and the door opened. All climbed out except the tiny one. She was waiting until all had left so they might not laugh at her.

"Uncle Rufus. What is a miracle?"

He did not reply.

She paused a moment and then stepping down from the bus ran into the grocery. "Merry Christmas," she called. "Uncle Rufus is asleep."

"Asleep?"

They went out to wake him. They called Doctor Wilson from next door and he climbed into the bus. But soon he shook his head.

136

"Looks like an attack. Can't do anything now. You should have called me an hour ago. He's been dead for some time."

"But the bus just arrived this minute," argued the grocer.

The doctor shook his head. "I know what I am talking about. He's been dead at least an hour."

Then the tiny one spoke up. "He was asleep at the school when we left and he wouldn't wake up. All the way he was sleeping."

The large wet flakes of snow brought an added whiteness to his face. And the tops of the graceful elms were lost in the sky.

Eminence

RUTH SUCKOW

M R. AND Mrs. Watkins were going to church on Christmas Eve. Mr. Watkins was proudly carrying Florentine. Her little white legs, dangling, bumped against his coat. Her curls were carefully covered. Mrs. Watkins was carrying, wrapped from the snow, the star and crown of silver paper.

"Be careful of her slippers, daddy!"

"I'm being careful."

Florentine took one bare hand from her muff and stretched it out to the snow flakes. They were like dim soft little stars. They melted with a cool delicious tingle upon her warm skin. The flimmer of misty snow hushed for a moment the high excitement of being on the program.

"Oh, keep your hands covered, darling!"

The church was brilliant with lighted windows in the snowfall. With preoccupied faces, taking only an instant to smile and half nod to this one and that, Mr. and Mrs. Watkins made their way through the people flocking up the church steps. They were thrillingly aware of the whispers all around them. A man called out jovially, "What's that you've got there, Watkins?" Mr. Watkins said proudly, "That's part of the program!" Above all the heads was Florentine's small pale face with starry eyes.

They went straight to the Infant Room, where the children who were going to take part on the program were crowded. Instantly they were surrounded. "Oh, here she is! They've brought her!" Faces of Sunday-school teachers, of older girls, delighted, eager, were all around them. Boys watched, while they pretended not to, with aloof and silent admiration. At the edge of the

138

group, withdrawn, solemn and watchful, were the other little girls in Florentine's class.

Mr. Watkins set Florentine on her feet. Mrs. Watkins sent him to find seats for them in the audience room. Her face was tensely absorbed as she laid aside Florentine's white wavy furs, drew off her white coat, and undid the scarf. She brushed out the pale-gold curls that were flattened, the little fine surface hairs roughened and glinting, from the pressure. She knelt to place the crown of silver paper, tipped at the center with a star, upon Florentine's head. Florentine was all in white. She wore white slippers and stockings and a little white silk dress with puffed sleeves.

"How darling! How dear! Mrs. Watkins, what is she?"

"The Christmas Fairy," Mrs. Watkins said.

She led Florentine over to the register, murmuring, "Come, darling, you must get warm!" The girls from the older classes circled around her in delight, with coos and cries of ecstasy, reaching out adoring fingers to brush Florentine's floating curls, to fondle her little soft wrists, and touch her silken skirts. "Oh, Mrs. Watkins, can't we look after her?" Florentine Watkins was the prettiest child in the Sunday-school. She stood on the register, a little princess, small, calm and sure of herself, but her face pale and her eyes like dark blue stars. She let one hold her hand and another lay all her curls straight, with one curl over each shoulder. Beneath her little smile, the glory of the occasion, of the moment, of the worship, was shining and singing through her—almost ready to break into fiery sparkles, as when she dragged her feet across the rug and touched the cat's fur. She was well aware of being the star of the evening. The scarf her mother had anxiously put about her floated and clung to her puffed sleeves and her small chilly arms. The heat from the register billowed out her full skirt, that clung like milkweed floss to the fingers of the girls, when they pushed it down. All the boys were aware of her, but awed, looking sidelong at her and standing apart.

139

"Mrs. Watkins, let us take care of her!"

"Will you stay with the girls, darling?"

Florentine consented royally.

"You remember your piece, darling. You remember what to do."

"I remember."

Still on the edge of the group stood the other girls in the class, Lola, Kitty, Amy, Mary Louise. They were in their winter dresses, black stockings and high shoes. They had walked to the church. Their hair was crimped or braided, and they wore big red ribbons. They eyed Florentine.

The noise in the audience room was growing louder. It was almost time for the program to begin. The teachers were beginning to marshal the classes. "Now, Miss Morrison's class!" That was the one to which Florentine belonged. She stepped into line with a thrill of shining fear and expectation.

Lola, Kitty, Amy and Mary Louise huddled together behind her with giggles and excited whispers. They clung to each other. "What if I should forget!" "I know your part, I'll prompt you." Florentine stood at the head. Now her fear had become a great cold blankness that left her, in the midst of the envy and the worship, all alone. The girls looked at her, but did not cling to her. Her face was white and her eyes dark under her silver star. If she forgot, none of them could help her. She had the principal part. The exercise depended upon her.

The organ was almost hidden behind the Christmas tree, that was dark glistening green, laden with white packages, shredded over with sparkles of tinsel. The opening march sounded out through the branches. It spread through the air heated from the big registers and chilled by the wintry drafts from the door, spiced with evergreen, thick with the odors of the crowd in their winter clothing damp from the snow. All the heads turned to watch the Sunday-school march in.

Mr. and Mrs. Watkins sat near the front. Their eyes were set in a glaze of expectation. Mrs. Watkins clasped her hands until

the knuckles were strained to white. In all the marching ranks
—little boys and little girls, bigger, smaller, fair-haired, black-
haired, awkward, pretty—they could see only one child. "There
comes Florentine!" She had a little space to herself, as if made
by the shining of her silver star and the dainty floating of her
silken skirts. Just for one transported instant the little face
passed them, pale, unconscious of them, under the silver star.
Then they sat back. With shovings, rustlings, scuffings, and
orders from teachers, the Sunday-school was seated. She was lost
to them among the other children.

The exercises began.
"Joy to the world, the Lord has come . . ."
The music roared through the branches of the Christmas tree
and filled the room. When the audience sat down again, the
front seats reserved for the Sunday-school quivered with hair
ribbons.

All bowed their heads, but they were not listening to the
minister's prayer. It was just something that came at this time
on the program. Parents were craning and straining their eyes
to see their own children. The children had their eyes on the
packages heaped about the tree. They nudged one another to
see that big package propped at its foot. "Wonder whose that
is?" The prayer ended, the audience moved and shuffled, and the
superintendent stepped forward and announced the first real
number of the program. Now those who were to take part became self-conscious, looked down and twisted their shaking
fingers, with their lips silently repeating the opening lines of
their pieces.

"A song by the Infant Department."
Pulling back, stopping and wandering, whimpering or looking about with widely innocent eyes, the infants were herded
upon the platform. The little ones were pulled to their places
in front. Some were too large and awkward among the others.

A shock-headed boy, with holes in his stockings that showed

141

white patches of winter underwear, stood grinning at the end of the line. The little threads of voices followed the voice of the primary teacher, on and off the key. When the song was over none of the infants knew enough to go down. They stood smiling with engaging foolishness at the audience until the teacher began to marshal them off the platform. Some wandered down, others came with quick little steps, while the audience laughed and clapped, the men grinning, but ashamed, at the exhibition of ingenuousness.

Mr. and Mrs. Watkins smiled slightly and clapped perfunctorily. They could not give ready applause until Florentine had had hers.

Exercises, songs and recitations—pieces by children whose mothers would be offended if they were left off the program: good or bad, the audience clapped. Here a clear little voice got a momentary sharpness of applause; or a lisp or a stutter drew a ripple of laughter. Mrs. Watkins listened, clasping her hands. Once she was angry. It was when Howard Hopkins "forgot." He stood staring at the audience with a bright, bold, unabashed gaze, and when he could not go on, suddenly grinned and said, "Guess that's all!" and marched nonchalantly down. The roar of laughter and appreciation beat upon Mrs. Watkins' jealous ears. It was not fair. It did not really belong to the program. This boy had no right to come in, not even able to speak his piece, and take away some of the applause from Florentine.

In the third row from the front, Miss Morrison's class waited, all crowded together. Their exercise came near the end of the program. It was the principal one. They were old enough now to know how to do things, but still small enough to be "cute." And then, they had Florentine Watkins. They wiggled and squirmed through the earlier numbers. The other girls whispered together. But Florentine sat still, her eyes brightly fixed, whispering over and over to herself with rapt intentness the first line of her piece. At times she forgot about it, and it fled away from her, and then, after a cold moment when the world shook, it

142

sounded clear and true in her mind. She felt all the eyes upon her silver star. Through the earlier part of the program, that elated her and made her hold her small golden head high. But now it quivered through her with terror. Her turn was almost here. She was Florentine Watkins. The whole church expected her to do well. The teacher depended upon her. The girls would wait for her. Her mother and father were listening. Her lines started to vanish and her mind made a leap and caught them. The lights and the sparkles on the Christmas tree dazzled together. She could not breathe or live until this was over. She moistened her lips and moved one cold little hand. She was the most miserable one on the program. If she could be Kitty with only four lines to speak, that girl in front of her who had already given her recitation—be a child of whom no one expected anything—Beany Watters, that boy with the holes in his stockings! The shining of the silver star on her forehead was a bright terror. The next . . . her heart began to thump . . .

"'The Christmas Fairy'—an exercise by Miss Morrison's class."

Florentine rose at the head of her line, made her way daintily down the aisle and up the steps, padded with white and bordered with evergreen, and crossed the enormous space of the platform. Her knees were trembling, but a strange spacious coolness was upon her. She would get through her part, and then die.

In shaking silence the little girls took their places about Florentine. Mr. and Mrs. Watkins were staring straight ahead. Mr. Watkins cleared his throat. Mrs. Watkins saw her child through a wavering shimmer of dizziness: little delicate white figures in the flimsy shine of the silken dress, silver star tipping the golden head—was the dress all right? Long enough? the crown straight on her head? Mrs. Watkins dug her nails in ecstatic agony into her palms. Then silence. Florentine stepped forward. Her voice came out clear and small, tremulous—like the shaking of a tiny bell—in the rustling hush of the room.

"Dear children all, I heard your wishes,
And o'er the world I flew
To bring my happy Christmas message
To all the world and you. . . ."

Her mother's eyes were fixed in an agony of watchfulness on that small face. Every word seemed to turn and twist in her own heart.

Florentine was getting through it. Her little bell-like voice rang out the words small and clear and pure. Her knees had stopped trembling. Her coolness was fired with happiness. Why, it was going to be over too soon! In a blaze of elation she wanted to go all through it again. Now the eyes upon her were a bright intoxication. Just for this little moment, she was the Fairy—silver star and white slippers, silken dress and silver crown—herself and beyond herself. . . . It was over. She had spoken the last word. She was standing—she was going down the steps—sliding into her pew. The applause was a roaring sea in her ears. It was not until she was seated, breathing quickly and clasping her warm trembling hands in her silken lap, that she realized in a burning glory that the applause was for her!

Mr. Watkins was smiling broadly, unable to hold in his pride. Mrs. Watkins' heart steadied into a happy, elated beat as she drank in the applause. Their child, their child—the best on the whole program! Moisture stung in the mother's eyes, and warmth flowed over her. Now she could be happy. Now she could be easy. She could smile at the rest of the program.

The children were growing restless. They did not want to hear the superintendent's announcements. They were watching, turning—but the little ones shrieked when they heard a jingle of bells from the entry and a stamping of feet. Santa Claus came running down the aisle. He shouted in an enormous jovial voice, "Well, children, Merry Christmas! Did you think old Santy wouldn't come?"

144

Clapping, laughter and cat-calls answered him.

"Well, Santy pretty nearly thought so himself. I'll tell you how it was. One of Santy's reindeer got a stone in its hoof and we had to stop and see the blacksmith down there at Grover. Well sir, and all the presents I was bringing to the good little girls and boys in Mahaska—Santy don't give any presents to bad children, no sir, but you're all good, ain't you? (A little trusting voice piped up, "Yes, Santy!") Sure you are! I knew it! Well, all the presents rolled out, and those children in Grover—I guess, they hadn't seen anything like those!—they came pretty near getting the whole lot of them."

The little children sat with starry eyes of wonder and expectation. It was Mr. Heggy. The big boys were whispering that it was only Mr. Heggy. And yet, could they be sure? There were the buffalo coat and the fur cap, the white wooly beard and rosy cheeks, the jingle of sleighbells from up his sleeve. . . . They watched breathlessly while the first presents were taken from the Christmas tree. "Aw, it ain't either Santy. It's just Mr. Heggy. Because there's another Santy at the Methodists! They ain't two Santys, is they?" Still the little ones were not convinced. They murmured, "I bet it *could* be Santy, though!"

The big boys in Mr. Pendleton's class were distributing the candy—hard Christmas candy, little colored curley-cues and squares and round white logs with flowers in the center glistening red and sticky white. Every child—visitors and all—got one of the little cardboard packages. Florentine accepted hers. She was glad to sit back for a little while in the obscurity that Santa's speech made for her, but still with the radiance of her great moment warmly upon her.

Santa had come to the packages. He was reading the names in a loud voice as he took them from the tree.

" 'Helen Vincent!' Anybody know Helen? Oh, that's Helen, is it? Hold up your hand, Helen, this looks like a pretty nice present. . . . . 'Mamie Runkle!' Now I wonder who could have given Mamie a present like that? Must have been some one who likes her pretty well! . . . 'Mrs. Peabody. From her Sunday-school class!' Well, well, I guess those boys know a good teacher when they get one."

The boys rushed about, waving the packages, sending them down the aisles from hand to hand. Children were gnawing at the hard candy, with loud snaps, as if teeth were breaking. Papers were strewed untidily over the church. The Christmas tree was shining but disheveled. Santa was just calling the names now. The big box at the foot of the tree had not yet been given out. It had been saved for the last. The children were still pointing to it, and hoping and whispering about it.

Santa lifted it. A hush in the buzzing and talking and rustling followed. The package was big enough to catch the last jaded attention of the audience. He looked it all over for a name. The room became still. Respectful, wondering, eager glances were turned toward the box. Santa took his time.

"Well, this is quite a little bundle! Glad Santy didn't have to carry this very far. Guess this must go to Santy himself—must be a token of appreciation. . . . No, sir! I'm mistaken there. This seems to belong to a little girl. I'd oughta brought my specs along from the North Pole to read this. Let's see if I can make it out. . . . 'Florentine Watkins!' Well, well! A big box for a little girl! Here, boys! The little girl with the silver star on her head."

The sound of wonder, envy, disappointment, and excited laughter swelled. Mr. and Mrs. Watkins sat suffused with happy pride. Florentine's face was pale as she held out her arms to take the package. "Open it, open it!" she heard the whispers all around her. The girls pressed close. Some one had to help her untie the string. . . . The string was loose, the white paper off—tissue paper, crackling and soft, and wadded into it, an enormous doll! . . . There was a long sigh from the children crowding to see. The doll lay revealed—closed, waxy-lidded eyes and golden curls matted upon its cold bisque forehead, dress of pink satin, pink stockings, gold buckles on its tiny shoes. . . .

146

"Oh look!" A moan came from the girls. They crowded about to touch the hair and satin gown. "Florentine, will you let me see? Is she jointed all over? Can I just *touch* her?" Heads through the audience craned to see, people half rose, the room was a buzz.

Florentine sat holding the big box. She was mute with a surfeit of bliss. Nothing else could happen after this.

In the loud hubbub of leaving, people were all crowded and talking at the door. Children came running on padding little feet up the sloping aisles, and bumped joyously into parents. "Oh, here you are, are you?" A father put his arm around a little shoulder, squeezed a flaxen head against him and held it there while he went on talking, and the other persons smiled. "See all the things I got, papa!"

"Well, well!" He didn't really see them. "Santy Claus was pretty good to you!"

Mothers had gone down to the front rows to find their own infants. They sat down in convenient pews and tried to drag small, stiff, black overshoes over little feet limp in their laps. The white sheeting on the platform was marked all over with footprints, the evergreen trimmings were pulled out from their tacks. The Christmas tree stood sparkling but denuded. From it spread the odors of pine needles, hot wax, popcorn and paper.

Mrs. Watkins had taken Florentine at once into the Infant Room to find her wraps. Mr. Watkins waited in the audience room near the register. He talked in a manly way with Mr. Hollister—also waiting—about the effect this snow would have upon the ground; but his ears were straining with shamed eagerness for the words that were occasionally spoken to him: "I should think you'd be pretty proud of that little girl tonight, Mr. Watkins!"

In the Infant Room, where tired mothers were finding wraps in the piled mountain shaking and toppling on an old discarded pew—"How can we *ever* find our own things in this jam!" Mrs.

Watkins took down Florentine's white wraps from their special hook. "Are you tired, darling?" she mourned. Even when she was drawing on the little coat, and her back was turned to the room, she was tinglingly aware of the notice of the others and the glory shed upon her by her child. She pretended to think only of the hurry of getting home. As soon as she turned toward the room, she expected the congratulations to break out. With careful, proud, reluctant hands she lifted off the silver crown and star.

A woman came searching through the Infant Room with a big-eyed little child clinging to her hand. "Oh, here she is!" She encouraged the child, "Ask her! I think she will"; and then she said to Mrs. Watkins, "Here's a little girl, Mrs. Watkins, who thinks she can't go home until she's seen Florentine Watkins' big doll!"

"Why, of course!" Mrs. Watkins said with radiant graciousness. "It's in the other room. Mr. Watkins has it. You come in with us, Lucy. Florentine will show it to you."

"I want to see that, too! Mamma, I want to see it, too! I want to see the big doll."

Now all the crowd who had been pawing over the wraps and staying away from Mrs. Watkins and Florentine out of respect, diffidence and envy, came flocking around them.

"These children want to see the doll, daddy!"

"Want to see the doll?"

Mr. Watkins opened the box. The little children gave great sighs. Mothers had to clutch little reaching hands and warn, "Oh, mustn't touch!" while Mrs. Watkins smiled graciously, but alertly. Mr. Watkins set the box upright, and the bright blue eyes of the doll flew open between its golden-brown lashes. Lola Hollister cried with an anguish of longing, "Oh, mamma, look! The doll's got *real* little gold buckles on its shoes!" Mrs. Hollister said in a slight, withdrawn voice, "Yes, I see!", and gave a painful little smirk. She compared this doll with the doll Lola was going to get in the morning. Her heart was rent with a painful anguish of jealousy for her child. Mr. Hollister tried to be admiring, but it shamed him, shamed his adequacy as a father, when he too compared this doll with Lola's doll, which he had bought. Some of the crowding faces were artlessly adoring. Others had a look of reserve which Mrs. Watkins' alert eyes caught. At last all the wondering childish eyes were satiated with the vision. Hands of mothers drew little figures gently back and voices murmured: "Well, are you satisfied? Have you seen the big doll?"

Long-drawn sighs answered them.

But there was something that made Florentine wonder. Mary Louise did not come to look at the doll. "I saw it before!" she said snippily to Lola, and ran off. The doll was too much. The Watkinses, on the very peak of glory in showing it off, did not know. Even some of the admiring ones went away from the church saying: they shouldn't have bought the doll; they shouldn't have put it on the Christmas tree; it was too expensive for a little girl; the Watkinses made them tired trotting out that child; next year they hoped some other child would get a chance.

The chief families of the church, with the minister and his wife, stood talking at the door. Mr. Watkins had set Florentine in a pew, and she stood leaning against him while he kept his arm around her. As people passed him, going to the door, they stopped. "My, but you must be proud of her tonight!" Florentine touched his cheek with a little princess air. The great doll was asleep in its closed box. The room glittered in tinsel and evergreen, and her presents were heaped on the pew beside her.

Freddy Perkins, being dragged out by a father who wanted to get home, called back eagerly. "G'night Flor'ntine!"

"Goodnight!" she answered with starry graciousness.

Old ladies moving slowly to the door, stopping to pat her little woolly sleeve with thin fingers, murmured, "Wasn't she dear? Just *like* a little fairy!" Florentine accepted the homage with sweet, childish royalty. But in her mind, under all the

149

glory, was a tremulous, shining wonder that craved to be re-assured.

Mrs. Watkins was flushed. She drank down the praise that burned her like a fiery wine. "She was simply perfect, Mrs. Watkins!" "I know you're proud tonight!" But the first perfect bliss of the applause that followed Florentine's exercise was marred. Florentine had won, and yet there were people who went away unconvinced, who seemed to have other, strange values. Already the atmosphere of universal praise had slackened. She was jealous of the laughter that still followed any mention of Howard Hopkins. "Wasn't that kid funny? Say, he was great!" Could there be people who had enjoyed him more than Florentine? She hated the minister's wife, who kept repeating, with effervescing tactfulness:

"They were *all* good!"

It was time to close up the church. The people who were talking over the program, the expenses, the success of the evening, began to look about for their children; and the Watkinses were beginning to realize that they had heard all the praise they were likely to hear for this evening. Lola and Mary Louise and Kitty were playing a game, chasing each other through the pews and down the aisles. "Come! It's time to go home! Remember, tomorrow is Christmas!" They came scampering up to the register, flushed, with disordered hair, panting and giggling together. "What are you little girls up to?" some one asked tolerantly. Kitty pinched Lola, and they laughed; but when they looked at Florentine, their eyes grew sober and aloof, considering.

"You go get your wraps on, young lady!"

Kitty ran off. She turned to call back to Mary Louise, "Don't you forget about tomorrow!" Mary Louise answered, "I won't! Don't *you* forget, Lola!" "I won't." They were going to see each other's presents. Lola gave a timid look at Florentine, but did not ask her to come. Florentine's big doll was so wonderful —finer than anything they would get. Florentine, in her white dress and slippers, noticed by every one, was no longer one of them.

Florentine stood silent and cool. She could not make a move toward the other girls, but she looked after them with a strange loneliness; and all at once it seemed to her that they had been having the most fun in the world playing together. She was suddenly very tired. Her eyes blinked under the dazzle of the lights. She no longer cared what people said to her. The program was over. She had her doll. What more was there? Christmas would be nothing after this evening.

Mrs. Watkins said commiseratingly, "Hurry up, daddy. She's tired."

Mr. Watkins picked Florentine up in his arms again. As they went outside the warm church into the snow, her disheveled little head drooped upon his shoulder. Mrs. Watkins was carrying the doll, and she was saying with anxious caution, "I was so afraid some of those children would do something to this doll! Daddy and mother had to send away off for it. It isn't to play with every day—just on special occasions. And Florentine, you must never let any of the girls handle it, no matter if they do ask you. You can't trust other children with it. Remember how Kitty ruined your little piano! This doll is much too expensive for that."

Florentine did not answer. All down the silent street—it had stopped snowing now, the ground where the corner light shone was covered with a soft, white, diamondy fluff—she snuggled down against her father's shoulder. To be carried by her father, and give way to the strong shelter of his arms, was all she wanted now. When they came up onto their own porch, stamping the snow from their rubbers, he set her down. They were going into the house, proud, happy and satisfied; but by the hall light they saw her sleepy face under the bright dishevelment of hair, drunk with the glories of the evening, forlorn now and bewildered, able to bear no more. Her eyes almost closed. It was as if they had never realized until now how small she was.

Her father said heartily, "Well, the big night's over!"

But her mother cried, in an anguish of adoring pity: "She must go to bed this minute! She'll be all tired out if she doesn't. We mustn't forget that tomorrow will be here."

As Ye Sow...

DOROTHY CANFIELD FISHER

CASUALLY, not that she was especially interested, just to say something, she asked as she handed out the four o'clock pieces of bread and peanut-butter, "Well, what Christmas songs are you learning in your room this year?"

There was a moment's pause. Then the three little boys, her own and the usual two of his playmates, told her soberly, first one speaking, then another, "We're not going to be let to sing." "Teacher don't want us in the Christmas entertainment." Their round, eight-year-old faces were grave.

"Well—!" said the mother. "For goodness' sakes, why not?"

Looking down at his feet, her own small David answered sadly, "Teacher says we can't sing good enough."

"Well enough," corrected his mother mechanically.

"Well enough," he repeated as mechanically.

One of the others said in a low tone, "She says we can't carry a tune. She's only going to let kids sing in the entertainment that can carry a tune."

David, still hanging his head humbly, murmured, "She says we'd spoil the piece our class is going to sing."

Inwardly the mother broke into a mother's rage at a teacher. "So that's what she says, does she? What's she *for*, anyhow, if not to teach children what they don't know. The idea! As if she'd say she would teach arithmetic only to those who are good at it already."

The downcast children stood silent. She yearned over their shame at failing to come up to the standards of their group. "Teachers are callous, that's what they are, insensitively callous. She is deliberately planting an inferiority feeling in them. It's

153

a shame to keep them from going up on the platform and standing in the footlights. Not to let them have their share of being applauded! It's cruel."

She drew in a deep breath, and put the loaf of bread away. Then she said quietly, "Well, lots of kids your age can't carry a tune. Not till they've learned. How'd you like to practice your song with me? I could play the air on the piano afternoons, after school. You'd get the hang of it that way."

They brightened, they bit off great chunks of their snacks, and said, thickly, that that would be swell. They did not say they would be grateful to her, or regretted being a bother to her, busy as she always was. She did not expect them to. In fact it would have startled her if they had. She was the mother of four.

So while the after-school bread-and-butter was being eaten, washed down with gulps of milk, while the November-muddy rubbers were taken off, the mother pushed to the back of the stove the interrupted rice pudding, washed her hands at the sink, looked into the dining room where her youngest, Janey, was waking her dolls up from naps taken in the dining-room chairs, and took off her apron. Together the four went into the living room to the piano.

"What song is it, your room is to sing?"

"It came upon the midnight—" said the three little boys, speaking at once.

"That's a nice one," she commented, reaching for the battered songbook on top of the piano. "This is the way it goes." She played the air, and sang the first two lines. "That'll be enough to start on," she told them. "*Now—*" she gave them the signal to start.

They started. She had given them food for body and heart. Refreshed, heartened, with unquestioning confidence in a grown-up's ability to achieve whatever she planned, they opened their mouths happily and sang out.

As Ye Sow . . .

"It came upon the midnight clear
That glorious song of old."

They had evidently learned the words by heart from hearing them.

At the end of that phrase she stopped abruptly, and for an instant bowed her head over the keys. Her feeling about Teacher made a right-about turn. There was a pause.

But she was a mother, not a teacher. She lifted her head, turned a smiling face on the three bellowing children. "I tell you what," she said. "The way, really, to learn a tune, is just one note after another. The reason why a teacher can't get *every*body in her room up to singing in tune, is because she'd have to teach each person separately—unless they happen to be naturally good at singing. That would take too much time, you see. A teacher has such a lot of children to see to."

They did not listen closely to this. They were not particularly interested in having justice done to Teacher, since they had not shared the mother's brief excursion into indignation. But they tolerated her with silent courtesy. They were used to parents, teachers, and other adults, and had learned how to take with patience and self-control their constantly recurring prosy explanations of things that did not matter.

"Listen," said the mother, "I'll strike just the two first notes on the piano—'It came—'" She struck the notes, she sang them clearly. Full of good will the little boys sang with her. She stopped. Breathed hard.

"Not quite," she said, with a false smile, "pret-t-ty good. Close to it. But not quite, yet. I think we'd better take it *one* note at a time. Bill, *you* try it."

They had been in and out of her house all their lives, they were all used to her, none of them had reached the age of self-consciousness. Without hesitation, Bill sang, "I-i-it—" loudly.

After he had, the mother, as if fascinated, kept her eyes fixed on his still open mouth. Finally, "Try again," she said.

"But first, *listen.*" Oracularly she told them, "Half of carrying a tune is listening first."

She played the note again. And again. And again. Then, rather faintly, she said, "Peter, you sing it now."

At the note emitted by Peter, she let out her breath, as if she had been under water and just come up. "Fine!" she said. "Now we're getting somewhere! David, your turn." David was her own. "Just that one note. No, not *quite*. A little higher. Not quite so high." She was in a panic. What could she do? "Wait," she told David. "Try just breathing it out, not loud at all. Maybe you can get it better."

The boys had come in a little after four. It was five when the telephone rang—Bill's mother asking her to send Bill home because his Aunt Emma was there. The mother turned from the telephone to say, "Don't you boys want to go along with Bill a ways, and play around for a while outdoors? I've got to get supper ready." Cheerful, sure that she, like all adults, knew just what to do, relieved to see a door opening before them that had been slammed shut in their faces, and very tired of that one note, they put on their muddy rubbers and thudded out.

That evening when she told her husband about it, after the children had gone to bed, she ended her story with a vehement "You never heard anything like it in your life, Harry. Never. It was appalling! You can't *imagine* what it was!"

"Oh, yes I can too," he said over his temporarily lowered newspaper. "I've heard plenty of tone-deaf kids hollering. I know what they sound like. There *are* people, you know, who really *can't* carry a tune. You probably never could teach them. Why don't you give it up?"

Seeing, perhaps, in her face, the mulish mother-stubbornness, he said, with a little exasperation, "What's the use of trying to do what you *can't* do?"

That was reasonable, after all, thought the mother. Yes, that was the sensible thing to do. She would be sensible, for once, and give it up. With everything she had to do, she would just be reasonable and sensible about this.

So the next morning, when she was downtown doing her marketing, she turned in at the public library and asked for books about teaching music to children. Rather young children, about eight years old, she explained.

The librarian, enchanted with someone who did not ask for a light, easy-reading novel, brought her two books, which she took away with her.

At lunch she told her husband (There were just the two of them with little Janey; the older children had their lunch at school.), "Musical experts say there really is no such thing as a tone-deaf person. If anybody seems so, it is only because he has not had a chance to be carefully enough trained."

Her husband looked at her quickly. "Oh, all right," he said, "all *right!* Have it your own way." But he leaned to pat her hand. "You're swell," he told her. "I don't see how you ever keep it up as you do. Gosh, it's one o'clock already."

During the weeks between then and the Christmas entertainment, she saw no more than he how she could ever keep it up. The little boys had no difficulty in keeping it up. They had nothing else to do at four o'clock. They were in the indestructible age, between the frailness of infancy and the taut nervous tensions of adolescence. Wherever she led they followed her cheerfully. In that period of incessant pushing against barriers which did not give way, she was the one whose flag hung limp.

Assiduous reading of those two reference books on teaching music taught her that there were other approaches than a frontal attack on the tune they wanted to sing. She tried out ear-experiments with them, of which she would never have dreamed, without her library books. She discovered to her dismay that sure enough, just as the authors of the books said, the little boys were musically so far below scratch that, without seeing which piano keys she struck, they had no idea whether a note was higher or lower than the one before it. She adapted and invented musical "games" to train their ear for this. The boys standing in a row, their backs to the piano, listening to hear whether the second note was "up hill or down hill" from the first note, thought it as good a game as any other, rather funnier than most because so new to them. They laughed raucously over each other's mistakes, kidded and joshed each other, ran a contest to see who came out best, while the mother, aproned for cooking, her eye on the clock, got up and down for hurried forays into the kitchen where she was trying to get supper.

David's older brother and sister had naturally good ears for music. That was one reason why the mother had not dreamed that David had none. When the two older children came in from school, they listened incredulously, laughed scoffingly, and went off to skate, or to rehearse a play. Little Janey, absorbed in her family of dolls, paid no attention to these male creatures of an age so far from hers that they were as negligible as grown-ups. The mother toiled alone, in a vacuum, with nobody's sympathy to help her, her great stone rolling down hill as fast as she toilsomely pushed it up.

Not quite in a vacuum. Not even in a vacuum. Occasionally the others made a comment, "Gee, Mom, those kids are fierce. You can't do anything with them." "Say, Helen, an insurance man is coming to the house this afternoon. For heaven's sake keep those boys from screeching while he is here. A person can't hear himself think."

So, she thought, with silent resentment, her task was not only to give up her own work, to invent and adapt methods of instruction in an hour she could not spare, but also to avoid bothering the rest. After all, the home was for the whole family. They had the right to have it the background of what *they*

158

wanted to do, needed to do. Only not she. Not the mother. Of course.

She faltered. Many times. She saw the ironing heaped high, or Janey was in bed with a cold, and as four o'clock drew near, she said to herself, "Now today I'll just tell the boys that I can *not* go on with this. We're not getting anywhere, anyhow."

So when they came storming in, hungry and cheerful and full of unquestioning certainty that she would not close that door she had half-opened for them, she laid everything aside and went to the piano.

As a matter of fact, they were getting somewhere. She had been so beaten down that she was genuinely surprised at the success of the exercises ingeniously devised by the authors of those books. Even with their backs to the piano, the boys could now tell, infallibly, whether a second note was above or below the first one. Sure. They even thought it distinctly queer that they had not been able to, at first. "Never paid any attention to it, before," was their own accurate surmise as to the reason.

They paid attention now, their interest aroused by their first success, by the incessant practicing of the others in their classroom, by the Christmas-entertainment thrill which filled the schoolhouse with suspense. Although they were allowed no part in it, they also paid close attention to the drill given the others, and sitting in their seats, exiled from the happy throng of singers, they watched how to march along the aisle of the Assembly Hall, decorously, not too fast, not too slow, and when the great moment came for climbing to the platform how not to knock their toes against the steps. They fully expected— wasn't a grown-up teaching them?—to climb those steps to the platform with the others, come the evening of the entertainment.

It was now not on the clock that the mother kept her eye during those daily sessions at the piano, it was on the calendar. She nervously intensified her drill, but she remembered carefully not to yell at them when they went wrong, not to screw her face into the grimace which she felt, not to clap her hands over her ears and scream, "Oh, horrible! *Why* can't you get it right!" She reminded herself that if they knew how to get it right, they would of course sing it that way. She knew (she had been a mother for sixteen years) that she must keep them cheerful and hopeful, or the tenuous thread of their interest and attention would snap. She smiled. She did not allow herself even once to assume the blighting look of patience.

Just in time, along about the second week of December, they did begin to get somewhere. They could all sound—if they remembered to sing softly and to "listen to themselves"—a note, any note, within their range, she struck on the piano. Little Peter turned out, to his surprise and hers, to have a sweet clear soprano. The others were—well, all right, good enough.

They started again, very cautiously, to sing that tune, to begin with "It ca-ame—" having drawn a deep breath, and letting it out carefully. It was right. They were singing true.

She clapped her hands like a girl. They did not share her overjoyed surprise. That was where they had been going all the time. They had got there, that was all. What was there to be surprised about?

After that it went fast; the practicing of the air, their repeating it for the first skeptical, and then thoroughly astonished Teacher, their triumphant report at home, "She says we can sing it good enough. She says we can sing with the others. We practiced going up on the platform this afternoon."

Then the Christmas entertainment. The tramping of class after class up the aisle to the moment of foot-lighted glory; the big eighth-graders' Christmas pantomime, the first graders' wavering performance of a Christmas dance as fairies—or were they snowflakes? Or perhaps angels? It was not clear. They were tremendously applauded, whatever they were. The swelling hearts of their parents burst into wild hand-clapping as the first grade began to file down the steps from the platform. Little

Janey, sitting on her mother's lap, beat her hands together too, excited by the thought that next year she would be draped in white cheesecloth, would wear a tinsel crown and wave a star-tipped wand.

Then it was the turn of the third grade, the eight- and nine-year-olds, the boys clumping up the aisle, the girls switching their short skirts proudly. The careful tiptoeing up the steps to the platform, remembering not to knock their toes on the stair-treads, the two lines of round faces facing the audience, bland and blank in their ignorance of—oh, of everything! thought David's mother, her hand clutching her handbag tensely.

The crash from the piano giving them the tone, all the mouths open,

> "It came upo-on the midnight clear
> That glorious song of old."

The thin pregnant woman sitting in front of the mother, leaned to the shabbily-dressed man next to her, with a long breath of relief. "They do real *good*, don't they?" she whispered proudly.

They did do real good. Teacher's long drill and hers had been successful. It was not howling, it was singing. It had cost the heart's blood, thought the mother, of two women, but it was singing. It would never again be howling, not from those children.

It was even singing with expression—some. There were swelling crescendos, and at the lines

> "The world in solemn stillness lay
> To hear the angels sing."

the child-voices were hushed in a diminuendo. Part of the mother's very life had been spent in securing her part of that diminuendo. She ached at the thought of the effort that had gone into teaching that hushed tone, of the patience and self-control and endlessly repeated persistence in molding into something shapely the boys' puppy-like inability to think of anything but aimless play. It had taken hours out of her life, crammed as it was far beyond what was possible with work that must be done. Done for other people. Not for her. Not for the mother.

This had been one of the things that must be done. And she had done it. There he stood, her little David, a fully accredited part of his corner of society, as good as anybody, the threat of the inferiority-feeling averted for this time, ready to face the future with enough self-confidence to cope with what would come next. The door had been slammed in his face. She had pushed it open, and he had gone through.

The hymn ended. The burst of parental applause began clamorously. Little Janey, carried away by the festival excitement, clapped with all her might—"learning the customs of her corner of society" thought her mother, smiling tenderly at the petal-soft noiselessness of the tiny hands.

The third grade filed down the steps from the platform and began to march back along the aisle. For a moment, the mother forgot that she was no longer a girl, who expected recognition when she had done something creditable. David's class clumped down the aisle. Surely, she thought, David would turn his head to where she sat and thank her with a look. Just this once.

He did turn his head as he filed by. He looked full at his family, at his father, his mother, his kid sister, his big brother and sister from the high school. He gave them a formal, small nod to show that he knew they were there, to acknowledge publicly that they were his family. He even smiled, a very little, stiffly, fleetingly. But his look was not for her. It was just as much for those of his family who had been bored and impatient spectators of her struggle to help him, as for her who had given part of her life to roll that stone up hill, a part of her life she never could get back.

She shifted Janey's weight a little on her knees. Of course.

Did mothers ever expect to be thanked? They were to accept what they received, without bitterness, without resentment. After all, that was what mothers worked for—not for thanks, but to do their job. The sharp chisel of life, driven home by experience, flaked off expertly another flint-hard chip from her blithe, selfish girlhood. It fell away from the woman she was growing to be, and dropped soundlessly into the abyss of time.

After all, she thought, hearing vaguely the seventh-graders now on the platform (none of her four was in the seventh grade), David was only eight. At that age they were, in personality, completely cocoons, as in their babyhood they had been physical cocoons. The time had not come yet for the inner spirit to stir, to waken, to give a sign that it lived.

It certainly did not stir in young David that winter. There was no sign that it lived. The snowy weeks came and went. He rose, ravenously hungry, ate an enormous breakfast with the family, and clumped off to school with his own third-graders. The usual three stormed back after school, flinging around a cloud of overshoes, caps, mittens, windbreakers. For their own good, for the sake of their wives-to-be, for the sake of the homes which would be dependent on them, they must be called back with the hard-won, equable reasonableness of the mother, and reminded to pick up and put away. David's special two friends came to his house at four to eat her cookies, or went to each other's houses to eat other cookies. They giggled, laughed raucously, kidded and joshed each other, pushed each other around. They made snow-forts in their front yards, they skated with awkward energy on the place where the brook overflowed the meadow, took their sleds out to Hingham Hill for coasting, made plans for a shack in the woods next summer.

In the evening, if the homework had been finished in time, they were allowed to visit each other for an hour, to make things with Meccano, things which were a source of enormous pride to the eight-year-olds, things which the next morning fell over, at the lightest touch of the mother's broom.

At that age, thought the mother, their souls, if any, were certainly no more than seeds, deep inside their hard, muscular, little-boy flesh. How do souls develop, she wondered occasionally, as she washed dishes, made beds, selected carrots at the market, answered the telephone. How do souls develop out of those rough-and-ready little males? If they do develop?

David and Peter, living close to each other, shared the evening play-hour more often than the third boy who lived across the tracks. They were allowed to go by themselves, to each other's house, even though it was winter-black at seven o'clock. Peter lived on the street above theirs, up the hill. There was a short-cut down across a vacant lot, which was in sight of one or the other house, all the way. It was safe enough, even for youngsters, even at night. The little boys loved that downhill short-cut. Its steep slope invited their feet to fury. Never using the path, they raced down in a spray of snow kicked up by their flying overshoes, arriving at the house, their cheeks flaming, flinging themselves like cannon-balls against the kitchen door, tasting a little the heady physical fascination of speed, on which, later, as ski-runners, they would become wildly drunken.

"Sh! *David!* Not so *loud!*" his mother often said, springing up from her mending at the crash of the banged-open door. "Father's trying to do some accounts," or "Sister has company in the living room."

Incessant acrobatic feat—to keep five people of different ages and personalities, all living under the same roof, from stepping on each other's feet. Talk about keeping five balls in the air at the same time! That was nothing compared to keeping five people satisfied to live with each other, to provide each one with approximately what he needed and wanted without taking away something needed by one of the others. (Arithmetically con-

sidered, there were of course six people living under that roof.
But she did not count. She was the mother. She took what she
got, what was left. . . .)

That winter, as the orbits of the older children lay more
outside the house, she found herself acquiring a new psycho-
logical skill that was almost eerie. She could be in places where
she was not, at all. She had an astral body which could go anywhere. Anywhere, that is, where one of her five was. She was
with her honey-sweet big daughter in the living room, playing
games with high-school friends (was there butter enough, she
suddenly asked herself, for the popcorn the young people would
inevitably want, later?). She was upstairs where her husband
sat, leaning over the desk, frowning in attentiveness at a page
of figures—that desk-light was not strong enough. Better put
the flood-light up there tomorrow. She was in the sun-porch of
the neighbor's house, where her little son was bolting Meccano-
strips together with his square, strong, not-very-clean hands—
his soul, if any, dormant far within his sturdy body. She floated
above the scrimmage in the high-school gym, where her first-
born played basketball with ferocity, pouring out through that
channel the rage of maleness constantly gathering in his big
frame which grew that year with such fantastic rapidity that he
seemed taller at breakfast than he had been when he went to
bed. She sent her astral body upstairs to where her little daughter, her baby, her darling, slept with one doll in her arms, and
three others on the pillow beside her. That blanket was not
warm enough for Janey. When she went to bed, she would put
on another one.

She was all of them. First one, then another. When was she
herself? When did *her* soul have time to stretch its wings?

One evening this question tried to push itself into her mind,
but was swept aside by her suddenly knowing, as definitely as
if she had heard a clock strike, or the doorbell ring, that the
time had passed for David's return from his evening play-hour

165

with Peter. She looked at her watch. But she did not need to. A sixth sense told her heart, as with a blow, that he should before this have come pelting home down the hill, plowing the deep snow aside in clouds, hurling himself against the kitchen door. He was late. Her astral self, annihilating time and space, fled out to look for him. He must have left the other house some time ago. Peter's mother always sent him home promptly.

She laid down the stocking she was darning, stepped into the dark kitchen, and put her face close to the window to look out. It was a cloudless cold night. Every detail of the back-yard world was visible, almost transparent, in the pale radiance that fell from the stars. Not a breath of wind. She could see everything: the garbage pail at the woodshed door, the trampled snow of the driveway, the clothes she had washed that morning and left on the line, the deep unbroken snow beyond the yard, the path leading up the hill.

Then she saw David. He was standing half way down, as still as the frozen night around him.

But David never stood still.

Knee-deep in the snow he stood, looking all around him. She saw him slowly turn his head to one side, to the other. He lifted his face towards the sky. It was almost frightening to see *David* stand so still. What could he be looking at? What was there he could be seeing? Or hearing? For as she watched him, the notion crossed her mind that he seemed to be listening. But there was nothing to hear. Nothing.

She did not know what was happening to her little son. Nor what to do. So she did nothing. She stood as still as he, her face at the window, lost in wonder.

She saw him, finally, stir and start slowly, slowly down the path. But David never moved slowly. Had he perhaps had a quarrel with Peter? Had Peter's mother been unkind to him?

It could do no harm now to go to meet him, she thought, and by that time, she could not, anxious as she was, not go to meet him. She opened the kitchen door and stepped out into the dark, under the stars.

He saw her, he came quickly to her, he put his arms around her waist. With every fiber of her body which had borne his, she felt a difference in him.

She did not know what to say, so she said nothing.

It was her son who spoke. "It's so still," he said quietly in a hushed voice, a voice she had never heard before. "It's so still!"

He pressed his cheek against her breast as he tipped his head back to look up. "All those stars," he murmured dreamily, "they shine so. But they don't make a sound. They—they're *nice*, aren't they?"

He stood a little away from her to look up into her face. "Do you remember—in the song—'the world in solemn stillness lay'?" he asked her, but he knew she remembered.

The starlight showed him clear, his honest, little-boy eyes wide, fixed trustingly on his mother's. He was deeply moved. But calm. This had come to him while he was still so young that he could be calmed by his mother's being with him. He had not known that he had an inner sanctuary. Now he stood in it, awe-struck at his first sight of beauty. And opened the door to his mother.

As naturally as he breathed, he put into his mother's hands the pure rounded pearl of a shared joy. "I thought I heard them singing—sort of," he told her.

Christmas Eve's Day

BARRY BENEFIELD

ONE WINTER Lige Dunklin loaded his wife and four-year-old son into his wagon and left the hills of Arkansas for the flat lands of Louisiana, which he had heard were fertile and easy to cultivate. His visible wealth was forty-odd dollars, a green-bodied wagon, Rhoda, the young white mare tinily spotted with red hairs which gave her that appearance called flea-bitten, and the old black mule named Tom.

In seven years Lige had cropped on five plantations in as many parishes. He kept moving on from farm to farm because there never was anything noticeable left over after he had sold his cotton and paid for his supplies. It seemed to him that things worked in a vicious circle so far as he was concerned. If the crop was good the price was low, and if the price was high the yield was scanty. It often infuriated him to think of it. "Hit's the beatin'est thing," he would say to Amanda, his enormous sharp-pointed Adam's apple working up and down in his long brown neck and his grey eyes blinking rapidly. Maybe on another plantation things would, somehow, go better.

He had with him now not only the boy Kilmer, the name taken from a trusted kidney remedy, but a daughter of four. She was Peruna; and Lige, having begun to christen his children from medicine bottles, had already selected other revered names for future children—Lydia, Hood, Carter and Hostetter—because, being a farmer, he hoped for more boys than girls. But his wife died leaving him only Kilmer and Peruna.

Lige's spirit did not recover from the blow of her death. There was near him now not a single person intimately acquainted with and interested in the details of his life and work and he was very lonesome, and full of something he called "jandice," and so a year after her loss he started back in his wagon for the Arkansas hills, where he said he had "kinfolks." The old black mule, Tom, had laid his body down permanently one spring night following a hard day's plowing, but Rhody had providentially been philandering in the woods the autumn before and her son Buster, now a leggy yearling, yellow and very tame, walked with his aged mother along the white roads leading back to Arkansas.

Kilmer did most of the driving and whatever other work was necessary, for his pappy, saying frequently with faint bitterness that he "felt like the devil before day," lay on the bedding under the canvas cover while the wagon worked slowly northward. Lige had waited to gather and sell his crops, so that it was December when the Dunklins reached Asphodel, in southern Arkansas.

Having crossed the state line, Lige's spirit revived somewhat and he began calling up at Kilmer on the high spring-seat to get along faster. Leaving Asphodel late one afternoon, the Dunklins camped for the night on the banks of a bayou three miles north of town. The next day Lige could not go on, and the following week he died.

For a few days Asphodel was keenly interested in Dunklin affairs. The sheriff put the wagon and team in Beamer's wagon-yard, pending the settlement of the Elijah Dunklin estate, including the bills of the doctor and the undertaker. While vague efforts were being made to locate his unknown relatives in the hills, whose surnames and addresses Kilmer did not know, and while letters were being sent to several institutions that cared for orphaned children the twelve-year-old boy was taken in by one family and Peruna by another on the opposite side of town.

She received an outfit of clothes, mostly new, of which she was ecstatically proud, and Kilmer too was polished up considerably. A barber removed the whitey-colored shag of hair that almost covered his ears and extended well down over his coat collar. His brass-toed brogans, his trousers that had been cut down from a pair of his pappy's, so that the two hip pockets stood abutting each other and were no longer hip pockets, his ancient and holey brown felt hat, all these and more were replaced with things entirely new, since the two sons of his host were smaller than he.

But within a week the two little Dunklins had lost their delightful center-stage position for Asphodel's adults and children alike. The grown-ups were busy with other matters, and the children with whom Peruna and her brother came in contact were soon subjecting them to various juvenile barbarities by way of initiation.

Peruna dared not pour out her grievances to the awesome adults of the family that had taken her in, but Kilmer came over every day to see her and at some time while he was there she would get him away from the other children and passionately unburden herself.

Many things struggled in him to get said, though he could find few words in which to put them; and besides he talked so slowly that the more articulate Peruna had run on into a new subject before he had barely touched the one a minute older. Still he could sum up what he wanted to say by slipping his arm around her and squeezing her hard against him; and she understood, for always after that her wistful little kitten face would relax and brighten and presently she would be lightheartedly playing with the temporarily friendly enemy.

There was no comforter for Kilmer. Before his father died he had felt responsibility touch his shoulders, and he had unconsciously braced himself to meet the strain. Vaguely he had the notion that now he was the head of the family, that he was the court of last resort as to Dunklin matters, and that there was no one to whom he could complain or to whom he could transfer his multitude of worries. The lonely brave child's necessarily stoic philosophy was developing rapidly.

Adult Asphodel would have been amazed to know that he had any worries, he and Peruna were deemed children of luck, the hills being held in scant esteem by the lowlanders. Kilmer covered his troubles with a sallow mask, his gray eyes seeking to see all things and to reveal nothing. For he was among strangers, he was suspicious, and he had caught dim intimations of something appalling that was about to befall him and Peruna.

One night at the supper table he noticed that Mr. Turley looked meaningly at his wife and then at him. She sent her own three children to a neighbor's house across the street with a message about the Christmas tree to be at the Baptist church. When they were gone she began talking in a voice sweeter, it seemed to Kilmer, than she had ever used before to him.

"Wouldn't you like to go away on the train, Kilmer, an' live in a great big buildin' where there were a lot of other nice boys, an' learn to be a carpenter or somethin'? Wouldn't that just be fine? Then you could be a rich man, maybe, an' come back an' take care of your little sister, an' buy her all kinds of pretty things. Wouldn't you just like to do that?"

Kilmer looked down at his plate a long time and under the table his big bony hands were twisting together and he felt his neck and ears and face getting prickly hot. He wanted to separate the question so that he could answer yes and no, but after a moment he whispered, without raising his head, "Yessum."

"That's a good boy. I knew you would."

"Would she be with me, Mis' Turley?" He still stared down at his plate, hanging on the answer, though he knew what it would be. She had said, "Come *back* an' take care of your sister."

"No, Kilmer. Will Nevins is as rich as all outdoors an' they're goin' to keep her on; for a while, anyway, until she is bigger. But she'll have a good home until you can take care of her, an' we'll

171

write you all about what happens. You needn't worry about your sister, Kilmer; she'll be looked after. You must trust us all for that."

He had heard only her "No"; the rest of it had been a mere murmuring in his ears. And before she had finished speaking he stood up, his head turned away from her, and mumbled, " 'Scuse me," and went out into the dark hall. Putting on his overcoat and hat, he waited for a moment to steady himself.

"Downtown a minute," he called back into the dining-room. "See the things in the store." These were the words he had heard her own two boys use the night before.

Outside the air was clear and chilly. Turning his overcoat collar up about his neck and pulling his new black hat down over his eyes, Kilmer walked slowly down the sidewalk. Town, meaning the half-dozen business streets, was only five blocks away. He had had no mind to see the things in the stores; he had felt an overmastering desire to get away by himself and he had been afraid that if he didn't hurry Bob and Hal Turley would come back and want to drag him off with them.

Christmas was close at hand. Kilmer heard small firecrackers popping here and there about him—a mere foretaste of what was to come on Christmas Eve— and the wind bore faint whiffs of inciting powder scent to his nostrils and he heard the excited calls of gangs of boys. But he went on his way, his head down, scuttling through dark alleys to escape notice. He was bound for Beamer's wagon-yard.

On that side of town, where the stores were all closed at night, there was a quiet darkness welcome to him. Opening the gate, he slipped in, latching it behind him. In the long line of stalls running around three sides of the yard he heard horses and mules steadily crunching, one of them now and then squealing furiously at a nosy neighbor, following with a futile grunting kick. Locating Rhody's stall, he eased himself up into the shallow feedbox for small grain that was now empty. Rhody had passed on to her dessert of hay in the deep box next to the little one.

It was dark in the stall, the musky smell of animals and the sharp ammoniac odor of manure were good in his nostrils, and he sat there recklessly banging his new shoes against the slanting planks underneath the box. Old Rhody knew that here was a creature who had often supplied her with food and water, and tickled her skin delightfully with curry-comb and brush; she was not afraid, and she began making up to him, whinnying huskily far down in her throat and nuzzling his shoulder with her nose. But even here, all by himself, Kilmer could see no way out of the horror that awaited him; and presently he reached his arms around her neck, laid his cheek against her warm head and cried as if the old mare were really his mother.

Two days later came Christmas Eve's Day, as it is called in the South, and the excited Turley household was early astir. Mr. Turley looked forward to a big day in his "notion" store, his wife was flutteringly concerned about cakes and pies and the church Christmas tree, and Bob and Hal were to peddle oranges and apples and firecrackers from baskets, "on commission," they grandly explained.

By nine o'clock the house was empty except for the negro cook fuming in the kitchen and Kilmer. He was in the boys' room feverishly removing the new clothes that had been given him and putting on the old ones that had come up with him from Louisiana; his face set and his lips moving with half-sensed words that rushed about his head and tumbled out in jerky mumblings.

Many people were coming and going through Mr. Beamer's store, and the yard was nearly full of wagons and buggies. No one paid any attention to the silent boy who now and then ran into the big barn-like store, picked up an armful of bedding or kitchen utensils and loaded them into a canvas-covered wagon that stood near the gate. And no hand was raised to stop Kilmer when finally he drove out and away.

Somehow he had gathered the impression that though the wagon and horses had been his pappy's they were now not exactly his, and he had the feeling that in taking them he was doing something forbidden and dangerous. Troubled but unhesitant, he moved swiftly and surely, a hard fierce look in his slate-gray eyes.

Standing behind the seat and under the canvas to hide himself as much as possible, he drove down the street as if he meant to leave town, expecting every moment to hear somebody come yelling after him to stop. But presently he was well away from the yard, and no one had hailed him. Urging Rhody and Buster to a trot, he circled the town and eased the wagon cautiously into the alley behind the Nevins home, putting the cowbarn and the garage between it and the great white house.

When he had found Peruna and whispered his message to her he still had to wait while she found and put on her old clothes and slipped away.

But by twelve o'clock they were a mile out of town, going north along a road that Lige had followed as far as he could. That seemed a very long time ago to Kilmer.

"Whur air we a-goin' to buddie? I reckin you can tell me now."

"Sitta, we air a-goin home to pappy's kinfolks, whur he wuz aimin' to go, away up yander in the mountings. I ricollect a little bit about hit, and he tole me a whole lot more."

"What's our kinfolks names, buddie? Same as ourn?"

"I reckon so, sitta. I know Uncle Buck an' Aunt Emmy an' Cousin Lem, but I don't ricollect nary a hind name if ever I knowed 'em."

"How come you decide to go?"

Peruna's pale-faced brother looked a long time out in front

of him before he tried to answer. He wasn't sure he ought to tell her anything about what had threatened them. But she caught his right arm in both of hers and shook it. "How come, buddie?"

"Would you want me to go away, sitta, on a railroad train an' stay I don't know how long, hundreds o' miles from whur you air?"

"How come I couldn't go on the railroad train along with you, buddie?"

"I reckin I couldn' tell you that, sitta; for I jist don't rightly know. Anyhow, Mis' Turley an' Mr. Turley an' ever'body, I reckin, wuz a-aimin' to send me away an' keep you in Asphodel." His voice had the ring of fierce certitude about it.

Kilmer stared out along in the road in front of him, and no word came from his little sister standing by his side behind the seat. He wished she would say something. After a while he looked down at her, but the faded pink sunbonnet hid her face; and when he stooped down and peered under the bonnet brim her lips were pressed tremblingly together and her darkened blue eyes were welling round tears over their lower lids.

"Don't you mind, sitta, don't you mind a durn bit whut they been a-aimin' to do, 'cause they hain't a-goin' to do it." He put his right arm around her shoulder and pulled her hard against him. "Now, now, sitta, don't cry. We air a-goin home to pappy's kinfolks away up yander in the mountings; you an' me, sitta, together. We air that."

Kilmer could say no more, and she stumbled back and lay on the pile of bedding crying. He yelled furiously at Rhody and Buster, snatching the lines to make them trot.

"How come," he called back over his shoulder presently, "how come you cry now, sitta? Don't you *want* to come along with me?"

"I'm afeared—I'm jist afeared they might ketch us yit an' send you away on the railroad train."

175

"Giddap, Rhody," he bellowed. "Giddap, Buster, afore I bust you wide open." He wiped the back of his right hand across his eyes.

In the middle of the afternoon, stopping at a wayside store standing among three or four weather-grayed houses in a clearing of the pine forest that circled blackly around the horizon in all directions, Kilmer spent some of Lige's last ten dollars that he had held on to grimly through his Asphodel days. With a bushel of corn in the shuck, a dime's worth of crackers, two bits' worth of cheese and three of those tremendous brown ginger cakes called stage planks, he pushed on into the dimly known North.

Now and then a wagon or a rattling car passed him, going away from town, but no one questioned him and he was beginning to feel easier about possible pursuit and recapture, though he "calculated" that when Mr. Beamer's nigger set out to feed Rhody and Buster that night the flight would be discovered. He aimed, though, to be far away in the woods by then, and besides, neither Mr. Beamer nor the sheriff nor the mayor nor anybody at all would know for a day or so which road he had taken. By dogs, he'd beat 'em yit. He quit his standing position behind the high spring seat, and helping Peruna up on it he settled himself comfortably beside her and clucked almost gayly at Rhody and Buster, very proud of himself and quietly exalted.

After a while, the sharp chill of coming night settling through the woods, Kilmer began thinking of a fire and preparations for camping. Camping would not be so simple now, he felt, as when his pappy was with him, for he would have to hide, lest pursuers come upon him off his guard. From time to time streams of water, which he called branches, crossed the dipping road, and when the country boy's sense of time told him that the day was nearly done he left his sister in charge of the team while he followed a branch back into the pine forest, behind a little hill, to see if he could find a place "fitten to camp in";

and presently Rhody and Buster, free of harness, stood grinding corn for themselves in the feedbox bolted on the tailpiece of the wagonbed, and Peruna and her brother Kilmer sat before the camp fire watching the fat pine knots spout red pointed flames up into the early black night.

The fearful runaways had merely nibbled at the cheese and crackers and one stage plank during the afternoon, but now they could take their ease as they dined. On the edge of the light Kilmer sat, bareheaded, his back against a tree-trunk, his knees drawn up and soft little Peruna between them. Their left hands each held a big piece of cheese and their right hands an installment of the complementary crackers, and by the side of them were the reserves of crackers, two whole stage planks and, mercifully, a tin bucket filled with water to wash their dinners down.

They had been hungry and now they were eating. They had been afraid and now they felt secure. Peace and freedom and piercing happiness were with Peruna and her brother Kilmer by the red fire, and all manner of wild things struggled within them to get said, but they had no words to fit the great white joys fluttering in their hearts. So Kilmer could only pat his right foot on the ground as if he were keeping time with some tune lilting through the woods, the long slim crescent of brass on the toe of his brogan winking in the light; and Peruna could only lean her black head against his chest and look up at him now and then with worshipful eyes crowding with shining words that needed no saying.

"Like it, sitta?"

"Uh-huh!" She knocked her head vigorously against his chest for emphasis, and a light was on his face that did not come from the fire.

Occasionally they noted a homebound wagon passing along the road on the other side of the little hill—the thin voices of children, the loud ringing voices of extremely exhilarated men, the high clear voices of women sometimes singing, the clink of

177

trace-chains, a new accordion or banjo or fiddle tried out, tin horns, thumping little drums.

Once after a wagon had passed Peruna looked inquiringly at Kilmer. "You reckin, buddie, *he* will find us away out here in the woods tonight?"

"We wouldn't mind if *he* did find us, would we, sitta?"

"You reckin he *will*, buddie? We ain't got no chimbley or nothin', an' we ain't been here long. Maybe he won't know whur we're *at*."

The head of the Dunklin family felt vaguely that the conversation was on dangerous ground; not because he disbelieved in the existence of the saint of childhood but because the circumstances were certainly unpropitious. So he fell back upon the ancient trick of avoiding a question with a question. "What you want him to fetch you, sitta?"

"Well, last Christmas he fotch me a doll, an' a napple, an' a norange, an' a big stick o' banana candy, an' I reckin maybe I'd kinda like them same things again; only if he *could* jist drap in a breastpin with blue sparklin' di'monds hit'd be mighty nice."

"Breastpin! Shucks, little gals don't wear no breastpins, sitta."

"Yes-siree-bob, they do so, buddie; an' besides couldn't I keep it till I'm a grown lady, answer me that?"

Well he knew there was no adequate answer to that, and he attempted none, but sat staring wistfully over her head into the fire.

"Now, buddie, tell whut you want him to fetch you."

"A knife with a corkscrew in the back o' the handle, an' a red necktie, an' a package of firecrackers, an' a napple, an' a norange, an' a stick of lemon candy so as we could swap each other an' have two kinds apiece."

"My, *wouldn't* that be fine!"

"An' he ought to fetch Buster somethin', too, if he's a-comin', 'cause Buster ain't nothin' but a little ole boy-horse. Why, sitta, he ain't nigh as old as you."

"Let's ask him to, buddie; an' pore ole Rhody, maybe she'd cry like ever'thing if he left her out."

"Buster 'ud jist about tear up gourd vines if he had a string o' them little bells on his collar like I seen 'em in the store."

"Yes, an' I know ole Rhody 'ud priss along the road to beat six bits if bells wuz a-jinglin on her collar too. Come on, buddie, let's *do* somethin' about hit."

It appeared doubtful to tidy little Peruna that the great visitor would have any "truck" with stockings not freshly laundered, so in a bucket of water from the branch she washed hers and Kilmer's, standing barelegged in her shoes and tinily shrieking at the coldness of the water on her toy white arms. Kilmer planted two forked sticks close to the fire and placed a pole on them to hold the stockings until they should dry. Then he went down to the branch and cut a small holly tree, dug out a hole in the ground, set the tree in it and after much pounding of the loosened earth with the axe made it reasonably safe against any wind that might come or the weight of any gift that might be put upon it during the night.

No pencil could be found in the pockets of the runaways or in the supply-box of the wagon, so the collars of Rhody and Buster were laid in the light on the ground by the tree in the desperate hope that they would be hints not too delicate to be effective. As for themselves, in default of specific requests put clearly upon paper, they hung both their stockings prominently in strong limbs of the tree and decided to be satisfied with any changes that might be made in their two lists of wants, though with mystic faith they several times casually repeated in rather loud self-conscious voices all the items for the benefit of whomsoever might hear. They had known of such messages into the void to have effect.

And now they were ready. Kilmer had built up the fire afresh, clearing away the pine straw from around it so that it could not spread, and stacking a great pile of fat knots and hard wood near-by to keep it going through the night. The light glistened on the glossy green leaves and the red berries of the holly tree, the wind sank low far up in the nodding pine-tops, the branch at the foot of the hill hurried along its course, pishing and pshawing and clucking at the sticks and stones in its way, like a busy and hearty old woman enjoying her own voice.

Kilmer and Peruna stood by the wagon a while looking and listening, and then they slowly climbed over a front wheel, laid a thick slab of bedding smelling of hay on the floor of the wagon, inserted themselves between its folds, and prepared to await the issue with whatever patience they could command. They did not, alas, say their prayers, and there was no one to remind them, but surely some things may be taken for granted.

They were not afraid. As for Peruna, she lay close to her brother Kilmer; and as for him, he was the head of the family, he was used to the woods, and besides, listen as hard as he could, he heard nothing to alarm him.

Presently Kilmer felt the taut small body relax against him. Peruna moistened her mouth, murmured something about a doll with long yellow hair and drifted swiftly away into a sleep as sweet and sound and deep as, according to much testimony in fine black type, should have been connoted by her name.

But he lay awake for a long time. He must make up the fire once more after a while, he told himself, and besides he was already trying to think what he might say to soften the shock for her if indeed no visible miracle came to pass that night by his camp fire. The air was keen on his face, the covering was warm, it was softly dark under the canvas, and several times he caught himself dropping off to sleep. "Shucks!" he always said at himself, and if he could have looked in a mirror he would have seen his lips curled in scorn at his weakness.

An hour or so later he stole from under the covers, slipped on his shoes, and piled wood high on the fire so that well into the night it might remain a flaming signal in lieu of a chimney and continue a spot of beckoning red until the lighted morning of Christmas Day. Then he ran back to the warm bed, his teeth knocking together and his back all goosey, and after that the long rolling waves of the dark night closed in on him, and when again sleep stole near to call him he gave up and let himself go and go, oh so gladly.

And while the two innocents with the famous names slept in secret security countless miracles came to pass outside the wagon. Great red and yellow flames, and now and then a thin green one, leaped and wheeled and danced, and at the heart of the fire a thousand towering castles shaped themselves and faded unseen into gray ashes. At the foot of the hill where the branch ran into a little clearing of the forest, starlight that had been on the way for years and years fell upon the face of a ripple, burst into shining beauty for an unnoted fraction of a second and helped a minnow around a dangerous turning of his course. Under the earth pine trees were making from sand and water giant dark plumes to wave at the moon, and high above the earth golden suns marched on through that stately figure begun millions of years ago and to be finished millions of years hence. And though at daybreak no miracle had come to the tree of the sleepers, a wonderful story had been given to one of them and, more wonderful still, quick words to tell it with.

Rising stealthily and peeping through the puckered hole in the back of the canvas, just to make sure, Kilmer sighed and slipped back under the quilts, hoping that Peruna would not be awake. But he felt her hand searching for his, and turning he saw in the dim light that her questioning eyes were upon him.

"Did he come, buddie? Did he come at all?"

"Long, long time ago he come, he did. It was all black and cold outside, an' I got up to put some wood on the fire, an' he slided down right through the trees with little bells a-jinglin' an' a-janglin'. I was a-standin there by the fire a-lookin' at him, but he went right on a-liftin' things outen a big bran sack in his sleigh. I seen him slip into the stockin's your doll with the long

181

yaller hair an' my knife an' ever'thing an' a lots more besides; an' then, kinda smilin' in his white whiskers, he laid a brown strop all covered with shiny tinklin' bells on ole Rhody's collar an' one on Buster's. After that he stood a while, like he was a-studyin' somethin'; an' all at once he begun puttin' the things back in the bran sack.

" 'How come you takin' 'em all back, mister?' I called to him. An' he said, 'I'm a-goin to save 'em for you an' your little sister. Nobody else shall have a single one o' them,' he said, 'ain't a-goin' to lose nary a one o' them, no-siree-bob, you ain't,' he said, kinda laughin' in his white whiskers.

"An' then them reindeers of hisn, six or eight or maybe ten o' them, set in to pawin' at the ground an' a-shakin their heads so as you could hear their horns a-knockin' an' a-scrapin' together, like they knowed it wuz time to go; an' he jumped in his sleigh, all red it wuz, an' went slidin' out through the pines, risin' higher an' higher, the little bells a-jinglin' an' a-janglin', an' then he wuz gone."

Kilmer waited breathlessly to hear what Peruna might say. "I 'lowed I heard bells in the night, buddie." She whispered it.

"I shore am glad he's a-savin' our things till we git settled, ain't you, sitta? An' I believe ever' word he said. Don't you, sitta? He was a good ole man; I could tell by the look o' him. Do you believe, sitta?"

"I believe, buddie." She was looking into his eyes, and hers were round and solemn and clear. "My, but I wisht *I'd* a-seen them deers."

Before the sun had risen halfway to the tops of the tall pines two automobiles overtook the covered wagon. The fussy buzzing little sheriff put a negro on the wagon to drive it, and he spluttered away in Mr. Beamer's small car. For passengers back to Asphodel Mr. Nevins had only Peruna and her brother Kilmer, who slid about on the vast deeply cushioned rear seat, his right arm firmly clasping her waist. Mr. Nevins kept looking back at them, and after a while he said, this time without turning his head, "Hold her tight, Kilmer; you two must stick together."

"Yes, sir; we aim to."

The next morning Peruna and her brother Kilmer had evidence that the good old man had discovered the fact that they were already settled.

☆

"GREAT TIDINGS, STRANGE AND TRUE"

☆

From Far Away

OLD ENGLISH CAROL

From far away we come to you.
  The snow in the street, and the wind on the door,
To tell of great tidings, strange and true.
  Minstrels and maids, stand forth on the floor.
From far away we come to you,
  To tell of great tidings, strange and true.

For as we wandered far and wide,
  The snow in the street, and the wind on the door,
What hap do you deem there should us betide?
  Minstrels and maids, stand forth on the floor.

Under a bent when the night was deep,
  The snow in the street, and the wind on the door,
There lay three shepherds, tending their sheep.
  Minstrels and maids, stand forth on the floor.

"O ye shepherds, what have ye seen,
  The snow in the street, and the wind on the door,
To stay your sorrow and heal your teen?"
  Minstrels and maids, stand forth on the floor.

"In an ox stall this night we saw,
  The snow in the street, and the wind on the door,
A Babe and a maid without a flaw.
  Minstrels and maids, stand forth on the floor.

187

Old English Carol

"There was an old man there beside;
The snow in the street, and the wind on the door,
His hair was white, and his hood was wide.
Minstrels and maids, stand forth on the floor.

"And as we gazed this thing upon,
The snow in the street, and the wind on the door,
Those twain knelt down to the little one.
Minstrels and maids, stand forth on the floor.

"And a marvellous song we straight did hear,
The snow in the street, and the wind on the door,
That slew our sorrow and healed our care."
Minstrels and maids, stand forth on the floor.

News of a fair and marvellous thing,
The snow in the street, and the wind on the door,
Nowell, Nowell, Nowell, we sing.
Minstrels and maids, stand forth on the floor.

The Other Wise Man

HENRY VAN DYKE

YOU KNOW the story of the Three Wise Men of the East, and how they traveled from far away to offer their gifts at the manger cradle in Bethlehem. But have you ever heard the story of the Other Wise Man, who also saw the star in its rising, and set out to follow it, yet did not arrive with his brethren in the presence of the young child Jesus? Of the great desire of this fourth pilgrim, and how it was denied, yet accomplished in the denial; of his many wanderings and the probations of his soul; of the long way of his seeking and the strange way of his finding the One whom he sought—I would tell the tale as I have heard fragments of it in the Hall of Dreams, in the palace of the Heart of Man.

I

In the days when Augustus Caesar was master of many kings and Herod reigned in Jerusalem, there lived in the city of Ecbatana, among the mountains of Persia, a certain man named Artaban. His house stood close to the outermost of the walls which encircled the royal treasury. From his roof he could look over the sevenfold battlements of black and white and crimson and blue and red and silver and gold, to the hill where the summer palace of the Parthian emperors glittered like a jewel in a crown.

Around the dwelling of Artaban spread a fair garden, a tangle of flowers and fruit trees, watered by a score of streams descending from the slopes of Mount Orontes, and made musical by innumerable birds. But all color was lost in the soft and odorous darkness of the late September night, and all sounds

189

were hushed in the deep charm of its silence, save the plashing of the water, like a voice half sobbing and half laughing under the shadows. High above the trees a dim glow of light shone through the curtained arches of the upper chamber, where the master of the house was holding council with his friends.

He stood by the doorway to greet his guests—a tall, dark man of about forty years, with brilliant eyes set near together under his broad brow, and firm lines graven around his fine, thin lips; the brow of a dreamer and the mouth of a soldier, a man of sensitive feeling but inflexible will—one of those who, in whatever age they may live, are born for inward conflict and a life of quest.

His robe was of pure white wool, thrown over a tunic of silk; and a white, pointed cap, with long lapels at the sides, rested on his flowing black hair. It was the dress of the ancient priesthood of the Magi, called the fire worshipers.

"Welcome!" he said, in his low, pleasant voice, as one after another entered the room—"welcome, Abdus; peace be with you, Rhodaspes and Tigranes, and with you, my father, Abgarus. You are all welcome. This house grows bright with the joy of your presence."

There were nine of the men, differing widely in age, but alike in the richness of their dress of many-colored silks, and in the massive golden collars around their necks, marking them as Parthian nobles, and in the winged circles of gold resting upon their breasts, the sign of the followers of Zoroaster.

They took their places around a small black altar at the end of the room, where a tiny flame was burning. Artaban, standing beside it, and waving a barsom of thin tamarisk branches above the fire, fed it with dry sticks of pine and fragrant oils. Then he began the ancient chant of the Yasna, and the voices of his companions joined in the hymn to Ahura-Mazda:

We worship the Spirit Divine,
   all wisdom and goodness possessing,

Surrounded by Holy Immortals,
 the givers of bounty and blessing;
We joy in the work of His hands,
 His truth and His power confessing.

We praise all the things that are pure,
 for these are His only Creation;
The thoughts that are true and the words
 and the deeds that have won approbation;
These are supported by Him,
 and for these we make adoration.

Hear us, O Mazda! Thou livest
 in truth and in heavenly gladness;
Cleanse us from falsehood, and keep us
 from evil and bondage to badness;
Pour out the light and the joy of Thy life
 on our darkness and sadness.

Shine on our gardens and fields,
 shine on our working and weaving;
Shine on the whole race of man,
 believing and unbelieving;
Shine on us now through the night,
Shine on us now in Thy might,
The flame of our holy love
 and the song of our worship receiving.

The fire rose with the chant, throbbing as if the flame responded to the music, until it cast a bright illumination through the whole apartment, revealing its simplicity and splendor.

The floor was laid with tiles of dark blue veined with white; pilasters of twisted silver stood out against the blue walls; the clerestory of round-arched windows above them was hung with azure silk; the vaulted ceiling was a pavement of blue stones, like the body of heaven in its clearness, sown with silver stars. From the four corners of the roof hung four golden magic wheels, called the tongues of the gods. At the eastern end, behind the altar, there were two dark-red pillars of porphyry; above them a lintel of the same stone, on which was carved the figure of a winged archer, with his arrow set to the string and his bow drawn.

The doorway between the pillars, which opened upon the terrace of the roof, was covered with a heavy curtain of the color of a ripe pomegranate, embroidered with innumerable golden rays shooting upward from the floor. In effect the room was like a quiet, starry night, all azure and silver, flushed in the east with rosy promise of the dawn. It was, as the house of a man should be, an expression of the character and spirit of the master.

He turned to his friends when the song was ended, and invited them to be seated on the divan at the western end of the room.

"You have come tonight," said he, looking around the circle, "at my call, as the faithful scholars of Zoroaster, to renew your worship and rekindle your faith in the God of Purity, even as this fire has been rekindled on the altar. We worship not the fire, but Him of whom it is the chosen symbol, because it is the purest of all created things. It speaks to us of one who is Light and Truth. Is it not so, my father?"

"It is well said, my son," answered the venerable Abgarus. "The enlightened are never idolaters. They lift the veil of form and go in to the shrine of reality, and new light and truth are coming to them continually through the old symbols."

"Hear me, then, my father and my friends," said Artaban, "while I tell you of the new light and truth that have come to me through the most ancient of all signs. We have searched the secrets of Nature together, and studied the healing virtues of water and fire and the plants. We have read also the books of prophecy in which the future is dimly foretold in words that are hard to understand. But the highest of all learning is the knowledge of the stars. To trace their course is to untangle the threads of the mystery of life from the beginning to the end. If we could follow them perfectly, nothing would be hidden from us. But is not our knowledge of them still incomplete? Are there not many stars still beyond our horizon—lights that are known only to the dwellers in the far southland, among the spice trees of Punt and the gold mines of Ophir?"

There was a murmur of assent among the listeners.

"The stars," said Tigranes, "are the thoughts of the Eternal. They are numberless. But the thoughts of man can be counted, like the years of his life. The wisdom of the Magi is the greatest of all wisdoms on earth, because it knows its own ignorance. And that is the secret of power. We keep men always looking and waiting for a new sunrise. But we ourselves understand that the darkness is equal to the light, and that the conflict between them will never be ended."

"That does not satisfy me," answered Artaban, "for, if the waiting must be endless, if there could be no fulfillment of it, then it would not be wisdom to look and wait. We should become like those new teachers of the Greeks, who say that there is no truth, and that the only wise men are those who spend their lives in discovering and exposing the lies that have been believed in the world. But the new sunrise will certainly appear in the appointed time. Do not our own books tell us that this will come to pass, and that men will see the brightness of a great light?"

"That is true," said the voice of Abgarus; "every faithful disciple of Zoroaster knows the prophecy of the Avesta, and carries the word in his heart. 'In that day Sosiosh the Victorious shall arise out of the number of the prophets in the east country. Around him shall shine a mighty brightness, and he shall make life everlasting, incorruptible, and immortal, and the dead shall rise again.' "

"This is a dark saying," said Tigranes, "and it may be that we shall never understand it. It is better to consider the things that are near at hand, and to increase the influence of the Magi in their own country, rather than to look for one who may be a stranger, and to whom we must resign our power."

The others seemed to approve these words. There was a silent feeling of agreement manifest among them; their looks responded with that indefinable expression which always follows when a speaker has uttered the thought that has been slumbering in the hearts of his listeners. But Artaban turned to Abgarus with a glow on his face, and said:

"My father, I have kept this prophecy in the secret place of my soul. Religion without a great hope would be like an altar without a living fire. And now the flame has burned more brightly, and by the light of it I have read other words which also have come from the fountain of Truth, and speak yet more clearly of the rising of the Victorious One in his brightness."

He drew from the breast of his tunic two small rolls of fine parchment, with writing upon them, and unfolded them carefully upon his knee.

"In the years that are lost in the past, long before our fathers came into the land of Babylon, there were wise men in Chaldea, from whom the first of the Magi learned the secret of the heavens. And of these Balaam the son of Beor was one of the mightiest. Hear the words of his prophecy: 'There shall come a star out of Jacob, and a scepter shall arise out of Israel.'"

The lips of Tigranes drew downward with contempt, as he said:

"Judah was a captive by the waters of Babylon, and the sons of Jacob were in bondage to our kings. The tribes of Israel are scattered through the mountains like lost sheep, and from the remnant that dwells in Judea under the yoke of Rome neither star nor scepter shall arise."

"And yet," answered Artaban, "it was the Hebrew Daniel, the mighty searcher of dreams, the counselor of kings, the wise Belteshazzar, who was most honored and beloved of our great

King Cyrus. A prophet of sure things and a reader of the thoughts of the Eternal, Daniel proved himself to our people. And these are the words that he wrote." (Artaban read from the second roll:) " 'Know, therefore, and understand that from the going forth of the commandment to restore Jerusalem, unto the Anointed One, the Prince, the time shall be seven and threescore and two weeks.' "

"But, my son," said Abgarus, doubtfully, "these are mystical numbers. Who can interpret them, or who can find the key that shall unlock their meaning?"

Artaban answered: "It has been shown to me and to my three companions among the Magi—Caspar, Melchior and Balthasar. We have searched the ancient tablets of Chaldea and computed the time. It falls in this year. We have studied the sky, and in the spring of the year we saw two of the greatest planets draw near together in the sign of the Fish, which is the house of the Hebrews. We also saw a new star there, which shone for one night and then vanished. Now again the two great planets are meeting. This night is their conjunction. My three brothers are watching by the ancient Temple of the Seven Spheres, at Borsippa, in Babylon, and I am watching here. If the star shines again, they will wait ten days for me at the temple, and then we will set out together for Jerusalem, to see and worship the promised one who shall be born King of Israel. I believe the sign will come. I have made ready for the journey. I have sold my possessions, and bought these three jewels—a sapphire, a ruby and a pearl—to carry them as tribute to the King. And I ask you to go with me on the pilgrimage, that we may have joy together in finding the Prince who is worthy to be served."

While he was speaking he thrust his hand into the inmost fold of his girdle and drew out three great gems—one blue as a fragment of the night sky, one redder than a ray of sunrise, and one as pure as the peak of a snow mountain at twilight— and laid them on the outspread scrolls before him.

But his friends looked on with strange and alien eyes. A veil of doubt and mistrust came over their faces, like a fog creeping up from the marshes to hide the hills. They glanced at each other with looks of wonder and pity, as those who have listened to incredible sayings, the story of a wild vision, or the proposal of an impossible enterprise.

At last Tigranes said: "Artaban, this is a vain dream. It comes from too much looking upon the stars and the cherishing of lofty thoughts. It would be wiser to spend the time in gathering money for the new fire temple at Chala. No king will ever rise from the broken race of Israel, and no end will ever come to the eternal strife of light and darkness. He who looks for it is a chaser of shadows. Farewell."

And another said: "Artaban, I have no knowledge of these things, and my office as guardian of the royal treasure binds me here. The quest is not for me. But if thou must follow it, fare thee well."

And another said: "In my house there sleeps a new bride, and I cannot leave her nor take her with me on this strange journey. This quest is not for me. But may thy steps be prospered wherever thou goest. So, farewell."

And another said: "I am ill and unfit for hardship, but there is a man among my servants whom I will send with thee when thou goest, to bring me word how thou farest."

So, one by one, they left the house of Artaban. But Abgarus, the oldest and the one who loved him the best, lingered after the others had gone, and said, gravely: "My son, it may be that the light of truth is in this sign that has appeared in the skies, and then it will surely lead to the Prince and the mighty brightness. Or it may be that it is only a shadow of the light, as Tigranes has said, and then he who follows it will have a long pilgrimage and a fruitless search. But it is better to follow even the shadow of the best than to remain content with the worst. And those who would see wonderful things must often be ready to travel alone. I am too old for this journey, but my heart shall be a companion of thy pilgrimage day and night, and I shall know the end of thy quest. Go in peace."

Then Abgarus went out of the azure chamber with its silver stars, and Artaban was left in solitude.

He gathered up the jewels and replaced them in his girdle. For a long time he stood and watched the flame that flickered and sank upon the altar. Then he crossed the hall, lifted the heavy curtain, and passed out between the pillars of porphyry to the terrace on the roof.

The shiver that runs through the earth ere she rouses from her night sleep had already begun, and the cool wind that heralds the daybreak was drawing downward from the lofty, snow-traced ravines of Mount Orontes. Birds, half-awakened, crept and chirped among the rustling leaves, and the smell of ripened grapes came in brief wafts from the arbors.

Far over the eastern plain a white mist stretched like a lake. But where the distant peaks of Zagros serrated the western horizon the sky was clear. Jupiter and Saturn rolled together like drops of lambent flame about to blend in one.

As Artaban watched them, a steel-blue spark was born out of the darkness beneath, rounding itself with purple splendors to a crimson sphere, and spiring upward through rays of saffron and orange into a point of white radiance. Tiny and infinitely remote, yet perfect in every part, it pulsated in the enormous vault as if the three jewels in the Magian's girdle had mingled and been transformed into a living heart of light.

He bowed his head. He covered his brow with his hands.

"It is the sign," he said. "The King is coming, and I will go to meet him."

II

All night long, Vasda, the swiftest of Artaban's horses, had been waiting, saddled and bridled, in her stall, pawing the

ground impatiently and shaking her bit as if she shared the
eagerness of her master's purpose, though she knew not its
meaning.

Before the birds had fully roused to their strong, high, joyful chant of morning song, before the white mist had begun to
lift lazily from the plain, the Other Wise Man was in the saddle, riding swiftly along the highroad, which skirted the base
of Mount Orontes, westward.

How close, how intimate is the comradeship between a man
and his favorite horse on a long journey. It is a silent, compre-
hensive friendship, an intercourse beyond the need of words.
They drink at the same wayside springs, and sleep under the
same guardian stars. They are conscious together of the sub-
duing spell of nightfall and the quickening joy of daybreak.
The master shares his evening meal with his hungry companion,
and feels the soft, moist lips caressing the palm of his hand
as they close over the morsel of bread. In the gray dawn he is
roused from his bivouac by the gentle stir of a warm, sweet
breath over his sleeping face, and looks up into the eyes of his
faithful fellow traveler, ready and waiting for the toil of the day.
Surely, unless he is a pagan and an unbeliever, by whatever
name he calls upon his God, he will thank Him for this voice-
less sympathy, this dumb affection, and his morning prayer
will embrace a double blessing—God bless us both, the horse
and the rider, and keep our feet from falling and our souls
from death!

Then, through the keen morning air, the swift hoofs beat
their tattoo along the road, keeping time to the pulsing of two
hearts that are moved with the same eager desire—to conquer
space, to devour the distance, to attain the goal of the journey.

Artaban must indeed ride wisely and well if he would keep
the appointed hour with the other Magi; for the route was a
hundred and fifty parasangs, and fifteen was the utmost that
he could travel in a day. But he knew Vasda's strength, and
pushed forward without anxiety, making the fixed distance

every day, though he must travel late into the night, and in the morning long before sunrise.

He passed along the brown slopes of Mount Orontes, furrowed by the rocky courses of a hundred torrents.

He crossed the level plains of the Nicaeans, where the famous herds of horses, feeding in the wide pastures, tossed their heads at Vasda's approach, and galloped away with a thunder of many hoofs, and flocks of wild birds rose suddenly from the swampy meadows, wheeling in great circles with a shining flutter of innumerable wings and shrill cries of surprise.

He traversed the fertile fields of Concabar, where the dust from the threshing floors filled the air with a golden mist, half hiding the huge temple of Astarte with its four hundred pillars.

At Baghistan, among the rich gardens watered by fountains from the rock, he looked up at the mountain thrusting its immense rugged brow out over the road, and saw the figure of King Darius trampling upon his fallen foes, and the proud list of his wars and conquests graven high upon the face of the eternal cliff.

Over many a cold and desolate pass, crawling painfully across the wind-swept shoulders of the hills; down many a black mountain gorge, where the river roared and raced before him like a savage guide; across many a smiling vale, with terraces of yellow limestone full of vines and fruit trees; through the oak groves of Carine and the dark Gates of Zagros, walled in by precipices; into the ancient city of Chala, where the people of Samaria had been kept in captivity long ago; and out again by the mighty portal, riven through the encircling hills, where he saw the image of the High Priest of the Magi sculptured on the wall of rock, with hand uplifted as if to bless the centuries of pilgrims; past the entrance of the narrow defile, filled from end to end with orchards of peaches and figs, through which the river Gyndes foamed down to meet him; over the broad rich fields, where the autumnal vapors spread their deathly mists; following along the course of the river, under tremulous shadows of poplar and tamarind, among the lower hills; and out upon the flat plain, where the road ran straight as an arrow through the stubble fields and parched meadows; past the city of Ctesiphon, where the Parthian emperors reigned, and the vast metropolis of Seleucia which Alexander built; across the swirling floods of Tigris and the many channels of Euphrates, flowing yellow through the cornlands—Artaban pressed onward until he arrived, at nightfall on the tenth day, beneath the shattered walls of populous Babylon.

Vasda was almost spent, and Artaban would gladly have turned into the city to find rest and refreshment for himself and for her. But he knew that it was three hours' journey yet to the Temple of the Seven Spheres, and he must reach the place by midnight if he would find his comrades waiting. So he did not halt, but rode steadily across the stubble fields.

A grove of date palms made an island of gloom in the pale yellow sea. As she passed into the shadow Vasda slackened her pace, and began to pick her way more carefully.

Near the farther end of the darkness an access of caution seemed to fall upon her. She scented some danger or difficulty; it was not in her heart to fly from it—only to be prepared for it, and to meet it wisely, as a good horse should do. The grove was close and silent as the tomb; not a leaf rustled, not a bird sang.

She felt her steps before her delicately, carrying her head low, and sighing now and then with apprehension. At last she gave a quick breath of anxiety and dismay, and stood stock-still, quivering in every muscle, before a dark object in the shadow of the last palm tree.

Artaban dismounted. The dim starlight revealed the form of a man lying across the road. His humble dress and the outline of his haggard face showed that he was probably one of the Hebrews who still dwelt in great numbers around the city. His pallid skin, dry and yellow as parchment, bore the mark of the deadly fever which ravaged the marshlands in autumn. The chill of death was in his lean hand, and, as Artaban released it, the arm fell back inertly upon the motionless breast.

He turned away with a thought of pity, leaving the body to that strange burial which the Magians deemed most fitting— the funeral of the desert, from which the kites and vultures rise on dark wings, and the beasts of prey slink furtively away. When they are gone there is only a heap of white bones on the sand.

But, as he turned, a long, faint, ghostly sigh came from the man's lips. The bony fingers gripped the hem of the Magian's robe and held him fast.

Artaban's heart leaped to his throat, not with fear, but with a dumb resentment at the importunity of this blind delay.

How could he stay here in the darkness to minister to a dying stranger? What claim had this unknown fragment of human life upon his compassion or his service? If he lingered but for an hour he could hardly reach Borsippa at the appointed time. His companions would think he had given up the journey. They would go without him. He would lose his quest.

But if he went on now, the man would surely die. If Artaban stayed, life might be restored. His spirit throbbed and fluttered with the urgency of the crisis. Should he risk the great reward of his faith for the sake of a single deed of charity? Should he turn aside, if only for a moment, from the following of the star, to give a cup of cold water to a poor, perishing Hebrew?

"God of truth and purity," he prayed, "direct me in the holy path, the way of wisdom which Thou only knowest."

Then he turned back to the sick man. Loosening the grasp of his hand, he carried him to a little mound at the foot of the palm tree.

He unbound the thick folds of the turban and opened the garment above the sunken breast. He brought water from one of the small canals near by, and moistened the sufferer's brow and mouth. He mingled a draught of one of those simple but potent remedies which he carried always in his girdle—for the Magians were physicians as well as astrologers—and poured it slowly between the colorless lips. Hour after hour he labored as only a skillful healer of disease can do. At last the man's strength returned; he sat up and looked about him.

"Who art thou?" he said, in the rude dialect of the country, "and why hast thou sought me here to bring back my life?"

"I am Artaban the Magian, of the city of Ecbatana, and I am going to Jerusalem in search of one who is to be born King of the Jews, a great Prince and Deliverer of all men. I dare not delay any longer upon my journey, for the caravan that has waited for me may depart without me. But see, here is all that I have left of bread and wine, and here is a potion of healing herbs. When thy strength is restored thou canst find the dwellings of the Hebrews among the houses of Babylon."

The Jew raised his trembling hand solemnly to heaven.

"Now may the God of Abraham and Isaac and Jacob bless and prosper the journey of the merciful, and bring him in peace to his desired haven. Stay! I have nothing to give thee in return—only this: that I can tell thee where the Messiah must be sought. For our prophets have said that he should be born not in Jerusalem, but in Bethlehem of Judah. May the Lord bring thee in safety to that place, because thou hast had pity upon the sick."

It was already long past midnight. Artaban rode in haste, and Vasda, restored by the brief rest, ran eagerly through the silent plain and swam the channels of the river. She put forth the remnant of her strength and fled over the ground like a gazelle.

But the first beam of the rising sun sent a long shadow before her as she entered upon the final stadium of the journey, and the eyes of Artaban, anxiously scanning the great mound of Nimrod and the Temple of the Seven Spheres, could discern no trace of his friends.

The many-colored terraces of black and orange and red and yellow and green and blue and white, shattered by the convulsions of nature, and crumbling under the repeated blows of human violence, still glittered like a ruined rainbow in the morning light.

Artaban rode swiftly around the hill. He dismounted and climbed to the highest terrace, looking out toward the west.

The huge desolation of the marshes stretched away to the horizon and the border of the desert. Bitterns stood by the stagnant pools and jackals skulked through the low bushes; but there was no sign of the caravan of the Wise Men, far or near.

At the edge of the terrace he saw a little cairn of broken bricks, and under them a piece of papyrus. He caught it up and read: "We have waited past the midnight, and can delay no longer. We go to find the King. Follow us across the desert."

Artaban sat down upon the ground and covered his head in despair.

"How can I cross the desert," said he, "with no food and with a spent horse? I must return to Babylon, sell my sapphire, and buy a train of camels, and provision for the journey. I may never overtake my friends. Only God the merciful knows whether I shall not lose the sight of the King because I tarried to show mercy."

III

There was a silence in the Hall of Dreams, where I was listening to the story of the Other Wise Man. Through this silence I saw, but very dimly, his figure passing over the dreary undulations of the desert, high upon the back of his camel, rocking steadily onward like a ship over the waves.

The land of death spread its cruel net around him. The stony waste bore no fruit but briers and thorns. The dark ledges of rock thrust themselves above the surface here and there, like the bones of perished monsters. Arid and inhospitable mountain ranges rose before him, furrowed with dry channels of ancient torrents, white and ghastly as scars on the face of nature. Shifting hills of treacherous sand were heaped like tombs along the horizon. By day the fierce heat pressed its intolerable burden on the quivering air. No living creature moved on the dumb, swooning earth, but tiny jerboas scuttling through the parched bushes, or lizards vanishing in the clefts of the rock. By night the jackals prowled and barked in the distance, and the lion made the black ravines echo with his hollow roaring, while a bitter, blighting chill followed the fever of the day. Through heat and cold, the Magian moved steadily onward.

Then I saw the gardens and orchards of Damascus, watered by the streams of Abana and Pharpar, with their sloping swards inlaid with bloom, and their thickets of myrrh and roses. I saw the long, snowy ridge of Hermon, and the dark groves of cedars, and the valley of the Jordan, and the blue waters of the Lake of Galilee, and the fertile plain of Esdraelon, and the hills of Ephraim, and the highlands of Judah. Through all these I followed the figure of Artaban moving steadily onward, until he arrived at Bethlehem. And it was the third day after the three Wise Men had come to that place and had found Mary and Joseph, with the young child, Jesus, and had laid their gifts of gold and frankincense and myrrh at his feet.

Then the Other Wise Man drew near, weary, but full of hope, bearing his ruby and his pearl to offer to the King. "For now at last," he said, "I shall surely find him, though I be alone, and later than my brethren. This is the place of which the Hebrew exile told me that the prophets had spoken, and here I shall behold the rising of the great light. But I must inquire about the visit of my brethren, and to what house the star directed them, and to whom they presented their tribute."

The streets of the village seemed to be deserted, and Artaban wondered whether the men had all gone up to the hill pastures to bring down their sheep. From the open door of a cottage he heard the sound of a woman's voice singing softly. He entered and found a young mother hushing her baby to rest. She told him of the strangers from the far East who had appeared in the village three days ago, and how they said that a star had guided them to the place where Joseph of Nazareth was lodging with his wife and her new-born child, and how they had paid reverence to the child and given him many rich gifts.

"But the travelers disappeared again," she continued, "as suddenly as they had come. We were afraid at the strangeness of their visit. We could not understand it. The man of Nazareth took the child and his mother, and fled away that same night secretly, and it was whispered that they were going to Egypt. Ever since, there has been a spell upon the village; something evil hangs over it. They say that the Roman soldiers are coming from Jerusalem to force a new tax from us, and the men have driven the flocks and herds far back among the hills, and hidden themselves to escape it."

Artaban listened to her gentle, timid speech, and the child in her arms looked up in his face and smiled, stretching out its rosy hands to grasp at the winged circle of gold on his breast. His heart warmed to the touch. It seemed like a greeting of love and trust to one who had journeyed long in loneliness and perplexity, fighting with his own doubts and fears, and following a light that was veiled in clouds.

"Why might not this child have been the promised Prince?" he asked within himself, as he touched its soft cheek. "Kings have been born ere now in lowlier houses than this, and the favorite of the stars may rise even from a cottage. But it has not seemed good to the God of wisdom to reward my search so soon and so easily. The one whom I seek has gone before me; and now I must follow the King to Egypt."

The young mother laid the baby in its cradle, and rose to minister to the wants of the strange guest that fate had brought into her house. She set food before him, the plain fare of peasants, but willingly offered, and therefore full of refreshment for the soul as well as for the body. Artaban accepted it gratefully; and, as he ate, the child fell into a happy slumber, and murmured sweetly in its dreams, and a great peace filled the room.

But suddenly there came the noise of a wild confusion in the streets of the village, a shrieking and wailing of women's voices, a clangor of brazen trumpets and a clashing of swords, and a desperate cry: "The soldiers! The soldiers of Herod! They are killing our children."

The young mother's face grew white with terror. She clasped her child to her bosom, and crouched motionless in the darkest corner of the room, covering him with the folds of her robe, lest he should wake and cry.

But Artaban went quickly and stood in the doorway of the house. His broad shoulders filled the portal from side to side, and the peak of his white cap all but touched the lintel.

The soldiers came hurrying down the street with bloody hands and dripping swords. At the sight of the stranger in his imposing dress they hesitated with surprise. The captain of the band approached the threshold to thrust him aside. But Artaban did not stir. His face was as calm as though he were watching the stars, and in his eyes there burned that steady radiance before which even the half-tamed hunting leopard shrinks, and the bloodhound pauses in his leap. He held the soldier silently for an instant, and then said in a low voice:

"I am all alone in this place, and I am waiting to give this jewel to the prudent captain who will leave me in peace."

He showed the ruby, glistening in the hollow of his hand like a great drop of blood.

The captain was amazed at the splendor of the gem. The pupils of his eyes expanded with desire, and the hard lines of greed wrinkled around his lips. He stretched out his hand and took the ruby.

"March on!" he cried to his men; "there is no child here. The house is empty."

The clamor and the clang of arms passed down the street as the headlong fury of the chase sweeps by the secret covert where the trembling deer is hidden. Artaban re-entered the cottage. He turned his face to the east and prayed:

"God of truth, forgive my sin! I have said the thing that is not, to save the life of a child. And two of my gifts are gone. I have spent for man that which was meant for God. Shall I ever be worthy to see the face of the King?"

But the voice of the woman, weeping for joy in the shadow behind him, said very gently:

"Because thou hast saved the life of my little one, may the Lord bless thee and keep thee; the Lord make His face to shine upon thee and be gracious unto thee; the Lord lift up His countenance upon thee and give thee peace."

I V

Again there was a silence in the Hall of Dreams, deeper and more mysterious than the first interval, and I understood that the years of Artaban were flowing very swiftly under the stillness, and I caught only a glimpse, here and there, of the river of his life shining through the mist that concealed its course.

I saw him moving among the throngs of men in populous Egypt, seeking everywhere for traces of the household that had come down from Bethlehem, and finding them under the spreading sycamore trees of Heliopolis, and beneath the walls of the Roman fortress of New Babylon beside the Nile—traces so faint and dim that they vanished before him continually, as footprints on the wet river sand glisten for a moment with moisture and then disappear.

I saw him again at the foot of the pyramids, which lifted their sharp points into the intense saffron glow of the sunset sky, changeless monuments of the perishable glory and the imperishable hope of man. He looked up into the face of the crouching Sphinx and vainly tried to read the meaning of the calm eyes and smiling mouth. Was it, indeed, the mockery of all effort and all aspiration, as Tigranes had said—the cruel jest of a riddle that has no answer, a search that never can succeed? Or was there a touch of pity and encouragement in that inscrutable smile—a promise that even the defeated should attain a victory, and the disappointed should discover a prize, and the ignorant should be made wise, and the blind should see, and the wandering should come into the haven at last?

I saw him again in an obscure house of Alexandria, taking counsel with a Hebrew rabbi. The venerable man, bending over the rolls of parchment on which the prophecies of Israel were written, read aloud the pathetic words which foretold the sufferings of the promised Messiah—the despised and rejected of men, the man of sorrows and acquainted with grief.

"And remember, my son," said he, fixing his eyes upon the face of Artaban, "the King whom thou seekest is not to be found in a palace, nor among the rich and powerful. If the light of the world and the glory of Israel had been appointed to come with the greatness of earthly splendor, it must have appeared long ago. For no son of Abraham will ever again rival the power which Joseph had in the palaces of Egypt, or the magnificence of Solomon throned between the lions in Jerusalem. But the light for which the world is waiting is a new light, the glory that shall rise out of patient and triumphant suffering. And the kingdom which is to be established forever is a new kingdom, the royalty of unconquerable love.

"I do not know how this shall come to pass, nor how the turbulent kings and peoples of earth shall be brought to acknowledge the Messiah and pay homage to him. But this I know. Those who seek him will do well to look among the poor and the lowly, the sorrowful and the oppressed."

So I saw the Other Wise Man again and again, traveling from place to place, and searching among the people of the Dispersion, with whom the little family from Bethlehem might, perhaps, have found a refuge. He passed through countries where famine lay heavy upon the land, and the poor were crying for bread. He made his dwelling in plague-stricken cities where the sick were languishing in the bitter companionship of helpless misery. He visited the oppressed and the afflicted in the gloom of subterranean prisons, and the crowded wretchedness of slave markets, and the weary toil of galley ships. In all this populous and intricate world of anguish, though he found none to worship, he found many to help. He fed the hungry, and clothed the naked, and healed the sick, and comforted the captive; and his years passed more swiftly than the weaver's shuttle that flashes back and forth through the loom while the web grows and the pattern is completed.

It seemed almost as if he had forgotten his quest. But once I saw him for a moment as he stood alone at sunrise, waiting at the gate of a Roman prison. He had taken from a secret resting place in his bosom the pearl, the last of his jewels. As he looked at it, a mellower luster, a soft and iridescent light, full of shifting gleams of azure and rose, trembled upon its surface. It seemed to have absorbed some reflection of the lost sapphire and ruby. So the secret purpose of a noble life draws into itself the memories of past joy and past sorrow. All that has helped it, all that has hindered it, is transfused by a subtle magic into its very essence. It becomes more luminous and precious the longer it is carried close to the warmth of the beating heart.

Then, at last, while I was thinking of this pearl, and of its meaning, I heard the end of the story of the Other Wise Man.

V

Three-and-thirty years of the life of Artaban had passed away, and he was still a pilgrim and a seeker after light. His hair, once darker than the cliffs of Zagros, was now white as the wintry snow that covered them. His eyes, that once flashed like flames of fire, were dull as embers smoldering among the ashes.

Worn and weary and ready to die, but still looking for the King, he had come for the last time to Jerusalem. He had often visited the Holy City before, and had searched all its lanes and crowded hovels and black prisons without finding any trace of the family of Nazarenes who had fled from Bethlehem long ago. But now it seemed as if he must make one more effort, and something whispered in his heart that, at last, he might succeed.

It was the season of the Passover. The city was thronged with strangers. The children of Israel, scattered in far lands, had returned to the Temple for the great feast, and there had been a confusion of tongues in the narrow streets for many days.

But on this day a singular agitation was visible in the multitude. The sky was veiled with a portentous gloom. Currents of excitement seemed to flash through the crowd. A secret tide was sweeping them all one way. The clatter of sandals and the soft, thick sound of thousands of bare feet shuffling over the stones, flowed unceasingly along the street that leads to the Damascus gate.

Artaban joined a group of people from his own country, Parthian Jews who had come up to keep the Passover, and inquired of them the cause of the tumult, and where they were going.

"We are going," they answered, "to the place called Golgotha, outside the city walls, where there is to be an execution. Have you not heard what has happened? Two famous robbers are to be crucified, and with them another, called Jesus of Nazareth, a man who has done many wonderful works among the people, so that they love him greatly. But the priests and elders have said that he must die, because he gave himself out to be the Son of God. And Pilate has sent him to the cross because he said that he was the 'King of the Jews.' "

How strangely these familiar words fell upon the tired heart of Artaban! They had led him for a lifetime over land and sea. And now they came to him mysteriously, like a message of despair. The King had arisen, but he had been denied and cast out. He was about to perish. Perhaps he was already dying. Could it be the same who had been born in Bethlehem thirty-three years ago, at whose birth the star had appeared in heaven, and of whose coming the prophets had spoken?

Artaban's heart beat unsteadily with that troubled, doubtful apprehension which is the excitement of old age. But he said within himself: "The ways of God are stranger than the thoughts of men, and it may be that I shall find the King, at last, in the hands of his enemies, and shall come in time to offer my pearl for his ransom before he dies."

So the old man followed the multitude with slow and painful steps toward the Damascus gate of the city. Just beyond the entrance of the guardhouse a troop of Macedonian soldiers came down the street, dragging a young girl with torn dress and disheveled hair. As the Magian paused to look at her with compassion, she broke suddenly from the hands of the tormentors, and threw herself at his feet, clasping him around the knees. She had seen his white cap and the winged circle on his breast.

"Have pity on me," she cried, "and save me, for the sake of the God of Purity! I also am a daughter of the true religion which is taught by the Magi. My father was a merchant of Parthia, but he is dead, and I am seized for his debts to be sold as a slave. Save me from worse than death!"

Artaban trembled.

It was the old conflict in his soul, which had come to him in the palm grove of Babylon and in the cottage at Bethlehem —the conflict between the expectation of faith and the impulse of love. Twice the gift which he had consecrated to the worship of religion had been drawn to the service of humanity. This was the third trial, the ultimate probation, the final and irrevocable choice.

Was it his great opportunity, or his last temptation? He could not tell. One thing only was clear in the darkness of his mind —it was inevitable. And does not the inevitable come from God?

One thing only was sure to his divided heart—to rescue this helpless girl would be a true deed of love. And is not love the light of the soul?

He took the pearl from his bosom. Never had it seemed so luminous, so radiant, so full of tender, living luster. He laid it in the hand of the slave.

"This is thy ransom, daughter! It is the last of my treasures which I kept for the King."

While he spoke, the darkness of the sky deepened, and shuddering tremors ran through the earth heaving convulsively like the breast of one who struggles with mighty grief.

The walls of the houses rocked to and fro. Stones were loosened and crashed into the street. Dust clouds filled the air. The soldiers fled in terror, reeling like drunken men. But Artaban and the girl whom he had ransomed crouched helpless beneath the wall of the Praetorium.

What had he to fear? What had he to hope? He had given away the last remnant of his tribute for the King. He had parted with the last hope of finding him. The quest was over, and it had failed. But even in that thought, accepted and embraced, there was peace. It was not resignation. It was not submission. It was something more profound and searching. He knew that all was well, because he had done the best that he could from day to day. He had been true to the light that had been given to him. He had looked for more. And if he had not found it, if a failure was all that came out of his life, doubtless that was the best that was possible. He had not seen the revelation of "life everlasting, incorruptible and immortal." But he knew that even if he could live his earthly life over again, it could not be otherwise than it had been.

One more lingering pulsation of the earthquake quivered through the ground. A heavy tile, shaken from the roof, fell and struck the old man on the temple. He lay breathless and pale, with his gray head resting on the young girl's shoulder, and the blood trickling from the wound. As she bent over him, fearing that he was dead, there came a voice through the twilight, very small and still, like music sounding from a distance, in which the notes are clear but the words are lost. The girl turned to see if someone had spoken from the window above them, but she saw no one.

Then the old man's lips began to move, as if in answer, and she heard him say in the Parthian tongue:

"Not so, my Lord! For when saw I thee an hungered and fed

212

thee? Or thirsty, and gave thee drink? When saw I thee a stranger, and took thee in? Or naked, and clothed thee? When saw I thee sick or in prison, and came unto thee? Three-and-thirty years have I looked for thee; but I have never seen thy face, nor ministered to thee, my King."

He ceased, and the sweet voice came again. And again the maid heard it, very faint and far away. But now it seemed as though she understood the words:

"Verily I say unto thee, Inasmuch as thou hast done it unto one of the least of these my brethren, thou hast done it unto me."

A calm radiance of wonder and joy lighted the pale face of Artaban like the first ray of dawn on a snowy mountain peak. A long breath of relief exhaled gently from his lips.

His journey was ended. His treasures were accepted. The Other Wise Man had found the King.

Mr. Huffam

HUGH WALPOLE

ONCE upon a time (it doesn't matter when it was except that it was long after the Great War), young Tubby Winsloe was in the act of crossing Piccadilly just in front of Hatchard's Bookshop. It was three days before Christmas and there had been a frost, a thaw, and then a frost again. The roads were treacherous, traffic nervous and irresponsible, while against the clifflike indifference of brick and mortar a thin faint snow was falling from a primrose-colored sky. Soon it would be dark and the lights would come out. Then things would be more cheerful.

It would, however, take more than lights to bribe Tubby's cheerfulness. Rubicund of face and alarmingly stout of body for a youth of twenty-three, he had just then the spirit of a damp face towel for, only a week ago, Diana Lane-Fox had refused to consider for a moment the possibility of marrying him. "I like you, Tubby," she had said. "I think you have a kind heart. But marry you! You are useless, ignorant, and greedy. You're disgracefully fat and your mother worships you."

He had not known, until Diana had refused him, how bitterly alone he would find himself. He had money, friends, a fine roof above his head; he had seemed to himself popular wherever he went. "Why, there's old Tubby!" everyone had cried. It was true that he was fat, it was true that his mother adored him. He had not until now known that these were drawbacks. He had seemed to himself until a week ago the Friend of All the World. Now he appeared a pariah.

Diana's refusal of him had been a dreadful shock. He had

been quite sure that she would accept him. She had gone with him gladly to dances and the pictures. She had, it seemed, approved highly of his mother, Lady Winsloe, and of his father, Sir Roderick Winsloe, Bart. All, it had seemed to him, that was needed was for him to say the word. He could choose his time. Well, he *had* chosen his time—at the Herries dance last Wednesday evening. This was the result.

He had expected to recover. His was naturally a buoyant nature. He told himself, again and again, that there were many other fish in the matrimonial sea. But it appeared that there were not. He wanted Diana, and only Diana.

He halted at the resting place halfway across the street and sighed so deeply that a lady with a little girl and a fierce-looking Chow dog looked at him severely as though she would say: "Now this is Christmas time—a gloomy period for all concerned. It is an unwarranted impertinence for anyone to make it yet more gloomy."

There was someone else clinging to this small fragment of security. A strange-looking man. His appearance was so unusual that Tubby forgot his own troubles in his instant curiosity. The first unusual thing about this man was that he had a beard. Beards are very seldom worn today. Then his clothes, although they were clean and neat, were most certainly old-fashioned. He was wearing a high sharp-pointed collar, a black stock with a jeweled waistcoat, purple in color and covered with little red flowers. He was carrying a large, heavy-looking brown bag. His face was bronzed and he made Tubby think of a retired sea captain.

But the most remarkable thing of all about him was the impression that he gave of restless driving energy. It was all that he could do to keep quiet. His strong, wiry figure seemed to burn with some secret fire. The traffic rushed madly past, but at every moment when there appeared a brief interval between the cars and the omnibuses this bearded gentleman with the bag made a little dance forward, and once he struck the Chow with his bag and once nearly thrust the small child into the road.

The moment came when, most unwisely, he darted forth. He was almost caught by an imperious, disdainful Rolls Royce. The lady gave a little scream and Tubby caught his arm, held him, drew him back.

"That nearly had you, sir!" Tubby murmured, his hand still on his arm. The stranger smiled—a most charming smile that shone from his eyes, his beard, his very hands.

"I must thank you," he said, bowing with old-fashioned courtesy. "But damn it, as the little boy said to the grocer, 'there's no end to the dog,' as he saw the sausages coming from the sausage machine."

At this he laughed very heartily and Tubby had to laugh, too, although the remark did not seem to him very amusing.

"The traffic's very thick at Christmas time," Tubby said. "Everyone doing their shopping, you know."

The stranger nodded. "Splendid time, Christmas!" he said. "Best of the year!"

"Oh, do you think so?" said Tubby. "I doubt if you'll find people to agree with you. It isn't the thing to admire Christmas these days!"

"Not the thing!" said the stranger, amazed. "Why, what's the matter?"

This was a poser, because so many things were the matter. Tubby was saved for the moment from answering.

"Now there's a break," he said. "We can cross now."

Cross they did, the stranger swinging his body as though at any instant he might spring right off the ground.

"Which way are you going?" Tubby asked. It astonished him afterwards when he looked back and remembered this question. It was not his way to make friends of strangers, his theory being that everyone was out to "do" everyone.

"To tell you the truth I don't quite know," the stranger said. "I've only just arrived."

"Where have you come from?"

The stranger laughed. "I've been moving about for a long time. I'm always on the move. I'm considered a very restless man by my friends."

They were walking along very swiftly, for it was cold and the snow was falling fast now.

"Tell me," said the stranger. "About it's being a bad time. What's the matter?"

What was the matter? What a question!

Tubby murmured: "Why, everything's the matter. Unemployment, no trade—*you* know."

"No, I don't. I've been away. I think everyone looks very jolly."

"I say, don't you feel cold without an overcoat?" Tubby asked.

"Oh, that's nothing," the stranger answered. "I'll tell you when I *did* feel cold, though. When I was a small boy I worked in a factory putting labels on to jam bottles. It was cold *then*. Never known such cold. Icicles would hang on the end of your nose!"

"No!" said Tubby.

"They did, I assure you, and the jam bottles would be coated with ice!"

By this time they had reached Berkeley Street. The Winsloe mansion was in Hill Street.

"I turn up here," said Tubby.

"Oh, do you?" the stranger smiled and held out his hand.

Then Tubby did another extraordinary thing. He said: "Come in and have a cup of tea. Our place is only five yards up the street."

"Certainly," the stranger said. "Delighted."

As they walked up Berkeley Street he went on confidentially—

217

"I haven't been in London for a long time. All these vehicles are very confusing. But I like it. I like it immensely. It's so lively, and then the town's so quiet compared with what it was when I lived here."

"Quiet!" said Tubby.

"Certainly. There were cobbles and the cabs and drays screamed and rattled like the damned."

"But that's years ago!"

"Yes. I am older than I look."

"Isn't that bag a terrible weight?" Tubby asked.

"I've carried worse things than this," said the stranger. "I carried a trunk full of broken crockery once all the way from one end of the Marshalsea to the other."

They were outside the house now and Tubby realized for the first time his embarrassment. It wasn't his way to bring anyone into the house unannounced, and his mother could be very haughty with strangers. However, here they were and it was snowing hard. So in they went.

The Winsloe mansion was magnificent, belonging in all its features to an age that is gone. There was a marble staircase, and up this the stranger almost ran, carrying his bag like a feather. Tubby toiled behind him but was, unhappily, not in time to prevent the stranger from entering through the open doors of the drawing room.

Here, seated in magnificent state, was Lady Winsloe, a roaring fire encased with marble on one side of her, a beautiful tea table in front of her and walls hung with magnificent imitations of the Great Masters.

Lady Winsloe was a massive woman with snow-white hair, a bosom like a small skating rink and a little face that wore a look of perpetual astonishment. Her dress of black and white silk fitted her so tightly that one anticipated with excitement the moment when she would be compelled to rise. She moved as little as possible; she said as little as possible; she thought as

218

little as possible. She had a kind heart and was sure that the world was going straight to the devil.

The stranger put his bag on the floor and went over to her with his hand outstretched.

"How are you?" he said. "I'm delighted to meet you!"

By good fortune Tubby arrived in the room at this moment.

"Mother," he began. "This is a gentleman—"

"Oh, of course," said the stranger. "You don't know my name. My name's Huffam," and he caught the small white pudgy hand and shook it. At this moment two Pekinese dogs, one brown and one white, advanced from somewhere, violently barking. Lady Winsloe found the whole situation so astonishing that she could only whisper: "Now, Bobo! Now, Coco!"

"You see, mother," Tubby went on, "Mr. Huffam was nearly killed by a motor car and it began to snow heavily."

"Yes, dear," Lady Winsloe said in her queer husky little voice that was always a surprise coming from so vast a bosom. Then she pulled herself together.

For some reason Tubby had done this amazing thing, and whatever Tubby did was right.

"I do hope you'll have some tea, Mr. . . . ?" she hesitated.

"Huffam, ma'am. Yes, thank you. I *will* have some tea!"

"Milk *and* sugar?"

"All of it!" Mr. Huffam laughed and slapped his knee. "Yes, milk *and* sugar. Very kind of you indeed. A perfect stranger as I am. You have a beautiful place here ma'am. You are to be envied."

"Oh, do you think so?" said Lady Winsloe in her husky whisper. "Not in these days—not in these terrible days. Why, the taxes alone! You've no idea, Mr. . . . ."

"Huffam."

"Yes, how stupid of me! Now, Bobo. Now, Coco!"

Then a little silence followed and Lady Winsloe gazed at her strange visitor. Her manners were beautiful. She never looked

directly at her guests. But there was something about Mr.
Huffam that *forced* you to look at him. It was his energy. It
was his obvious happiness (for happy people are so very rare).
It was his extraordinary waistcoat.

Mr. Huffam did not mind in the least being looked at. He
smiled back at Lady Winsloe as though he had known her all
his life.

"I'm so very fortunate," he said, "to find myself in London at
Christmas time. And snow, too! The very thing. Snowballs,
mistletoe, holly, the pantomime—nothing so good in life as
the pantomime!"

"Oh, do you think so?" said Lady Winsloe, faintly. "I can't,
I'm afraid, altogether agree with you. It lasts such a *very* long
time and is often exceedingly vulgar!"

"Ah, it's the sausages!" said Mr. Huffam, laughing. "You
don't like the sausages! For my part, I dote on 'em. I know it's
silly at my age, but there it is—Joey and the sausages—I
wouldn't miss them for anything."

At that moment a tall and exceedingly thin gentleman entered. This was Sir Roderick Winsloe. Sir Roderick had been
once an Under-Secretary, once a chairman of a company, once
famous for his smart and rather vicious repartees. All these were
glories of the past. He was now nothing but the husband of
Lady Winsloe, the father of Tubby, and the victim of an uncertain and often truculent digestion. He now regarded Mr.
Huffam, his bag and his waistcoat with unconcealed astonishment.

"This is my father," said Tubby.

Mr. Huffam rose at once and grasped his hand.

"Delighted to meet you, sir," he said.

Sir Roderick said nothing but "Ah." Then he sat down.
Tubby was suffering now from a very serious embarrassment. The
odd visitor had drunk his tea and it was time that he should go.
Yet it seemed that he had no intention of going. With his legs
spread apart, his head thrown back, his friendly eyes taking

everyone in as though they were all his dearest friends, he was asking for his second cup.

Tubby waited for his mother. She was a mistress of the art of making a guest disappear. No one knew quite how she did it. There was nothing so vulgarly direct as a glance at the clock or a suggestion as to the imminence of dressing for dinner. A cough, a turn of the wrist, a word about the dogs, and the thing was done. But *this* guest, Tubby knew, was a little more difficult than the ordinary. There was something old-fashioned about him. He took people most naively at their word. Having been asked to tea, he considered that he *was* asked to tea. None of your five minutes' gossip and then hastening on to a cocktail party. However, Tubby reflected, the combination of father, mother, *and* the drawing-room with its marble fireplace and row of copied Old Masters was, as a rule, enough to ensure brief visitors. On this occasion also it would have its effect.

And then—an amazing thing occurred! Tubby perceived that his mother *liked* Mr. Huffam, that she was smiling and even giggling; that her little eyes shone, her tiny mouth was parted in expectation as she listened to her visitor.

Mr. Huffam was telling a story, an anecdote of his youth. About a boy whom he had known in his own childhood, a gay, enterprising, and adventurous boy who had gone as page boy to a rich family. Mr. Huffam described in a marvellous manner his adventures, his *rencontre* with the second footman who was a snob and Evangelical; of how he had handed biscuits through the pantry window to his little sister; of the friendship that he had made with the cook; and as Mr. Huffam told these things, all these people lived before your eyes; the pompous mistress with her ear trumpet, the cook's husband who had a wooden leg, the second footman who was in love with the pastry cook's daughter. The house of this young page boy took on life, and all the furniture in it, the tables and chairs, the beds and looking glasses—everything down to the very red woolen muffler that the footman wore in bed because he was subject to colds in the neck. Then Lady Winsloe began to laugh and Sir Roderick even laughed, and the butler, a big, red-faced man, coming in to remove the tea, could not believe his parboiled eyes but stood there, looking first of all at his mistress, then at his master, then at Mr. Huffam's bag, then at Mr. Huffam himself, until he remembered his manners and with a sudden apologetic cough set sternly (for himself this disgraceful behavior of his employers was no laughing matter) about his proper duties.

The best of all perhaps was the pathos at the end of Mr. Huffam's story. Pathos is a dangerous thing in these days. We so easily call it sentimentality. Mr. Huffam was a master of it. Quite easily and with no exaggeration he described how the sister of the little page boy lost some money entrusted to her by her only-too-bibulous father, of her terror, her temptation to steal from her aged aunt's purse, her final triumphal discovery of the money in a bandbox!

How they all held their breath! How vividly they saw the scene! How real was the sister of the little page boy! At last the story was ended. Mr. Huffam rose.

"Well, ma'am, I must thank you for a very happy hour," he said.

Then the most remarkable thing of all occurred, for Lady Winsloe said:—

"If you have not made any other arrangements, why not stay here for a night or two—while you are looking about you, you know! I'm sure we should be delighted—would we not, Roderick?"

And Sir Roderick said: "Ah . . . Ah . . . Certainly."

II

On looking back, as he so often did afterwards, into the details of this extraordinary adventure, Tubby was never able to arrange the various incidents in their proper order. The whole affair had the inconsequence, the colored fantasy of a dream—

one of those rare and delightful dreams that are so much more true and reasonable than anything in one's waking life.

After that astounding invitation of Lady Winsloe's, in what order did the events follow—the cynical luncheon party, the affair of Mallow's young woman (Mallow was the butler), the extraordinary metamorphosis of Miss Allington. All of these were certainly in the first twenty-four hours after Mr. Huffam's arrival. The grand sequence of the Christmas tree, the Mad Party, the London Vision were all part of the tremendous climax.

At once, Tubby realized, the house itself changed. It had never been a satisfactory house; always one of those places rebelliously determined not to live. Even the rooms most often inhabited—the drawing room, the long, dusky dining-room, Sir Roderick's study, Tubby's own bedroom—sulkily refused to play the game. The house was too large, the furniture too heavy, the ceilings too high.

Nevertheless, on the first evening of Mr. Huffam's visit the furniture began to move about. After dinner on that evening there was only the family present. Agatha Allington, an old maid, a relation with money to be left, an unhappy old woman suffering from constant neuralgia, had not yet arrived. There they were in the drawing room and, almost at once, Mr. Huffam had moved some of the chairs away from the wall, had turned the sofa with the gilt spikey back more cosily toward the fire.

He was not impertinent nor officious. Indeed on this first evening he was very quiet, asking them some questions about present-day London, making some rather odd social inquiries about prisons and asylums and the protection of children. He was interested, too, in the literature of the moment and wrote down in a little notebook an odd collection of names, for Lady Winsloe told him that Ethel Dell, Warwick Deeping, and a lady who wrote poetry, called Wilhelmina Stitch, were her favorite writers, while Tubby suggested that he should look into

the work of Virginia Woolf, D. H. Lawrence, and Aldous Hux-
ley. They had, in fact, a quiet evening which ended with Mr.
Huffam having his first lesson in Bridge. (He had been, he told
them, when he had last "tried" cards an enthusiastic whist
player.) It was a quiet evening, but as Tubby went up the long,
dark staircase to his room, he felt that in some undefined way
there was excitement in the air. Before undressing he opened
his window and looked out on to the roofs and chimney pots of
London. Snow glittered and sparkled under a sky that quivered
with stars. Dimly he heard the recurrent waves of traffic as
though the sea gently beat at the feet of the black, snow-crowned
houses.

"*What* an extraordinary man!" was his last thought before
he slept.

Before he had known that he would have Mr. Huffam as his
guest, Tubby had invited a few of his clever young friends to
luncheon—Diana, Gordon Woolley, Ferris Bland, Mary Polk-
inghome. Gathered round the Winsloe luncheon table, Tubby
regarded them with new eyes. Was it because of the presence
of Mr. Huffam? He, gaily flaunting his tremendous waistcoat,
was in high sprits. He had, all morning, been recovering some of
his old haunts. He was amazed. He could not conceal, he did
not attempt to conceal, his amazement. He gave them, as they
sat there, languidly picking at their food, a slight notion of what
East-End London had once been—the filth, the degradation,
the flocks of wild haggard-eyed homeless children. Mary Polk-
inghome, who had a figure like an umbrella-handle, an Eton
crop, and an eye-glass, gazed at him now with an expression of
bemused amazement.

"But they say our slums are awful. I haven't been down there
myself, but Bunny Carlisle runs a Boys' Club and *he* says . . ."

Mr. Huffam admitted that he had seen some slums that
morning but they were nothing, nothing at all to the things he
had seen in his youth.

"Who *is* this man?" Ferris Bland whispered to Diana.

"I don't know," she answered. "Someone Tubby picked up. But I like him."

And then this Christmas!

"Oh dear!" young Woolley sighed. "Here's Christmas again! Isn't it awful; I'm going to bed. I shall sleep, and I hope dream, until this dreadful time is over."

Mr. Huffam looked at him with wonder. "Hang up your stocking and see what happens," he said. Everyone screamed with laughter at the idea of young Woolley hanging up his stocking.

Afterwards, in the drawing-room, they discussed literature.

"I've just seen," Ferris Bland explained, "the proofs of Hunter's new novel. It's called 'Pigs in Fever.' It's quite marvellous. The idea is a man has scarlet fever and it's an account of his ravings. Sheer poetry."

There was a book on a little table. He picked it up. It was a first edition of "Martin Chuzzlewit," bound in purple leather.

"Poor old Dickens," he said. "Hunter has a marvellous idea. He's going to rewrite one or two of the Dickens books."

Mr. Huffam was interested.

"Rewrite them?" he asked.

"Yes. Cut them down to about half. There's some quite good stuff in them, hidden away, he says. He'll cut out all the sentimental bits, bring the humor up to date, and put in some stuff of his own. He says it's only fair to Dickens to show people that there's something there."

Mr. Huffam was delighted.

"I'd like to see it," he said. "It will make quite a new thing of it."

"That's what Hunter says," Bland remarked. "People will be surprised."

"I should think they will be," Mr. Huffam remarked.

The guests stayed a long time. Mr. Huffam was something quite new in their experience. Before she went, Diana said to Tubby: "What a delightful man! Where *did* you find him?"

225

Tubby was modest. She was nicer to him than she had ever been before.

"What's happened to you, Tubby?" she asked. "You've woken up suddenly."

During the afternoon, Miss Agatha Allington arrived with a number of bags and one of her worst colds.

"How are you, Tubby? It's kind of you to ask me. What horrible weather! What a vile thing Christmas is! You won't expect me to give you a present, I hope."

Before the evening, Mr. Huffam made friends with Mallow, the butler. No one knew quite how he did it. No one had ever made friends with Mallow before. But Mr. Huffam went down to the lower domestic regions and invaded the world of Mallow, Mrs. Spence, the housekeeper, Thomas, the footman, Jane and Rose, the housemaids, Maggie, the scullery maid. Mrs. Spence, who was a little round woman like a football, was a Fascist in politics, and said that she was descended from Mary Queen of Scots, permitted no one, except Lady Winsloe, in her sitting room, but she showed Mr. Huffam the photographs of the late Mr. Spence and her son, Darnley, who was a steward in the Cunard line. She laughed immeasurably at the story of the organ-grinder and the lame monkey. But Mallow was Mr. Huffam's great conquest. It seemed (no one had had the least idea of it) that Mallow was hopelessly in love with a young lady who assisted in a flower shop in Dover Street. This young lady, it seemed, admired Mallow very much and he had once taken her to the pictures. But Mallow was shy (no one had conceived it!) wanted to write her a letter, but simply hadn't the courage. Mr. Huffam dictated a letter for him. It was a marvellous letter, full of humor, poetry, and tenderness.

"But I can't live up to this, sir," said Mallow. "She'll find me out in no time."

"That's all right," said Mr. Huffam. "Take her out to tea tomorrow, be a little tender. She won't worry about letters after that."

Mr. Huffam went out after tea and returned, powdered with snow, in a taxicab filled with holly and mistletoe.

"Oh, dear," whispered Lady Winsloe, "we haven't decorated the house for years. I don't know what Roderick will say. He thinks holly so messy."

"I'll talk to him," said Mr. Huffam.

He did, with the result that Sir Roderick came himself and assisted. Through all this Mr. Huffam was in no way dictatorial. Tubby observed that he had even a kind of shyness—not in his opinions, for here he was very clear-minded indeed, seeing exactly what he wanted, but he seemed to be aware, by a sort of ghostly guidance, of the idiosyncrasies of his neighbors. How did he know, for instance, that Sir Roderick was afraid of a ladder! When he, Mallow, Tubby, and Sir Roderick were festooning the hall with holly, he saw Sir Roderick begin, timidly, with trembling shanks to climb some steps. He went to him, put his hand on his arm and led him safely to ground again.

"I know you don't like ladders," he said. "Some people can't stand 'em. I knew an old gentleman once terrified of ladders, and his eldest son, a bright promising lad, *must* become a steeplejack. Only profession he had a liking for."

"Good heavens!" cried Sir Roderick, paling. "What a horrible pursuit! Whatever did the father do?"

"Persuaded him to be a diver instead," said Mr. Huffam. "The lad took to it like a duck to water. Up or down it was all the same to him, he said."

In fact Mr. Huffam looked after Sir Roderick as a father his child and, before the day was out, the noble Baronet was asking Mr. Huffam's opinion upon everything. Tubby, as he listened, could not help wondering where Mr. Huffam had been all these years, in some *very* remote South Sea Island surely! So many things were new to him. But his kindness and energy carried him forward through everything. There was much of the child about him, much of the wise man of the world also, and behind these a hint of melancholy, of loneliness. Tubby was no sentimentalist about his own sex, but he had to confess that he was growing very fond of Mr. Huffam. It was almost as though he had known him before. There were in fact certain phrases, certain tones in the voice that were curiously familiar and reminded Tubby in some dim way of his innocent, departed childhood.

And then, after dinner, there was the conquest of Agatha Allington. Agatha had taken an instant dislike to Mr. Huffam. She prided herself on her plain speech. "My dear," she said to Lady Winsloe, "What a ruffian! "He'll steal the spoons."

"I don't think so," said Lady Winsloe with dignity. "We like him very much."

He seemed to perceive that Agatha disliked him. He sat beside her at dinner—he wore a tailcoat of strange old-fashioned cut and carried a large gold fob. He was, as Tubby perceived, quite different with Agatha. He was almost, you might say, an old maid himself—or, rather, a confirmed old bachelor. He discovered that she had a passion for Italy; she visited Rome and Florence every year—and he described to her some of his own Italian journeys taken years ago; confessed to her that he didn't care for frescoes which he described as "dim virgins with mildewed glories"—but Venice! ah! Venice! with its prisoners and dungeons and lovely iridescent waters! All the same, he was always homesick when he was out of London and he described the old London to her, the fogs and the muffin-bell and the "growlers," and enchanted her with a story about a shy little bachelor and how he went out one evening to dine with a vulgar cousin and be kind to a horrible godchild. Then, after dinner, he insisted that they should dance. They made a space in the drawing room, brought up a gramophone and set about it. Then how Mr. Huffam laughed when Tubby showed him a one-step.

"Call that dancing!" he cried. Then, humming a polka, he caught Agatha by the waist and away they polka-d. Then Lady Winsloe, who had adored the polka once, joined in. Then the Barn Dance. Then, few though they were, Sir Roger . . .

"I know!" Mr. Huffam cried. "We must have a party!"

"A party!" almost screamed Lady Winsloe. "What kind of a party?"

"Why, a children's party, of course. On Christmas night."

"But we don't know any children! And children are bored with parties. And they'll all be engaged anyway."

"Not the children I'll ask!" cried Mr. Huffam. "Not the party I'll have! It shall be the best party London has seen for years!"

III

It is well known that good humored, cheerful, and perpetually well-intentioned people are among the most tiresome of their race. Tubby often wondered afterwards why Mr. Huffam was *not* tiresome. It was perhaps because of his childlikeness; it was also, most certainly, because of his intelligence. Most of all was it because of the special circumstances of the case. In ordinary daily life Mr. Huffam *might* be a bore—most people are at one time or another. But on this occasion no one was a bore, not even Agatha.

It was as though the front wall of the Hill Street house had been taken away and all the details and incidents of those two days—Christmas Eve and Christmas Day became part of it. It seemed that Berkeley Square was festooned with crystal trees —that candles, red and green and blue—blazed from every window, that small boys instead of chanting "King Wenceslas" in the usual excruciating fashion, carolled with divine voices, that processions of Father Christmas, with snowy beards and red gowns, marched from Selfridge and Harrods and Fortnums carrying in their hands small Christmas trees, and were attended by reindeer, as though brown paper parcels tied with silver bands and decorated with robins fell in torrents through the chimneys and gigantic Christmas puddings rolled on their own stout bellies down Piccadilly, attended by showers of almonds and raisins. And upon all this first a red-faced sun, then a moon, cherry-colored and as large as an orange, smiled down, upon a world of crusted glittering snow while the bells pealed and once again the Kings of the Earth, having surrendered all their tariffs, came to the stable with gifts in their hands . . .

Of course it was not like that, but most certainly the Winsloe house was transformed. For one thing there was not the usual present-giving. At breakfast on Christmas Day everyone gave everyone else presents that must not cost more than sixpence apiece—Mr. Huffam had discovered some marvelous things— toy dogs that barked, Father Christmases glistening with snow, a small chime of silver bells, shiny pieces of sealing wax.

Then they all went to church at St. James's, Piccadilly. At the midday meal Sir Roderick had turkey and Christmas pudding which he hadn't touched for many a day.

In the evening came the party. Tubby had been allowed to invite Diana—for the rest of the guests were to be altogether Mr. Huffam's . . . No one knew what was in his mind.

At 7:15 exactly came the first ring of the doorbell. When Mallow opened the portals there on the steps were three very small children, two girls and a little boy.

"Please, sir, this was the number the gentleman said," whispered the little girl, who was very frightened.

Then up Hill Street the children came, big children, little children, children who could scarcely walk, boys as bold as brass, girls mothering their small relations, some of them shabby, some of them smart, some with shawls, some with mufflers, some with collars, some brave, some frightened, some chatting like monkeys, some silent and anxious—all coming up Hill Street, crowding up the stairs, passing into the great hall.

It was not until they had all been ushered up the stairs by Mallow, were all in their places, that Sir Roderick Winsloe, Bart., Lady Winsloe his wife, Tubby Winsloe their son, were permitted to see their own drawing-room. When they did they gasped with wonder. Under the soft and shining light the great floor had been cleared and, at one end of the room, all the children were gathered. At the other end was the largest, the strongest, the proudest Christmas tree ever beheld, and this tree shone and gleamed with candles, with silver tissue, with blue and gold and crimson balls, and so heavily weighted was it with dolls and horses and trains and parcels it was a miracle that it could support its burden. So there it was, the great room shining with golden light, the children massed together, the gleaming floor like a sea, and only the crackle of the fire, the tick of the marble clock, the wondering whispers of the children for sound.

A pause and from somewhere or another Father Christmas appeared. He stood there, looking across the floor at his guests.

"Good evening, children," he said, and the voice was the voice of Mr. Huffam.

"Good evening, Father Christmas," the children cried in chorus.

"It's all his own money," Lady Winsloe whispered to Agatha. "He wouldn't let me spend a penny."

He summoned them then to help with the presents. The children (who behaved with the manners of the highest of the aristocracy—even *better* than that, to be truthful) advanced across the shining floor. They were told to take turn according to size, the smallest first. There was no pushing, no cries of "I want *that!*" as so often happens at parties. At last the biggest girl and the biggest boy received their gifts. The tree gave a little quiver of relief at its freedom from its burden, and the candles, the silver tissue, the red and blue and golden balls shook with a shimmer of pleasure.

Games followed. Tubby could never afterward remember what the games had been. The room was alive with movements, with cries of joy and shouts of triumph, with songs and kisses and forfeits. Tubby never knew. He only knew that he saw his mother with a paper cap on her head, his father with a false nose, Agatha beating a child's drum—and on every side of him

231

children and children and children, children dancing and singing and running and sitting and laughing.

There came a moment, when Diana, her hair dishevelled, her eyes shining, caught his arm and whispered: "Tubby, you are a dear. Perhaps—one day—if you keep this up—who knows?"

And then there was sudden quiet. Mr. Huffam, no longer Father Christmas, arranged all the children round him. He told them a story, a story about a circus and a small child who, with her old grandfather, wandered in the company of these strange people—of the fat lady and the skeleton man, the jugglers and the beautiful creatures who jumped through the hoops, and the clown with the broken heart and how his heart was mended.

"And so they all lived happily ever after," he ended.

Everyone said goodnight. Everyone went away.

"Oh, dear, I *am* tired!" said Mr. Huffam. "But it *has* been a jolly evening!"

Mallow, in his excitement, forgot to draw the curtains, so the moon looked in through the window and saw the strong dark tree and the long shiny floor covered with silver tissue and brown paper and torn crackers and caps of gold and crimson . . .

"Yes, it *has* been a jolly evening!" said the Tree to the Moon.

"So it appears," said the Moon.

Next morning when Rose, the housemaid, woke Lady Winsloe with her morning cup of tea, she had startling news.

"Oh, dear, my lady, the gentleman's gone!"

"What gentleman?" said Lady Winsloe.

"Mr. Huffam, my lady. His bed's not been slept in and his bag's gone. There isn't a sign of him anywhere."

Alas, it was only too true. Not a sign of him anywhere.

At least one sign only.

The drawing room was as it had always been, every chair in its proper place, the copied Old Masters looking down solemnly from the dignified walls.

One thing was different. The First Edition of "Martin

Chuzzlewit," in its handsome blue binding, was propped up against the marble clock.

"How very strange!" said Lady Winsloe.

But opening it, she found that on the first page these words were freshly written:—

> "For Lady Winsloe
> with gratitude
> from her friend
> the Author."

And under this, the signature, above a scrawl of thick black lines:—

> *"Charles Dickens"*

The Christmas Shadrach

FRANK STOCKTON

WHENEVER I make a Christmas present I like it to mean something; not necessarily my sentiments toward the person to whom I give it, but sometimes an expression of what I should like that person to do or to be. In the early part of a certain winter not very long ago I found myself in a position of perplexity and anxious concern regarding a Christmas present which I wished to make.

The state of the case was this. There was a young lady, the daughter of a neighbor and old friend of my father, who had been gradually assuming relations toward me which were not only unsatisfactory to me, but were becoming more and more so. Her name was Mildred Bronce. She was between twenty and twenty-five years of age, and as fine a woman in every way as one would be likely to meet in a lifetime. She was handsome, of a tender and generous disposition, a fine intelligence, and a thoroughly well-stocked mind. We had known each other for a long time, and when fourteen or fifteen Mildred had been my favorite companion. She was a little younger than I, and I liked her better than any boy I knew. Our friendship had continued through the years, but of late there had been a change in it; Mildred had become very fond of me, and her fondness seemed to have in it certain elements which annoyed me.

As a girl to make love to, no one could be better than Mildred Bronce; but I had never made love to her—at least not earnestly —and I did not wish that any permanent condition of loving should be established between us. Mildred did not seem to share this opinion; for every day it became plainer to me that

234

she looked upon me as a lover, and that she was perfectly willing to return my affection.

But I had other ideas upon the subject. Into the rural town in which my family passed the greater part of the year there had recently come a young lady, Miss Janet Clinton, to whom my soul went out of my own option. In some respects, perhaps, she was not the equal of Mildred, but she was very pretty; she was small, she had a lovely mouth, was apparently of a clinging nature, and her dark eyes looked into mine with a tingling effect that no other eyes had ever produced. I was in love with her because I wished to be, and the consciousness of this fact caused me a proud satisfaction. This affair was not the result of circumstances, but of my own free will.

I wished to retain Mildred's friendship, I wished to make her happy; and with this latter intent in view I wished very much that she should not disappoint herself in her anticipations of the future.

Each year it had been my habit to make Mildred a Christmas present, and I was now looking for something to give her which would please her and suit my purpose.

When a man wishes to select a present for a lady which, while it assures her of his kind feeling toward her, will at the same time indicate that not only has he no matrimonial inclinations in her direction, but that it would be entirely unwise for her to have any such inclinations in his direction; that no matter with what degree of fondness her heart is disposed to turn toward him, his heart does not turn toward her, and that, in spite of all sentiments induced by long associations and the natural fitness of things, she need never expect to be to him anything more than a sister, he has, indeed, a difficult task before him. But such was the task which I set for myself.

Day after day I wandered through the shops. I looked at odd pieces of jewelry and bric-à-brac, and at many a quaint relic or bit of art work which seemed to have a meaning, but nothing had the meaning I wanted. As to books, I found none which satisfied me; not one which was adapted to produce the exact impression that I desired.

One afternoon I was in a little basement shop kept by a fellow in a long overcoat, who, so far as I was able to judge, bought curiosities but never sold any. For some minutes I had been looking at a beautifully decorated saucer of rare workmanship for which there was no cup to match, and for which the proprietor informed me no cup could be found or manufactured. There were some points in the significance of an article of this sort, given as a present to a lady, which fitted to my purpose, but it would signify too much: I did not wish to suggest to Mildred that she need never expect to find a cup. It would be better, in fact, if I gave her anything of this kind, to send her a cup and saucer entirely unsuited to each other, and which could not, under any conditions, be used together.

I put down the saucer, and continued my search among the dusty shelves and cases.

"How would you like a paper-weight?" the shopkeeper asked. "Here is something a little odd," handing me a piece of dark-colored mineral nearly as big as my fist, flat on the under side and of a pleasing irregularity above. Around the bottom was a band of arabesque work in some dingy metal, probably German silver. I smiled as I took it.

"This is not good enough for a Christmas present," I said. "I want something odd, but it must have some value."

"Well," said the man, "that has no real value, but there is a peculiarity about it which interested me when I heard of it, and so I bought it. This mineral is a piece of what the iron-workers call shadrach. It is a portion of the iron or iron ore which passes through the smelting-furnaces without being affected by the great heat, and so they have given it the name of one of the Hebrew youths who was cast into the fiery furnace by Nebuchadnezzar, and who came out unhurt. Some people think there is a sort of magical quality about this shadrach, and that it can give out to human beings something of its power to keep their minds cool when they are in danger of being overheated. The old gentleman who had this made was subject to fits of anger, and he thought this piece of shadrach helped to keep him from giving way to them. Occasionally he used to leave it in the house of a hot-tempered neighbor, believing that the testy individual would be cooled down for a time, without knowing how the change had been brought about. I bought a lot of things of the old gentleman's widow, and this among them. I thought I might try it some time, but I never have."

I held the shadrach in my hand, ideas concerning it rapidly flitting through my head. Why would not this be a capital thing to give to Mildred? If it should, indeed, possess the quality ascribed to it, if it should be able to cool her liking for me, what better present could I give her? I did not hesitate long.

"I will buy this," I said; "but the ornamentation must be of a better sort. It is now too cheap and tawdry-looking."

"I can attend to that for you," said the shopkeeper. "I can have it set in a band of gold or silver filigree-work like this, if you choose."

I agreed to this proposition, but ordered the band to be made of silver, the cool tone of that metal being more appropriate to the characteristics of the gift than the warmer hues of gold.

When I gave my Christmas present to Mildred, she was pleased with it; its oddity struck her fancy.

"I don't believe anybody ever had such a paperweight as that," she said, as she thanked me. "What is it made of?"

I told her, and explained what shadrach was; but I did not speak of its presumed influence over human beings, which, after all, might be nothing but the wildest fancy. I did not feel altogether at my ease, as I added that it was merely a trifle, a thing of no value except as a reminder of the season.

"The fact that it is a present from you gives it value," she said, as she smilingly raised her eyes to mine.

I left her house—we were all living in the city then—with a

troubled conscience. What a deception I was practicing upon this noble girl, who, if she did not already love me, was plainly on the point of doing so. She had received my present as if it indicated a warmth of feeling on my part, when, in fact, it was the result of a desire for cooler feeling on her part.

But I called my reason to my aid, and I showed myself that what I had given Mildred—if it should prove to posses any virtue at all—was, indeed, a most valuable boon. It was something which would prevent the waste of her affections, the wreck of her hopes. No kindness could be truer, no regard for her happiness more sincere, than the motives which prompted me to give her the shadrach.

I did not soon again see Mildred, but now as often as possible I visited Janet. She always received me with a charming cordiality, and if this should develop into warmer sentiments I was not the man to wish to cool them. In many ways Janet seemed much better suited to me than Mildred. One of the greatest charms of this beautiful girl was a tender trustfulness, as if I were a being on whom she could lean and to whom she could look up. I liked this; it was very different from Mildred's manner: with the latter I had always been well satisfied if I felt myself standing on the same plane.

The weeks and months passed on, and again we were all in the country; and here I saw Mildred often. Our homes were not far apart, and our families were very intimate. With my opportunities for frequent observation I could not doubt that a change had come over her. She was always friendly when we met, and seemed as glad to see me as she was to see any other member of my family, but she was not the Mildred I used to know. It was plain that my existence did not make the same impression on her that it once made. She did not seem to consider it important whether I came or went; whether I was in the room or not; whether I joined a party or stayed away. All this had been different. I knew well that Mildred had been used to consider my presence as a matter of much importance, and I now felt sure that my Christmas shadrach was doing its work. Mildred was cooling toward me. Her affection, or, to put it more modestly, her tendency to affection, was gently congealing into friendship. This was highly gratifying to my moral nature, for every day I was doing my best to warm the soul of Janet. Whether or not I succeeded in this I could not be sure; Janet was as tender and trustful and charming as ever, but no more so than she had been months before.

Sometimes I thought she was waiting for an indication of an increased warmth of feeling on my part before she allowed the temperature of her own sentiments to rise. But for one reason and another I delayed the solution of this problem. Janet was very fond of company, and although we saw a great deal of each other, we were not often alone. If we two had more frequently walked, driven, or rowed together, as Mildred and I used to do, I think Miss Clinton would soon have had every opportunity of making up her mind about the fervor of my passion.

The summer weeks passed on, and there was no change in the things which now principally concerned me, except that Mildred seemed to be growing more and more indifferent to me. From having seemed to care no more for me than for her other friends, she now seemed to care less for me than for most people. I do not mean that she showed a dislike, but she treated me with a sort of indifference which I did not fancy at all. This sort of thing had gone too far, and there was no knowing how much further it would go. It was plain enough that the shadrach was overdoing the business.

I was now in a state of much mental disquietude. Greatly as I desired to win the love of Janet, it grieved me to think of losing the generous friendship of Mildred—that friendship to which I had been accustomed for the greater part of my life, and on which, as I now discovered, I had grown to depend.

In this state of mind I went to see Mildred. I found her in the library writing. She received me pleasantly, and was sorry her father was not at home, and begged that I would excuse her finishing the note on which she was engaged, because she wished to get it into the post-office before the mail closed. I sat down on the other side of the table, and she finished her note, after which she went out to give it to a servant.

Glancing about me, I saw the shadrach. It was partly under a litter of papers, instead of lying on them. I took it up, and was looking at it when Mildred returned. She sat down and asked me if I had heard of the changes that were to be made in the time-table of the railroad. We talked a little on the subject, and then I spoke of the shadrach, saying carelessly that it might be interesting to analyze the bit of metal; there was a little knob which might be filed off without injuring it in the least.

"You may take it," she said, "and make what experiments you please. I do not use it much; it is unnecessarily heavy for a paper-weight."

From her tone I might have supposed that she had forgotten that I had given it to her. I told her that I would be very glad to borrow the paper-weight for a time, and, putting it into my pocket, I went away, leaving her arranging her disordered papers on the table, and giving quite as much regard to this occupation as she had given to my little visit.

I could not feel sure that the absence of the shadrach would cause any diminution in the coolness of her feelings toward me, but there was reason to believe that it would prevent them from growing cooler. If she should keep the shadrach she might in time grow to hate me. I was very glad that I had taken it from her.

My mind was easier on this subject, my heart turned more freely toward Janet, and, going to her house, the next day I was delighted to find her alone. She was as lovely as ever, and as cordial, but she was flushed and evidently annoyed.

"I am in a bad humor today," she said, "and I am glad you came to talk to me and quiet me. Dr. Gilbert promised to take me to drive this afternoon, and we were going over to the hills where they find the wild rhododendron. I am told that it is still in blossom up there, and I want some flowers ever so much —I am going to paint them. And besides, I am crazy to drive his new horses; and now he sends me a note to say that he is engaged."

This communication shocked me, and I began to talk to her about Dr. Gilbert. I soon found that several times she had been driving with this handsome young physician, but never, she said, behind his new horses, nor to the rhododendron hills.

Dr. Hector Gilbert was a fine young fellow, beginning practice in town, and one of my favorite associates. I had never thought of him in connection with Janet, but I could now see that he might make a most dangerous rival. When a young and talented doctor, enthusiastic in his studies, and earnestly desirous of establishing a practice, and who, if his time were not fully occupied, would naturally wish that the neighbors would think that such was the case, deliberately devotes some hours on I know not how many days to driving a young lady into the surrounding country, it may be supposed that he is really in love with her. Moreover, judging from Janet's present mood, this doctor's attentions were not without encouragement.

I went home; I considered the state of affairs; I ran my fingers through my hair; I gazed steadfastly upon the floor. Suddenly I rose. I had had an inspiration; I would give the shadrach to Dr. Gilbert.

I went immediately to the doctor's office, and found him there. He too was not in a very good humor.

"I have had two old ladies here nearly all the afternoon, and they have bored me to death," he said. "I could not get rid of them because I found they had made an appointment with each other to visit me today and talk over a hospital plan which I proposed some time ago and which is really very important to me, but I wish they had chosen some other time to come here. What is that thing?"

"That is a bit of shadrach." I said, "made into a paper-weight." And then I proceeded to explain what shadrach is, and what peculiar properties it must possess to resist the power of heat, which melts other metal apparently of the same class; and I added that I thought it might be interesting to analyze a bit of it and discover what fire-proof constituents it possessed.

"I should like to do that," said the doctor, attentively turning over the shadrach in his hand. "Can I take off a piece of it?"

"I will give it to you," said I, "and you can make what use of it you please. If you do analyze it. I shall be very glad indeed to hear the results of your investigations."

The doctor demurred a little at taking the paper-weight with such a pretty ring around it, but I assured him that the cost of the whole affair was trifling, and I should be gratified if he would take it. He accepted the gift, and was thanking me, when a patient arrived, and I departed.

I really had no right to give away this paper-weight, which, in fact, belonged to Mildred, but there are times when a man must keep his eyes on the chief good, and not think too much about other things. Besides, it was evident that Mildred did not care in the least for the bit of metal, and she had virtually given it to me.

There was another point which I took into consideration. It might be that the shadrach might simply cool Dr. Gilbert's feelings toward me, and that would be neither pleasant nor advantageous. If I could have managed matters so that Janet could have given it to him, it would have been all right. But now all that I could do was to wait and see what would happen. If only the thing would cool the doctor in a general way, that would help. He might then give more thought to his practice and his hospital ladies, and let other people take Janet driving.

About a week after this I met the doctor; he seemed in a hurry, but I stopped him. I had a curiosity to know if he had analyzed the shadrach, and asked him about it.

"No," said he; "I haven't done it. I haven't had time. I knocked off a piece of it, and I will attend to it when I get a chance. Good day."

Of course if the man was busy, he could not be expected to give his mind to a trifling matter of that sort, but I thought he need not have been so curt about it. I stood gazing after him as he walked rapidly down the street. Before I resumed my walk I saw him enter the Clinton house. Things were not going on well. The shadrach had not cooled Dr. Gilbert's feeling toward Janet.

But because the doctor was still warm in his attentions to the girl I loved, I would not in the least relax my attentions to her. I visited her as often as I could find an excuse to do so. There was generally some one else there, but Janet's disposition was of such gracious expansiveness that each one felt obliged to be satisfied with what he got, much as he may have wished for something different.

But one morning Janet surprised me. I met her at Mildred's house, where I had gone to borrow a book of reference. Although I had urged her not to put herself to so much trouble, Mildred was standing on a little ladder looking for the book, because, she said, she knew exactly what I wanted, and she was sure she could find the proper volume better than I could. Janet had been sitting in a window-seat, reading, but when I came in she put down her book and devoted herself to conversation with me. I was a little sorry for this, because Mildred was very kindly engaged in doing me a service, and I really wanted to talk to her about the book she was looking for. Mildred showed so much of her old manner this morning that I would have been very sorry to have her think that I did not appreciate her returning interest in me. Therefore, while under other circumstances I would have been delighted to talk to Janet, I did not wish to give her so much of my attention then. But Janet Clinton was a girl who insisted on people attending to her when she wished them to do so, and, having stepped through an open door into the garden, she presently called me to her. Of course I had to go.

"I will not keep you a minute from your fellow-student," she said, "but I want to ask a favor of you." And into her dark, up-lifted eyes there came a look of tender trustfulness clearer than any I had yet seen there. "Don't *you* want to drive me to the rhododendron hills?" she said. "I suppose the flowers are all gone by this time, but I have never been there, and I should like ever so much to go."

I could not help remarking that I thought Dr. Gilbert was going to take her there.

"Dr. Gilbert, indeed!" she said with a little laugh. "He promised once, and didn't come, and the next day he planned for it it rained. I don't think doctors make very good escorts, anyway, for you can't tell who is going to be sick just as you are about to start on a trip. Besides, there is no knowing how much botany I should have to hear, and when I go on a pleasure-drive I don't care very much about studying things. But of course I don't want to trouble you."

"Trouble!" I exclaimed. "It will give me the greatest delight to take you that drive or any other, and at whatever time you please."

"You are always so good and kind," she said, with her dark eyes again upraised. "And now let us go in and see if Mildred has found the book."

I spoke the truth when I said that Janet's proposition de-lighted me. To take a long drive with that charming girl, and at the same time to feel that she had chosen me as her com-panion, was a greater joy than I had yet had reason to expect; but it would have been a more satisfying joy if she had asked me in her own house and not in Mildred's; if she had not al-lowed the love which I hoped was growing up between her and me to interfere with the revival of the old friendship between Mildred and me.

But when we returned to the library Mildred was sitting at

a table with a book before her, opened at the passage I wanted.

"I have just found it," she said with a smile. "Draw up a chair, and we will look over these maps together. I want you to show me how he traveled when he left his ship."

"Well, if you two are going to the pole," said Janet, with her prettiest smile, "I will go back to my novel."

She did not seem in the least to object to my geographical researches with Mildred, and if the latter had even noticed my willingness to desert her at the call of Janet, she did not show it. Apparently she was as much a good comrade as she had ever been. This state of things was gratifying in the highest degree. If I could be loved by Janet and still keep Mildred as my friend, what greater earthly joys could I ask?

The drive with Janet was postponed by wet weather. Day after day it rained, or the skies were heavy, and we both agreed that it must be in the bright sunshine that we would make this excursion. When we should make it, and should be alone together on the rhododendron hill, I intended to open my soul to Janet.

It may seem strange to others, and at the time it also seemed strange to me, but there was another reason besides the rainy weather which prevented my declaration of love to Janet. This was a certain nervous anxiety in regard to my friendship for Mildred. I did not in the least waver in my intention to use the best endeavors to make the one my wife, but at the same time I was oppressed by a certain alarm that in carrying out this project I might act in such a way as to wound the feelings of the other.

This disposition to consider the feelings of Mildred became so strong that I began to think that my own sentiments were in need of control. It was not right that while making love to one woman I should give so much consideration to my relations with another. The idea struck me that in a measure I had shared the fate of those who had thrown the Hebrew youths into the fiery furnace. My heart had not been consumed by the flames, but in throwing the shadrach into what I supposed were Mildred's affections it was quite possible that I had been singed by them. At any rate my conscience told me that under the circumstances my sentiments toward Mildred were too warm; in honestly making love to Janet I ought to forget them entirely.

It might have been a good thing, I told myself, if I had not given away the shadrach, but kept it as a gift from Mildred. Very soon after I reached this conclusion it became evident to me that Mildred was again cooling in my direction as rapidly as the mercury falls after sunset on a September day. This discovery did not make my mercury fall; in fact, it brought it for a time nearly to the boiling-point. I could not imagine what had happened. I almost neglected Janet, so anxious was I to know what had made this change in Mildred.

Weeks passed on, and I discovered nothing, except that Mildred had now become more than indifferent to me. She allowed me to see that my companionship did not give her pleasure.

Janet had her drive to the rhododendron hills, but she took it with Dr. Gilbert and not with me. When I heard of this it pained me, though I could not help admitting that I deserved the punishment; but my surprise was almost as great as my pain, for Janet had recently given me reason to believe that she had a very small opinion of the young doctor. In fact, she had criticised him so severely that I had been obliged to speak in his defense. I now found myself in a most doleful quandary, and there was only one thing of which I could be certain—I needed cooling toward Mildred if I still allowed myself to hope to marry Janet.

One afternoon I was talking to Mr. Bronce in his library, when, glancing toward the table used by his daughter for writing purposes, I was astounded to see, lying on a little pile of letters, the Christmas shadrach. As soon as I could get an opportunity I took it in my hand and eagerly examined it. I had not been mistaken. It was the paper-weight I had given Mildred. There was the silver band around it, and there was the place where a little piece had been knocked off by the doctor. Mildred was not at home, but I determined that I would wait and see her. I would dine with the Bronces; I would spend the evening; I would stay all night; I would not leave the house until I had had this mystery explained. She returned in about half an hour and greeted me in the somewhat stiff manner she had adopted of late; but when she noticed my perturbed expression and saw that I held the shadrach in my hand, she took a seat by the table, where for some time I had been waiting for her, alone.

"I suppose you want to ask me about that paper-weight," she remarked.

"Indeed I do," I replied. "How in the world did you happen to get it again?"

"Again?" she repeated satirically. "You may well say that. I will explain it to you. Some little time ago I called on Janet Clinton, and on her writing-desk I saw that paper-weight. I remembered it perfectly. It was the one you gave me last Christmas and afterward borrowed of me, saying that you wanted to analyze it, or something of the sort. I had never used it very much, and of course was willing that you should take it, and make experiments with it if you wanted to, but I must say that the sight of it on Janet Clinton's desk both shocked and angered me. I asked her where she got it, and she told me a gentleman had given it to her. I did not need to waste any words in inquiring who this gentleman was, but I determined that she should not rest under a mistake in regard to its proper ownership, and told her plainly that the person who had given it to her had previously given it to me; that it was mine, and he had no right to give it to any one else. 'Oh, if that is the case,' she exclaimed, 'take it, I beg of you. I don't care for it, and, what is more, I don't care any more for the man who gave it to me than I do for the thing itself.' So I took it and brought it home with me. Now you know how I happened to have it again."

For a moment I made no answer. Then I asked her how long

it had been since she had received the shadrach from Janet Clinton.

"Oh, I don't remember exactly," she said; "it was several weeks ago."

Now I knew everything; all the mysteries of the past were revealed to me. The young doctor, fervid in his desire to please the woman he loved, had given Janet this novel paper-weight. From that moment she had begun to regard his attentions with apathy, and finally—her nature was one which was apt to go to extremes—to dislike him. Mildred repossessed herself of the shadrach, which she took, not as a gift from Janet, but as her rightful property, presented to her by me. And this horrid little object, probably with renewed power, had cooled, almost frozen indeed, the sentiments of that dear girl toward me. Then, too, had the spell been taken from Janet's inclinations, and she had gone to the rhododendron hills with Dr. Gilbert.

One thing was certain. I must have that shadrach.

"Mildred," I exclaimed, "will you not give me this paper-weight? Give it to me for my own?"

"What do you want to do with it?" she asked sarcastically. "Analyze it again?"

"Mildred," said I, "I did not give it to Janet. I gave it to Dr. Gilbert, and he must have given it to her. I know I had no right to give it away at all, but I did not believe that you would care; but now I beg that you will let me have it. Let me have it for my own. I assure you solemnly I will never give it away. It has caused trouble enough already."

"I don't exactly understand what you mean by trouble," she said, "but take it if you want it. You are perfectly welcome." And picking up her gloves and hat from the table she left me.

As I walked home my hatred of the wretched piece of metal in my hand increased with every step. I looked at it with disgust when I went to bed that night, and when my glance lighted upon it the next morning I involuntarily shrank from it, as if it had been an evil thing. Over and over again that day I asked myself why I should keep in my possession something which would make my regard for Mildred grow less and less; which would eventually make me care for her not at all? The very thought of not caring for Mildred sent a pang through my heart.

My feelings all prompted me to rid myself of what I looked upon as a calamitous talisman, but my reason interfered. If I still wished to marry Janet it was my duty to welcome indifference to Mildred.

In this mood I went out, to stroll, to think, to decide; and that I might be ready to act on my decision I put the shadrach into my pocket. Without exactly intending it I walked toward the Bronce place, and soon found myself on the edge of a pretty pond which lay at the foot of the garden. Here, in the shade of a tree, there stood a bench, and on this lay a book, an ivory paper-cutter in its leaves as marker.

I knew that Mildred had left that book on the bench; it was her habit to come to this place to read. As she had not taken the volume with her, it was probable that she intended to return. But then the sad thought came to me that if she saw me there she would not return. I picked up the book; I read the pages she had been reading. As I read I felt that I could think the very thoughts that she thought as she read. I was seized with a yearning to be with her, to read with her, to think with her. Never had my soul gone out to Mildred as at that moment, and yet, heavily dangling in my pocket, I carried—I could not bear to think of it. Seized by a sudden impulse, I put down the book; I drew out the shadrach, and, tearing off the silver band, I tossed the vile bit of metal into the pond.

"There!" I cried. "Go out of my possession, out of my sight! You shall work no charm on me. Let nature take its course, and let things happen as they may." Then, relieved from the weight on my heart and the weight in my pocket, I went home.

Nature did take its course, and in less than a fortnight from that day the engagement of Janet and Dr. Gilbert was announced. I had done nothing to prevent this, and the news did not disturb my peace of mind; but my relations with Mildred very much disturbed it. I had hoped that, released from the baleful influence of the shadrach, her friendly feelings toward me would return, and my passion for her had now grown so strong that I waited and watched, as a wrecked mariner waits and watches for the sight of a sail, for a sign that she had so far softened toward me that I might dare to speak to her of my love. But no such sign appeared.

I now seldom visited the Bronce house; no one of that family, once my best friends, seemed to care to see me. Evidently Mildred's feelings toward me had extended themselves to the rest of the household. This was not surprising, for her family had long been accustomed to think as Mildred thought.

One day I met Mr. Bronce at the post-office, and, some other gentlemen coming up, we began to talk of a proposed plan to introduce a system of water-works into the village, an improvement much desired by many of us.

"So far as I am concerned," said Mr. Bronce, "I am not now in need of anything of the sort. Since I set up my steam-pump I have supplied my house from the pond at the end of my garden with all the water we can possibly want for every purpose."

"Do you mean," asked one of the gentlemen, "that you get your drinking-water in that way?"

"Certainly," replied Mr. Bronce. "The basin of the pond is kept as clean and in as good order as any reservoir can be, and the water comes from an excellent, rapid-flowing spring. I want nothing better."

A chill ran through me as I listened. The shadrach was in that pond. Every drop of water which Mildred drank, which touched her, was influenced by that demoniacal paper-weight, which, without knowing what I was doing, I had thus bestowed upon the whole Bronce family.

When I went home I made diligent search for a stone which might be about the size and weight of the shadrach, and having repaired to a retired spot I practised tossing it as I had tossed the bit of metal into the pond. In each instance I measured the distance which I had thrown the stone, and was at last enabled to make a very fair estimate of the distance to which I had thrown the shadrach when I had buried it under the waters of the pond.

That night there was a half-moon, and between eleven and twelve o'clock, when everybody in our village might be supposed to be in bed and asleep, I made my way over the fields to the back of the Bronce place, taking with me a long fish-cord with a knot in it, showing the average distance to which I had thrown the practice stone. When I reached the pond I stood as nearly as possible in the place by the bench from which I had hurled the shadrach, and to this spot I pegged one end of the cord. I was attired in an old tennis suit, and, having removed my shoes and stockings, I entered the water, holding the roll of cord in my hand. This I slowly unwound as I advanced toward the middle of the pond, and when I reached the knot I stopped, with the water above my waist.

I had found the bottom of the pond very smooth, and free from weeds and mud, and I now began feeling about with my bare feet, as I moved from side to side, describing a small arc; but I discovered nothing more than an occasional pebble no larger than a walnut.

Letting out some more of the cord, I advanced a little farther into the centre of the pond, and slowly described another arc. The water was now nearly up to my armpits, but it was not cold, though if it had been I do not think I should have minded it in the ardor of my search. Suddenly I put my foot on something hard and as big as my fist, but in an instant it moved away from under my foot; it must have been a turtle. This occurrence made me shiver a little, but I did not swerve from my purpose, and, loosing the string a little more, I went farther into the pond. The water was now nearly up to my chin, and there was something weird, mystical, and awe-inspiring in standing thus in the

251

depths of this silent water, my eyes so near its gently rippling surface, fantastically lighted by the setting moon, and tenanted by nobody knew what cold and slippery creatures. But from side to side I slowly moved, reaching out with my feet in every direction, hoping to touch the thing for which I sought.

Suddenly I set my right foot upon something hard and irregular. Nervously I felt it with my toes. I patted it with my bare sole. It was as big as the shadrach! It felt like the shadrach. In a few moments I was almost convinced that the direful paper-weight was beneath my foot.

Closing my eyes, and holding my breath, I stooped down into the water, and groped on the bottom with my hands. In some way I had moved while stooping, and at first I could find nothing. A sensation of dread came over me as I felt myself in the midst of the dark solemn water,—around me, above me, everywhere,—almost suffocated, and apparently deserted even by the shadrach. But just as I felt that I could hold my breath no longer my fingers touched the thing that had been under my foot, and, clutching it, I rose and thrust my head out of the water. I could do nothing until I had taken two or three long breaths; then, holding up the object in my hand to the light of the expiring moon, I saw that it was like the shadrach; so like, indeed, that I felt that it must be it.

Turning, I made my way out of the water as rapidly as possible, and, dropping on my knees on the ground, I tremblingly lighted the lantern which I had left on the bench, and turned its light on the thing I had found. There must be no mistake; if this was not the shadrach I would go in again. But there was no necessity for re-entering the pond; it *was* the shadrach.

With the extinguished lantern in one hand and the lump of mineral evil in the other, I hurried home. My wet clothes were sticky and chilly in the night air. Several times in my haste I stumbled over clods and briers, and my shoes, which I had not taken time to tie, flopped up and down as I ran. But I cared for none of these discomforts; the shadrach was in my power.

Crossing a wide field I heard, not far away, the tramping of hoofs, as of a horseman approaching at full speed. I stopped and looked in the direction of the sound. My eyes had now become so accustomed to the dim light that I could distinguish objects somewhat plainly, and I quickly perceived that the animal that was galloping toward me was a bull. I well knew what bull it was; this was Squire Starling's pasture-field, and that was his great Alderney bull, Ramping Sir John of Ramapo II.

I was well acquainted with that bull, renowned throughout the neighborhood for his savage temper and his noble pedigree —son of Ramping Sir John of Rampo I., whose sire was the Great Rodolphin, son of Prince Maximus of Granby, one of whose daughters averaged eighteen pounds of butter a week, and who, himself, had killed two men.

The bull, who had not perceived me when I crossed the field before, for I had then made my way with as little noise as possible, was now bent on punishing my intrusion upon his domains, and bellowed as he came on. I was in a position of great danger. With my flopping shoes it was impossible to escape by flight; I must stand and defend myself. I turned and faced the furious creature, who was not twenty feet distant, and then, with all my strength, I hurled the shadrach, which I held in my right hand, directly at his shaggy forehead. My ability to project a missile was considerable, for I had held, with credit, the position of pitcher in a base-ball nine, and as the shadrach struck the bull's head with a great thud, he stopped as if he had suddenly run against a wall.

I do not know that actual and violent contact with the physical organism of a recipient accelerates the influence of a shadrach upon the mental organism of said recipient, but I do know that the contact of my projectile with that bull's skull instantly cooled the animal's fury. For a few moments he stood and looked at me, and then his interest in me as a man and trespasser appeared to fade away, and, moving slowly from me, Ramping Sir John of Ramapo II. began to crop the grass.

I did not stop to look for the shadrach; I considered it safely disposed of. So long as Squire Starling used that field for a pasture, connoisseurs in mineral fragments would not be apt to wander through it, and when it should be prolonged, the shadrach, to ordinary eyes no more than a common stone, would be buried beneath the sod. I awoke the next morning refreshed and happy, and none the worse for my wet walk.

"Now," I said to myself, "nature shall truly have her own way. If the uncanny comes into my life and that of those I love, it shall not be brought in by me."

About a week after this I dined with the Bronce family. They were very cordial, and it seemed to me the most natural thing in the world to be sitting at their table. After dinner Mildred and I walked together in the garden. It was a charming evening, and we sat down on the bench by the edge of the pond. I spoke to her of some passages in the book I had once seen there.

"Oh, have you read that?" she asked with interest.

"I have seen only two pages of it," I said, "and those I read in the volume you left on this bench, with a paper-cutter in it for a marker. I long to read more and talk with you of what I have read."

"Why, then, didn't you wait? You might have known that I would come back."

I did not tell her that I knew that because I was there she would not have come. But before I left the bench I discovered that hereafter, wherever I might be, she was willing to come and to stay.

Early in the next spring Mildred and I were married, and on our wedding trip we passed through a mining district in the mountains. Here we visited one of the great ironworks, and were both much interested in witnessing the wonderful power of man, air, and fire over the stubborn king of metals.

"What is this substance?" asked Mildred of one of the officials who was conducting us through the works.

"That," said the man, "is what we call shad——"

"My dear," I cried, "we must hurry away this instant or we shall lose the train. Come; quick; there is not a moment for delay." And with a word of thanks to the guide I seized her hand and led her, almost running, into the open air.

Mildred was amazed.

"Never before," she exclaimed, "have I seen you in such a hurry. I thought the train we decided to take did not leave for at least an hour."

"I have changed my mind," I said, "and think it will be a great deal better for us to take the one which leaves in ten minutes."

My Grandmother's Grandmother's Christmas Candle

HEZEKIAH BUTTERWORTH

THERE were no Christmas celebrations in my old Puritan home in Swanzey, such as we have in all New England homes to-day. No church bells rung out in the darkening December air; there were no children's carols learned in Sunday-schools; no presents, and not even a sprig of box, ivy, or pine in any window. Yet there was one curious custom in the old town that made Christmas Eve in many homes the merriest in the year.

It was the burning of the Christmas candle; and of this old, forgotten custom of provincial towns I have an odd story to tell.

The Christmas candle? You may never have heard of it. You may fancy that it was some beautiful image in wax or like an altar-light. This was not the case. It was a candle containing a quill filled with gunpowder, and its burning excited an intense interest while we waited for the expected explosion.

I well remember Dipping Candle Day; it was a very interesting day to me in my boyhood, because it was then that the Christmas candle was dipped.

It usually came in the fall, in the short, lonesome days of November, just before the new school-master opened the winter term of the school.

My grandmother brought down from the garret her candle-rods and poles. The candle-rods were light sticks of elder, some fifty in number, and the poles were long pine bars. These poles were tied two each to two chairs, and the rods, after they had been wicked, were laid upon them at short distances apart.

256

My Grandmother's Grandmother's Christmas Candle

Wicking the candle-rods is a term of which few people to-day know the meaning. Every country store in old times contained a large supply of balls of cotton candle-wick. This wick was to be cut, put upon the candle-rods, twisted, and tallowed or waxed, so as to be convenient for dipping.

How many times have I seen my grandmother, on the long November evenings, wicking her candle rods! She used to do the work, sitting in her easy-chair before the great open fire. One side of the fireplace was usually hung with strings of dried or partly dried apples, and the other with strings of red peppers. Over the fireplace were a gun and the almanac; and on the hearth there were usually, in the evening, a few sweet apples roasting; and at one end of it was the dog, and at the other the cat.

Dipping candles would seem a comical sight to-day. My grandmother used to sit over a great iron kettle of melted tallow, and patiently dip the wicks on the rods into it, until they grew to the size of candles. Each rod contained about five wicks, and these were dipped together. The process was repeated perhaps fifty or more times.

A quill of powder was tied to the wick of the Christmas candle before dipping, and the wick was so divided at the lower end that the candle should have three legs. The young people took a great interest in the dipping as well as the burning of the Christmas candle.

My grandmother's candle-rods had belonged to her grandmother, who had lived in the early days of the Plymouth Colony. They had been used since the days of King Philip's war.

There was a story of the dark times of the Indian war that my grandmother used to relate on the night that we burned our Christmas candle; a story that my grandmother told of her grandmother, and of the fortunate and timely explosion of one of that old lady's Christmas candles in the last days of Philip's war, when the sight of a hostile Indian was a terror to the unarmed colonist.

257

"It was well that candle went off when it did," my grand-mother used to say. "If it had not, I don't know where any of us would have been to-night; not here, telling riddles and roasting apples and enjoying ourselves, I imagine. I have dipped a powder-candle every season since, not that I believe much in keeping holidays, but because a powder-candle once saved the family."

She continued her story:

"My grandmother was a widow in her last years. She had two children, Benjamin and my mother, Mary. She lived at Pocassett, and the old house overlooked Mount Hope and the bay. Pocassett was an Indian province then, and its Indian queen was named Wetamoo.

"My grandmother was a great-hearted woman. She had a fair amount of property, and she used it for the good of her less fortunate neighbors. She had kept several poor old people from the town-house by giving them a home with her. Her good deeds caused her to be respected by every one.

"The Indians were friendly to her. She had done them so many acts of kindness that even the haughty Wetamoo had once called to see her and made her a present. The old house was near an easy landing-place for boats on the bay; and the Indians, as they came from their canoes, passed through the yard, and often stopped to drink from the well. It was no un-common thing, on a hot summer's day, to find an Indian asleep in the street or under the door-yard trees.

"Among the great men of the tribe was an Indian named Squammaney; Warmmesley he was sometimes called—also Warmmesley-Squammaney. He was a giant in form, but his greatness among his people arose from his supposed magical power and his vigorous voice. It was believed that he could whoop and bellow so loud and long as to frighten away evil spirits from the sick, so that the patient would recover. All the Indians regarded old Squammaney with fear and awe, and he was very proud of his influence over them.

"When an Indian fell sick, Warmmesley-Squammaney was called to the bed-side. If old Warmmesley could not drive the evil spirits away, the patient believed that he must die.

"Squammaney did his supposed duty in such cases. He was a faithful doctor. He covered himself with dried skins, shells, and feathers, and approached the hut of the patient with as mysterious and lofty an air as one of the old-time physicians of the gig and saddle-bags. As he drew near the hut, he would rattle the dried skins, and howl. He would look cautiously into the hut, then run away from it a little distance, leap into the air, and howl. Then he would cautiously return, and if the case were a bad one, he would again run away, leap into the air, and howl. At last he would enter the hut, examine the sick man or woman, and utter mysterious cries. He would fix the mind of the sufferer entirely upon himself by a kind of mesmeric influence; then he would begin to move in a circle around the patient, shaking the dried skins and beads, bobbing his plumes, and chanting an Indian ditty. Gradually his movements would become more swift; he would howl and leap, his voice rising higher at every bound; he would continue this performance until he fell down all in a heap, like a tent of dried skins. But by this time the mind of the patient was usually so withdrawn from his sufferings as to quite forget them; and consequently it often happened that the invalid and old Warmmesley-Squammaney rose up together, and indulged in hand-shaking, thus concluding an exhibition of some of the remarkable effects of mesmeric influence, which were possible in those old times as well as now.

"In his peculiar way, old Warmmesley once cured of rheumatism a Puritan deacon who rewarded him by calling him a 'pagan.' The deacon had been confined to his room for weeks. Some Indians called to see him, and, pitying his condition, set off in great haste for Warmmesley. The latter came, in his dried skins, with his head bristling with horns and feathers. The astonished deacon forgot his infirmities at the first sight of the terrible object; and as soon as Warmmesley began to leap and howl, and shake his beads, shells, and dried skins, the white man leaped from his bed, and, running to the barn, knelt down and began to pray. There his wife found him.

" 'It is old Warmmesley,' said she.

" 'The old pagan!' said he, rising up. 'What was it, Ruth, that was the matter with me?'

"My grandmother had caught the spirit of Eliot, the Indian apostle, and she used to hold in the old kitchen a religious meeting, each week, for the instruction of the 'praying Indians' of the town. The Indians who became Christians were called 'praying Indians' by their own people, and came to be so called by the English. Among the Indians who came out of curiosity, was the beautiful Princess Amie, the youngest daughter of the great chief Massasoit, who protected Plymouth Colony for nearly forty years.

"Warmmesley came once to my grandmother's meetings, and tried to sing. He wished to outsing the rest, and he did, repeating over and over again:

> " 'He lub poor Indian in de wood,
> An' me lub God, and dat be good;
> I'll praise him two times mo'!'

"Just before the beginning of the Indian war, my grandmother offended Warmmesley. The English had taught him bad habits, and he had become a cider drinker. He used to wander about the country, going from farm-house to farmhouse, begging for 'hard' cider, as old cider was called.

"One day my grandmother found him lying intoxicated under a tree in the yard, and she forbade the giving of Warmmesley any more cider from the cellar. A few days afterward, he landed from his canoe in front of the grounds, and came to the workmen for cider. The workmen sent him to my grandmother.

" 'No, Warmmesley, no more,' said she firmly. 'Steal your wits. Wicked!'

"Warmmesley begged for one porringer—just one.

260

" 'Me sick,' he pleaded.

" 'No, Warmmesley. Never. Wrong.'

" 'Me pay you!' said he, with an evil look in his eye. 'Me pay you!'

"Just then a flock of crows flew past. Warmmesley pointed to them and said:

" 'It's coming—fight—look up there! Ugh, ugh!'—pointing to the crows. 'Fight English. Look over'—pointing to the bay— 'fight, fight—me pay you! Ugh! Ugh!'

"My grandmother pointed up to the blue sky, as much as to say that her trust was in a higher power than man's.

"Warmmesley turned away reluctantly, looking back with a half-threatening, half-questioning look, and saying 'Ugh! Ugh!' He evidently hoped that my grandmother would call him back, but she was firm.

"The upper windows of the old house overlooked the bay.

"It was fall. The maples flamed and the oak-leaves turned to gold and dust. The flocks of birds gathered and went their unknown way. The evenings were long. It was harvest time. The full moon rose in the twilight, and the harvesters continued their labors into the night.

"Philip, or Pometacom, was now at Mount Hope, and Wetamoo had taken up her residence on the high shores of Pocassett. The hills of Pocassett were in full view of Mount Hope, and between lay the quiet, sheltered waters of the bay. Philip had cherished a strong friendship for Wetamoo, who was the widow of his brother Alexander.

"Night after night the harvesters had noticed canoes crossing and recrossing the bay, moving like shadows silently to and fro. The moon waned; the nights became dark and cloudy; the movement across the water went on; the boats carried torches now, and the dark bay became picturesque as the mysterious lines of light were drawn across it.

"From time to time a great fire would blaze up near the high rocks at Mount Hope, burn a few hours, and then fade.

"It was whispered about among the English that Philip was holding war-dances, and that Wetamoo and her warriors were attending them. Yet Philip had just concluded a treaty of peace with the English, and Wetamoo professed to be a friend to the Colony.

"War came on the following summer, stealthily at first. Englishmen were found murdered mysteriously in the towns near Mount Hope. Then came the killing of the people in Swanzey as they were going home from church, about which all the histories of the Colonies tell; then the open war.

"Philip flashed like a meteor from place to place, murdering the people and burning their houses. No one could tell where he would next appear, or who would be his next victim. Every colonist during the year 1675, wherever he might be, lived in terror of lurking foes. There were dreadful cruelties everywhere, and towns and farm-houses vanished in smoke.

"Wetamoo joined Philip. She had some six hundred warriors. Philip had made her believe that the English had poisoned her husband Alexander, who was also his brother, and who had succeeded the good Massasoit. Alexander had died suddenly while returning from Plymouth, on the Taunton river. The mysterious lights on the bay were now explained.

"Before Wetamoo joined Philip, one of her captains had sent word to my grandmother that, as she had been a friend to the Indians, she should be protected.

" 'I have only one fear,' said my grandmother often, during that year of terror,— 'Warmmesley.'

"Warmmesley-Squammaney had gone away with Philip's braves under Wetamoo. He was one of Wetamoo's captains. Wetamoo herself had joined Philip like a true warrior queen.

"The sultry August of 1676 brought a sense of relief to the Colonies. The warriors of Philip were defeated on every hand. His wife and son were captured, and, broken-hearted, he returned to Mount Hope—the burial ground of his race for unknown generations—to die. Wetamoo, too, became a fugitive,

and was drowned in attempting to cross to the lovely hills of Pocassett on a raft.

"The war ended. Where was Warmmesley-Squammaney? No
one knew. Annawon, Philip's great captain, had been captured,
and nearly all the principal leaders of the war were executed; but
old Squammaney had mysteriously disappeared.

"Peace came. October flamed, as Octobers flame, and November faded, as Novembers fade, and the snows of December fell.
The Colonies were full of joy and thanksgivings.

" 'I am thankful for one thing more than all others,' said my
grandmother on Thanksgiving Day; 'and that is that I am now
sure that old Squammaney is gone where he will never trouble
us again. I shall never forget his evil eye as he said, "I will pay
you!" It has troubled me night and day.'

"That fall, when my grandmother was dipping candles, she
chanced to recall the old custom of the English town from
which she had come, of making a powder-candle for Christmas.
The spirit of merrymaking was abroad upon the return of peace,
and she prepared one of these curious candles, and told her
family that they might invite the neighbors' children on Christmas Eve to see it burn and explode. The village school-master,
Silas Sloan, was living at the old house, and he took the liberty
to invite the school, which consisted of some ten boys and girls.

"Christmas Eve came, a clear, still night, with a white earth
and shining sky. Some twenty or more people, young and old,
gathered in the great kitchen to see the Christmas candle 'go
off.' During the early part of the evening 'Si' Sloan entertained
the company with riddles. Then my grandmother brought in the
Christmas candle, an odd-looking object, and set it down on its
three legs. She lighted it, blew out the other candles, and asked
Silas to tell a story.

"Silas was glad of the opportunity to entertain such an audience. The story that he selected for this novel occasion was
awful in the extreme, such as were usually told in those times
before the great kitchen fires.

"Silas—'Si,' as he was called—was relating an account of a so-called haunted house, where, according to his silly narrative, the ghost of an Indian used to appear at the foot of an old woman's bed; and some superstitious people declared that the old lady one night, on awaking and finding the ghostly Indian present, put out her foot to push him away, and pushed her foot directly *through him*. What a brave old lady she must have been, and how uncomfortable it must have been for the ghost! —But, at this point of Silas's foolish story, the dog suddenly started up and began to howl.

"The children, who were so highly excited over Si's narrative that they hardly dared to breathe, clung to one another with trembling hands as the dog sent up his piercing cry. Even Si himself was startled. The dog seemed listening.

"The candle was burning well. The children now watched it in dead silence.

"A half-hour passed. The candle was burning within an inch of the quill, and all eyes were bent upon it. If the candle 'sputtered,' the excitement became intense. 'I think it will go off in ten minutes now,' said my grandmother.

"There was a noise in the yard. All heard it distinctly. The dog dashed round the room, howled, and stopped to listen at the door.

"People who relate so-called ghost stories are often cowardly, and it is usually a cowardly nature that seeks to frighten children. 'Si' Sloan was no exception to the rule.

"The excitement of the dog at once affected Silas. His tall, thin form moved about the room cautiously and mysteriously. He had a way of spreading apart his fingers when he was frightened, and his fingers were well apart now.

"A noise in the yard at night was not an uncommon thing, but the peculiar cry of the dog and the excited state of the company caused this to be noticed. My grandmother arose at last, and, amid dead silence, opened the shutter.

" 'I think that there is some one in the cider mill,' said she.

"She looked toward the candle, and, feeling confident that some minutes would elapse before the explosion, she left the room, and went upstairs, and there looked from the window.

From the window she could see in the moonlight, Mount Hope, where Philip had so recently been killed, and also the arm of the bay, where Wetamoo had perished. She could see the bay itself, and must have remembered the lights that a year before had so often danced over it at night. She lingered there a moment. Then she called:

" 'Silas—Silas Sloan!'

"Silas hurried up the stairs.

"They both came down in a few minutes. Silas's face was as white as the snow.

" 'What is it?' the children whispered.

"There was another painful silence. Grandmother seemed to have forgotten the candle. All eyes were turned to her face.

"Then followed a sound that sent the blood from every face. It was as if a log had been dashed against the door. The door flew open, and in stalked two Indians. One of them was Warmmesley-Squammaney.

" 'Ugh!' said Warmmesley.

" 'What do you want?' demanded my grandmother.

" 'Me pay you now!—Old Squammaney pay you. Cider!'

"He sat down by the fire, close to the candle. The other Indian stood by his chair, as though awaiting his orders. The young children began to cry, and Silas shook like a man with the palsy.

" 'Me pay you!—Me remember! Ugh!' said Squammaney. 'Braves all gone. Me have revenge—old Squammaney die hard. Ugh! Ugh!'

"The door was still partly open, and the wind blew into the room. It caused the candle to flare up and to burn rapidly.

"Squammaney warmed his hands. Occasionally he would turn his head, slowly, with an evil look in his black eye, as it swept the company.

265

"The candle was forgotten. The only thought of each one was what Squammaney intended to do.

"All the tragedies of the war just ended were recalled by the older members of the company. Were there other Indians outside?

"No one dared to rise to close the door, or to attempt to escape.

"Suddenly Squammaney turned to my grandmother.

" 'White squaw get cider. Go—go!'

"The Indians threw open their blankets. They were armed.

"The sight of these armed warriors caused Silas to shake in a strange manner, and his fear and agitation became so contagious that the children began to tremble and sob. When the sound of distress became violent, Squammaney would sweep the company with his dark eyes, and awe it into a brief silence.

"My grandmother alone was calm.

"She rose, and walked around the room, followed by the eyes of the two Indians.

"As soon as the attention of the Indians, attracted for a moment by the falling of a burnt stick on the hearth, was diverted from her, she whispered to Silas:

" 'Go call the men.'

"The attitude of Silas on receiving this direction, as she recalled it afterward, was comical indeed. His hands were spread out by his side, and his eyes grew white and wild. He attempted to reply in a whisper, but he could only say:

" 'Ba-b-b-ba!'

"Squammaney's eyes again swept the room. Then he bent forward to push back some coals that had rolled out upon the floor.

" 'Go call the men,' again whispered my grandmother to Silas; this time sharply.

" 'Ba—b—b—b—ba!' His mouth looked like a sheep's. His hands again opened, and his eyes fairly protruded. His form was tall and thin, and he really looked like one of the imaginary specters about whom he delighted to tell stories on less perilous occasions.

"Squammaney heard Grandmother's whisper, and became suspicious. He rose, his dark form towering in the light of the fire. He put his hand on the table where burned the candle. He turned, and faced my grandmother with an expression of hate and scorn.

"What he intended to do was never known, for just at that moment there was a fearful explosion. It was the powder-candle.

"A stream of fire shot up to the ceiling. Then the room was filled with the smoke of gunpowder. The candle went out. The room was dark.

" 'White man come! Run!' my grandmother heard one of the Indians say. There was a sound of scuffling feet; then the door closed with a bang. As the smoke lifted, the light of the fire gradually revealed that the Indians had gone. They evidently thought that they had been discovered, pursued, and that the house was surrounded by soldiers.

"At last my grandmother took a candle from the shelf and lighted it. Silas, too, was gone. Whither? Had the Indians carried him away?

"Late in the evening the neighbors began to come for their children, and were told what had happened. The men of the town were soon under arms. But old Warmmesley-Squammaney was never seen in that neighborhood again, nor was his fate ever known to the town's-people. That was the last fright of the Indian war.

"Silas returned to the school-room the next day, but he never visited the old house again. Whatever may have been his real belief in regard to people of the air, he had resolved never again to put himself under a roof where he would be likely to meet Warmmesley-Squammaney.

"After this strange event, two generations of grandmothers continued to burn, on each Christmas Eve, the old powder-candle."

267

Twilight of the Wise

JAMES HILTON

E were talking, on Christmas night, about other Christmas nights. I had said that twenty years ago I was in the trenches somewhere in France. "And I," Middleton countered, "was somewhere in the Bavarian Alps."

It seemed a queer place for an Englishman to have been during the war years, until he explained, with a smile: "I was escaping. We managed it, you know—thanks to luck and Manny Stewart's German."

I guessed then that this fellow Middleton had deliberately stayed up to talk after the others had gone to bed; he knew I had known Manny from the conversation at dinner. I had quoted one of Manny's last poems, and we had all argued about what it probably meant—all of us, that is, except Middleton, who didn't seem the kind of person to argue much about a poem, anyway.

"You must have known him well?" I suggested.

"Not exactly. But it came as a personal loss when I read of his death last year, and again to-night when you quoted that poem. I suppose an experience of the kind he and I had, even if it only lasts a few days, counts for more than years of just 'knowing' somebody."

"Maybe."

"Ordinarily, of course, Manny and I wouldn't have had much in common—even at the prison-camp he'd been with us at least a month before I exchanged more than a few words with him. He had his own friends—chaps interested in art and books and all that. Then one day he came up to me when I was alone and said: 'Is it true you nearly got away once?' It *was* true, and I told him all about it, how I'd been within a mile of the Dutch frontier when things went wrong, all because I didn't know that *Eisenstange* means a sort of iron rod. I was hiding in a railway wagon full of them . . . but that's another story. Manny laughed when I told it him. 'My German's pretty good,' he said. 'How would you like to have another try with me?' I looked at him and I knew damn well I'd like it, and he knew I knew, too—it was a sort of sudden contact between us that didn't have to be argued about."

"Yes," I said. "He made a good many of those contacts."

"So we fixed it right away, and began to make plans. Manny thought we ought to try an escape in midwinter, because of the long nights; and we had an idea that the third week of December might be lucky for us, because even in war-time Germany the Christmas spirit had its manifestations—feasting and jollification and a general slackening of vigilance. The food shortage wasn't too bad in our part of Bavaria, and the people were a comfortable lot compared with the Prussians—as I knew myself from experience. And then, too, he thought we might try to get across the mountains instead of keeping to lowland routes— the idea, you see, being to do just what nobody would expect. Actually, we could be among the mountains within a couple of hours of leaving camp—if we dared risk it. Do you know the Bavarian Alps? I didn't, and neither did Manny, but we had a map, and we both found we'd had plenty of pre-war climbing experience in Switzerland. It was just a matter of nerve, endurance, food-supply, and luck with the weather. Well, we thought we had the first two, and we prayed for the others. We began to hide food till we had a store; then we collected warm clothing and white coats made of bed-linen, so that we shouldn't be spotted against a snow background. Then we had to make plans for the actual escape, but I needn't tell you of these, partly because they weren't very different from the other escapes I've read of, and also because the get-away was pretty easy. We were six thousand feet above the camp when dawn broke. We had put on dark glasses because of the snow dazzle, and we ate chocolate and chaffed each other and stared down at the camp below—just a few littered roofs among the pine forests.

"Of course, by that time the hue and cry must surely have been raised, but it didn't worry us much. You can't chase two men over high alps in midwinter, and in practice you don't consider it—because you don't believe the two men would ever be such fools. *We* were, though, and we were quite happy about it. I don't believe I've ever had a feeling of such almighty ecstasy as that morning as we climbed farther and higher up the snow-slopes till we reached the steep rocks.

"The day was glorious, and we lay out in the sun during the afternoon and slept, knowing that it would be bitterly cold at night, and that we should have to keep moving all the time. We didn't talk very much, except that Manny tried to brush up my German. We climbed an icy ridge, and descended the other side. There was no trace after that of any inhabited world—the mountains enclosed us on every hand. Manny led the way, and at nightfall the moon rose so that we went on without a halt.

"Of course we might have known that it wouldn't be all as easy as that. The next day there was no sunshine at all, and a freezing wind blew; we were utterly exhausted and slept for odd minutes in any sheltered place we could find, until our stiffening limbs awakened us. We began to walk and climb in a daze; Manny recited poetry, and I told him, I remember, about my horses and dogs at home. We were really talking to ourselves—not to each other. That night we began to realize, though neither of us put it into words, the pretty awful chance we were taking. We ate our food, primed ourselves with brandy, smoked our pipes, and drew what consolation we could from the map. It was a good map, and Manny knew exactly the place he was making for. Nevertheless, our spirits sank lower, and lowest of all during the early hours of the morning. But afterwards, when the sun came out, we grew cheerful again.

"I won't try to detail each day as it passed—partly because I

270

can't be sure how many days did pass. During the sunshine we lived; during the cold, dark hours we slipped into a kind of coma. I think there was an exact moment when we both felt that our number was up—though whether this came on the third or the fifth or the seventh day I can't be sure. We had come to the end of our food, we were chilled and utterly wearied, and—to make things worse—the comparatively fine weather broke down and snowstorms began. I think Manny saw the future as I did, for he said once, in that wry way of his: 'I'm afraid we've been guarding against the wrong sort of danger with these white coats of ours. The trouble's going to be that we *shan't* be found, not that we *shall*. All the same, we kept going, though I believe I was the first to collapse, and had to be given what was left of the brandy. The next thing I recollect is a clearing sky and a valley vista opening at our feet, and far down, almost as if we could have jumped on skis to it, a cluster of lights. Rather like Lauterbrunnen seen from Wengenalp, if you happen to know that."

I said I did, and he went on: "There was no discussion about what we should do—we had planned it so many times in our heads. We'd comforted ourselves by thinking that as soon as we came to a house we'd wait till the occupants had gone to bed, break in, and take some food. So with this new and exciting hope we staggered down the slope, running when we came to the level of the pinewoods, and checking our pace by wild grabs from tree to tree. I can remember how dark it was in those woods, and rather terrifying; we kept stumbling and scratching our hands and faces. Then, just ahead of us—almost as if it hadn't been there before, if you know the feeling—we saw the lighted window of a house, shining out exactly like a Christmas card. Yes, and smoke curling up from the chimney. *Exactly* like a Christmas card. Warm and comforting and sentimental.

"But, of course, the light at the window meant that there were still people out of bed, so there was nothing for us to do but

271

wait—and as it was Christmas night, we guessed we might have to wait a long time. Still, there would be some heavy sleeping afterwards, and that would help us. So we crouched down on a sort of grassy ledge, rather like a golf green, where the snow was half melted, and the moonlight lay over it like a sort of trembling sea. I suppose it was *we who* were trembling, really—you know how it feels when you've been hurrying downhill and you come to a level stretch again—your legs seem to sink under you. We were so exhausted we threw ourselves on the grass and rested a minute or two, and as I looked back at the pinewoods reaching up the side of the mountain, I noticed a star touching the dark edge of the tree-tops—just one little star. I'm not much of a person for noticing things like that, but it's a queer thing—I can almost see those woods and that star now, if I shut my eyes.

"I dare say we waited a couple of hours—it seemed twice as long. What began to puzzle us was that there was no sound from the house. We were quite close, and the night was still—surely there ought to have been voices or a dog barking or something? But there wasn't. At last Manny whispered: 'I can't stand this hanging about any longer—I'm going to scout round.'

"We crept to the outside wall, and saw that the place was a mountain chalet, timbered and heavily gabled. We listened awhile but there still wasn't a sound—but I'll tell you what there was. There was a most luscious, and to us an infuriating smell of cooking. In the end that settled it. We groped round to the doorway, and Manny tried the handle. It turned—the door was unlocked. A gust of warm air reached us and—more overpowering than ever—a definite smell of sizzling meat and roasting poultry. I looked at Manny and my look meant: Let's take a chance. . . .

"We entered the house and tiptoed along a corridor. There was a room that had a strip of light under the door, but still no sound. Manny was trying to deduce where the larder was—we daren't strike matches. And then suddenly we heard footsteps on the inside of the lighted room, the door opened, and a young girl came walking straight into us—actually she'd have collided if we hadn't stepped away. I don't think my heart has ever jumped as much as it did at that moment. Manny had the presence of mind to say 'Guten Abend.'

"The light from the doorway shone full on us then, and it suddenly occurred to me what a grim and frightening sight we must look—torn, scratched, dirty, eyes bloodshot, unshaven for days. But she didn't seem alarmed—she just said, in a tranquil voice: 'You are strangers?'

"Manny answered her, and they exchanged a few sentences in such rapid German that I couldn't properly follow it. Then I realized that we were being invited into the room. . . . That room . . . I shall never forget it. . . . It dazzled me, its firelight and lamplight, for the moment; then, as I gathered my wits, I saw a table set for two and food for a banquet warming in front of the long fire. Roast chicken, slices of veal, beans, potatoes. Cheese and a bottle of wine. A little Christmas tree. . . . I just stared and stared and left Manny to do the talking. It seemed to me we'd probably have to surrender and make the best of it—we certainly weren't prepared to terrorize a girl; and for myself, the thought of immediate things that surrender would bring—food, sleep, warmth—nearly outweighed the disappointment I knew I should feel afterward. I wondered whether Manny felt the same, especially as the girl went on talking. At last she smiled and went out of the room. Then Manny turned to me and said: 'It's all right. You can sit down and make yourself at home.'

"I must have looked rather stupid about it, for he added: 'Draw your chair to the table and don't guzzle too much all at once.'

" 'But—have you—told her who—who we are?' I whispered.

" ' Sssh,' he answered. 'I don't have to. Can't you see . . . she's blind.'

" 'Blind?'

273

" 'Simply the most incredible piece of luck,' he went on. 'She's alone here—her father's one of the frontier guards—he's out on the mountains with a search-party. The frontier's quite close, too—that's another piece of luck. There's a whole platoon of them looking for the two escaped Englishmen—apparently we've been well advertised.'

"I asked him who she thought we really were. He answered: 'Why, part of the search-party, of course—I've explained to her that we got lost, and are dead tired and hungry. And what's more to the point, my lad, she's going to give us our Christmas dinner!'

" 'But if her father returns?'

" 'Then we shall just be a little less in luck, that's all.'"

"The girl came back then, and laid extra places at the table. She had a very serene face and beautiful hands. Now that the idea was put in my head, it seemed obvious that she was blind. Yet her movements were scarcely less quick and accurate than if she had had sight. She helped us to food and Manny carved the chicken. They talked and laughed a lot together, and though I could follow what they were saying more or less, sometimes they talked too quickly or used words I didn't understand. But the food—and the wine— and the fire! I've never had a dinner that was as good as that. I know now I never shall. . . . The girl showed us photographs of her father and her two brothers who were at the Front. We drank their health and the healths of the German Army and—in our hearts—of the British Army, and of all brave men. Then she and Manny began an argument about the whole war business, and how damsilly it was that men should spend Christmas hunting other men over the mountains instead of feasting at home. She agreed, and then added something that made my heart miss another beat. She said: 'I thought at first you were the two English prisoners.'

" ' That would have been awkward for you,' said Manny.

" 'Oh, no, I expect they would have wanted food, just the same.'

" 'They certainly would.'

" 'Because, after all, there's not as much difference between English and German as between tired and hungry people and those who aren't.'

" 'Other people mightn't see that,' said Manny, laughing.

" 'They see other things instead.' "

Middleton glanced around the room as if to reassure himself of privacy before he continued: "I remembered this rather strange conversation, because at the time it scared me—I thought it was just the sort of too-clever-by-half stuff that a fellow like Manny would give himself away by, instead of sticking to the proper part of the simple German soldier. Because, you see, I was getting more and more panicky over an idea that had just struck me—that the girl was leading us on with all that sort of talk, that she already suspected who we were, and was deliberately trying to keep us till her father and probably some of the other searchers came back. As soon as she next went out of the room, ostensibly to fetch another bottle of wine, I whispered to Manny just what I felt about it. He seemed surprised, and told me then that the girl had offered to show us a short cut over the mountain that would lead us exactly where he wanted to go.

"I was scared again by that. 'I wouldn't trust a yard of that short cut,' I told Manny. 'She's obviously going to lead us straight into a trap.' He answered, in that dreamy way of his: 'Well, you may be right. Wisdom or cleverness—which are we up against?—that's the question, always.'

" 'That just irritated me—it didn't seem to be the right moment to be so damned philosophical. But he only kept saying: 'You may be right, and I may be wrong—time will show.'

"But time never did—nor anything else. Because while we were still arguing we heard a commotion outside in the corridor, then the girl's sudden cry amidst men's voices. Both Manny and I took it that our number was up and that the girl was telling them all about us. But she wasn't. We could see what was happening through the gap in the hinge of the door. She was crying because they had brought her father home—on an improvised stretcher.

"Apparently he'd fallen pretty badly somewhere—had a nasty headwound and an arm was limp. He was in a lot of pain, and we heard the girl imploring the men who had brought him in— there were two of them—to hurry down to the village and bring a doctor. And that would take them a couple of hours at least.

"Well, there isn't much more to tell you. Manny, as you may or may not know, was born to be a surgeon if he hadn't been a poet with a private income, and those soldiers hadn't done a good job with the broken arm. Manny refixed it, and we made the old boy as comfortable as we could before we left. He was semi-conscious and obviously didn't care a damn who we were —you don't know, if things are hurting and somebody's help- ing. . . . So we said 'Guten Abend' again, and made off into the woods. We didn't find the short cut, but we did, after sundry other adventures, manage to wriggle across the frontier. And that's the end of the story. I've no doubt Manny would have told it better."

"The odd thing is," I said, "that he never told it at all."

Middleton answered after a pause: "I wonder if he felt about it as I did afterwards—that it all happened in another sort of world? Mind you, it *did* happen—we escaped all right. That much is on the record. And the roast chicken was real enough, I'll swear. And yet . . . oh, well, we were dazed with exhaustion, and sick with anxiety, and wild with hunger. And the girl was blind and her father half-crazy with pain. Things don't happen *to* you when you're like that—as Manny said, they happen *in* you."

I agreed, and we smoked awhile, and then he went on: "That's the worst and the best of war—you feel a brotherhood with the other side that you can't get away from, and equally that you can't give way to. I often wonder what became of the old boy—whether he got better; I hope he did. He was really quite a veteran—far too old and fat to be chasing youngsters like us over the mountains. A few years after the Armistice, Manny was in Munich and tried to trace both the man and the girl, but he had no luck—couldn't even find the chalet on the hillside. Anyway, it's twenty years ago now—too late to hold an inquiry over it. But you can perhaps understand how . . . I felt . . . when you quoted that poem at dinner."

"Oh, the poem we were all arguing about?"

"Yes, As a matter of fact, I never knew Manny had written it—poetry, I must admit, isn't much in my line. But the poem . . . well, it reminded me."

I nodded. The volume of Manny Stewart's last poems, issued after his death, lay on the shelf at my elbow, and I reached for it, found the page, and leaned forward to catch the firelight as I read, in a sense for the first time:

> You do not know our ways are strange
>   In war-perverted brotherhood;
> How white the snow upon the range,
>   How warm the window in the wood.
> You do not know, you have not seen
> The moonlight trembling on the green;
> Nor have you watched a single star
> Rise over shades where terrors are.
> Yet in that world whose beauty lies
>   Beyond the eye and in the mind,
> Yours is the twilight of the wise,
>   And ours the noonday of the blind.

The Christmas Guest

KENNETH IRVING BROWN

THERE are times when new scenes pall and strange faces affright, when a man yearns for his home and the companionship of his friends. I had reached such a state of mind after four months in South America, during which I had ravaged the Guianas, Venezuela, and Colombia in search of flora for my botanical museum. My collection was complete except for a specimen of the *Cocos comosa*, and I was loath to leave the country until I had secured it. All of my search for it had been fruitless. As a final endeavor, I set out with Pedro, a native Carib guide whom I engaged at Cartagena, down the Gulf of Darien to the mouth of the Mulatto River, and up the Mulatto into the Colombian wilderness, hoping that here at last I might find that rara avis.

I lay back in the native dugout, lost in pleasant thoughts of home and a land where Nature was tamed. Pedro, between the lazy strokes of his paddle, had told me, in lingo of distorted English and incomprehensible Spanish, of Cispatia, a tiny Carib town inland on the Mulatto which he knew, of the villagers' "heart warmness," which I interpreted to mean hospitality, and of their isolation. If I understood him correctly, no white man had visited them for twenty years. I smiled to myself at the thought of the fright I should cause them with my pale complexion—pale in comparison, in spite of the tanning of the sun —and my American clothes, for the town was ahead and we should be there by nightfall.

"And this is the day before Christmas," I mused half aloud. "We shall spend our Christmas Eve at Cispatia; I shall be their Christmas guest."

278

The thought was ironical, and I smiled bitterly. Pedro smiled in return; I doubt if he understood my words, but his sympathy and good nature were apparent.

The Mulatto is a sluggish stream, mud-brown, with a current whose movement is barely perceptible. High luxuriant tropic-growth lines both sides of the winding river, vegetation in fulsome abundance, and yet its very voluptuousness suggests stagnation. The air seemed heavy with that stillness, that impenetrable calm, which is so characteristic of the Southern lands. The sun rose high and glared with fury; passed meridian splendor and slowly sank. Pedro paddled on leisurely; the great muscles of his bare black back moved with lazy regularity. For a long time neither of us spoke; the silence was broken only by the shrill calling of some wild bird in the palm trees.

It was approaching twilight—the twilight of Christmas Eve —when the camp enclosure of Cispatia came into view. From the coast the river had meandered willfully and vagrantly; each turn had revealed a new turn only a few rods ahead; but when the tiny village came into sight the stream ran in a straight course for several hundred yards, as if, near this oasis in the midst of yawning stretches of forest land, its conduct must be circumspect.

The first view of the enclosure was not prepossessing. The village consisted of a score or more of small huts with their novel grass-roofs, many of them built on stilts for protection against the attack of wild animals. An area of some two or three acres, containing the buildings, was surrounded by a high wooden stockade and on the fourth by the river. There was only one man visible: an old father, bent low with age. His grizzled hair fell over his misshapen back like an enveloping cloak, and his beard reached to his knees.

He espied us and stood as if rooted to the spot, staring intently at us. Then with a wild shout, such as I have never heard from beast or human being, he cried: *"Hombres, hombres! Venid!"* and straightway running from the huts came men and

women. They stopped abruptly when they saw us; with one accord they fell upon their knees and bowed their faces in the
dust, all the while making a rhythmic moan, uncanny at first,
and then strangely harmonious and beautiful.

I knew not what to make of this strange performance and my
guide offered no information. Our canoe came nearer and as it
hugged the bank I stepped ashore. Not a person stood, nor even
peered at me through half-closed eyes; evidently that which I
had taken for a moan was a prayer.

"Can you give a night's lodging to a weary traveler?" I asked.

The old man I had first seen raised himself on his knees and
extended his arms to me, but he uttered not a word.

"They no speak English," my guide said.

"Tell them we want to spend the night here," I answered.

He turned to them with my message, and no sooner had he
spoken than their prayer—if such it was—ceased, and they
rushed toward me. In no human eye have I ever seen expressed
such a wildness of emotion as was written in theirs—amazement, fear, childish simplicity, and passion. They seemed to be
searching for something in me, some special quality, for their
eyes scanned my face with a hunger and avidity quite discon-
certing. When I raised my arms to them to signify that I would
be their friend, they fell at my feet; one even kissed my sandals
and another my trousers.

When a second time my guide explained that we would
spend the night with them, their delight was pitiful, and one
and all ran to the largest of the several huts to make ready my
bed.

The entire performance was incomprehensible to me. The
hamlet's reputation for hospitality, of which Pedro had told me,
failed to explain their strange actions; even amazement at the
presence of a white man hardly accounted for the apparent worship. I recalled stories, from grammar-school readers of Romans
who were taken to be gods when they were cast shipwrecked
upon an unknown shore; but I laughed aloud. Did they take me

for an Olympian? How far was an academically sheltered botan-
ist from qualifying as a relative of Jupiter and Juno! Rather
this must be their way of paying respect to the white man's
superiority.

The ancient Carib chieftain, the old man whom we had seen
on the shore, came forward and bowed us to a bench before a
narrow table near the steps of the main hut. We seated ourselves,—Pedro and I,—but our host was troubled. He made
strange motions to my guide, and then came to whisper something in his ear. Pedro rose solemnly and, with a gaze half of
regret and half of reverence, moved to another table, leaving me
alone. Then the *muchachas* brought the food; but while they
served Pedro, all the dishes intended for me were given to my
host, who himself served me. Although I dared not attempt to
thank him in my meager Spanish, I tried to show him by smile
and friendly nod that I appreciated his generosity. The dishes
set before me were many and, to a wayfaring man, delicious: a
soup of beef, fried plantains, and a roasted bull-steak. I was
hungry and ate greedily. When I had finished I strolled down
to the bank of the little stream and sat in wonder, while the
shadows of twilight thickened, and the matted growth across
the river, higher than the height of a man, assumed strange
forms as it swayed in the gentle night breezes.

I could see the *hombres* and *mujeres* in the distance. They
were talking in low soft tones. Suddenly from the group I saw
a figure emerge. It was one of the muchachas, young and slender,
but she walked with difficulty, leaning heavily upon a staff at
each step. She was partially shrouded in the dusk, so that I
could not see her distinctly, but as she drew nearer I thought
her left side was paralyzed. Her foot dragged as a leaden weight,
and her arm hung useless. She came forward alone, stumbling
and with visible hesitation. No one moved among the group
in the background, and yet I could see they were watching her
intently. What could it mean?

The young girl was too much in earnest to be acting a part

in any heathen ceremonial. She was trembling violently and now I could see that she was coming toward me. I rose, wondering what was expected of me, and even as I did she stumbled. Her staff fell from her hand and she pitched forward, her right arm stretched out for help. I caught her easily, and held her trembling body for a moment. Eyes like the eyes of a young lioness when first entrapped—soft, yearning, wondering, before she knows the cruelty of her position—met mine in a look which years of scientific training had brought me no means of understanding. Then, with a cry of ecstasy, the young thing leaped from my arms and flew back to the shadows. As if waiting for this moment, her friends raised their voices with hers and there arose on the night air a solemn chanting, crude and unmusical, yet beautiful in its absolute sincerity and resplendent in its recurring note of joy. I watched, listening, and waited, longing to know the secret of the mystery.

The muchacha's staff lay at my feet. Could it be that these poor people, hearing of our progress in medicine believed in the white man's miraculous power to heal? Faith is the ability to believe the incredible, I had heard it said. Was this the solution?

I did not see my guide again that night. I was so astounded at what had taken place, and so disconcerted by the plaintive chanting, that I hurried to absent myself and made signs to my host that I would retire. He understood and led me to the hut, where they had prepared a spreading of fresh palm-leaves with a blanket covering—the choicest sleeping-accommodation the camp offered, I knew—and I accepted with gracious heart.

I was weary from my journey, and the cool night air brought refreshing sleep. It was dawn when I awoke.

Christmas Day—yet how unbelievable! What was Christmas Day in a land of wilderness and black folk? What could it mean to these dark-skinned Carib Indians? Not even a name, I suspected, to them who would worship a white man as they would a god, who instinctively bowed before a stranger from the fairyland of success.

It was with a feeling of wretchedness and discontent that I recalled the past Christmases, and knew that for the love of leaves and grass I had deprived myself of another such exquisite pleasure. My thoughts were willful truants: a jolly Christmas Day; outside, the ground white with snow, inside, the tree bulging with gifts and tempting eatables; the children were probably shouting as they opened their presents, and their mother—she too was lonely, even as I was lonely, for she had expected me to return before the holiday season. And all for a *Cocos comosa.*

The dream was dispelled as I became conscious of the voices which had awakened me, harsh and untuneful, even as the night before, yet they stirred something within me which quieted the loneliness of my heart. I bethought me of the old Christmas minstrels—but the very unlikeness of their carols to the present crying caused me to smile. I rose from my pallet; there about the hut were gathered the inhabitants of the camp, with their arms laden. At sight of me they bowed themselves to the ground; then slowly one by one they came and laid their offerings at my feet. I stood as a man in a dream, insensible to what was going on. I looked for my guide to explain, but Pedro was nowhere near. At the foot of my ladder were heaped great skins of tiger and lynx, bananas and plantains, curiously carved images, and a reed basket woven in intricate design and filled with stone charms. In my amazement I wondered if this were my Christmas dream come true!

I did my best to express my thanks by smiles and gestures, and the natives appeared to understand, but my confusion was turning to puzzled incredulity. I wanted to get away from it all; I wanted to question my guide. Was this Cispatia's tribute to civilization and nothing more?

They brought me food, when I had thanked them as best I could; and when I had eaten I sought my guide.

"Pedro, we must away."

He looked at me in awe and surprise. *"Hoy, Señor?"*

"Yes, today; at once."

He acquiesced and went to my host with word that we were going. The old man hurried to my side and through Pedro and pantomime begged me to stay. Then, seeing I was resolute, he motioned me to remain for a moment while he called the villagers together.

They came quickly, for at no time did they seem to be far away, and, grouping themselves about me, they fell on their knees. My host stood before me, and by frantic gesticulation, spreading his hands out in front of him, endeavored to communicate an idea to me, but I could not understand. I turned to Pedro for assistance.

"Bless," he said.

They wanted me to bless them. I, an old, homesick, botany professor, with theological notions too vague or too radical to be bound by creed or formula, was called upon to bless this little community which had housed me in the best of their homes! I lifted my hands and, with eyes raised to Heaven, I repeated over them the words which came to my mind from childhood days, like a voice heard from afar: *"The Lord watch between me and thee, when we are absent one from another."* Then, turning to my companion, I entered the dugout, and we pushed off.

Pedro took his place at the fore and began to paddle with his long, lazy strokes. By a turn in the stream the tiny enclosure was soon lost to sight.

"Pedro, what did it all mean?"

He looked at me with eyes filled with amazement and doubt. "You know."

"I don't know; tell me."

He hesitated, but something in my face must have warned him that I wanted an answer, for at last he spoke.

"Christ come."

No white man ever uttered such words with deeper reverence.

"Christ come!" I echoed, as I remembered their greeting and the incident of the night before.

"Yes, old miss'nary tell—Christ come. He come day 'fore Christmas; come up river at shade-time in dugout with hombre. He stay all night at Cispatia. They know at Cispatia."

I sat stunned by the thought. This then was the reason for their reception and their gifts: this the reason for the muchacha's confidence.

It was an idea which made me tremble. How inconceivable their childish faith, how perfect their adoration! And I had taken their homage as a white man's due!

Very, very silent I sat, awed and oppressed by an overburdening sense of impotence. If only the King might have come to receive His Christmas tribute!

The canoe moved on. The tall grasses rustled in the breeze; in the distance I heard music. It was the solemn chant they had sung for me when I came; they were singing it again as I left them. Clear, sometimes shrill, ever tuneless, and yet motivated by a strangely recurring theme of joy, it came to me on the morning air. Fainter and fainter it grew, as the recessional fades in the anteroom of the cathedral; then the hushed pause, silence, and that sense of unutterable loneliness, of loss, even as when a star falls from the heavens and the light of the world seems dimmed.

Pedro leaned toward me.

"It is true, *no es verdad?* You are, you are—He?"

☆

CHRISTMAS
EVERYWHERE

☆

Teacher Jensen

KARIN MICHAELIS

I F THE school children had cared to look about them while they were playing hide-and-seek during recess, they would have seen the sharp tower of a mighty building piercing the air beyond a distant clump of trees. Unless you knew better, you would have believed that it was a castle where knights and beautiful ladies ate game off golden plates and on Sundays regaled themselves with macaroons. But the school children did know better. They knew, forgot, and remembered again, that it was a prison standing near them, where prisoners lived, each in his own cell, never seeing each other except at church, where black masks disguised their faces. They knew and forgot and remembered again.

Lauritz Thomsen belonged there. Not that he had done anything to be ashamed of—God forbid! But his father was the cook for the prison, and Lauritz knew what the prisoners got to eat— and what they did not get. He lived, so to speak, in prison, but apart from these men with the black masks. He was so accustomed to taking the short cut across the fields to the high red wall and walking through the entrance portal, which was immediately closed and bolted after him, that it all seemed like nothing extraordinary. He could see it in no other light. But if his schoolmates began to ask him questions he would hold his peace and blush to the roots of his hair.

His mother worried and grieved about the prison, and sought as best she could to forget what was going on. Filling her windows with flowers, she tried to silence her unpleasant thoughts about the poor creatures breathing the deathly cellar air behind

289

those iron bars. She laid by penny upon penny in the hope of saving enough to buy a little country inn, or any kind of establishment far away from the Living Cemetery, as the prison was called. During her dreams she cried aloud, waking her children, for she always saw people with black masks on their faces swarming behind walls and windows and threatening to kill her. Evil dreams arise from evil thoughts, it is said, but Frau Thomsen could have no evil thoughts. She had only once in her life gone through the prison. It still froze her with terror to think of it, and she could not understand how her husband could sing and enjoy himself at the end of his day's work. Nor could she comprehend how he could speak of the prisoners as if they were friends or comrades. When he began to carry on in this way she would leave the room and not come back until he had promised to talk about something else.

Children are children. They can accustom themselves to wading in a river where crocodiles sleep, or to playing in a jungle where snakes hang from the trees. Children become accustomed to living near a prison just as they get used to a father who drinks or a mother who scolds. They think of it, forget it, and remember it again. Thoughts glide across their minds like shadows; for a moment everything seems dark, and suddenly the sun shines once more.

Whenever a prisoner escaped, the school children were thrown into a great commotion. They followed the pursuit from afar, listening to the shots, the alarm signals, the whistles. They leaned out of windows and saw the prison wardens rushing in all directions, on foot, and on horseback. Nothing was so exciting as a man hunt, either over winter snow or over green summer fields. When the fugitive was taken, peace descended upon all their souls. Now the only question was what punishment would be meted out to the victim, and all eyes were turned toward Lauritz. But Lauritz said nothing. He was ashamed without quite knowing why.

Prison and prisoners would be forgotten save when a boy

or girl at play would suddenly gape at the high towers to the east, jutting up there above the forest.

The children had a new teacher. He was called Teacher Jensen —nothing more. If he had a Christian name, he was never called by it. Just Teacher Jensen. And Teacher Jensen was little and frail, and Teacher Jensen's voice was as little and frail as he. But there was a wonderful quality in his voice, like a violin that makes a much louder noise than anyone would believe possible. The children did not sleep in his classes. They were not even drowsy. In his classes they forgot to write notes to each other or secretly to eat bread and butter behind their desks. They only listened and asked questions. Teacher Jensen had an answer for everything. They could ask Teacher Jensen all kinds of questions. But sometimes he would shake his head and say: "I seem to have forgotten it. Let me think a minute." Or worse yet: "I don't know. I never knew it. But I will look it up. It is to be found in some book, or a friend will tell me the answer." The children found that there was something splendid about having a teacher of whom you could ask all kinds of questions and who sometimes did not know the answer offhand.

Teacher Jensen talked about new things and old, and his speech was not like pepper shaken from a pepper pot. Even while the children were playing in the fields, they would remember what he had said. Yes, it remained fast in their minds.

One day Teacher Jensen said that murder was by no means the worst thing a man could do, and that it was much worse to think or say or do evil to another human being, or to make a defenseless animal suffer. And the children were full of wonder. It seemed that a new door had been opened to them, and each passed through it, one after another. Yes, it was true, what he said. They understood his meaning clearly, but they cast their eyes down, for all of them knew they had often done what was much worse than murder. Perhaps they would do it again, but not willingly, never willingly. Yet there was another thing worse than murder, and that was to act without using your will.

One day Teacher Jensen brought with him a sick, whining little cat which he had found on his way to school. He had put it under his cloak to keep it warm, and he stroked its back and its sharp little head. It was an ugly, gray, dirty cat. Teacher Jensen did not tell the children what he was going to do with it, but simply sat with the cat in his lap and rubbed his cheek against its head. To the children this poor little sick gray cat was the whole world. They took a silent vow that they would cure it. Through Teacher Jensen's little gray cat they had peered deep into the soul of an animal, and what they saw was more beautiful and more pure than a human soul.

Teacher Jensen often went on Sunday excursions with the children. Whoever wanted to could come, and all of them wanted to. It so happened that one Sunday morning in the autumn they were walking among falling leaves, and the earth clung to their shoes in little lumps. It had been raining, and was likely to rain again. Traversing a bit of open country, they soon entered the big forest in the distance. Ahead of them was the "castle" that was a prison. Lauritz ran in to get a scarf. Teacher Jensen saw him and drew his hand over his eyes, and as he cast down his eyes it was clear that he had been crying; but no one asked anything, no one spoke. They arrived at a vast grove of fir trees standing in long rows, with their evergreen branches above and their yellow trunks below. Teacher Jensen explained that such a forest could grow from a mere handful of tiny grains. The children knew this perfectly well; yet it sounded quite new. They suddenly understood that trees lived, breathed, and thought, that they strove for the light as poor people strive for bread.

"Now let's begin the game," said Teacher Jensen. "Let's imagine that this forest of fir trees is a prison, and that we are all prisoners, each in his own cell. Let us do this for one hour. I am holding a watch in my hand. During that hour let no one speak, for we are prisoners, and speech is forbidden."

This was a new game, a peculiar game. The rain had stopped some time ago, but drops were still falling from the high trees.

The children stood, each under his own tree, and felt the water dripping and dripping on cheeks and hands. The children stood with the water dripping off them, laughing and shouting to each other side by side cell by cell. Slowly the laughter died and their faces became serious. All eyes were directed toward Teacher Jensen, who stood with the watch in his hand. He seemed to see nobody, and did not announce when the hour should begin.

The children felt as if they ought to hold their breath, for surely something important and serious was afoot. It was not like the times when they had gone out with other teachers, when hatred and pride cropped up as soon as the school door was closed. This was serious, and each breath was like a bucketful of water from a deep, deep well. Was time standing still? Had not many hours already passed? Were they really prisoners after all? They did not crawl away, though there was nothing to stop them. Teacher Jensen did not look around him at all, yet as soon as any of the children thought of creeping away they could not help remembering what happened when a prisoner escaped and they heard the shots ring out, the alarm bells clang, the whistles blow, and saw the wardens riding off in all directions hunting the fugitive. Their feet would not obey them—they were bound fast by Teacher Jensen's word; the outstretched hand with the watch held them in their places. Yes, they were prisoners, each in his own cell, and darkness settled and a gentle mist descended, veil upon veil.

Was this what it was like being a prisoner?

The hour was up.

Every one sighed with relief, yet they all stood quiet for a moment, as if they could not really believe that they had regained their freedom. Then they sprang up and clustered around Teacher Jensen, asking him questions. It was growing dark, and he put his watch in his pocket, saying: "It is just as hard to be a prison watchman as to be a prisoner."

The children had never thought of this before, and after a long pause Teacher Jensen added: "The lot of the prison warden

293

is the hardest of all, for he can do nothing for the prisoners; and in his heart he wants to help them all he can, yet they are not able to read his thoughts."

And after another pause he said: "I knew a man who spent seventeen years in prison and then died there."

When Lauritz reached home his mother was sitting at the piano playing and singing. The smell of freshly baked cake filled the room. On the table stood a glass bowl of apples. Lauritz's father sat on a chair smoking his pipe. Without knowing just what he said or why he said it, Lauritz went up to the piano and whispered in his mother's ear: "When I am a big man I shall be a prison warden."

"What did you say" she cried. "A prison warden, Lauritz? In there with those people? Never!"

Lauritz repeated: "When I am a big man I shall be a prison warden."

And then something happened that was never explained. Who had the idea first no one knew. Perhaps it entered all those little heads at the same time, in that hour when they were standing, each a prisoner under his own tree, each in his own cell—just in a single hour.

When Teacher Jensen was told about the plan, he only nodded as if he had known about it long ago. But when they begged him to talk to the prison inspector, since their scheme was contrary to all regulations, he shook his head, saying: "It is your idea. You must carry it out. It is up to you, if you believe in yourselves, to stand fast by your beliefs."

That was two months before Christmas, and all the school children, big and little, boys and girls, were there. Money was the first necessity, and it had to be collected in modest amounts and earned in an honorable way. Teacher Jensen said that if the gift was not honest no good came of it. The children all saved the money that they would ordinarily have spent on sweets and on stamps for their albums. They went on little errands, chopped wood, carried water, and scrubbed milk cans, wooden buckets, and copper tubs. The money was put into a big earthenware pig that Teacher Jensen had put in the wardrobe at school. No one knew who gave the most or who gave the least.

Lauritz announced that, including the seventeen sick people, there were three hundred and ten prisoners in the jail.

In the middle of December the pig was broken and the money was counted over and over, but it did not amount to much. Then a little fellow came with his little private savings bank, and a girl with a little earthen receptacle in which she kept her spare pennies. That started them off. Many little hoardings destined for Christmas presents were emptied into the great common fund at school. See how it grew! Shiny paper was now brought, and flags and walnuts. Every day the whole school stayed until supper time cutting out and pasting. The little girls made white and red roses. They wove baskets, gilded walnuts, pasted flags on little sticks, and cut out cardboard stars, painting them gold and silver. The little ones made, out of clay, birds' nests with eggs in them, and little horses and cows that they covered with bright colors so they looked like real live animals. The boys cut out photographs and made little boxes. With jig saws they fashioned napkin rings and paper weights.

Christmas trees were bought—three hundred and ten real fir trees, for which the gardner charged only twenty-five pfennigs apiece.

Teacher Jensen emptied his purse on the desk. It had once been black, but it had long since turned brown, and was full of cracks. "That belonged to the man who spent seventeen years in prison," he announced. "He had it there with him. He kept it there for seventeen long years."

No one asked who the man was, but the money had to be counted over many times, for the children's eyes were moist and they had to keep wiping the tears away.

On the Sunday before Christmas the children went with Teacher Jensen to the local store and bought a lot of tobacco and chocolate, almonds and raisins, playing cards and brightly colored handkerchiefs, and writing paper. And they got a lot of old Christmas books too, which were given to them free because they were at the bottom of the pile and were out of date.

The parents of the children had to contribute whether they wanted to or not, and bags full of cookies and nuts, playing cards and books, came out of each house.

Lauritz's father had spoken in all secrecy to the prison chaplain, who went as a representative to the inspector. But the inspector hemmed and hawed saying: "That goes against all regulations. It's impossible. It can't be allowed on any ground whatever." The chaplain was to have told this to Lauritz's father, and Lauritz was to have brought the news to the children that the plan had to be abandoned. But the chaplain said nothing to Lauritz's father, and the children did not know that it was impossible and could never be allowed.

All the parents, no matter how much they had to do, made a point of going into the schoolhouse the day before Christmas and seeing the three hundred little sparkling Christmas trees, each laden with joy, each with its star on the top, each with its white and red roses, white and red flags, and white and red candles, each decorated with tinsel and hung with gifts. To every tree a little letter was fastened, written by a boy or a girl. What was in this letter only the writer and perhaps Teacher Jensen knew—for Teacher Jensen had to help the little ones who only knew how to print numbers and capital letters.

The church bells rang over the town and called the faithful to God's worship. The prison bells rang out over the prison and called the prisoners to the prison church. Before the school was drawn up a row of wagons which had been laden with the little Christmas trees. Each child then took his tree under his arm and set out, following the wagons, singing as he went. It was a Christmas party without snow, but a Christmas party just the same.

Stopping before the prison, they rang the bell, and asked to speak to the inspector. He came out, and the moment he appeared Teacher Jensen and all the children began to sing: *O du fröhliche, o du selige, gnadenbringende Weihnachtszeit. . . .*"

The inspector shook his head sadly and raised his hands in the air. It was impossible, absolutely impossible—he had said so. But the children kept right on singing, and seemed not to hear him. As the inspector afterward said, when the director of all the prisons in that district demanded an explanation: "A man is only human, and had you been in my place, Mr. Director, you would have done as I did, even if it had cost you your position."

Thus it came to pass that this one time Christmas was celebrated in each cell of the big prison—a good, happy, cheerful Christmas. When the prisoners came back from the worship of God with their black masks on their faces they found a Christmas tree in every cell, and the cell doors stood open until the candles had burned out, and the prisoners received permission to go freely from cell to cell all through the corridor to look at each other's Christmas trees and gifts—to look at them and to compare them. But each prisoner thought that his little tree and his present were the most beautiful and the best of all.

When the last light had burned out, the doors were closed, and far into the night the prisoners sang the Christmas carols of their childhood, free from distress, grief, and all spitefulness.

And as the last light flickered out behind the high walls the thin figure of a man with his coat collar up over his ears and his hat pulled over his face crept along the prison wall. Through the night air he heard the voices singing, *"Stille Nacht, heilige Nacht."*

Clasping his hands tightly together and raising them aloft into the darkness, he cried: "I thank thee, father. Thy guilt has been atoned for ten times over."

"Song from Heaven"

HERTHA PAULI

ON THE 24th of December, 1818, in Hallein, an age-old village in the Austrian Alps, Father Joseph Mohr sat alone in his study, reading the Bible. All through the valley the children were filled with excitement, for it was Holy Eve, and they could stay up for Midnight Mass. On their way down the open, frozen trails they carried rush lights, so that from the village the valley looked like a huge Christmas tree with a hundred moving candles.

The young priest had no eyes for the valley that was so festively lighted. With open Bible, he sat at his oaken study table working on a sermon for the midnight service. He read again the story of the shepherds in the fields to whom the angel came and said: "Unto you is born this day in the City of David a Saviour . . ."

Just as Father Mohr read this passage a knock sounded at his door. He admitted a peasant woman wrapped in a coarse shawl who told him of a child born earlier that day to a poor charcoal-maker's wife living on one of the highest alps in his parish. The parents had sent her to ask the priest to come and bless the infant, that it might live and prosper.

Father Mohr was strangely moved on his visit to the poorly lighted ramshackle hut where the young mother lay on the crude bed smiling happily, with her baby asleep in her arms. The scene certainly did not resemble the manger in the City of David, yet the last words he had read in his Bible suddenly seemed to be addressed to him. When he returned to the valley, he saw that the dark slopes were alight with the torches of the mountaineers on their way to church, and from all the villages far and near bells began to ring.

To Father Mohr a true Christmas miracle had come to pass. Sitting in his study after the midnight service he tried to put down on paper what had happened to him. The words kept turning into verse, and when dawn broke Father Mohr had written a poem. And on Christmas Day his friend, Franz Xaver Gruber, music teacher in the village school, composed music to fit the verses.

Village children heard the priest and the teacher singing. The church organ was out of order, so the pair were using what they had—two voices and a guitar, which Franz Gruber played. "After all," Gruber said, "the Lord can hear us without an organ."

They did not know that this anniversary of Christ's birthday was also the birthday of a great Christmas hymn that would be known in all lands where there is a Christmas, and that four little children would one day start it on its way to fame.

Of all the youngsters in the Zillertal valley in the Austrian Tyrol, the ones with the most beautiful voices were the four Strasser children, Caroline, Joseph, Andreas and little Amalie, who was called Maly, and was so young that she couldn't pronounce the words correctly. "Those Strassers," the townspeople used to say, "sing just like the nightingales."

Like the nightingales, too, every spring the four children traveled northward to Leipzig, in the kingdom of Saxony, the site of the great annual Trade Fair. For their parents were glovemakers, and it was the children's chore to display and sell the soft chamois gloves that were sought far and wide.

Leipzig, at Fair time, was an exciting city and the youngsters from the Zillertal at times felt lost in the bright and curious crowd. But they did just what they did at home when their spirits needed lifting—they sang together. The song they sang most, because it was their favorite, was "Song from Heaven."

Karl Mauracher, far-famed Zillertal organ builder, had taught the children the song. Once he had been called to a neighborhood village to repair an organ, and when his work was done he had asked the organist to try it out. The organist was Franz Gruber and somehow he slipped into the Christmas melody he had composed for Father Mohr.

"I never heard that song before," the organ builder said, with awe in his voice. "Would you mind if I took it with me? Folks back where I live would appreciate it." Gruber had offered to write it down, but Mauracher told him not to bother—he had hundreds of songs in his head and one more would make no difference.

The song quickly became popular in his valley, and was called "Song from Heaven." The organ builder didn't realize that he had brought back a truly valuable gift from two unknown composers to the entire world.

The children found the song's charm worked in the busy city; passers-by stopped to listen and were enchanted by the beautiful, melodious tune. One day an elderly gentleman, who introduced himself as Mr. Pohlenz, Director General of Music in the kingdom of Saxony, gave them tickets to one of the concerts that he conducted regularly in the Gewandhaus—the ancient guild house of the drapers of Leipzig. The youngsters were delighted.

When they entered the brilliantly lighted auditorium filled with silk-hatted gentlemen and ladies in rustling gowns, they felt timid and were glad to be led to inconspicuous seats beneath the platform. They were still rapt and glowing at the concert's end, when the shock came. For Mr. Pohlenz rose to announce that there were four children present, with the finest voices he had heard in years. They might be persuaded to treat Their Royal Majesties, the King and Queen of Saxony, who were present, and the audience to some of their lovely Tyrolean airs.

The announcement took the youngsters' breath away, and their faces flamed as people began to applaud. "Let's just shut our eyes and pretend we're singing at home," Maly whispered to the others.

Their first song was "Song from Heaven," and when they had finished it there was a moment of almost reverent quiet before applause broke loose. They sang all the songs they knew, and when they knew no more, they sang "Song from Heaven" again.

The audience was still shouting for more when a gentleman in uniform came up on the platform and said that Their Majesties desired to receive the singers.

"That was very pretty indeed," the King said after the children had been introduced. "We've never heard that Christmas song before. What is it?"

"It is a Tyrolean folk song, Your Highness," said Joseph.

"Won't you come to the castle and sing it on Christmas?" the Queen asked. "Our children will love it."

So it happened that on Holy Eve of the year 1832, in the Royal Saxon Court Chapel in Pleissenburg Castle, the Strasser children sang at the end of the Christmas services:

> Silent night, holy night—
> All is calm, all is bright,
> Round yon Virgin, Mother and Child;
> Holy Infant, so tender and mild,
> Sleep in heavenly peace—
> Sleep in heavenly peace.

And on that Christmas Eve the song bid the children farewell, to spread quietly around the world.

For years, on each Holy Eve, "Silent Night" was sung in the village of Hallein, in the house where Gruber lived and died, by a choir accompanied by Gruber's grandson, who used his grandfather's original guitar in the accompaniment. Later this yearly performance was carried round the world by radio—until a day in 1938 when the land of Austria was wiped off the map and the little song of peace became "undesirable."

But the great land of music from which it hails knows no frontiers. And the "Song from Heaven," like the Christmas message itself, still rings for all men of good will.

Silent Night! Holy Night!

JOSEPH MOHR

Silent night! holy night!
All is calm, all is bright;
Round yon virgin mother and Child,
Holy Infant so tender and mild;
Sleep in heavenly peace,
Sleep in heavenly peace.

Silent night! holy night!
Darkness flies, all is light;
Shepherds hear the angels sing:
"Alleluia! hail the King!
Christ the Saviour is born,
Christ the Saviour is born."

Silent night! holy night!
Guiding Star, lend thy light!
See the eastern wise men bring
Gifts and homage to our King!
Christ the Saviour is born,
Christ the Saviour is born.

Silent night! holy night!
Wondrous Star, lend thy light!
With the angels let us sing
Alleluia to our King!
Christ the Saviour is born,
Christ the Saviour is born.

Two Brothers

A Victorian Story

AUTHOR UNKNOWN

THE COLD Christmas moon was shining on the sleeping village of Cheriton. It lit up the long, straggling street, and made every object almost as distinctly visible as at noonday. But in the spiritual light they appeared very different. A beautiful quietude, solemn yet serene, seemed to rest on all things. The quaint houses, with their high roofs and oddly clustered chimneys, looked as if they brooded over the recollection of the long past times they had known; and the grand old church looked doubly reverend, with the frost-work glittering about its Norman-arched windows, and on the boughs of the huge cedar which towered beside the doorway. The moonbeams lingered lovingly about the gray walls; they fell, too, on the white gravestones in the churchyard, and made each one shine as with a still, calm smile—happy and holy. It was a night upon which thoughtful men might gaze, and feel rising in their hearts simultaneous hope for earth and aspiration to heaven.

Very quiet was the place, as the moon went on her way, looking down with her clear, chill lustre of gaze. And there was one house, isolated from the others by a somewhat extensive domain of shrubbery and garden, about which the moonlight seemed to play as if in curiosity. It was a primitive, old-fashioned abode; window-shutters and blinds were few, save to the lower rooms, and the moonbeams penetrated unhindered into the chambers, and played fantastic tricks upon the walls and floors. Into one little room the elfish rays darted on a sudden, as the moon, rising higher in the heavens, escaped the shadow of a projecting buttress in the wall; and the pale light fell full upon a little white draped bed, wherein lay two young boys. One, the eldest by some years, was asleep, and the quivering light fell on his face—a face every lineament of which was so full of nervous energy, that even in sleep it did not wear an expression of repose. His brother's pale, delicate features were, on the contrary, distinguished by a sort of sculptural calm. He had a high, straight, thoughtful brow, and that sensitive mouth, which to the most masculine face always adds an almost womanlike sweetness of expression.

The two boys seemed apt illustrations of two differently constituted beings. The one all action, the other all thought; if the life of the first might be a picture, that of the second would be a poem.

The younger brother was awake. His eyes of dark, deep, liquid hazel were thoughtfully fixed upon the sleeping face beside him, and now and again, as with a tender impulse, his hands gently put aside the clustering brown curls from the broad forehead of the sleeper. Presently he drew back the white curtain, and looked out at the quiet, homely scene stretched out in the moonlight—at the foreground of trees, leafless, but clothed in a fairy robe of rime, and (in the far distance, strangely clear that night) the wide wonder of the silent sea. He looked— his face lit up—glowed with a nameless rapture. Unuttered prayers swelled in the young heart—instinctive hopes—blessed beliefs rose unbidden to his mind.

And even while he thus gazed, and felt, and pondered in the stillness of that wintry midnight, the stillness was broken. Vibrating on the frosty air came solemn strains of music, played with untaught skill on two or three old-fashioned instruments. It was an ancient English air, with a kind of patriarchal simplicity in its character, half carol, half hymn, which harmonized well with the place and the time. As the very voice of the quaint and peaceful village came the clear, sweet sounds, blending like a visible actuality with the wintry stars dotting the dark sky, with the snow-covered roofs, and walls, and trees, and with the pure, passionless moonlight shining over them all.

"Laurence, wake! Listen to the Waits!"

It was some time before the subdued voice and the gentle touch disturbed the sleeper from his dreams. When at last he was aroused, he started up suddenly, crying aloud—

"Who calls? Oh, Willie, is it you?" he added, in a sleepy tone. "What do you wake me for? 'Tisn't morning!"

"Hush! speak low! Don't you hear the music?"

There was a pause. The two boys listened in silence.

"It's old Giles Headforth, with his violoncello," at length broke in Laurence, "and John Read, with his cracked hautboy, and little——"

"Ah, don't!" cried the younger boy, with a gesture almost of pain; "never mind *who* plays. It sounds so solemn now, so——"

His words died away in the intentness of his listening.

"Queer old tune, isn't it?" presently said Laurence, "and queer old figures they look, I'll be bound, standing in the street, with red noses, and frozen eyelashes, and muffled in worsted comforters up to the chin."

He laughed, and then yawned.

"I think I shall go to sleep again. These fellows don't seem inclined to leave off. I shall be tired of listening before they are of playing, I expect."

"Keep awake a little longer, Laurence dear," pleaded the other. "It's only for one night, and 'tis so nice for us to hear the music, and look out upon the moonlight *together*."

"Very well, Willie," assented the elder boy, nipping a fresh yawn in the bud, "anything to please you, old fellow."

"There—put your arm round me—*so*," pursued Willie, always in the same hushed, whispering tone, "and let me lean my head upon your shoulder. Now, that is pleasant. We love each other; don't we, Laurence?"

And the tender, childish face looked upwards, askingly.

"I should think so—slightly! You're a dear old chap, Will, though you *have* rather odd, old-fashioned notions."

He stooped down, and pressed a hearty kiss on his young brother's delicate face.

And then the two boys remained silent, watching the flickering moon-rays, and listening to the simple music without.

There are some recollections, oftentimes trivial enough in themselves, which yet remain impressed upon the mind through a whole life, outlasting the memory of events far more striking, and more recent in their occurrence.

Laurence and William Carr grew to be men, went out into the world, and were battlers for fortune; and one of them, alas! in fighting that hard fight became hardened in nature, so that scarce a trait remained of the generous, loving boy of yore. His soul was chilled in the stony routine of that life which is so scrupulously practical—one might almost say, material—the life of a London merchant, devoted heart and soul to his calling, and to the ambitions of his class. His old instincts were almost dead within him; his old aspirations, his boyish predilections, were crushed out, effaced, as though they had never been. And yet the cold, hard, money-getting man of the world never lost the vivid remembrance of that Christmas night, years and years ago, when his little brother lay with his head leaning on his shoulder, and they listened together to the village waits.

The brothers were separated now—worse, they were estranged. The world came between them, and stifled the frank, free love which each, though in so widely different a way, had felt for the other, ever since the childish days when they had played together about the old house at Cheriton, and prayed, night and morning, at their mother's knee.

The two boys were left orphans before William was twenty years old, and with but little with which to begin life. Laurence's desires had been all for a life of change, adventure, and travel; but instead, he was compelled to take the only opening which offered to him; and, before his father's death, was established in the counting-house of a wealthy relative. He soon learned contentment with his fate. To pursue an object, be it fame, or power, or wealth, seems an inherent instinct in man's nature. It fills his energies, satisfies his restlessness, and insensibly, but gratefully, ministers to that vague yearning for dominion which is the inevitable birthright of every man since the beginning of the world. Laurence, shut out from worthier aspirations, found his ambition run high—to be *great* in the sense by which all those around him understood greatness. He would be rich. He would work his way to fortune, to position, to influence. Keeping that goal ever in view, he would struggle through every difficulty, force his way over every obstacle, but he would gain it at last. So he said to himself, silently, many times, during the weary time of probation, when obscurity and hard work appeared to be his allotted portion then and always. But this dark period did not last long; it was not likely that it should continue. He had talents, quickness, vigor, untiring perseverance, and unfailing health. His progress was rapid. He climbed the hill with footsteps swift as they were sure, and when his father died the old man felt easy on the score of his eldest's son's prospects and ultimate success.

But meanwhile William had remained at home, pursuing his self-imposed and dearly loved studies; reading, thinking, dreaming his hours away in perfect happiness.

From this content he was rudely aroused to the dread realities of death and poverty. The pleasant home and the familiar faces which made it so dear, seemed to slide from him, and left him standing alone in the bleak world, which was so new and strange; like one who, reared in an Arcadia, is on a sudden thrust into the midst of the fierce turmoil of a battle.

He sought his brother—but the two natures, always different, were doubly so now, when a life of active business had hardened the one, rendering it more than ever stern and uncompromising; while years of quiet retirement had made the other yet more refined, more visionary, more sensitive. And from Laurence, the younger brother met with no sympathy in all those innermost feelings of his soul; the closest, dearest portion of himself. There was in William Carr that inexplicable, intangible *somewhat,* which marks one man among his fellows—the Poet—even though he be dumb to his life's end.

The man of business shrugged his shoulders, knitted his brows at "William's strange fancies." He did not comprehend— he did not care to do so, it seemed. The first step towards their estrangement was taken when William declined, gently and thankfully, but decisively, a situation in the same house where Laurence was now high in trust.

"It is of no use, brother; it would not be right to accept it. I am not fit for such a responsibility. It would be wrong to my employers to burden them with my incapacity."

"You will improve. You may leave them to protect their own interests, believe me."

William shook his head.

And in brief, the elder brother found the delicate-looking youth immutable in his decision, and left him, with words of impatience and anger on his lips.

His heart reproached him for it afterwards. He was not all encrusted as yet with the ossification of worldliness. The next day he again went to his brother's lodgings. But William was no longer there—he had left London, they told him; and it was not till he reached his own home that he received a letter of explanation:—

"Dear Laurence—I thought it best to go. Forgive me if you think it wrong. I am not able to struggle with the fierce multitude of money-getters in this dreary London. My old master, Dr. K——, has offered me a situation as classical tutor in his school. I have accepted it. It is the best thing I see to do. So farewell.
              "Ever yours,
                      "William."

A *Victorian* Story

"And *my* brother will be the paltry usher in a country school!" muttered Laurence, as he crushed the letter in his hand. "Gone, too, without consulting me, his elder, his natural adviser. It is badly done."

And so the cloud between the brothers grew dark and palpable. They occasionally corresponded; but each succeeding letter, instead of drawing them nearer together, seemed only to widen the gap. They did not understand one another. Besides, Laurence was becoming a rich man, had become partner in the house where once he was a clerk; while William still remained poor and obscure, with no prospect of his circumstances improving. And when the breach between two brothers or friends once exists, difference of worldly position fatally, icily increases it.

Laurence married brilliantly, choosing his wife from a noble but impoverished family, who were glad enough to ally their aristocratic poverty with his wealth, merchant and plebeian though he was. It was while on his wedding tour, with his handsome but somewhat *passée* bride, that he received a letter from his brother, forwarded to him from London.

"From William—my brother," he remarked explanatorily, as he opened it; "in answer, I presume, to the announcement of my marriage."

The frigidly high-bred lady responded by a slight bend of her long neck, and busied herself with her chocolate and muffins, while her husband perused the letter. When he had finished, he refolded it carefully, and placed it in his pocket, then turned in silence to his breakfast. His wife never noticed any peculiarity in his manner; she was one of those by whom it is seldom considered good *ton* to be observant of other people's emotions, even a husband's. Lady Henrietta Carr was scrupulous in her attention to such points of etiquette. One more loving than she was might possibly have divined how much was concealed under the pale face, the bent brow, and the remarkably quiet voice of Laurence Carr that morning. One more tender might

310

even have drawn the secret disturbance forth, and pleaded the cause of the absent offender, instead of leaving the wrath to ferment hiddenly in the stern man's breast.

"I will never forgive him—never, never! I will never look on his face again. I will never give him help—we are strangers from this hour. Let him travel his own road—and starve."

These hard, terrible words the brother passionately uttered, as he trod the room to and fro, when he was alone, and after again reading the letter.

"Dear Brother Laurence" (it ran)—"Your letter, with its brief announcement of your marriage, gave me great pleasure, not only for the sake of its intelligence, but because of the kindly manner in which you conveyed it to me. Perhaps, brother, it is an equal reproach to both of us, that the cordiality was strange as well as pleasant. Let us be friends again, in heart as in name; we were so once—but it is a long while ago. In our new happiness we may surely drown all past offenses. For I also am married—not to a peer's daughter; no, Laurence, with you alone will rest all the brilliances and grandeur of life; I only ask for a little quiet—I am easily content. My wife you may remember; we all knew her when we were boys at school—Mary Elliot, who, though her father was a village tradesman, has had the education, and innately possesses the refinement of any lady in the land. I have loved her, and she me, for six years. She is an orphan, too, and has been a governess all that time. We are rich enough to commence housekeeping, though on a modest scale. We are very happy; I pray that you may be the same with my new sister, to whom I beg to offer my affectionate regards. Mary also joins me in the same to yourself, my dear brother. And believe me ever yours faithfully,

"William Carr."

"The daughter of a country shopkeeper and the daughter of the Earl of Tynford to call each other sisters? And he has done

311

this! He will repent it; he must, he shall. He is a disgrace, a shame to me. He might have been an aid—he might have helped my plans. But now—to marry *thus!*"

Such were some of Laurence's disjointed exclamations, as he tore the letter in pieces, and flung them into the fire. Then he joined his bride. In the course of the day he informed her that his brother had irremediably offended him, and that he would never speak to him or see him more. Lady Henrietta elevated her handsome eyebrows in a momentary amazement, then restored her features to their habitual expressionless composure, and, without any remark, suffered her husband to turn the conversation.

Time passed on. The wealth of Laurence Carr increased yearly; his name grew glorious in the ears of business men. His house was a palace; his wife was jewelled like a queen. He himself still burrowed daily in dusty city holes, whence all his riches seemed to spring; and every year he became harder and more impassible, and more devoted to the one aim and end of his life—money-getting.

It was his sole ambition now—he had no hope, no joy in anything beyond. There was no happiness in his gorgeous home, no tenderness in his majestic and aristocratic wife. No one who looked on him would have imagined that he felt the want of love; that there was any remnant of the generous, warmhearted boy's nature still lingering in the old grim merchant—old before his time, but hard, and cold, and piercing as a steel poniard yet. But it was so. There were moments when his thoughts wandered at their own will—when he *remembered*. The face of his mother shone on him sometimes; and then would come a flash of memory—of the old childish days. And ah, so strange! the childish feelings of those days.

And his two children. The boy he often pictured to himself as born to continue the greatness of his family—as enjoying, like a prince, the wealth and luxury he had labored to acquire.

And the fair, gentle girl, whose progress to womanhood he had followed in his thoughts; whose birth softened his harsh heart to absolute tenderness. She it was who would cling to him lovingly in after years—whose soft lips would press upon the wrinkles of his worn face—whose gentle voice would always have the power to win him out of his harder, sterner self. If either of his children had lived, Laurence Carr might have been a different man; but both these blessings which he had prayed for—dreamed of as the solace and delight of his old age, were only granted to him for a brief space, and then—left his sight for ever.

The blow rent his heart sorely. It was so deep a grief, even, that at first he forgot the check to his ambition it involved. No son of his would carry his name into future ages—no descendants of his were destined to make illustrious the plebeian family *he* had first raised from obscurity. When this remembrance came, it added to his affliction a something that was cold, stony, and almost defiant. Bereaved love mourns, but blighted ambition erects its head in very impotence of pride against the hand that chastises. Laurence's heart grew hardened. He buried himself anew in his grim pursuits; they seemed the be-all and end-all of his existence now. He said to himself that it was enough; he would make it enough.

Yet, spite of all his inward protestations, he looked enviously, and sometimes with a feeling less selfish than envy, at the happy parents of blooming children. He would have given well nigh all his hard-won wealth for one such boon as was so freely granted to many. Against his will he often found himself musing thus, sorrowfully, yearningly. He would awake himself with stern resolve; the one half of his nature would shrink into itself, while the other looked on it with a sardonic kind of pity.

Yet again and again came these softening reveries. It was in the midst of one of them, in the twilight of a dreary December evening, that he was roused by receiving a letter from William. It was the first since many years, during which the stern elder brother had suspended all intercourse, and had never sought to know what had become of the other. He had known somewhat, however; for William had come to London and had commenced the new life of authorship, and Laurence had occasionally met his name in passing periodicals. But direct communication between the two had altogether ceased. He frowned as he recognized the hand.

Perhaps, had this letter come at any other time, he might have returned it unopened. Oh, men! ye who pray, pray for your fellow men *whose hearts are hardened*. Oh, angels! plead for them, strive for them; for verily if there be a place in all His works where God does not dwell, and where no saving spark of divinity can linger, it must be in the sterile heart of a world-hardened man.

Laurence frowned; but he tore the letter open so soon as the servant had left the room, and he read:

"I had almost sworn never to address you again, after that last letter you sent. In that you bade me never to trouble you more; you told me that you would neither listen to me nor assist me, however sore my strait might be. I forgot you were my brother when I read those words; the devil rose within me, and I had uttered—what hereafter it might have withered me to think of, only my wife came up to me, and looked in my face, and, God bless her, while her eyes rested on me, I could not speak, nor even think of what was hissing at my heart. I tell you this that you may judge what it costs me to write to you now. 'I might starve,' you said. Laurence Carr, since then I have learned what starvation is like—I have traveled very near its utmost brink; it is a word the meaning of which I *know*. That would not drag me one quarter inch towards your threshold; its worst agony is not within a twentieth part of that which even the thought of addressing you for help would have cost me. But that anguish now is swallowed in a greater. I ask your help—I entreat you, I beseech you to assist me. Laurence, we are brothers, the children of one mother; do not deny me. Give to me as you would to a beggar—fling me some money into the street. I care not how, so you be not deaf to my cry—only be prompt, for Death is pitiless.

"Brother! God look on you as you hearken to me. *My child is dying for want of food.* I wait.

"WILLIAM CARR."

Laurence rose from his gilded chair, and traversed the luxurious chamber wherein he had sat, stately and solitary. He opened the door—there he paused. Then, as if with new resolution, he stepped forth into the hall.

In a remote corner, which even the brilliant lamp failed to clearly illumine, he distinguished a tall, thin figure—a pale, pinched face, with grey hair falling tangled over the broad brow. Did Laurence see *then* the vision of the bright-haired child, who slept on his breast one Christmas night long years back? Who can tell!

Howbeit, he retreated into the room before he was recognized, or even seen by his brother; and it was by a servant that he sent to William a small but heavy packet. He eagerly seized it, with a kind of smothered cry, almost like a sob, and the next instant had left his brother's house.

The child was saved; and then William had time to think on the sacrifice he had made to save it. His proud heart was torn at the remembrance that he had been a waiting petitioner in the hall of his brother's house, and had been relieved at the hands of his brother's lackey. He could not know that Laurence, hard man as he was, had tried to face him, but could not; that he had watched him as he darted away through the street; that he had thought of him often, since, with something almost approaching tenderness.

He did not know this; so he strove and toiled with desperate energy, till he could give back his brother's gold, and then returned it with a brief acknowledgment. He added—"It is best

315

for us both to forget our humiliation, for you degraded both in me. Let us be strangers again."

The returned money found Laurence Carr a ruined man. Sudden political troubles abroad, with their inevitable consequences —two or three mistakes in home commercial policy—had brought about this great change, and he was bankrupt. A day— two or three hours in that day—saw the fall, saw the ruin to its climax. The merchant prince was worse than penniless; for there were large debts which all his vast possessions, all his accumulated wealth, would fail to satisfy. His wife, naturally incensed at his misfortunes, betook herself and her liberal jointure to the parental roof, and he remained alone to combat with ruin.

Then came out the finer part of his character. With courage he encountered the host of difficulties that pressed crushingly upon him. With scrupulous (some people called it Quixotic) integrity he gave up all he had, and quietly and simply announced his intention of paying off the residue of his debt to the uttermost farthing, if he lived. Then with proud, silent bravery, he accepted a clerkship in some brother merchant's office, took a humble lodging, and began again the life he had commenced in his early youth.

The world—even the world of business and money-getting— is not so wholly bad as we read of in novels. Laurence received many offers of assistance, and one or two good hearts persisted for a long time in following him with their active friendship. But he was not great enough to feel gratitude, or even to thoroughly appreciate their goodness. His pride was but the pride of a strong, bold, determined man. He disdained sympathy, and sullenly repulsed all proffered generosity.

The wheel of fortune had made a complete revolution. While depressing one brother, she elevated the other. William was growing into that *rara avis*, a flourishing author. He was sufficiently far from being wealthy, certainly; he was at an equally safe distance from want. And now—Oh, beware! ye who hastily write resentment—he felt as though he would gladly return to his old poverty, if he could only recall the few lines he had sent awhile since to his now ruined brother.

It was long before he dared to approach him with attempts at reconciliation. *He* felt keenly, with anguish, the fresh bitterness he had himself added to the former estrangement. If desperate then, it was surely hopeless now. Yet he tried. He wrote again and again, and his letters were returned with their seals unbroken. He laid in wait often, and essayed to speak to him— to grasp his hand. He was coldly thrust aside, without a word, without a look. He was always denied admittance at the door, when time after time he sought the poor abode where the former millionaire had his shelter.

One less tender, less patient than William, had been effectually repulsed with half the rebuffs he met with. But his exceeding love and yearning over his brother, besides the consciousness of having outraged that brother's pride, now that he was fallen from his high estate, smote him with an intense, sharp remorse. Only a *man* can wholly sympathize in a man's pride. William's own heart, different as it was, told him how great was the barrier he had set between them.

At length William and his wife bethought themselves of another plan. Their child, the girl that Laurence's assistance had saved from death, was now grown into a fair damsel, of some fourteen years. She was like her father, with golden hair and brown eyes, such as he had.

"He cannot turn *her* from him," said the father and mother, as with glistening eyes they watched her on her way. She led her little brother by the hand, and these two presented themselves before Laurence, as he sat reading in the quiet sunshine of a Sabbath afternoon.

"We are Willie and Alice," said the girl, timidly, looking in his face.

He knew them at once, though his eyes had never rested on them before. Alice was his mother's name, and his mother's face seemed bent on him now, longingly, yearningly.

William and his wife were right—he could not turn her from him.

"Uncle, won't you look at us?" said the pleading voice again; "won't you speak to us—me and little Willie?"

"Papa's own little Willie," chimed in the boy inopportunely.

"Go home to your father," said Laurence in a harsh, constrained voice; "I have nothing to say to you. Go home. I do not wish," he added in a softer tone, "to be unkind to you, but—but—you must leave me."

The girl stood drooping and tearful; the little boy gazed at him with wondering eyes. He was fain to escape from them, and so passed from the room.

After that William grew hopeless. He had exhausted his stock of expedients: all his patience, endurance, seemed in vain. He despaired of ever softening his obdurate heart.

Time passed on, and Laurence was untroubled by his brother. His persevering industry was working its own way, too, and he was already clear of the barren poverty he had at first experienced after his ruin. Each succeeding year found him advancing to ease again, if not to affluence; and he was stern, cold, and unbending as ever.

Another Christmastide drew near—forty-five years after that Christmas when the moon shone on the little white bed at Cheriton. It was Christmas Eve, and Laurence had been detained late in the city, balancing some complex accounts. It was past midnight as he wended his way homewards. It was a frosty night, and moonlight, and the suburban streets were quiet and slumberous; Laurence's footsteps, echoing on the pavement, alone breaking the stillness. Somehow, without his own will, almost in spite of it, indeed, his thoughts turned back to old times, and there arose before him a vision of the quaint

318

house in the country, where his boyhood had been passed; the large rambling garden, the big mulberry trees, and the wood near the village where he and Willie had used to gather nuts. He and Willie!—there he frowned and sternly refused to dwell on the retrospection. He walked quickly on, with lips sturdily compressed and brows knitted, resolved to shut his mind on all softening influences; but he could not—the thoughts came again, and would not be repulsed. He lifted his eyes to the sky, and the myriad stars were shining down on him with a kind of smile—the same smile as that of long ago . . . He could not sleep that night. He lay very quiet, but with a world of busy thoughts fluttering about his heart, striving for entrance. The moonlight streamed in through a crack in the blind, and lit up the dreary, comfortless room. Laurence closed his eyes suddenly. The moonbeams brought a remembrance with them that he would not welcome.

There came a sound of music outside in the frosty street.

The Waits! And they played the old, old tune two boys had listened to years ago at Cheriton.

Very strangely it sounded on Lawrence's ears—strangest of all because it seemed so familiar. With a mysterious, irresistible power the sweet, solemn strain smote on his closed heart, and even before he recognized it he had yielded to its power, and, wondering the while, felt the hot tears bubbling thickly to his eyes.

And then came thronging the recollections of the olden days —vanished the intervening years, like an obscuring smoke, leaving clear and vivid the memory of the happy, innocent time, when he was a boy, and Willie was his dear brother. The pleasant home, the kind father, and—gentlest thought of all—the mother who had been wont every night to hang over her boys in their little white bed, and lingeringly kiss them ere they went to sleep. How plainly he remembered all—the childish face with its golden curls; he opened his eyes, almost expecting to see it on the pillow beside him. No! the moonlight only fell on his own thin, wrinkled hand, worn and shriveled with the troubles and the cares of well-nigh sixty years.

Prayerful thoughts, long strange to him, alas! came instinctively to his mind, and he heard, low and soft, but clear, and blending with the music in the street, the voice of his mother, sounding as of old when she read to her little sons from the large Book on her knee. He heard solemn, slow, and sweet, the Divine words—*"And this commandment I leave with you, that ye love one another."*

He saw the dear mother's eyes as they rested on her boys with such an infinite yearning tenderness in their depths. He could tell *now*, what that earnest look meant. He could guess, too, something of what were her thoughts, when often in their childish quarrels she would draw little Willie close to her side, and then pass her arm round the strong active, vigorous Laurence, whispering, "Don't be harsh with Willie; take care of Willie. Love each other always, my boys—my darlings."

The waits ceased—the air was silent—but there was music still in the heart of Laurence Carr.

Christmas Day at Cheriton was drawing to its close. The evening bells were ringing—the stars shone in the dark colorless sky. The murmur of the waves beating on the shore came ever and anon—a quiet sound and happy.

Only two days before William Carr had come to live at Cheriton in the old house. It was nothing altered; there were the same many-paned windows, quaint corners, and gabled ends; the same surrounding domain of garden, with the grove of trees beyond, behind which the icy moon was rising even now.

At the bay window of the oak-panelled parlor sat William and his wife, with their two children, watching the pale light trembling between the branches of the gloomy firs. The firelight flashed and glowed within the room, lighting up the pictures on the walls, the books, and prints, and drawings scattered on the table, and the graceful groups of winter flowers lavishly disposed, as women love to have them—everywhere. Alice rested beside her father—his hand wandered among her bright curls; but he was looking towards the fir grove, and his thoughts had traveled back, many, many years. His wife's eyes were fixed on his face; she could read the language of that sad wistful look; she knew how eloquently everything he saw spoke to his heart of the old happy childish days—tender, pathetic memories that she also loved so dearly for his sake. The children prattled gaily for some time, but at length their voices ceased; they were subdued into stillness by the unwonted gravity of their father. Never had they seen him so sorrowful, and they marveled in their innocent hearts; for he was happy, they knew, at coming back to Cheriton—to his old home. All the afternoon he had been pointing out to them his favorite haunts—his garden, his tree with the seat under it, and the little room where he used to sleep. He had been so happy and glad *then*. What could make Papa look grieved now?

Awed by the mystery, they gave their good-night kiss with added tenderness, but silently; and silently followed their mother from the room. But she returned almost immediately, and stole softly behind the chair wherein her husband sat, still looking forth with that silent, longing, regretful look. Even when he felt her arm round his neck he did not turn. But she spoke softly—

"Dearest, I *know*. But be comforted. It will be made right some day. Perhaps before another Christmas. God has been so good to us, he will not deny this one blessing you so crave, so pray for."

And William folded her to his heart, and smiled. Mary's voice never sounded in his ears but to create peace, or to add to content. When she left him again, the moonlight fell on his face, and showed it calm, hopeful, and serene.

There came a heavy tread on the stone steps, leading to the entrance door, and then the great bell rang startlingly through the quiet house. William rose, and himself went to meet the intruder.

Fairly, clearly, purely gleamed the moonlight in at the window; warm and generous glowed the fire, revealing the pleasant homelike aspect of the room.

So William threw back his gray hair from his brows—a boyish habit, continued ever since the time of golden curls—and went to the outer door, unbarred and opened it.

A gush of chill, sharp air—the sound of the sea, like a far-off chant—the moonbeams, white on the stone porch and pavement —and a dark figure standing motionless there; —this was what William felt, and heard, and saw, the first moment.

The next, a face looked on him, a hand was stretched towards him, and a voice uttered only one word—

"Brother!"

William's joyful cry answered him; then, like Joseph of old, "he fell upon his neck, and wept."

And at the door where the two children had so often entered from their play, the two gray-haired men stood, the Christmas stars shining on their faces.

A Journey in Search of Christmas

OWEN WISTER

THE GOVERNOR descended the steps of the Capitol
slowly and with pauses, lifting a list frequently to his eye.
He had intermittently penciled it between stages of the
forenoon's public business, and his gait grew absent as he re-
curred now to his jottings in their accumulation, with a slight
pain at their number, and the definite fear that they would be
more in seasons to come. They were the names of his friends'
children to whom his excellent heart moved him to give Christmas presents. He had put off this regenerating evil until the
latest day, as was his custom, and now he was setting forth to do
the whole thing at a blow, entirely planless among the guns and
rocking-horses that would presently surround him. As he reached
the highway he heard himself familiarly addressed from a distance, and turning, saw four sons of the alkali jogging into town
from the plain. One who had shouted to him galloped out from
the others, rounded the Capitol's enclosure, and approaching
with radiant countenance, leaned to reach the hand of the Governor, and once again greeted him with a hilarious "Hello,
Doc!"

Governor Barker, M.D., seeing Mr. McLean unexpectedly
after several months, hailed the horseman with frank and lively
pleasure, and inquiring who might be the other riders behind,
was told they were Shorty, Chalkeye, and Dollar Bill, come for
Christmas. "And dandies to hit town with," Mr. McLean added.
"Red-hot."

"I am acquainted with them," assented his Excellency.

"We've been ridin' trail fer twelve weeks," the cow-puncher
continued, "makin' our beds down anywheres, and eatin' the

323

same old chuck every day. So we've shook fried beef and heifer's delight, and we're goin' to feed high."

Then Mr. McLean overflowed with talk and pungent confidences, for the holidays already rioted in his spirit, and his tongue was loosed over their coming rites.

"We've soured on scenery," he finished, in his drastic idiom. "We're sick of moonlight and cow-dung, and we're heeled for a big time."

"Call on me," remarked the Governor, cheerily, "when you're ready for bromides and sulphates."

"I ain't box-headed no more," protested Mr. McLean. "I've got maturity, Doc, since I seen yu' in the summer, and I'm a heap older than them hospital days when I bust my leg on yu'. Three or four glasses, and quit. That's my rule."

"That your rule too?" inquired the Governor of Shorty, Chalk-eye, and Dollar Bill. These gentlemen of the saddle were sitting quite expressionless upon their horses.

"We ain't talkin', we're waitin'," observed Chalkeye, and the three cynics smiled amiably.

"Well, Doc, see yu' again," said Mr. McLean. He turned to accompany his brother cow-punchers, but in that particular moment Fate descended or came up from whatever place she dwells in, and entered the body of the unsuspecting Governor.

"What's your hurry?" said Fate, speaking in the official hearty manner. "Come along with me."

"Can't do it. Where're yu' goin'?"

"Christmasing," replied Fate.

"Well, I've got to feed my horse. Christmasing yu' say?"

"Yes; I'm buying toys."

"Toys! You? What for?"

"Oh, some kids."

"Yourn?" screeched Lin, precipitately.

His Excellency the jovial Governor opened his teeth in pleasure at this, for he was a bachelor, and there were fifteen upon his list, which he held up for the edification of the hasty McLean. "Not mine, I'm happy to say. My friends keep marrying and settling, and their kids call me uncle, and climb around and bother, and I forget their names, and think it's a girl, and the mother gets mad. Why, if I didn't remember these little folks at Christmas, they'd be wondering—not the kids, they just break your toys and don't notice; but the mother would wonder— 'What's the matter with Dr. Barker? Has Governor Barker gone back on us?'—that's where the strain comes!" he broke off, facing Mr. McLean with another spacious laugh.

But the cow-puncher had ceased to smile, and now, while Barker ran on exuberantly, McLean's wide-open eyes rested upon him, singular and intent, and in the hazel depths the last gleam of jocularity went out.

"That's where the strain comes, you see. Two sets of acquaintances. Grateful patients and loyal voters, and I've got to keep solid with both outfits, especially the wives and mothers. They're the people. So it's drums, and dolls, and sheep on wheels, and games, and monkeys on a stick, and the saleslady shows you a mechanical bear, and it costs too much, and you forget whether the Judge's second girl is Nellie or Susie, and—well, I'm just in for my annual circus this afternoon! You're in luck. Christmas don't trouble a chap fixed like you."

Lin McLean prolonged the sentence like a distant echo.

"A chap fixed like you!" The cow-puncher said it slowly to himself. "No, sure." He seemed to be watching Shorty and Chalkeye and Dollar Bill going down the road. "That's a new idea—Christmas," he murmured, for it was one of his oldest, and he was recalling the Christmas when he wore his first long trousers.

"Comes once a year pretty regular," remarked the prosperous Governor. "Seems often when you pay the bill."

"I haven't made a Christmas gift," pursued the cow-puncher, dreamily, "not fer—fer—Lord! it's a hundred years, I guess. I don't know anybody that has any right to look fer such a thing from me." This was indeed a new idea, and it did not stop the chill that was spreading in his heart.

"Gee whiz!" said Barker, briskly, "there goes twelve o'clock. I've got to make a start. Sorry you can't come and help me. Good-by."

His Excellency left the rider sitting motionless, and forgot him at once in his own preoccupation. He hastened upon his journey to the shops with the list, not in his pocket, but held firmly, like a plank in the imminence of shipwreck. The Nellies and Susies pervaded his mind, and he struggled with the presentiment that in a day or two he would recall some omitted and wretchedly important child. Quick hoof-beats made him look up, and Mr. McLean passed like a wind. The Governor absently watched him go, and saw the pony hunch and stiffen in the check of his speed when Lin overtook his companions. Down there in the distance they took a side street, and Barker rejoicingly remembered one more name, and wrote it as he walked. In a few minutes he had come to the shops and met face to face with Mr. McLean.

"The boys are seein' after my horse," Lin rapidly began, "and I've got to meet 'em sharp at one. We're twelve weeks shy on a square meal, yu' see, and our first has been a date from 'way back. I'd like to—" Here Mr. McLean cleared his throat, and his speech went less smoothly. "Doc, I'd like just for a while to watch yu' gettin'—them monkeys, yu' know."

The Governor expressed his agreeable surprise at this change of mind, and was glad of McLean's company and judgment during the impending selections. A picture of the cow-puncher and himself discussing a couple of dolls rose nimbly in Barker's mental eye, and it was with an imperfect honesty that he said, "You'll help me a heap."

And Lin, quite sincere, replied, "Thank yu'."

So together these two went Christmasing in the throng. Wyoming's Chief Executive knocked elbows with the spurred

and jingling waif, one man as good as another in that raw, hopeful, full-blooded cattle era, which now the sobered West remem-
bers as the days of its fond youth. For one man has been as
good as another in three places—Paradise before the fall; the
Rocky Mountains before the wire fence; and the Declaration of
Independence. And then this Governor, besides being young, almost as young as Lin McLean or the Chief Justice (who lately
had celebrated his thirty-second birthday), had in his doctoring
days at Drybone known the cow-puncher with that familiarity
which lasts a lifetime without breeding contempt; accordingly he
now laid a hand on Lin's tall shoulder and drew him among the
petticoats and toys.

Christmas filled the windows and Christmas stirred in mankind. Cheyenne, not over zealous in doctrine or litanies, and
with the opinion that a world in the hand is worth two in the
bush, nevertheless was flocking together, neighbor to think of
neighbor, and everyone to remember the children; a sacred assembly, after all, gathered to rehearse unwittingly the articles of
its belief, the Creed and Doctrine of the Child. Lin saw them
hurry and smile among the paper fairies; they questioned and
hesitated, crowded and made decisions, failed utterly to find the
right thing, forgot and hastened back, suffered all the various
desperations of the eleventh hour, and turned homeward, dropping their parcels with that undimmed good-will that once a
year makes gracious the universal human face. This brotherhood
swam and beamed before the cow-puncher's brooding eyes, and
in his ears the greeting of the season sang. Children escaped from
their mothers and ran chirping behind the counters to touch and
meddle in places forbidden. Friends dashed against each other
with rabbits and magic lanterns, greeted in haste, and were gone,
amid the sound of musical boxes.

Through this tinkle and bleating of little machinery the murmur of the human heart drifted in and out of McLean's hearing;
fragments of home talk, tenderness, economies, intimate first
names, and dinner hours; and whether it was joy or sadness, it

was in common; the world seemed knit in a single skein of home ties. Two or three came by whose purses must have been slender, and whose purchases were humble and chosen after much nice adjustment; and when one plain man dropped a word about both ends meeting, and the woman with him laid a hand on his arm, saying that the children must not feel this year was different, Lin made a step toward them. There were hours and spots where he could readily have descended upon them at that, played the rôle of clinking affluence, waved thanks aside with competent blasphemy, and tossing off some infamous whiskey, cantered away in the full self-conscious strut of the frontier. But here was not the moment; the abashed cow-puncher could make no such parade in this place. The people brushed by him back and forth, busy upon their errands, and aware of him scarcely more than if he had been a spirit looking on from the helpless dead; and so, while these weaving needs and kindnesses of man were within arm's touch of him, he was locked outside with his impulses. Barker had, in the natural press of customers, long parted from him, to become immersed in choosing and rejecting; and now, with a fair part of his mission accomplished, he was ready to go on to the next place, and turned to beckon McLean. He found him obliterated in a corner beside a life-sized image of Santa Claus, standing as still as the frosty saint.

"He looks livelier than you do," said the hearty Governor. " 'Fraid it's been slow waiting."

"No," replied the cow-puncher, thoughtfully. "No, I guess not."

This uncertainty was expressed with such gentleness that Barker roared. "You never did lie to me," he said, "long as I've known you. Well, never mind. I've got some real advice to ask you now."

At this Mr. McLean's face grew more alert. "Say, Doc," said he, "what do yu' want fer Christmas that nobody's likely to give yu'?"

"A big practice—big enough to interfere with my politics."

"What else? Things and truck, I mean."

"Oh—nothing I'll get. People don't give things much to fellows like me."

"Don't they? Don't they?"

"Why, you and Santa Claus weren't putting up any scheme on my stocking?"

"Well—"

"I believe you're in earnest!" cried his Excellency. "That's simply rich!" Here was a thing to relish! The Frontier comes to town "heeled for a big time," finds that presents are all the rage, and must immediately give somebody something. Oh, childlike, miscellaneous Frontier! So thought the good-hearted Governor; and it seems a venial misconception. "My dear fellow," he added, meaning as well as possible, "I don't want you to spend your money on me."

"I've got plenty all right," said Lin, shortly.

"Plenty's not the point. I'll take as many drinks as you please with you. You didn't expect anything from me?"

"That ain't—that don't—"

"There! Of course you didn't. Then, what are you getting proud about? Here's our shop." They stepped in from the street to new crowds and counters. "Now," pursued the Governor, "this is for a very particular friend of mine. Here they are. Now, which of those do you like best?"

They were sets of Tennyson in cases holding little volumes equal in number, but the binding various, and Mr. McLean reached his decision after one look. "That," said he, and laid a large muscular hand upon the Laureate. The young lady behind the counter spoke out acidly, and Lin pulled the abject hand away. His taste, however, happened to be sound, or at least it was at one with the Governor's; but now they learned that there was a distressing variance in the matter of price.

The Governor stared at the delicate article of his choice. "I know that Tennyson is what she—is what's wanted," he muttered; and, feeling himself nudged, looked round, and saw Lin's extended fist. This gesture he took for a facetious sympathy, and dolorously grasping the hand, found himself holding a lump of bills. Sheer amazement relaxed him, and the cow-puncher's matted wealth tumbled on the floor in sight of all people. Barker picked it up and gave it back. "No, no, no!" he said, mirthful over his own inclination to be annoyed. "You can't do that. I'm just as much obliged, Lin," he added.

"Jest as a loan, Doc. Some of it. I'm grass-bellied with spot cash."

A giggle behind the counter disturbed them both, but the sharp young lady was only dusting. The Governor at once paid haughtily for Tennyson's expensive works, and the cow-puncher pushed his discountenanced savings back into his clothes. Making haste to leave the book department of this shop, they regained a mutual ease, and the Governor became waggish over Lin's concern at being too rich. He suggested to him the list of delinquent taxpayers and the latest census from which to select indigent persons. He had patients, too, whose inveterate pennilessness he could swear cheerfully to—"since you want to bolt from your own money," he remarked.

"Yes, I'm a green horse," assented Mr. McLean, gallantly. "Ain't used to the looks of a twenty-dollar bill, and I shy at 'em."

From his face—that jocular mask—one might have counted him the most serene and careless of vagrants, and in his words only the ordinary voice of banter spoke to the Governor. A good woman, it may well be, would have guessed before this the sensitive soul in the blundering body; but Barker saw just the familiar, whimsical, happy-go-lucky McLean, and so he went gayly and innocently on, treading upon holy ground. "I've got it!" he exclaimed. "Give your wife something."

The ruddy cow-puncher grinned. He had passed through the world of woman with but few delays, rejoicing in informal and transient entanglements; and he welcomed the turn which the conversation seemed now to be taking. "If you'll give me her name and address," said he, with the future entirely in his mind.

"Why, Laramie!" and the Governor feigned surprise.

"Say, Doc," said Lin, uneasily, "none of 'em 'ain't married me since I saw yu' last."

"Then, she hasn't written from Laramie," said the hilarious Governor, and Mr. McLean understood, and winced in his spirit, deep down. "Gee whiz!" went on Barker; "I'll never forget you and Lusk that day!"

But the mask fell now. "You're talking of his wife, not mine," said the cow-puncher very quietly, and smiling no more. "And, Doc, I'm going to say a word to yu', for I know yu've always been my good friend. I'll never forget that day myself—but I don't want to be reminded of it."

"I'm a fool, Lin," said the Governor, generous instantly. "I never supposed—"

"I know yu' didn't, Doc. It ain't you that's the fool. And in a way—in a way—" Lin's speech ended among his crowding memories, and Barker, seeing how wistful his face had turned, waited. "But I ain't quite the same fool I was before that happened to me," the cow-puncher resumed. "Though maybe my actions don't show to be wiser. I know that there was better luck than a man like me had any call to look for."

The sobered Barker said, simply, "Yes, Lin." He was put to thinking by these words from the unsuspected inner man.

Out in the Bow Leg country Lin McLean had met a woman with thick red cheeks, calling herself by a maiden name; and this was his whole knowledge of her when he put her one morning astride a Mexican saddle, and took her fifty miles to a magistrate and made her his lawful wife to the best of his ability and belief. His sage-brush intimates were confident he would never have done it but for a rival. Racing the rival and beating him had swept Mr. McLean past his own intentions, and the marriage was an inadvertence. "He jest bumped into it before he could pull up," they explained; and this casualty resulting from Mr. McLean's sporting blood had entertained several hundred square miles of alkali. For the newmade husband the joke soon died. In the immediate weeks that came upon him he tasted a bitterness worse than in all his life before, and learned also how deep the woman, when once she begins, can sink beneath the man in baseness. That was a knowledge of which he had lived innocent until this time. But he carried his outward self serenely, so that citizens in Cheyenne who saw the cow-puncher with his bride argued shrewdly that men of that sort liked women of that sort; and before the strain had broken his endurance an unexpected first husband, named Lusk, had appeared one Sunday in the street, prosperous, forgiving, and exceedingly drunk. To the arms of Lusk she went back in the public street, deserting McLean in the presence of Cheyenne; and when Cheyenne saw this, and learned how she had been Mrs. Lusk for eight long, if intermittent, years, Cheyenne laughed loudly. Lin McLean laughed too, and went about his business, ready to swagger at the necessary moment, and with the necessary kind of joke always ready to shield his hurt spirit. And soon, of course, the matter grew stale, seldom raked up in the Bow Leg country where Lin had been at work; so lately he had begun to remember other things beside the smouldering humiliation.

"Is she with him?" he asked Barker, and musingly listened while Barker told him. The Governor had thought to make it a racy story, with the moral that the joke was now on Lusk; but that inner man had spoken and revealed the cow-puncher to him in a new and complicated light, hence he quieted the proposed lively cadence and vocabulary of his anecdote about the house of Lusk, but instead of narrating how Mrs. beat Mr. on Mondays, Wednesdays and Fridays, and Mr. took his turn the odd days, thus getting one ahead of his lady, while the kid Lusk had outlined his opinion of the family by recently skipping to parts unknown, Barker detailed these incidents more gravely, adding that Laramie believed Mrs. Lusk addicted to opium.

"I don't guess I'll leave my card on 'em," said McLean, grimly, "if I strike Laramie."

"You don't mind my saying I think you're well out of that scrape?" Barker ventured.

"Shucks, no! That's all right, Doc. Only—yu' see now. A man gets tired pretending—onced in a while."

Time had gone while they were in talk, and it was now half after one and Mr. McLean late for that long-plotted first square meal. So the friends shook hands, wishing each other Merry Christmas, and the cow-puncher hastened toward his chosen companions through the stirring cheerfulness of the season. His play hour had made a dull beginning among the toys. He had come upon people engaged in a pleasant game, and waited, shy and well-disposed, for some bidding to join, but they had gone on playing with each other and left him out. And now he went along in a sort of hurry to escape from that loneliness where his human promptings had been lodged with him useless. Here was Cheyenne, full of holiday for sale, and he with his pockets full of money to buy; and when he thought of Shorty and Chalkeye and Dollar Bill, those dandies to hit a town with, he stepped out with a brisk false hope. It was with a mental hurrah and a foretaste of a good time coming that he put on his town clothes, after shaving and admiring himself, and sat down to the square meal. He ate away and drank with a robust imitation of enjoyment that took in even himself at first. But the sorrowful process of his spirit went on, for all he could do. As he groped for the contentment which he saw around him he began to receive the jokes with counterfeit mirth. Memories took the place of anticipation, and through their moody shiftings he began to feel a distaste for the company of his friends and a shrinking from their lively voices. He blamed them for this at once. He was surprised to think he had never recognized before how light a weight was Shorty; and here was Chalkeye, who knew better, talking religion after two glasses. Presently this attack of noticing his friends' shortcomings mastered him, and his mind, according to its wont, changed at a stroke. "I'm celebrating no Christmas with this crowd," said the inner man; and when they had

333

next remembered Lin McLean in their hilarity he was gone.

Governor Barker, finishing his purchases at half past three, went to meet a friend come from Evanston. Mr. McLean was at the railway station, buying a ticket for Denver.

"Denver!" exclaimed the amazed Governor.

"That's what I said," stated Mr. McLean, doggedly.

"Gee whiz!" went his Excellency. "What are you going to do there?"

"Get good and drunk."

"Can't you find enough whiskey in Cheyenne?"

"I'm drinking champagne this trip."

The cow-puncher went out on the platform and got aboard, and the train moved off. Barker had walked out too in his surprise, and as he stared after the last car, Mr. McLean waved his wide hat defiantly and went inside the door.

"And he says he's got maturity," Barker muttered. "I've known him since seventy-six, and he's kept about eight right along." The Governor was cross, and sorry, and presently crosser. His jokes about Lin's marriage came back to him and put him in a rage with the departed fool. "Yes, about eight. Or six," said his Excellency, justifying himself by the past. For he had first known Lin, the boy of nineteen, supreme in length of limb and recklessness, breaking horses and feeling for an early mustache. Next, when the mustache was nearly accomplished, he had mended the boy's badly broken thigh at Drybone. His skill (and Lin's utter health) had wrought so swift a healing that the surgeon overflowed with the pride of science, and over the bandages would explain the human body technically to his wild-eyed and flattered patient. Thus young Lin heard all about tibia, and comminuted, and other glorious new words, and when sleepless would rehearse them. Then, with the bone so nearly knit that the patient might leave the ward on crutches to sit each morning in Barker's room as a privilege, the disobedient child of twenty-one had slipped out of the hospital and hobbled hastily to the hog ranch, where whiskey and variety waited for a languishing convalescent. Here he grew gay, and was soon carried back with the leg re-fractured. Yet Barker's surgical rage was disarmed, the patient was so forlorn over his doctor's professional chagrin.

"I suppose it ain't no better this morning, Doc" he had said, humbly, after a new week of bed and weights.

"Your right leg's going to be shorter. That's all."

"Oh, gosh! I've been and spoiled yer comminuted fee-mur! Ain't I a son of a gun?"

You could not chide such a boy as this; and in time's due course he had walked jauntily out into the world with legs of equal length after all, and in his stride the slightest halt possible. And Doctor Barker had missed the child's conversation. Today his mustache was a perfected thing, and he in the late end of his twenties.

"He'll wake up about noon tomorrow in a dive without a cent," said Barker. "Then he'll come back on a freight and begin over again."

At the Denver station Lin McLean passed through the shout-ings and omnibuses, and came to the beginning of Seventeenth Street, where is the first saloon. A customer was ordering Hot Scotch; and because he liked the smell and had not thought of the mixture for a number of years, Lin took Hot Scotch. Coming out upon the pavement he looked across and saw a saloon oppo-site with brighter globes and windows more prosperous. That should have been his choice; lemon peel would undoubtedly be fresher over there; and over he went at once, to begin the whole thing properly. In such frozen weather no drink could be more timely, and he sat, to enjoy without haste its mellow fitness. Once again on the pavement, he looked along the street toward uptown beneath the crisp, cold electric lights, and three little bootblacks gathered where he stood and cried, "Shine? Shine?" at him. Remembering that you took the third turn to the right to get the best dinner in Denver, Lin hit on the skilful plan of stopping at all Hot Scotches between; but the next occurred within a few yards, and it was across the street. This one being attained and appreciated, he found that he must cross back again or skip number four. At this rate he would not be dining in time to see much of the theater, and he stopped to consider. It was a German place he had just quitted, and a huge light poured out on him from its window, which the proprietor's father-land sentiment had made into a show. Lights shone among a well-set pine forest, where beery, jovial gnomes sat on roots and reached upward to Santa Claus; he, grinning, fat, and Teutonic, held in his right hand forever a foaming glass and forever in his left a string of sausages that dangled down among the gnomes. With his American back to this, the cow-puncher, wearing the same serious, absent face he had not changed since he ran away from himself at Cheyenne, considered carefully the Hot Scotch question, and which side of the road to take and stick to, while the little bootblacks found him once more and cried, "Shine? Shine?" monotonous as snow-birds. He settled to stay over here with the south-side Scotches, and the little one-note song reaching his attention, he suddenly shoved his foot at the nearest boy, who lightly sprang away.

"Dare you to touch him!" piped a snow-bird, dangerously. They were in short trousers, and the eldest enemy, it may be, was ten.

"Don't hit me," said Mr. McLean. "I'm innocent."

"Well, you leave him be," said one.

"What's he layin' to kick you for, Billy? 'Tain't yer pop, is it?"

"Naw!" said Billy in scorn. "Father never kicked me. Don't know who he is."

"He's a special!" shrilled the leading bird, sensationally. "He's got a badge, and he's goin' to arrest yer."

Two of them hopped instantly to the safe middle of the street, and scattered with practised strategy; but Billy stood his ground. "Dare you to arrest me!" said he.

"What'll you give me not to?" inquired Lin, and he put his hands in his pockets, arms akimbo.

"Nothing; I've done nothing," announced Billy firmly. But even in the last syllable his voice suddenly failed, a terror filled his eyes, and he, too, sped into the middle of the street.

"What's he claim you lifted?" inquired the leader, with eagerness. "Tell him you haven't been inside a store today. We can prove it!" they screamed to the special officer.

"Say," said the slow-spoken Lin from the pavement, "you're poor judges of a badge, you fellers."

His tone pleased them where they stood, wide apart from each other.

Mr. McLean also remained stationary in the bluish illumination of the window. "Why, if any policeman was caught wearin' this here," said he, following his sprightly invention, "he'd get arrested himself."

This struck them extremely. They began to draw together, Billy lingering the last.

"If it's your idea," pursued Mr. McLean, alluringly, as the three took cautious steps nearer the curb, "that blue clasped hands in a circle of red stars gives the bearer the right to put folks in the jug—why, I'll get somebody else to black my boots fer a dollar."

The three made a swift rush, fell on simultaneous knees, and clattering their boxes down, began to spit in an industrious circle.

"Easy!" wheedled Mr. McLean, and they looked up at him, staring and fascinated. "Not having three feet," said the cowpuncher, always grave and slow, "I can only give two this here job."

"He's got a big pistol and a belt!" exulted the leader, who had precociously felt beneath Lin's coat.

"You're a smart boy," said Lin, regarding him, "and yu' find a man out right away. Now you stand off and tell me all about myself while they fix the boots—and a dollar goes to the quickest through."

Young Billy and his tow-headed competitor flattened down,

337

each to a boot, with all their might, while the leader ruefully contemplated Mr. McLean.

"That's a Colt .45 you've got," ventured he.

"Right again. Some day, maybe, you'll be wearing one of your own, if the angels don't pull yu' before you're ripe."

"I'm through!" sang out Towhead, rising in haste.

Small Billy was struggling still, but leaped at that, the two heads bobbing to a level together; and Mr. McLean, looking down, saw that the arrangement had not been a good one for the boots.

"Will you kindly referee," said he, forgivingly, to the leader, "and decide which of them smears is the awfulest?"

But the leader looked the other way and played upon a mouth-organ.

"Well, that saves me money," said Mr. McLean, jingling his pocket. "I guess you've both won." He handed each of them a dollar. "Now," he continued, "I jest dassent show these boots uptown; so this time it's a dollar for the best shine."

The two went palpitating at their brushes again, and the leader played his mouth-organ with brilliant unconcern. Lin, tall and brooding, leaned against the jutting sill of the window, a figure somehow plainly strange in town, while through the bright plate-glass Santa Claus, holding out his beer and sausages, perpetually beamed.

Billy was laboring gallantly, but it was labor, the cow-puncher perceived, and Billy no seasoned expert. "See here," said Lin, stooping, "I'll show yu' how it's done. He's playin' that toon cross-eyed enough to steer anybody crooked. There. Keep your blacking soft, and work with a dry brush."

"Lemme," said Billy. "I've got to learn." So he finished the boot his own way with wiry determination, breathing and repolishing; and this event was also adjudged a dead heat, with results gratifying to both parties. So here was their work done, and more money in their pockets than from all the other boots and shoes of this day; and Towhead and Billy did not wish for further trade, but to spend this handsome fortune as soon as might be. Yet they delayed in the brightness of the window, drawn by curiosity near this new kind of man whose voice held them and whose remarks dropped them into constant uncertainty. Even the omitted leader had been unable to go away and nurse his pride alone.

"Is that a secret society?" inquired Towhead, lifting a finger at the badge.

Mr. McLean nodded. "Turruble," said he.

"You're a Wells & Fargo detective," asserted the leader.

"Play your harp," said Lin.

"Are you a—a desperaydo?" whispered Towhead.

"Oh, my!" observed Mr. McLean, sadly; "what hez our Jack been readin'?"

"He's a cattle-man!" cried Billy. "I seen his heels."

"That's you!" said the discovered puncher, with approval. "You'll do. But I bet you can't tell me what we wearers of this badge have sworn to do this night."

At this they craned their necks and glared at him.

"We—are—sworn—don't yu' jump, now, and give me away —sworn—to—blow off three bootblacks to a dinner."

"Ah, pshaw!" They backed away, bristling with distrust.

"That's the oath, fellers. Yu' may as well make your minds up —for I hev it to do!"

"Dare you to! Ah!"

"And after dinner it's the Opera-House, to see The Children of Captain Grant!"

They screamed shrilly at him, keeping off beyond the curb.

"I can't waste my time on such smart boys," said Mr. McLean, rising lazily to his full height from the window-sill. "I am goin' somewhere to find boys that ain't so turruble quick stampeded by a roast turkey."

He began to lounge slowly away, serious as he had been throughout, and they stopping their noise short, swiftly picked up their boxes and followed him. Some change in the current of electricity that fed the window disturbed its sparkling light, so that Santa Claus, with his arms stretched out behind the departing cow-puncher, seemed to be smiling more broadly from the midst of his flickering brilliance.

On their way to turkey the host and his guests exchanged but few remarks. He was full of good-will, and threw off a comment or two that would have led to conversation under almost any circumstances save these; but the minds of the guests were too distracted by this whole state of things for them to be capable of more than keeping after Mr. McLean in silence, at a wary interval, and with their mouths, during most of the journey, open. The badge, the pistol, their patron's talk, and the unusual dollars, wakened wide their bent for the unexpected, their street affinity for the spur of the moment; they believed slimly in the turkey part of it, but what this man might do next, to be there when he did it, and not to be trapped kept their wits jumping deliciously; so when they saw him stop, they stopped instantly too, ten feet out of reach. This was Denver's most civilized restaurant—that one which Mr. McLean had remembered, with foreign dishes and private rooms, where he had promised himself, among other things, champagne. Mr. McLean had never been inside it, but heard a tale from a friend; and now he caught a sudden sight of people among geraniums, with plumes and white shirt fronts, very elegant. It must have been several minutes that he stood contemplating the entrance and the luxurious couples which went in.

"Plumb French!" he observed at length; and then, "Shucks!" in a key less confident, while his guests ten feet away watched him narrowly. "They're eatin' patty de parley voo in there," he muttered, and the three bootblacks came beside him. "Say, fellers," said Lin, confidingly, "I wasn't raised good enough for them dude dishes. What do yu' say? I'm after a place where yu' can mention oyster stoo without givin' anybody a fit. What do yu' say, boys?"

That lighted the divine spark of brotherhood!

"Ah, you come along with us—we'll take yer! You don't want to go in there. We'll show yer the boss place in Market Street. We won't lose yer." So shouting together in their shrill little city trebles, they clustered about him, and one pulled at his coat to start him. He started obediently, and walked in their charge, they leading the way.

"Christmas is comin' now, sure," said Lin, grinning to himself. "It ain't exactly what I'd figured on." It was the first time he had laughed since Cheyenne, and he brushed a hand over his eyes, that were dim with the new warmth in his heart.

Believing at length in him and his turkey, the alert street faces, so suspicious of the unknown, looked at him with ready intimacy as they went along; and soon, in the friendly desire to make him acquainted with Denver, the three were patronizing him. Only Billy, perhaps, now and then stole at him a doubtful look.

The large Country Mouse listened solemnly to his three Town Mice, who presently introduced him to the place in Market Street. It was not boss, precisely, and Denver knows better neighborhoods; but the turkey and the oyster stew were there, with catsup and vegetables in season, and several choices of pie. Here the Country Mouse became again efficient; and to witness his liberal mastery of ordering and imagine his pocket and its wealth, which they had heard and partly seen, renewed in the guests a transient awe. As they dined, however, and found the host as frankly ravenous as themselves, this reticence evaporated, and they all grew fluent with oaths and opinions. At one or two words, indeed, Mr. McLean stared and had a slight sense of blushing.

"Have a cigarette?" said the leader, over his pie.

"Thank yu'," said Lin. "I won't smoke, if yu'll excuse me." He had devised a wholesome meal, with water to drink.

"Chewin's no good at meals," continued the boy. "Don't you use tobaccer?"

"Onced in a while."

The leader spat brightly. "He 'ain't learned yet," said he,

slanting his elbows at Billy and sliding a match over his rump. "But beer, now—I never seen anything in it." He and Towhead soon left Billy and his callow profanities behind, and engaged in a town conversation that silenced him, and set him listening with all his admiring young might. Nor did Mr. McLean join in the talk, but sat embarrassed by this knowledge, which seemed about as much as he knew himself.

"I'll be goshed," he thought, "if I'd caught on to half that when I was streakin' around in short pants! Maybe they grow up quicker now." But now the Country Mouse perceived Billy's eager and attentive apprenticeship. "Hello, boys!" he said, "that theater's got a big start on us."

They had all forgotten he had said anything about theater; and other topics left their impatient minds, while the Country Mouse paid the bill and asked to be guided to the Opera-house. "This man here will look out for your blackin' and truck, and let yu' have it in the morning."

They were very late. The spectacle had advanced far into passages of the highest thrill, and Denver's eyes were riveted upon a ship and some icebergs. The party found its seat during several beautiful lime-light effects, and that remarkable fly-buzzing of violins which is pronounced so helpful in times of peril and sentiment. The children of Captain Grant had been tracking their father all over the equator and other scenic spots, and now the north pole was about to impale them. The Captain's youngest child, perceiving a hummock rushing at them with a sudden motion, loudly shouted, "Sister, the ice is closing in!" and she replied, chastely, "Then let us pray." It was a superb tableau: the ice split, and the sun rose and joggled at once to the zenith. The act-drop fell, and male Denver, wrung to its religious deeps, went out to the rum-shop.

Of course Mr. McLean and his party did not do this. The party had applauded exceedingly the defeat of the elements, and the leader, with Towhead, discussed the probable chances of the ship's getting further south in the next act. Until lately Billy's doubt of the cow-puncher had lingered; but during this intermission whatever had been holding out in him seemed won, and in his eyes, that he turned stealthily upon his unconscious quiet neighbor shone the beginnings of hero worship.

"Don't you think this is splendid?" said he.

"Splendid," Lin replied, a trifle remotely.

"Don't you like it when they all get balled up and get out that way?"

"Humming," said Lin.

"Don't you guess it's just girls, though, that do that?"

"What, young feller?"

"Why, all that prayer-saying an' stuff."

"I guess it must be."

"She said to do it when the ice scared her, an' of course a man had to do what she wanted him."

"Sure."

"Well, do you believe they'd 'a' done it if she hadn't been on that boat, an' clung around an' cried an' everything, an' made her friends feel bad?"

"I hardly expect they would," replied the honest Lin, and then, suddenly mindful of Billy, "except there wasn't nuthin' else they could think of," he added, wishing to speak favorably of the custom.

"Why, that chunk of ice weren't so awful big anyhow. I'd 'a' shoved her off with a pole. Wouldn't you?"

"Butted her like a ram," exclaimed Mr. McLean.

"Well, I don't say my prayers any more. I told Mr. Perkins I wasn't a-going to, an' he—I think he is a flubdub anyway."

"I'll bet he is!" said Lin, sympathetically. He was scarcely a prudent guardian.

"I told him straight, an' he looked at me an' down he flops on his knees. An' he made 'em all flop, but I told him I didn't care for them putting up any camp-meeting over me; an' he

343

says, 'I'll lick you,' an' I says, 'Dare you to!' I told him mother kep' a-licking me for nothing, an' I'd not pray for her, not in Sunday-school or anywheres else. Do you pray much?"

"No," replied Lin, uneasily.

"There! I told him a man didn't, an' he said then a man went to hell. 'You lie; father ain't going to hell,' I says, and you'd ought to heard the first class laugh right out loud, girls an' boys. An' he was that mad! But I didn't care. I came here with fifty cents."

"Yu' must have felt like a millionaire."

"Ah, I felt all right! I bought papers an' sold 'em, an' got more an' saved, an' got my box an' blacking outfit. I weren't going to be licked by her just because she felt like it, an' she feeling like it most any time. Lemme see your pistol."

"You wait," said Lin. "After this show is through I'll put it on you."

"Will you, honest? Belt an' everything? Did you ever shoot a bear?"

"Lord! lots."

"Honest? Silvertips?"

"Silvertips, cinnamon, black, and I roped a cub onced."

"O-h! I never shot a bear."

"You'd ought to try it."

"I'm a-going to. I'm a-going to camp out in the mountains. I'd like to see you when you camp. I'd like to camp with you. Mightn't I some time?" Billy had drawn nearer to Lin, and was looking up at him adoringly.

"You bet!" said Lin; and though he did not, perhaps, entirely mean this, it was with a curiously softened face that he began to look at Billy. As with dogs, and his horse, so always he played with what children he met—the few in his sage-brush world; but this was ceasing to be quite play for him, and his hand went to the boy's shoulder.

"Father took me camping with him once, the time mother

was off. Father gets awful drunk, too. I've quit Laramie for good."

Lin sat up, and his hand gripped the boy. "Laramie!" said he, almost shouting it. "Yu'—yu'—is your name Lusk?"

But the boy had shrunk from him instantly. "You're not going to take me home?" he piteously wailed.

"Heaven and heavens!" murmured Lin McLean. "So you're her kid."

He relaxed again, down in his chair, his legs stretched their straight length below the chair in front. He was waked from his bewilderment by a brushing under him, and there was young Billy diving for escape to the aisle, like the cornered city mouse that he was. Lin nipped that poor little attempt and had the limp Billy seated inside again before the two in discussion beyond had seen anything. He had said not a word to the boy, and now watched his unhappy eyes seizing upon the various exits and dispositions of the theater; nor could he imagine anything to tell him that should restore the perished confidence. "Why did yu' head him off?" he asked himself unexpectedly, and found that he did not seem to know; but as he watched the restless and estranged runaway he grew more and more sorrowful. "I jest hate him to think that of me," he reflected. The curtain rose, and he saw Billy make up his mind to wait until they should all be going out in the crowd. While the children of Captain Grant grew hotter and hotter upon their father's geographic trail, Lin sat saying to himself a number of contradictions. "He's nothing to me; what's any of them to me?" Driven to bay by his bewilderment, he restated the facts of the past. "Why, she'd deserted him and Lusk before she'd ever laid eyes on me. I needn't to bother myself. He wasn't never even my step-kid." The past, however, brought no guidance. "Lord, what's the thing to do about this? If I had any home— This is a stinkin' world in some respects," said Mr. McLean, aloud, unknowingly. The lady in the chair beneath which the cow-puncher had his legs nudged her husband. They took it for emotion over the sad fortunes of

Captain Grant, and their backs shook. Presently each turned, and saw the singular man with untamed wide-open eyes glowering at the stage, and both backs shook again.

Once more his hand was laid on Billy. "Say!"

The boy glanced at him, and quickly away.

"Look at me, and listen."

Billy swervingly obeyed.

"I ain't after yu', and never was. This here's your business, not mine. Are yu' listenin' good?"

The boy made a nod, and Lin proceeded, whispering: "Yu've got no call to believe what I say to yu'—yu've been lied to, I guess, pretty often. So I'll not stop yu' runnin' and hidin', and I'll never give it away I saw yu', but yu' keep doin' what yu' please. I'll jest go now. I've saw all I want, but you and your friends stay with it till it quits. If yu' happen to wish to speak to me about that pistol or bears, you come around to Smith's Palace—that's the boss hotel here, ain't it? and if yu' don't come too late I'll not be gone to bed. But this time of night I'm liable to get sleepy. Tell your friends good-by for me, and be good to yourself. I've appreciated yer company."

Mr. McLean entered Smith's Palace, and engaging a room with two beds in it, did a little delicate lying by means of the truth. "It's a lost boy—a runaway." He told the clerk. "He'll not be extra clean, I expect, if he does come. Maybe he'll give me the slip, and I'll have a job cut out tomorrow. I'll thank yu' to put my money in your safe."

The clerk placed himself at the disposal of the secret service, and Lin walked up and down, looking at the railroad photographs for some ten minutes, when Master Billy peered in from the street.

"Hello!" said Mr. McLean, casually, and returned to a fine picture of Pike's Peak.

Billy observed him for a space, and receiving no further attention, came stepping along. "I'm not a-going back to Laramie," he stated, warningly.

"I wouldn't," said Lin. "It ain't half the town Denver is. Well, good-night. Sorry yu' couldn't call sooner—I'm dead sleepy."

"O-h!" Billy stood blank. "I wish I'd shook the darned old show. Say—lemme black your boots in the morning?"

"Not sure my train don't go too early."

"I'm up! I'm up! I get around to all of 'em."

"Where do yu' sleep?"

"Sleeping with the engine-man now. Why can't you put that on me to-night?"

"Goin' up stairs. This gentleman wouldn't let you go up stairs."

But the earnestly petitioned clerk consented, and Billy was the first to hasten into the room. He stood rapturous while Lin buckled the belt round his scanty stomach, and ingeniously buttoned the suspenders outside the accoutrement to retard its immediate descent to earth.

"Did it ever kill a man?" asked Billy, touching the six-shooter.

"No. It ain't never had to do that, but I expect maybe it's stopped some killin' me."

"Oh, leave me wear it just a minute! Do you collect arrowheads? I think they're bully. There's the finest one you ever seen." He brought out the relic, tightly wrapped in paper, several pieces. "I foun' it myself, camping with father. It was sticking in a crack right on top of a rock, but nobody'd seen it till I came along. Ain't it fine?"

Mr. McLean pronounced it a gem.

"Father an' me found a lot, an' they made mother mad laying around an' she threw 'em out. She takes stuff from Kelley's."

"Who's Kelley?"

"He keeps the drug store at Laramie. Mother gets awful funny. That's how she was when I came home. For I told Mr. Perkins he lied, an' I ran then. An' I knowed well enough she'd lick me when she got through her spell—an' father can't stop her, an' I —ah, I was sick of it! She's lamed me up twice beating me—an' Perkins wanting me to say 'God bless my mother!' a-getting up

347

and a-going to bed—he's a flub-dub! An' so I cleared out. But I'd just as leaves said for God to bless father—an' you. I'll do it now if you say it's any sense."

Mr. McLean sat down in a chair. "Don't yu' do it now," said he.

"You wouldn't like mother," Billy continued. "You can keep that." He came to Lin and placed the arrow-head in his hands, standing beside him. "Do you like birds' eggs? I collect them. I got twenty-five kinds—sage-hen, an' blue grouse, an' willow-grouse, an' lots more kinds harder—but I couldn't bring all them from Laramie. I brought the magpie's, though. D'you care to see a magpie egg? Well, you stay tomorrow an' I'll show you that an' some other things I got, the engine-man lets me keep there, for there's boys that would steal an egg. An' I could take you where we could fire that pistol. Bet you don't know what that is!"

He brought out a small tin box shaped like a thimble, in which were things that rattled.

Mr. McLean gave it up.

"That's kinni-kinnic seed. You can have that, for I got some more with the engine-man."

Lin received this second token also, and thanked the giver for it. His first feeling had been to prevent the boy's parting with his treasures, but something that came not from the polish of manners and experience made him know that he should take them. Billy talked away, laying bare his little soul; the street boy that was not quite come made place for the child that was not quite gone, and unimportant words and confidences dropped from him disjointed as he climbed to the knee of Mr. McLean, and inadvertently took that cow-puncher for some sort of parent he had not hitherto met. It lasted but a short while, however, for he went to sleep in the middle of a sentence, with his head upon Lin's breast. The man held him perfectly still, because he had not the faintest notion that Billy would be impossible to disturb. At length he spoke to him, suggesting that bed might prove more comfortable, and finding how it was, rose and undressed the boy and laid him between the sheets. The arms and legs seemed aware of the moves required of them, and stirred conveniently; and directly the head was upon the pillow the whole small frame burrowed down, without the opening of an eye or a change in the breathing. Lin stood some time by the bedside, with his eyes on the long curling lashes and the curly hair. Then he glanced craftily at the door of the room, and at himself in the looking-glass. He stooped and kissed Billy on the forehead, and rising from that, gave himself a hangdog stare in the mirror, and soon in his own bed was sleeping the sound sleep of health.

He was faintly roused by the church bells, and lay still, lingering with his sleep, his eyes closed, and his thoughts unshaped. As he became slowly aware of the morning, the ringing and the light reached him, and he waked wholly, and still lying quiet, considered the strange room filled with the bells and the sun of the winter's day. "Where have I struck now?" he inquired; and as last night returned abruptly upon his mind, he raised himself on his arm.

There sat Responsibility in a chair, washed clean and dressed, watching him.

"You're awful late," said Responsibility. "But I weren't a-going without telling you good-by."

"Go?" exclaimed Lin. "Go where? Yu' surely ain't leavin' me to eat breakfast alone?" The cow-puncher made his voice very plaintive. Set Responsibility free after all his trouble to catch him? This was more than he could do!

"I've got to go. If I'd thought you'd want for me to stay— why, you said you was a-going by the early train!"

"But the durned thing's got away on me," said Lin, smiling sweetly from the bed.

"If I hadn't a-promised them—"

"Who?"

"Sidney Ellis and Pete Goode. Why, you know them; you dined with them."

"Shucks!"

"We're a-going to have fun today."

"Oh!"

"For it's Christmas, an' we've bought some good cigars, an' Pete says he'll learn me sure. O' course I've smoked some, you know. But I'd just as leaves staid with you if I'd only knowed sooner. I wish you lived here. Did you smoke whole big cigars when you was beginning?"

"Do you like flapjacks and maple syrup?" inquired the artful McLean. "That's what I'm figurin' on inside twenty minutes."

"Twenty minutes! If they'd wait—"

"See here, Bill. They've quit expecting yu', don't yu' think? I'd ought to waked, yu' see, but I slep' and slep', and kep' yu' from meetin' your engagements, yu' see—for you couldn't go, of course. A man couldn't treat a man that way now, could he?"

"Course he couldn't," said Billy, brightening.

"And they wouldn't wait, yu' see. They wouldn't fool away Christmas, that only comes onced a year, kickin' their heels and sayin', 'Where's Billy?' They'd say, 'Bill hez sure made other arrangements, which he'll explain to us at his leesyure.' And they'd skip with the cigars."

The advocate paused, effectively, and from his bolster regarded Billy with a convincing eye.

"That's so," said Billy.

"And where would yu' be then, Bill? In the street, out of friends, out of Christmas, and left both ways, no tobaccer and no flapjacks. Now, Bill, what do yu' say to us putting up a Christmas deal together? Jest you and me?"

"I'd like that," said Billy. "Is it all day?"

"I was thinkin' of all day," said Lin. "I'll not make yu' do anything yu'd rather not."

"Ah, they can smoke without me," said Billy, with sudden acrimony. "I'll see 'em tomorro'."

"That's you!" cried Mr. McLean. "Now, Bill, you hustle down and tell them to keep a table for us. I'll get my clothes on and follow yu'."

The boy went, and Mr. McLean procured hot water and dressed himself, tying his scarf with great care. "Wished I'd a clean shirt," said he. "But I don't look very bad. Shavin' yesterday afternoon was a good move." He picked up the arrow-head and the kinni-kinnic, and was particular to store them in his safest pocket. "I ain't sure whether you're crazy or not," said he to the man in the looking-glass. "I ain't never been sure." And he slammed the door and went down stairs.

He found young Bill on guard over a table for four, with all the chairs tilted against it as warning to strangers. No one sat at any other table or came into the room, for it was late, and the place quite emptied of breakfasters, and the several entertained waiters had gathered behind Billy's important-looking back. Lin provided a thorough meal, and Billy pronounced the flannel cakes superior to flapjacks, which were not upon the bill of fare.

"I'd like to see you often," said he. "I'll come and see you if you don't live too far."

"That's the trouble," said the cow-puncher. "I do. Awful far." He stared out of the window.

"Well, I might come some time. I wish you'd write me a letter. Can you write?"

"What's that? Can I write? Oh yes."

"I can write, an' I can read too. I've been to school in Sidney, Nebraska, an' Magaw, Kansas, an' Salt Lake—that's the finest town except Denver."

Billy fell into that cheerful strain of comment which, unreplied to, yet goes on contented and self-sustaining, while Mr. McLean gave amiable signs of assent, but chiefly looked out of the window; and when the now interested waiter said respectfully that he desired to close the room they went out to the office, where the money was got out of the safe and the bill paid.

The streets were full of the bright sun, and seemingly at Denver's gates stood the mountains sparkling; an air crisp and

pleasant wafted from their peaks; no smoke hung among the
roofs, and the sky spread wide over the city without a stain; it
was holiday up among the chimneys and tall buildings, and
down among the quiet ground-stories below as well; and presently from their scattered pinnacles through the town the bells
broke out against the jocund silence of the morning.

"Don't you like music?" inquired Billy.

"Yes," said Lin.

Ladies with their husbands and children were passing and
meeting orderly yet gayer than if it were only Sunday, and the
salutations of Christmas came now and again to the cow-
puncher's ears; but today, possessor of his own share in this, Lin
looked at everyone with a sort of friendly challenge, and young
Billy talked along beside him.

"Don't you think we could go in here?" Billy asked. A church
door was open, and the rich organ sounded through to the pavement. "They've good music here, an' they keep it up without
much talking between. I've been in lots of times."

They went in and sat to hear the music. Better than the organ,
it seemed to them, were the harmonious voices raised from somewhere outside, like unexpected visitants; and the pair sat in their
back seat, too deep in listening to the Processional Hymn to
think of rising in decent imitation of those around them. The
crystal melody of the refrain especially reached their understand-
ings, and when for the fourth time "Shout the glad tidings, ex-
ultingly sing," pealed forth and ceased, both the delighted faces
fell.

"Don't you wish there was more?" Billy whispered.

"Wish there was a hundred verses," answered Lin.

But canticles and responses followed, with so little talking
between them they were held spellbound, seldom thinking to
rise or kneel. Lin's eyes roved over the church, dwelling upon the
pillars in their evergreen, the flowers and leafy wreaths, the texts
of white and gold. " 'Peace, Good-will toward Men,' " he read.
"That's so. Peace and Good-will. Yes, that's so. I expect they got

that somewheres in the Bible. It's awful good, and yu'd never think of it yourself."

There was a touch on his arm, and a woman handed a book to him. "This is the hymn we have now," she whispered, gently; and Lin, blushing scarlet, took it passively, without a word. He and Billy stood up and held the book together, dutifully reading the words:

> "It came upon the midnight clear,
> That glorious song of old,
> From angels bending near the earth
> To touch their harps of gold;
> Peace on the earth—"

This tune was more beautiful than all, and Lin lost himself in it, until he found Billy recalling him with a finger upon the words, the concluding ones:

> "And the whole world sent back the song
> Which now the angels sing."

The music rose and descended to its lovely and simple end; and, for a second time in Denver, Lin brushed a hand across his eyes. He turned his face from his neighbor, frowning crossly; and since the heart has reasons which Reason does not know, he seemed to himself a fool; but when the service was over and he came out, he repeated again, " 'Peace and Good-will.' When I run on to the Bishop of Wyoming I'll tell him if he'll preach on them words I'll be there."

"Couldn't we shoot your pistol now?" asked Billy.

"Sure boy. Ain't yu' hungry, though?"

"No. I wish we were away off up there. Don't you?"

"The mountains? They look pretty, so white! A heap better 'n houses. Why, we'll go there! There's trains to Golden. We'll shoot around among the foothills."

353

To Golden they immediately went, and after a meal there wandered in the open country until the cartridges were gone, the sun was low, and Billy was walked off his young heels—a truth he learned complete in one horrid moment, and battled to conceal.

"Lame!" he echoed, angrily. "I ain't."

"Shucks!" said Lin, after the next ten steps. "You are, and both feet."

"Tell you, there's stones here, an' I'm just a-skipping them."

Lin, briefly, took the boy in his arms and carried him to Golden. "I'm played out myself," he said, sitting in the hotel and looking lugubriously at Billy on a bed. "And I ain't fit to have charge of a hog." He came and put his hand on the boy's head.

"I'm not sick," said the cripple. "I tell you, I'm bully. You wait an' see me eat dinner."

But Lin had hot water and cold water and salt, and was an hour upon his knees bathing the hot feet. And then Billy could not eat dinner!

There was a doctor in Golden; but in spite of his light prescription and most reasonable observations, Mr. McLean passed a foolish night of vigil, while Billy slept quite well at first, and, as the hours passed, better and better. In the morning he was entirely brisk, though stiff.

"I couldn't work quick to-day," he said. "But I guess one day won't lose me my trade."

"How d'yu' mean?" asked Lin.

"Why, I've got regulars, you know. Sidney Ellis an' Pete Goode has theirs, an' we don't cut each other. I've got Mr. Daniels an' Mr. Fisher an' lots, an' if you lived in Denver I'd shine your boots every day for nothing. I wish you lived in Denver."

"Shine my boots? Yu'll never! And yu' don't black Daniels or Fisher, or any of the outfit."

A *Journey* in *Search* of *Christmas*

"Why, I'm doing first rate," said Billy, surprised at the swearing into which Mr. McLean now burst. "An' I ain't big enough to get to make money at any other job."

"I want to see that engine-man," muttered Lin. "I don't like yer smokin' friend."

"Pete Goode? Why, he's awful smart. Don't you think he's smart?"

"Smart's nuthin'," observed Mr. McLean.

"Pete has learned me and Sidney a lot," pursued Billy, engagingly.

"I'll bet he has!" growled the cow-puncher; and again Billy was taken aback at his language.

It was not so simple, this case. To the perturbed mind of Mr. McLean it grew less simple during that day at Golden, while Billy recovered, and talked, and ate his innocent meals. The cow-puncher was far too wise to think for a single moment of restoring the runaway to his debauched and shiftless parents. Possessed of some imagination, he went through a scene in which he appeared at the Lusk threshold with Billy and forgiveness, and intruded upon a conjugal assault and battery. "Shucks!" said he. "The kid would be off again inside a week. And I don't want him there, anyway."

Denver, upon the following day, saw the little boot-black again at his corner, with his trade not lost; but near him stood a tall singular man with hazel eyes and a sulky expression. And citizens during that week noticed, as a new sight in the streets, the tall man and the little boy walking together. Sometimes they would be in shops. The boy seemed happy as possible, talking constantly, while the man seldom said a word, and his face was serious.

Upon New Year's Eve, Governor Barker was overtaken by Mr. McLean riding a horse up Hill Street, Cheyenne.

"Hello!" said Barker, staring humorously through his glasses. "Have a good drunk?"

355

"Changed my mind," said Lin, grinning. "Proves I've got one. Struck Christmas all right, though."

"Who's your friend?" inquired his Excellency.

"This is Mister Billy Lusk. Him and me have agreed that towns ain't nice to live in. If Judge Henry's foreman and his wife won't board him at Sunk Creek—why, I'll fix it somehow."

The cow-puncher and his Responsibility rode on together towards the open plain.

"Suffering Moses!" remarked his Excellency.

Human

ZONA GALE

PRETTY soon the new-old Christmas will be here. I donno but it's here now. Here in the village we've give out time and again that our Christmas isn't going to be just trading (not many of us can call it "shopping" yet without stopping to think, any more than we can say "maid" for hired girl, real easy) and just an exchange of useless gifts. So in the "new" way, little by little the old Christmas is being uncovered from under the store-keepers' Christmas. Till at last we shall have the Christmas of the child in the manger and not of the three kings.

And then we're going to look back on the romance that Christmas had through the long time when meanings have measured themselves commercial. Just as we look back now on the romance of chivalry. And we'll remember all the kindness and the humor of the time that'll be outgrown—even though we wouldn't have the time come back when we looked for Christmas in things—things—things . . . and sometimes found it there.

The week before Christmas, the Friendship Village post-office, near closing, is regular Bedlam. We all stand in line, with our presents done up, while the man at the window weighs everybody else's, and we almost drop in our tracks. And our manners, times like this, is that we never get out of our place for no one. Not for no one! Only—once we did.

Two nights before Christmas that year I got my next-to-the-last three packages ready and stepped into the post-office with 'em about half-past seven. And at the post-office door I met Mis' Holcomb-that-was Mame Bliss. She had a work bag and a shopping bag and a suitcase, all of 'em bulging full.

"My land!" I says, "you ain't going to mail all them?"

"I am, too," she says, "and I'm that thankful I'm through, and my back aches that hard, I could cry. Twenty-one," she says, grim, "twenty-one presents I've got made out of thought and elbow work, and mighty little money, all ready to mail on time. Now," says she, "I can breathe."

"Kin I carry your satchel, Mis' Holcomb?" says somebody.

We looked down, and there's little Stubby Mosher, that's seven, and not much else to say about him. He ain't no father, nor much of any brother, except a no-account one in the city; and his mother has just been sent to the Wooster Hospital by the Cemetery Improvement Sodality that is extending our work to include the sick. We'd persuaded her to go there by Stubby's brother promising to send him to spend Christmas with her. And we were all feeling real tender toward Stubby, because we'd just heard that week that she wasn't going to get well.

"Well, Stubby," says Mis' Holcomb, kind, "yes, I'll be obliged for a lift, if not a lug. You well?" she asks.

"Yes'm," says Stubby, acting green, like a boy will when you ask after his health.

He picked up her suitcase and moved over toward the line. It was an awful long line that night, that reached 'way around past the public desk. In ahead of us was 'most everybody we knew—Abigail Arnold and Mis' Merriman and Libby Liberty and old rich Mis' Wiswell with a bag of packages looking like they might be jewelry, every one. And every one of them was talking as hard as they could about the Christmas things they couldn't get done.

"Might as well settle down for a good visit while we're waiting," I says to Mis' Holcomb, and she made her eyebrows sympathize.

No sooner was we stood up, neat and in line, than in come three folks that was total strangers to me and to the village as well. One was a young girl around twenty, with eyes kind of laughing *at* everything, dressed in blue, with ermine on her hat and an ermine muff as big as one of my spare-room pillows, and three big fresh pink roses on her coat. And one was a youngish fellow, some older than her, in a gray cap, and having no use of his eyes—being they were kept right close on the lady in blue. And the other, I judged, was her father—a nice, jolly, private Santa Claus, in a fur-lined coat. They were in a tearing hurry to get to the general-delivery window, but when they saw the line, and how there was only one window for mail and stamps and all, they fell in behind us, as nice as we was ourselves.

"Let me take you out and you wait in the car, Alison," says the youngish man, anxious.

"Hadn't you better, dear?" says her father, careful.

"Why, but I love this!" she says. "Isn't it *quaint?*" And she laughed again.

Now, I hate that word *quaint.* So does Mis' Holcomb. It always sounds to us like last year's styles. So though her and I had been looking at the three strangers—that we saw were merely passing through in an automobile, like the whole country seems to—with some interest, we both turned our backs and went on visiting and listening to the rest.

"I've got three more to get presents for," says Mis' Merriman in that before-Christmas conversation that everybody takes a hand at, "and what to get them I do *not* know. Don't you ever get up a stump about presents?"

"Stump!" says Libby Liberty, "I live on a stump from the time I start till I stick on the last stamp."

"I've got two more on my list," Mis' Wiswell says, worried, "and it don't seem as if I could take another stitch nor buy another spoon, hatpin *or* paper-knife. But I know they'll send me something, both of them."

I stood looking at us, tired to death with what we'd been a-making, but sending 'em off with a real lot of love and satisfaction wrapped up in 'em, too. And I thought how we covered up Christmas so deep with work that we hardly ever had time to get at the real Christmas down underneath all the stitches.

And yet, there we were, having dropped everything else that we were doing, just because it was Christmas week, and coming from all over town with little things we had made, and standing there in line to send 'em off to folks. And I thought of all the other folks in all the other post-offices in the world, doing the self-same thing that night. And I felt all kind of nice and glowing to think I was one of 'em. Only I did begin to wish we were enough civilized to get the glow some other way.

"I guess it's going to take a long time," says Mis' Holcomb, patient. "Stubby, you needn't wait if you've anything else to do."

"Oh," says Stubby, important, "I've got a present to mail."

A present to mail! When Sodality had been feeding him for five weeks among us!

Mis' Holcomb and I exchanged our next two glances.

"What is it, Stubby?" asks Mis' Holcomb, that is some direct by nature and never denies herself at it.

He looked up kind of shy—he's a nice little boy, when anybody has any time to pay any attention to him.

"It's just this," he said, and took it out from under his coat. It was about as big as a candy box, and he'd wrapped it up himself, and the string was so loose and the paper was so tore that they weren't going to stay by each other past two stations.

"Mercy!" says Mis' Holcomb, "leave me tie it up for you."

She took it. And in order to tie it she had to untie it. And when she done that, what was in it come all untied. And she see, and we both of us see, what was in it. It was a great big pink rose, fresh and real, with a lot of soaking wet paper wrapped round the stem.

"Stubby Mosher!" says Mis' Holcomb straight out, "where'd *you* get this?"

He colored up. "I bought it to the greenhouse," he says. "I'm a-goin' to shovel paths till the first of March to pay for it. And they gimme one path ahead for postage."

"Who you sending it to?" says Mis' Holcomb, blunt—and I

kind of wished she wouldn't, because the folks right around us
was beginning to listen.

"To mother," says Stubby.

Mis' Holcomb near dropped the box. "My land!" she said,
"why didn't you *take* it to her? You're goin' tomorrow to spend
Christmas with her, ain't you?"

Stubby shook his head and swallowed some.

"I ain't going," he told her.

"Ain't going!" Mis' Holcomb says. "*Why* ain't you goin', I'd
like to know, when you was promised?"

"My brother wrote he can't," said Stubby. "He's had some
money to pay. He can't send me. I——"

He stopped, and looked down on the floor as hard as ever he
could, and swallowed like lightning.

"Well, but that's how we got her there," Mis' Holcomb says.
"We promised her you'd come."

"My brother wrote he can't." Stubby said it over.

Mis' Holcomb looked at me for just one minute. Then her
thoughts took shape in her head, and out.

"How much money has Sodality got in the treasury?" she says
to me.

"Forty-six cents," says I, that's treasurer and drove to death
for a fund for us.

"How much is the fare to Wooster?"

"Three fifty-five each way," says Stubby, ready, but hopeless.

"My land!" says Mis' Holcomb, "they ain't a woman in Sodality that can afford the seven dollars—nor a man in the town'll
see it like we do. And no time to raise nothing. And that poor
woman off there. . . . "

She stared out over the crowd, kind of wild.

The line was edging along up to the window, and still talking
about it.

" . . . Elsie and Mame that I haven't sent a thing to," Mis'
Merriman was saying. "I just must get out and find something

tomorrow, if it does get there late. But I'm sure I dunno what.
. . ."

" . . . disappointed me last minute on two Irish crochet collars," Mis' Wiswell was holding forth, in her voice that talks like her vocal cords had gone flat, same as carwheels.

"I've got company coming tomorrow, and I just simply will *have* to let both presents go, if I stay awake all night about it, as stay awake I s'pose I shall."

Mis' Holcomb looked over at me steady for a minute, like she'd see a thing she couldn't name. Then she kind of give it up, and went on tying Stubby's package. And just then she see what he'd wrote for a Christmas card. It was on a piece of wrapping paper, and it said:

TO MY MOTHER
I CANT COM
MERY CRISMAS
STUB

"*Merry Christmas!*" Mis' Holcomb says over like she hadn't any strength. Then all of a sudden she stood up.

"Stubby," she says, "you run out a minute, will you? You run over to the grocery and wait for me there a minute—quick. I'll see to your package."

He went when she said that.

And swift as a flash, before I could think at all what she meant, Mis' Holcomb laid Stubby's present down by her suitcase, and wheeled around and whipped two packages out of her shopping bag, and faced the line of Friendship Village folks drawn up there to the window, taking their turns.

"Everybody!" she says, loud enough so's they all heard her, "I've got more Christmas presents than I need. I'll auction off some of 'em—all hand-made—to anybody that's short of presents. I'll show 'em to you. Come here and look at 'em, and make a bid."

They looked at her for a minute, perfectly blank; and she was beginning to undo one of 'em. . . . And then all of a sudden

362

I see her plan, what it was; and I walked right over beside of her.

"Don't you leave her undo 'em!" I calls out. "It's for Stubby Mosher," I says, "that can't go, after all, to his mother in the Wooster Hospital, that's going to die—count of his brother not sending him the money. She can't get well—we know that since last week. They's only forty-six cents in Sodality treasury. Let's us buy Mis' Holcomb's presents that she's made and is willing to auction off! Unsight-unseen let us buy 'em! I bid fifty cents."

The line had kind of wavered and broke, and was looking away from itself towards us. The man at the window had stopped weighing and had his head close up, looking out.

Everybody was hushed dumb for a minute. Then it kind of got to Mis' Wiswell—that's had so much trouble that things 'most always get to her easy—and she says out:

"Oh, land! *Is it?* Why, I bid seventy-five then."

"Eighty!" says I, reckless, to egg her on.

Then Libby Liberty kind of come to, and bid ninety, though everybody knew the most she has is egg-money—and finally it, whatever it was, went to Mis' Wiswell for a dollar.

"Is it a present would do for ladies?" she says, when she made her final bid. "I dunno, though, as that matters. One dollar!"

Well, then Mis' Holcomb up with another present, and Mis' Merriman started that one, and though dazed a little yet—some folks daze so terribly easy if you go off an inch from their stamping-ground!—the rest of us, including Abigail Arnold that hadn't ought to have bid at all, got that one up to another dollar, and it went to Mis' Merriman for that. But the next package stuck at fifty cents—not from lack of willingness, I know, but from sheer lack of ways—and it was just going at that when I whispered to Mis' Holcomb:

"What's in this one?"

"Towel with crochet work set in each end and no initial," she says.

"Really?" says a voice behind me.

And there was the young lady in blue, with the ermine and the roses. And I see all of a sudden that she didn't look to be laughing at us at all, but her eyes were bright, and she was kind of flushed up, and it come to me that she would have bidded before, only she was sort of watching us—mebbe because she thought we were *quaint*. But I didn't have time to bother with that thought much, not then.

"I'll give two dollars for that," she says.

"Done!" says Mis' Holcomb, real auctioneering-like, and with her cheeks red, and her hat on one ear, and her hand going up and down. "Now this one—who'll bid on this one?" says she, putting up another. "How much for this? How much——"

"How much is the fare to where he's going?" says somebody else strange, and there was the youngish fellow speaking, that was with her with the roses.

"Seven-ten round trip to Wooster," says Mis' Holcomb, instant.

"Why, then, I bid three-ten for whatever you have there," he says laughing.

But Mis' Holcomb, instead of flaming up because now the whole money for Stubby's fare was raised, just stood there looking at that youngish man, mournful all over her face.

"It's a hand-embroidered dressing-sack," she says melancholy. "You don't never want that!"

"Yes—yes, I do," he says, still laughing, "yes, I do. It's a straight bid."

"Oh, my land!" says Mis' Holcomb, her voice slipping, "then we've got it. We've got it all right here!"

But while she was a-saying it, a big, deep voice boomed out all over her and the rest that was exclaiming.

"Ticket to where?" says the private Santa-Claus-looking man in the fur coat.

"Wooster, this state," says I, being Mis' Holcomb was almost speechless.

"Well, now," says the private Santa Claus, "don't we go pretty close to Wooster? Where's that map we wore out? Well, I know we go pretty close to Wooster. Why can't we take your Master Stubby to Wooster in the car? We're going on tonight —if we ever get to that general-delivery window," he ends in a growl.

And *that* was the time the line made way—the line that never moves for no one. And the Santa Claus man went up and got his mail.

And while he was a-doing it, I run out after Stubby, setting on a barrel in the grocery, happy with three cranberries they'd give him. And as I come back in the door with him, I see Mis' Holcomb just showing his rose to the young lady with the ermine and the roses. And then I see for sure by the young lady's eyes that she wasn't the way I'd thought she was—laughing *at* us. Why, her eyes were as soft and understanding as if she didn't have a cent to her name. And I dunno but more so.

"Oh, father," I heard her say, "I'm glad we came in for the mail ourselves! *What* if we hadn't?"

And I concluded I didn't mind that word *quaint* half as much as I thought I did.

Every last one of the line went out of the post-office to see Stubby off, and the man at the window, he came too. They had a big warm coat they put the little boy into, and we wrapped up his rose and put that in the car, so's it would get there sooner and save the postage, same time, and they tucked him away as snug as a bug in a rug, his little face just shining out for joy.

"Oh, and you can buy your presents back now," says Libby Liberty to Mis' Holcomb right in the middle of it.

"No, sir," says Mis' Holcomb, proud. "A bargain is a bargain, and I made mine." And then she thought of something. "Oh," she says, leaning forward to the window of the car, "don't you want to sell your presents back again?"

"No!" they all told her together. "We made a straight bid, you know."

"Then," says Mis' Holcomb, "let's give Stubby the money to put in his pocket and take the one-way fare to his mother!"

And that was what they done. And the big car rolled off down Daphne Street, with Stubby in it going like a king.

And when we all got back in the post-office, what do you s'pose? There was the crocheted towel and the hand-embroidered dressing-sack slipped back all safe into Mis' Holcomb's shopping-bag!

But she wouldn't take the other things back—she would not, no matter what Mis' Wiswell and Mis' Merriman said.

"I can crochet a couple of things to-morrow like lightning," says Mis' Holcomb. "You don't want me to be done out of my share in Stubby's Christmas, do you?" she asks 'em.

And we all stood there, talking and laughing and going over it and clean forgetting all about the United States mails, till the man at the window called out:

"'Leven minutes and a quarter before the mail closes!"

We all started back to the window, but nobody could remember just exactly where anybody was standing before, and they all wanted everybody to go up first and step in ahead of them. And the line, instead of being a line with some of 'em ahead of others and all trying to hurry, was just a little group, with each giving everybody their turn, peaceful and good-willing. And all of a sudden it was like Christmas had come, up through all the work and the stitches, and was right there in the Friendship Village post-office with us.

"Goodness!" says Mis' Holcomb in my ear, "I was wore to the bone getting ready my Christmas things. But now I'm real rested."

"So am I," I says.

And so was every one of us, I know, falling back into line there by the window. All rested, and not feeling hurried nor nothing: only human.

Homesickness Night

RUDOLF KINAU

"CHRISTMAS Eve without carp in fresh butter with horse-radish," said Julius Bande. "That's no kind of Christmas Eve at all as far as I'm concerned."

"For carp, or plaice, or turbot, I don't give a hoot," said Paul Wittorf. "What I have to have on the blessed eve is green cabbage with bacon and after it a pair of apples and nuts—or I can't be happy."

"I don't want a thing to eat, hot or cold, on that evening," said Hein Tiemann, "if only I can see the tree and the lights, and can give a couple of presents and hear a little carol once in a while, then everything's dandy."

"But it must be a carol about the Christ child," said Albert Harms, "and it must be simply and plainly sung—by children. For Christmas is now just the children's feast. And where there are no children in the house . . ."

"Then the grown-ups will become children again, and the old folk will become childish," said Dieter Rolf. "I don't in any case need children racketing around me, or kids yelling. If I can just be at home, and can sit with my folks in a warm room, and now and then can yarn a bit, about everything that's going on in the world, then I won't ask anything more of Christmas."

"And I would just as soon be at sea on Christmas Eve," said old Jochen Fock, "or anywhere out in the open, far away, and quite alone. And then I creep into my own thoughts about myself, and once more am homesick—for—for long ago . . . when I too was young, and we were all still children."

"O, God, not that, above all not that!" said Klaus Wulf. "The last place to be is out in the open at Christmas. For the other feasts, it isn't so bad, and I don't really care one way or the other. Easter and Whitsun and engagements and birthdays and jubilees and all that stuff, those can be celebrated as well out as in or anywhere. But Christmas—never! For Christmas I must be at home. Christmas is a German feast, through and through. It's not celebrated as beautifully anywhere else."

Seven men, and each one said something different, and each one was right. But I think of them all, old Jochen Fock makes the most sense.

Homesick—that's what we all are, or wish we were, on December 24th. Homesick for . . . for long ago, when we were still children. And that is why this evening will always be a "holy" evening, even were people not to believe in the Christ child anymore. It would always be a "rue night," a "homesickness night," an evening and a night when everyone wishes something for himself and yearns for something.

He who is without, in war or in need, wishes to be home, and longs for joy and peace. He who is within, too well fed, and snugly warm, he would prefer at Christmas to go outside into the storm. The child wishes he were already grown up, and the old man would be young again, or at least in the prime of life, so that he could live the second half of his life over again. The poor man would like, at least at Christmas, to be rich and to be able to give gifts with full hands. The rich, spoiled man— he, just at Christmas, wishes he were poor and plain, and would like to believe in fairy tales and miracles. Each one of us has, at Christmas, beyond our small wishes, one great, big, unfulfillable wish, or a boundless longing, or, at least, a great big beautiful homesickness, either for his home or for the great outdoors.

And that's the way it should be. That's what we ought to have. "Or something's missing," said Adelheid Achner. And she should know—from experience. Adelheid has seven grown children, scattered all over the country and the great world. For twenty years she has had only one wish each Christmas, that on the holy eve they should all be at home with her once more. They all loved to come, they came from far away and brought much joy with them, but they never all came together at the same time. Year after year, one or two were missing. And then, at long last, when it finally came to the point that all the seven were sitting under the Christmas tree with their mother, poor old Adelheid Achner was quite overcome and confused. And when the children asked her what was wrong, she said, very sadly, "I really don't know where I shall send my thoughts to-day, since you are all here close to me." And the next morning she said to her neighbor, "Well, you know, if there's no one missing *at* Christmas, then something's missing *to* Christmas."

And that goes for many of us even if we don't put it quite that way; there has to be a little nostalgia, and there always is. Say what you will, even if a man's stiff and wooden.

That reminds me of a certain Christmas in the Seamen's Home in Bremen. About forty weatherbeaten sailors, from at least ten different ships, many fierce, rugged characters among them, all sitting like children around a great big table. They hear a brief, forthright address, sing with gruff voices, as best they can, a couple of songs, and look with great, big, hungry eyes not only at the lights, but also at the six young women and girls who, after first standing like angels under the tree, then with kind smiles, and so close you could almost touch them, come with coffee and cake and bring apples and nuts. And then they put a huge package on the table in front of every single man, and say "Merry Christmas," and then they add "A fair wind and a safe harbor," and the men reply "Thank you, thank you very much," and "the same to you." Follows a general unpacking, and much joyful astonishment. Then the voice of the superintendent is heard above everything, saying, "Listen, everyone. I have another small package, one that's come from somewhere by post, and on it is written "To the Seamen's Home, in Bremen," and it's a Christmas gift to the sailor who has been the longest away from home."

Everyone looks up, and grins and whispers, but no one says a word.

"The best way to find that out," says the superintendent, "is for me just to ask you! Who has been away from home for more than two years? Please raise your hands." He looks down the long row, and counts, "Two, four, six, twelve men. O.K. Thanks. Now, who has been away longer than three years? Two, four, six men. Longer than four? Three men. Longer than five years? One." A short, redhaired sailor with freckles and light gray eyes.

"Well, how long?" asks the superintendent.

"Eight and a half years," says the redhead, and he says it loudly and proudly, his hand still raised high in the air.

"Eight and a half years," repeats the superintendent approvingly, and comes a step nearer. "That's a long time. Where do you come from? From what far corner . . . ?"

"I come from—from somewhere near Sonderburg." He lets his arm drop.

"From Sonderburg in North Schleswig—but that's not very far from here! You could very easily—either from Hamburg or from Kiel . . .

"Don't you have any parents or relatives left?"

The redhead sounds a bit uncertain. "Father's dead, and my brothers and sisters are all scattered . . . "

"And your mother?"

"Mother?" He turns his face aside as though he were about to spit. Then he looks straight ahead, and says, in a harsh, loud voice, "Mother has married again. She has taken a Dane. The house and everything have become Danish there now. What would I be doing there?"

Everyone holds their breath.

"But your mother is still . . . your mother," says the superintendent. "And if she is still here, and if she is alive . . . Do you at least sometimes write to her?"

The redhead looks down at his clumsy hands and shakes his head. "No, I haven't done even that . . . not a word . . ."

"But you should have," says the superintendent, kindly. "You should have written. You really ought to have written, Mr. . . .? What was your name again?"

"Erichsen."

Then up gets a lanky seaman and pushing his parcel to one side he asks:

"Are you Henning Erichsen from Soderup near Sonderburg?"

"I am, yes; what of it?"

"You are? Well, in that case I have greetings for you from your mother, and she asked me to give you—just a moment . . . this letter. Here, take it; from your mother."

The redhead gets up and leans with both hands on the table. "From my mother? How did you get into this? I don't even know you."

"To be sure you don't," says the other, "and I've never set eyes on you before either. But your stepfather, your mother's second husband, is my uncle. And just lately—last October—I was over at their house—I was there for a whole day, and had a long talk with him, and with your mother. They talk of you and think about you a whole lot. And your mother is waiting night and day, because she thinks there's still a chance that you might come home or write. And that's why she gave me this letter. She said to me that if I should ever run into you, anywhere in the whole world—come on, here, take it."

The redhead reaches for the letter with shaking hands, and he looks at it, all over, and then he puts it on the table in front of him. And then he sits down in his place again. And he wipes his eyes with the back of his hand. No one moves at all.

"And here is your little package also," says the superintendent, "that, too, is for you, Mr. Erichsen. For the sailor who has been the longest away from home." And the boy unties the knot and unwraps the small parcel. A box of writing paper and a few post-cards and a pencil. And he puts them right next to his letter without saying another word.

"Thanks," then says Henning Erichsen. And he says it very

quietly and softly and looks at his letter again, nodding with his head a few times.

And then . . . and then the superintendent goes up front again, and gives them the chord. And then everyone sings—all with hoarse voices, and they sing as well as they know how, "This is the day that the Lord has made."

We are all a bit homesick at Christmas, for home, and for the old days when we were still children.

And that is why our Christmas will always be a holy evening and a "silent night."

TRANSLATED BY ANNE FREMANTLE

Christmas at Sea

ROBERT LOUIS STEVENSON

The sheets were frozen hard, and they cut the naked hand;
The decks were like a slide, where a seaman scarce could stand,
The wind was a nor'-wester, blowing squally off the sea;
And the cliffs and spouting breakers were the only things a-lee.

They heard the surf a-roaring before the break of day;
But 'twas only with the peep of light we saw how ill we lay.
We tumbled every hand on deck instanter, with a shout,
And we gave her the maintops'l, and stood by to go about.

All day we tack'd and tack'd between the South Head and the
    North;
All day we haul'd the frozen sheets, and got no further forth;
All day as cold as charity, in bitter pain and dread,
For very life and nature we tack'd from head to head.

We gave the South a wider berth, for there the tide-race roar'd;
But every tack we made we brought the North Head close
    aboard;
So's we saw the cliffs and houses, and the breakers running high,
And the coastguard in his garden, with his glass against his eye.

The frost was on the village roofs as white as ocean foam;
The good red fires were burning bright in every 'longshore home;
The windows sparkled clear, and the chimneys volley'd out;
And I vow we sniff'd the victuals as the vessel went about.

The bells upon the church were rung with a right jovial cheer;
For it's just that I should tell you how (of all days in the year)
This day of our adversity was blessèd Christmas morn,
And the house above the coastguard's was the house where I
    was born.

O well I saw the pleasant room, the pleasant faces there,
My mother's silver spectacles, my father's silver hair;
And well I saw the firelight, like a flight of homely elves
Go dancing round the china-plates that stand upon the shelves!

And well I knew the talk they had, the talk that was of me,
Of the shadow on the household and the son that went to sea;
And O the wicked fool I seem'd, in every kind of way,
To be here and hauling frozen ropes on blessèd Christmas Day.

They lit the high sea-light, and the dark began to fall.
"All hands to loose topgallant sails." I heard the captain call.
"By the Lord, she'll never stand it," our first mate Jackson cried.
. . . "It's the one way or the other, Mr. Jackson," he replied.

She stagger'd to her bearings, but the sails were new and good,
And the ship smelt up to windward just as though she under-
    stood.
As the winter's day was ending, in the entry of the night,
We clear'd the weary headland, and pass'd below the light.

And they heaved a mighty breath, every soul on board but me,
As they saw her nose again pointing handsome out to sea;
But all that I could think of, in the darkness and the cold,
Was just that I was leaving home and my folks were growing
    old.

Fifty Marks

HANS FALLADA

WE WERE newly married, Itzenplitz and I, and to all
intents and purposes we possessed absolutely nothing.
Now when you are very young and newly married
and very much in love into the bargain, this doesn't matter a
very great deal. True, we had our wistful moments, but always
one of us would laugh and say: "Why, there's no reason for
everything to come all at once! We've got all the time in the
world!" And the wistful moment was over.

Yet I do remember one particular conversation of ours in the
Park, when Itzenplitz sighed and said, "Oh, if only we hadn't to
watch every penny so carefully!"

I sought enlightenment. "Well?" I asked, "What then?"

"I'd buy myself something!" said Itzenplitz dreamily.

"Well, and what would you buy?"

Itzenplitz reflected. Believe it or not, she had to think before
she said, "For instance, a pair of warm woolly slippers!"

"Well, I'm blowed!" I said, completely staggered, and was
filled with awe at the remarkable reasoning of my wife Elizabeth,
alias Ibeth, alias Itzenplitz; for it was midsummer, the sun was
beating down, and for my part I wanted nothing better at the
moment than a cool shower and a cigarette. Yet it must have
been as the aftermath of this midsummer colloquy that our
Christmas Wish-List came into being.

"You know, Tim," said Itzenplitz, thoughtfully rubbing her
long, sharp nose, "we ought to start now putting down everything
that comes into our heads. Afterward, at Christmas, it'll be an
awful scramble and we shall quite probably give each other silly
things we don't need at all."

375

Accordingly we wrote down our first Christmas wish on a piece of paper torn from my order-book: "1 pair of warm woolly slippers for Itzenplitz"; and since we always made a point of being strictly impartial, I wrote underneath after much thought and frowning: "1 good book for Tim." "That's fine!" said Itzenplitz, and stared rapturously at the Wish-List as if slippers and book might pop out of it at any moment.

Midsummer gave place to late autumn; after the first slushy snow came the Christmas shop-windows, and all the time our Christmas Wish-List grew and grew and grew. "What does it matter if there is a terrible lot?" consoled Itzenplitz. "Then we shall have our choice. It's really more of a crossing-out list. Just before Christmas we'll cross out everything we can't manage, but wishing's still free, surely?" She reflected a moment and said, "I can wish what I like, can't I, Tim?"

"Yes," I said recklessly.

"Fine!" she said, and in a twinkling she had written: "1 blue silk evening frock (latest model)." She regarded me challengingly.

"Well, you know, Itzenplitz . . . " I observed.

"You said wishing was free!"

"All right," I said, and wrote: 1 four tube wireless set." And now I gave *her* a challenging look. Then we began a lively dispute, conducted with Machiavellian ingenuity, as to which we needed more, an evening frock or a wireless set— and all the time we were both perfectly well aware that for the next five years neither would even bear consideration.

But all this took place much later. For the time being we were still in the Park, and it was summer, and we had written down our first two wishes. Now Itzenplitz has a rather long, mischievous nose, which easily goes red with joy or indignation, hence her nose-rubbing; and on top of that she has the quickest eyes in the world. She is always finding something, and sure enough, at this moment she called: "Here it is! Oh, Tim, Tim, here's our first Christmas *groschen!*" And she touched it with her toe.

"Christmas *groschen?*" I said, picking it up, "I'm off right now to buy three cigarettes with it at the tea-room."

"You give it to me! It's our Christmas *groschen,* it's for our Christmas Savings Box!"

"*Have* you a Christmas Savings Box?" I asked derisively. "I've never seen you with one."

"I'll find something all right. Just let me look!" And her eyes darted about under the trees as if the search were due to start right away.

"We'll do it like this," I suggested. "We'll make a rough estimate of how much we want to spend on each other at Christmas, say for instance fifty marks . . . "

"You poor goop!" she said pityingly.

" . . . and there'll be six pay-days before Christmas, and each time we'll put by eight marks, no, eight marks fifty. That'll do the trick! And now I'm off for my three cigarettes."

"No, you don't! That *groschen* belongs to me!"

"Really!" I jeered.

"Oh, you're a stupid boy and I shan't speak a word to you for three days, and I won't walk with you at all, ever!"

Thereupon, snorting with rage, she left me standing and walked on alone. I followed her slowly; but when after a while we came to the streets, she walked on one side and I on the other as though we were perfect strangers. Only when a troop of really fat, respectable, Sunday-clad citizens came along, I was thoroughly low and called across the street: "Hey, miss! I say, miss!" The people made goggle-eyes, and she turned crimson and threw back her head.

But suddenly I had an idea, and I raced acrossed and shouted: "Itzenplitz, we'd quite forgotten, there's a fifty-mark bonus at Christmas, of course!"

Her first impulse was to bite my head off, and she did begin by inquiring who on earth would dream of giving a bonus to an idiot like myself; then, however, we considered our case seriously, deliberating whether, with times so bad, there would be any bonus at all, and the final verdict was: "We'll pretend there won't be one. But oh, it would be lovely . . . !"

Now I have still to relate why we were obliged to be so economical, and what we lived by, and what prospects we really had for the Christmas bonus. It is not at all easy to explain what I did. Recent as it all is, I shake my head and wonder how I managed to combine my manifold duties. At all events I spent all morning from seven o'clock onward in the editorial office of a local rag and wrote up half the local page, while Herr Pressbold, the Editor, sat opposite me, filling up the whole of the rest of the paper with the aid of pictures, matrices, correspondence, broadcasting programmes and a very defective typewriter. For this I was paid eighty marks a month, and that was our only regular source of income. However, having survived the morning, I set out to ensnare registered readers and secure advertisements on a commission basis 1.25 Reichsmarks per registered reader, and ten per cent of every advertisement. I was also treasurer of a voluntary sick-fund (three per cent of all subscriptions), entrusted by an Athletic Club with the collection of members' subscriptions, and to crown all, I functioned as secretary of the Town Improvements and Tourist Board. For this last, however, I got nothing save the glory and the somewhat remote prospect of these gentlemen doing something for me should anything ever happen to turn up.

Thus there was no lack of employment, only the depressing thing about the whole business was that all these combined activities hardly yielded enough to keep Itzenplitz and me alive. The verb "to buy" might have been Chinese for all it meant to us. Many were the times I came home listless and despondent, having tramped about the whole afternoon, knocked at fifty doors, and earned not fifty pfennigs. Today I am firmly convinced (however vehemently she may still deny it) that Itzenplitz's merry conceits were solely for the purpose of taking my mind off my troubles.

It must have been some time in the autumn—wet, foggy weather, and myself in the worst of humors, and our Christmas Box still a thing of fancy, when I came home and found Itzenplitz with a kitchen knife in one hand and a briquette, sawed through long-ways, in the other.

"What on earth are you up to?" I asked in astonishment, for she was engaged in hollowing out this half-briquette with the end of the knife. The other half lay before her on the table.

"Sh-h, Tim!" she whispered darkly, "the world is full of evildoers!" And she pointed with her knife to the door, pasted up with wall-paper, behind which dwelt the neighbor we referred to between ourselves as Jolly Roger.

"Well, what's the matter?" And then, in conspiratorial tones, she enlightened me; she had halved the briquette and was going to hollow it out and make a slit in it, and stick it together again with glue, and that was to be our Christmas Savings Box, and the idea was to put it among other briquettes, for—"There are lots and lots of great, big savage villains, all panting after our poor little money!" And her eyes sparkled. "And you're as mad as a hatter!" I said. "Besides, talking of Christmas, Heber says there's absolutely no question of any bonus this year. The Chief is as savage as the devil because business is bad!"

"That's fine!" she said. "Oh, Timothy-Titus, tell me all, so I'll know who gets the briquette at his head on Christmas Eve."

I have already mentioned that our editor was Herr Pressbold. A fine fellow he was too, pugnacious, blustering, daily increasing in girth; but he had no say. Herr Heber was the man. He kept the cash and the books, and had the ear of the Big Noise on whom we only set eyes once every six months. He spent his life being trundled about the country in his Rolls Royce, and had here a sawmill and there a little provincial paper and here some real estate and there a farm.

But on the paper his right hand man was Herr Heber, a dry, bony, long-shanked man of figures, and him I had tried to pump in a certain matter of Christmas bonuses and fifty marks. As well try to pump the Sahara desert! He had inquired whether the first cold spell had gone to my head, and whether I realized what it meant to work in a losing concern; and I could consider myself lucky if by the New Year the rotten rag wasn't washed out altogether.

And the worst of it was that Pressbold, on whom I was counting for support, had piped the same tune and actually reproved me for my "inflated ideas," telling me I ought to be glad if we weren't axed and that whatever we did we mustn't aggravate the Big Noise. And while the two of them jawed me, I thought that the losing concern and the boss's troubles were nothing to me, and the Wish-Lists sailed past my mind's eye like leaves in the wind, and away danced the warm woolly slippers and the evening frock and the good book and the Christmas Duck.

Ah, yes, the Christmas Duck! That reminds me. This is the moment for the official introduction of our neighbor beyond the wall-paper door, friend Jolly Roger. I don't suppose we ever knew Jolly Roger's real name, but he had the northern garret while we occupied the southern. He was a really black man. Indeed, I can only describe him by saying that he produced an effect of complete blackness; he had black bristly hair, black eyes that glittered wildly, and an untidy black beard. In town, and especially with the police, he was well-known and well-feared as a drunkard and a rowdy. In his spare time he was also a stoker at the Municipal Electricity Works. We could hardly have been closer neighbors; even when he turned over in bed we heard him, and so no doubt he heard all our business too.

At all events he heard our Christmas discussion about the duck. At her house, as in mine, the traditional Christmas fare had been goose, but in the course of the debate it occurred to us that a twelve-pound goose ("if it weighs less it's nothing but skin and bone") was rather a lot for two. So we decided on a duck—goose, so to speak, in octavo instead of folio. It would be just right for the two of us; but where to buy it and for how much . . . ?

At this moment a roar, a hoarse, unintelligible bellowing, issued from Jolly Roger's room, and a minute afterward a fist descended on our door. Swaying, but wild to look upon as a beast of the jungle, Jolly Roger stood in the doorway; he had come straight out of bed and was clad only in shirt and trousers, which he held up with a firm grip of the left hand.

"I'll get the Christmas bird for you!" croaked Jolly Roger, glaring from one to the other.

We were not a little startled, and embarrassed. Itzenplitz rubbed her nose and kept murmuring, "Very kind of you" and "Very nice of you," and I tried to explain that we were still undecided—perhaps we should plump for a goose or a turkey after all.

"Fools!" roared Jolly Roger, and the plaster flew from the ceiling, so hard did he slam the door. However, he evidently bore us no malice. He did not, it is true, renew his offer of a duck, but when, a week before Christmas, he met Itzenplitz on the landing endeavoring to nail two boards together as a stand for the Christmas tree, he took the boards away and declared: "I'll see to that. I've got a board already planed in the boiler room; make you a present of it for Christmas. Peach of a stand!"

But to return to the bonus question—my first attack then had been repulsed, and partly to console ourselves, we held an inquiry into our financial position. We ascertained what exactly we had put by since the great Christmas-Saving-Resolution. This was no easy task, for Itzenplitz had quite a system of separate funds—Housekeeping Money, Pocket Money, Tim's Money, the Fuel Fund, New Purchases Fund, Rent Fund and Christmas Fund, and since, thanks to our financial state, it was usually ebb-tide in most of the pots and tins, the few coins wandered from one fund to another and where they originally belonged it was impossible to tell.

Itzenplitz rubbed at her nose, which was growing rapidly redder, added a little here and a little there, abstracted a *groschen* and replaced a mark, while I leaned on the stove and made sarcastic remarks. Finally it seemed clear that within a period of three months the Christmas Fund had swollen 7.85 Reichsmarks, always assuming that the briquettes would last out the month. If not, then another two marks fifty would go to the Fuel Fund.

We looked at each other; but it never rains without pouring, and so in this moment of complete insolvence who should strike a chord in Itzenplitz's brain but my mother-in-law, and then Tutti and Johnny, nephew and niece. "I've always given Mummy and the children something for Christmas. We *must* manage it, I tell you!"

"Quite, quite; but you might tell me how!"

Itzenplitz disclosed nothing; instead she pulled off a masterstroke. She called on me one fine day at the paper, and engaged our old stick-in-the-mud of a Heber in a positively enchanting conversation. I still see him, with his long, dismal, horse-face, his cheeks actually tinged with red, sitting behind the dispatch counter, and Itzenplitz on the other side on our one cane chair; Itzenplitz in kid gloves—a pinafore frock with dotted silk blouse and a cheap summer coat. She put it over. She talked, she chatted, she prattled and she gossiped. She gave him the dope he wanted. She fed his old, dried-up, bachelor's heart with small talk. No sooner did a name fall than she invented the most intriguing stories on the spur of the moment. She chattered about people she had never seen, sealed engagements, broke them off, brought children into the world, killed off rich aunts, and as for Paradieser's cook . . . !

Heber's fishy old eyes grew really animated and down came

his bony fist on the counter. "I've always had my ideas about that feller! Well, I never!" And ever so gradually she worked her way from love to money, from Spieckermann's expensive new curtains and how on earth they could afford them and we certainly could not, and the Leisegang's were a bit shaky too, so people said, but here, God be praised, everything looked a marvel of prosperity, and no wonder with such a management! "And we're counting on you, you know, to put in a good word for us over the Christmas bonus. *You* can work the oracle, Herr Heber!"

But Heber, the six feet of misery, was, of course, quite unmoved; he merely cleared his throat and with a side glance at me loudly declared that he knew which way the wind blew, that good bait caught fine fish but not him, and that anyone anxious to burn his fingers was at perfect liberty to go to the Chief himself!

It was defeat, complete and ignominious. We fled with feeble stammerings from the Dispatch Department, and I was terribly sorry for Itzenplitz. For at least five minutes she said nothing, but merely snuffled disconsolately to herself, she was so crushed.

But however depressing this may have been, and however remote the prospect of a bonus, however gloomy our Christmas outlook, on the thirteenth of December it snowed for the first time that year. It was real dry, powdery snow that fell on frozen ground and lay, and needless to say we could not bear to stay indoors, but went out into the frost and swirling flakes.

Oh, that dreary, miserable little one-horse town! The gas-lamps burned in vain in the falling snow, and in our outlying street the people passed by like pale phantoms. When, however, we reached the High street, everything lay bathed in a magic light from the shop-windows, and the Christmas candles (electric ones) were burning, and we leaned our foreheads on the plate-glass and discussed this and pointed out that. "Look! That would be just right for us!" (Ninety-seven per cent of the articles exhibited were just right for us.)

And then we came to the worthy, old-established firm of Harland's the grocer's, and a wave of recklessness lifted us and carried us in, and we bought half a pound of hazel-nuts, half a pound of walnuts and half a pound of Brazil nuts: "Just to make it a bit Christmassy at home. No need for nut-crackers—we'll crack them in the door." Then we passed Ranf's the bookseller's, and there we saw a miracle: *Buddenbrooks* for two marks eighty-five. "Why, Itzenplitz, it's bound to have cost twelve before. Two marks eighty-five—that's a net economy of nine marks fifteen—and we're *bound* to land some Christmas ads!" So we bought *Buddenbrooks*; and passing Hämel's, we went in just to get some ideas for mother-in-law, Tutti and Johnny. For mother we bought a pair of very warm black gloves (five marks fifty); for Tutti a ball of remarkable size at one mark, and for Johnny a scooter (one mark ninety-five). And still the wave lifted and swept us on. I still see Itzenplitz standing before the mirror in a swarm of shoppers, trying on the little lace collar over her coat, her face a picture of happy absorption. "And you'll be giving me something for Christmas in any case, won't you, Tim? And perhaps later on the collar'll be gone. Isn't it sweet?"

It was still snowing as we strolled home: we walked close together, arm-in-arm, her hand in mine in my coat-pocket, and we had an armful of parcels as behooved true Christmas shoppers. And we were incredibly happy, and the advertisements would come—that was certain!

Being a man of almost meticulous tidiness, I undid the parcels and stacked our purchases while Itzenplitz fried the potatoes for supper. I then stuffed all the wrappings into our little cooking-stove called Roaring Rupert, and he roared and crackled exceedingly. But while we were happily lost in our fried potatoes, Itzenplitz suddenly sprang to her feet and called, "Don't be cross, Tim, but I really must try on that sweet little collar!"

I gave my leave, but—where was the collar? We searched and searched in vain.

"Oh, Tim, you must have burnt it with the wrappings!"

"I'm not such an idiot as to burn collars. You simply didn't bring it, that's all!"

She jerked open the stove, and stared and stared into the blaze—("It was *so* sweet") but I dashed back to the store, forced my way in long after closing-time and worried tired shop-girls in their packing-up for a vanished parcel—and went slowly and sadly home. And until bedtime we crept about the garret subdued and wordless.

But the new day came, and the snow still lay glistening and sparkling under a bright winter sky, and anyway, what's a collar? "Just wait and see how many collars we shall be able to buy before we're through! We're the right sort of people, aren't we! So rich that we can mend the fire with three-mark collars!"

My account of our first Christmas would not be complete without children to figure in it. If ever Itzenplitz and I talked of former Christmasses, it was those of our childhood that came back most vividly. The later ones were blurred and confused; never again had the Christmas tree sparkled so brightly. But I could still tell Itzenplitz exactly how it was when I got the doll's theater, and, two years later, the lead figures for Robinson Crusoe.

"There must be children for a really proper Christmas. It'll be lonely here, you know."

However, just before Christmas we got our baby after all. It was the eighteenth of December. Snow had turned to slush, frost to unpleasant, penetrating dampness—dismal days of fog that would not lift. On one of these afternoons that were neither day nor night, there had come a wailing, almost like a baby's cry, outside our door, and when Itzenplitz opened it, something cowered there, half-dead with wet and cold—a dirty-white kitten.

I did not see our guest till some hours later, when I came home from my advertisement-hunting. He was already fairly dry and not so rumpled, but even then it was plain that this dirty-white little fellow with the black patch half across his face was nothing but a common alley-cat. "Rumpelstiltskin," said Itzenplitz. "Our Rumpelstiltskin."

Well, there it was and there it stayed, and as Itzenplitz said, we had at least one youngster to share our Christmas.

On the twenty-third I hung round Heber as a bridegroom round his bride, but he was quite inscrutable and as bony and codlike as ever, and on the evening of the twenty-third Itzenplitz and I had our first real row; primarily because I had said nothing, secondly because Rumpelstiltskin had pulled out all the stalks of our one and only pot of heather, a present from Frau Pressbold—and thirdly because Jolly Roger, instead of delivering the Christmas-tree stand, had again put Itzenplitz off till the next day.

The new day dawned—December the twenty-fourth and Christmas Eve—an ordinary, grey, opaque winter day, neither warm nor cold. At ten o'clock Heber went to see the chief. As I sat there and waited for his return I wrote a stinking notice of the Christmas film running at the Cinema de Luxe and put my whole soul into it. Back came Heber, looking as bony and codlike as ever, sat down at his place and grumbled across at me: "Müller, you'll have to go at once to Ladewig's. He says he only took a quarter page and you wrote up half a page. Another of your muddles, I suppose!"

And as I trailed through the streets, my one thought was: "Poor Itzenplitz—poor Itzenplitz." All the life had gone out of me; but really, deep down, I had never believed in the Christmas bonus. When you really need something it never comes.

At Ladewig's I, of course, was right, and he remembered and was decent enough to admit it. I crept slowly back to the paper and told Heber, who said: "There you are! That's what I'm always saying. Those people call themselves business men! And by the way, just sign this receipt, will you? I've talked the Chief round again after all."

For one moment I felt giddy, and then everything grew bright, the sun shone, and I very nearly kissed the old shark on both cheeks. Then, with a shout of—"Just a second, Herr Heber," I signed for the fifty-mark note and raced, without hat or coat, the note in my hand, down the High Street into the Neuhäuser-strasse, over the Kirchplatz, through the Reepschlägergangste the Stradtrat-Hempel-Strasse, charged up the staircase, burst like a hurricane into our room, banged the note on the table and cried: "Make a list of what we're buying, Itzenplitz! Call for me at two!" And I kissed her and twizzled her round and was downstairs and back in the office before you could say "Knife!" Heber, the old fishface, had not yet recovered from his stupefaction and kept on muttering plaintively to himself: "I wouldn't like to be as crazy as you are even for an hour on Sundays, Müller!"

But at two o'clock, when Heber had departed, she came. And this is the list, our final Christmas Purchases List, that she gave me to read:

FOOD

1 Duck	R. M. 5.–
Red Cabbage	–.50
Apples	–.60
Nuts	2.–
Figs, dates and raisins	3.–
Sundries	5.–
	16.10

FOR THE TREE

Our tree	R. M. 1.–
12 Candles	–.60
Candle-holders	–.75
Tinsel	–.50
Magic candles	–.25
	3.10

FOR RUMPELSTILTSKIN

1 Bucket fresh sand	R. M. –.25
1 Kipper	–.15
	–.40

Hans Fallada

FOR TIM

Gloves	R. M.	4.–
Cigarettes		2.–
1 Shirt		4.–
1 Tie		2.–
Something else		2.–
		14.–

FOR ITZENPLITZ

1 Lottery ticket	R. M.	1.–
1 Pair scissors		2.50
1 LACE COLLAR (!)		3.–
1 Shawl		6.–
1 Hairdressing and waving		2.–
		14.50
OUR CHRISTMAS		48.10

"Listen!" began Itzenplitz at top speed (Heber's lunch hour was over at four and everything had to be done by then). "Listen, I know it's a terrible lot to spend on eating, but the duck'll last at least four days and there's only one Christmas a year. I *must* have some proper scissors for sewing now."

"What's 'something else'?" said I, interrupting her torrent of words.

"Oh, that means a little surprise for you."

"I want a couple of marks for 'something else' too!" I announced threateningly.

"Oh, Tim, we shall have only five marks left, and suppose the gas man comes? And I should be two marks fifty up on you then! Besides, it's not necessary, really it isn't—we're going to have *such* a merry Christmas!"

"I don't care, I'm having those two marks!" I persisted.

Then off went Itzenplitz to fetch old Lenzy, who had promised to deputize for me till four o'clock. For who was likely to come to the paper on the afternoon of the twenty-fourth? So off we dashed, and of course none of the prices were right.

Needless to say we were not finished by four; but we arranged that, having dashed back to the paper so that Heber might not notice my absence, I should ask leave to knock off at half past. Meanwhile Itzenplitz would have her hair cut and waved, and afterward we would do the rest of the shopping together.

At five minutes to four I arrived at the office to find that old Lenzy had actually got an engagement announcement from a young couple for nine marks eighty; that woman could do anything! When Heber came I gave him no peace till he handed over 98 pfennigs commission. He was horrified at my needing money so soon after my bonus; but I must admit that in the end he showed the true Christmas spirit and gave me a whole mark.

Soon after half-past four I really did get away and dashed off to the Steinmetzstrasse; and the worthy Unger, who three weeks before had broken off his engagement and retrieved his presents, was actually at home. So we came to terms and I bought the fine gold chain with the aquamarine pendant—three marks down (two marks "something else" plus one mark engagement commission) and fifteen weekly instalments of one mark as from the first of January.

My fears that Itzenplitz would be standing waiting for me outside the barber's were not realized. On this day of all days every woman and girl appeared to be having her hair cut. Yet in spite of my frozen feet I was not angry when she emerged with her waves and curls and ringlets, and we flung ourselves once more into the maelstrom of Christmas shoppers. And on my manly bosom reposed the aquamarine pendant.

It was long after nightfall when we arrived home. I seized the bucket and dashed off to the new building site for sand, and the caretaker growled mightily at me for turning up at a quarter to seven with such an order—sand for the cat, forsooth! But at home I found Itzenplitz in despair. Jolly Roger had still not reported with the Christmas-tree stand—and he was at home for we could hear noises. We crept out hand in hand to the dark landing and knocked at his door. We heard him tossing about in bed, heard sounds of snoring and opened softly. In an old bottle a cheap candle was burning, and over another half-empty one (the whole garret reeked of schnapps) Jolly Roger had dozed off. We were, of course, terribly afraid of him, but nevertheless we crept like Indians into his room to search for that stand. The search was soon over—it simply wasn't there. But just as Itzenplitz, with true feminine persistence, was engaged in opening a drawer which could never in this world secrete a Christmas-tree stand, there came a hoarse croak from the bed, "Well, yer young scallywags? Chrishmash-tree shtand? T'morrow fer certain!" He spoke—and slept again.

Five minutes to seven found me racing townward. At Günther's, the ironmonger's Christmas stands were sold out; at Mamlock's the iron shutters rattled down in front of my nose.

At ten minutes past seven I arrived home empty-handed, and there in Rumpelstiltskin's sand bucket, triumphantly draped with a white tablecloth, sparkling and radiant, stood our little Christmas-tree.

Wonderful Christmas, glorious Christmas . . . and Itzenplitz actually began to cry over the aquamarine pendant— "I haven't got anything nearly as nice for you, you know." But the lighter was a good one for all that. And then we stood and looked on while Rumpelstiltskin, with much cracking and tearing, worried his kipper; and Itzenplitz said softly: "We shan't need him next year."

Before the Paling of the Stars

CHRISTINA G. ROSSETTI

Before the paling of the stars,
   Before the winter morn,
Before the earliest cockcrow,
   Jesus Christ was born:
Born in a stable,
   Cradled in a manger,
In the world His hands had made
   Born a stranger.

Priest and king lay fast asleep
   In Jerusalem,
Young and old lay fast asleep
   In crowded Bethlehem;
Saint and Angel, ox and ass,
   Kept a watch together
Before the Christmas daybreak
   In the winter weather.

Jesus on His mother's breast
   In the stable cold,
Spotless Lamb of God was He,
   Shepherd of the fold:
Let us kneel with Mary maid,
   With Joseph bent and hoary,
With Saint and Angel, ox and ass,
   To hail the King of Glory.

Midnight in the Stable

ELIZABETH GOUDGE

IT WAS the snow that made that Christmas such an extra special one. They did not often see snow in the Channel Islands and never before in the children's memory had it come at Christmas Eve, spreading over their familiar home a beauty so new and so exciting that they could scarcely contain themselves. The farm's name of Bon Repos suited it in this weather; there was nothing to be heard but the faint murmur of the sea beyond their garden and the chirping of the robins about their door.

The children fed these robins to bursting point and it was the sight of the little redbreasts bobbing about on the snow like lighted lanterns that gave Colin du Frocq his bright idea. "Let *us* have lanterns, girls," he said to his four sisters, "and go out carol-singing."

"Carol-singing in the snow on Christmas Eve!" cried golden-haired Peronelle jigging for joy.

"We'd hang up our stockings," Colin continued blithely, "go to bed, say good night to the parents. And then we would get up again."

"But would the parents approve?" asked Michelle, the bespectacled eldest, a little primly.

"Can't say," said Colin. "Better not ask them. We've never been told not to go carol-singing."

But fat little Colette, the baby of the family and the only one who still believed in Father Christmas, waxed a little tearful. "If he comes and finds us gone," she wailed, "he won't put anything in our stockings!"

"Leave it to me, darling," consoled Jacqueline. "I'll see to it.

392

We'll write a note to Father Christmas. 'Dear sir, the du Frocqs are out but will be returning shortly. Please leave the customary seasonable gifts. Your truly, the du Frocqs.'"

It was after the midday dinner and the five of them stood outside the front door in the old cobbled courtyard, rosy-cheeked and radiant and apparently entirely oblivious to the cold.

"We'll spend the afternoon in the stable," said Colin. "No one hears us in the stable. We'll practice the carols there and make ourselves lanterns out of the mangel-wurzels. . . . Listen, is that the bus?"

"The bus!" yelled Colette in triumph.

At that time, the end of the nineteenth century, a few farms and a fishing hamlet were the only human habitations in the wild and beautiful part of the island where they lived and their one link with the town of Saint Pierre, a few miles away, was the daily horse bus. The children, cantering like young ponies, reached its stopping place, where four lanes met just beyond their farmhouse, just as Jean the driver brought the clattering old vehicle to a standstill. "Anything for us?" they yelled to Jean.

"Not today, praise be," said Jean winking one eye at them. "I've had my bus so weighed down with parcels for you youngsters this last week that the springs is broke."

"Oh!" chorused the children sadly, then they continued good-humoredly, "Merry Christmas!"

"Merry Christmas!" echoed Jean, and then, turning his head over his shoulder, "This is where you get out, Mamselle."

The children turned their attention to the girl whom Jean addressed as Mamselle. In spite of the clothes that she wore, the clothes of a beggar maid, she was attractive. Her dark eyes had the softness of black pansies in her white heart-shaped face and the hair that escaped from under the rusty shawl she wore over her head clung round her forehead in enchanting brown curls. She was like a flower, a snowdrop or a Christmas rose or a white camellia, and when she stumbled a little getting out of the bus, for she had a carpetbag in one hand and was holding something large and heavy in the folds of her shawl with the other, the children rushed to help her as though she had been the Queen.

"*Merci, mes enfants,*" she said laughing. "If you had not helped me I might have bumped my baby."

"Have you a baby?" they chorused in joy. "A baby? Quick! Let's see!" And they in their fresh young beauty closed in upon hers like the petals of a flower about the golden heart. And certainly it was an enchanting baby, as enchanting as its mother. Its eyes were dark and solemn but young as it was it laughed when Colette was lifted up to kiss it.

"A boy?" asked Peronelle holding out a slim forefinger to be gripped by engaging dimpled fingers.

"Of course," said the girl.

"Isn't he good!" whispered Jacqueline clasping a booted foot.

"He never cried the whole way over," triumphed his mother.

"Over?" asked Michelle. "Where have you come from?"

"From France, Mamselle," said the girl. "I have just landed."

"But where are you going?" demanded Colin. "Who are you?"

The girl's soft face suddenly hardened. "That is my affair, little M'sieur," she said. "And now I must ask you to let me go on my way."

"We'll take you," said Colin gallantly. "I'll carry your bag."

"No," she said firmly. "Do you live here? In this farmhouse? Your mother would not like you to be out in this bitter cold with so little on to keep you warm. I will watch you run home."

She had a strong will, it seemed, beneath her seeming softness, for they found themselves obeying her. At the door into the courtyard they turned round to wave and saw her still standing at the place where the four lanes met. "Good-by," they shouted. "Merry Christmas!"

"Merry Christmas!" she called back and nodded and smiled as they turned in and were hidden from her sight.

"She was very anxious to get rid of us, wasn't she?" said Jacqueline, aggrieved.

"I don't think she wanted us to see which way she was going," said Peronelle, a little puzzled.

"Clever!" mocked Colin. "She was just being grown-up and officious."

Further argument was quenched suddenly by Michelle's question: "How are we to get those lanterns made if we spend the whole afternoon here?"

They started running, everything forgotten except the night's adventure and the preparations for it.

"Come on!" they yelled to each other. "The stable and the mangel-wurzels! The carols! Get the kitchen cushions and the rug from Michelle's bed and come on!"

The moment they had shut the door behind them the du Frocq children knew that some strange change had come over their stable as well as over themselves. Outwardly it looked just the same, with its raftered cobwebby roof from which hung a lantern and bunches of dried herbs and those lovely orange seed pods that children call Chinese lanterns, its uneven floor of rounded cobbles and its dark velvety shadows that were not frightening shadows but deep cool wells of comfort and friendliness. And its smell was just the same—a smell of fields and gardens.

And the animals looked as usual: Lupin, the old fat horse who pulled the family carriage; Mathilde, the sprightly piebald person who did the milk round in the mornings; Albert, Grandpapa's little donkey who had been lent to them for over Christmas; Olivia, the lovely little fawn-colored Jersey cow, who had not been well lately and so had been promoted from the cow byre to the stable; Maximilian, their plumy black mongrel dog, and Marmalade the cat, who was ensconced in a box beneath Lupin's manger with a family of six ginger kits.

And yet it was all quite different. The animals were in a queer mood; aloof, even a little patronizing. The night-black eyes of Lupin and Mathilde were as mysterious as the shadows, and Albert the donkey, usually so meek, was brandishing his tail and stamping his hoofs as though he and not the lion were the king of beasts. Maximilian, though he lay quite still with his nose on his extended paws, was yet quivering with excitement, and the yellow eyes of Marmalade, sitting royally among her squirming kits, shone like lamps.

The children, with Michelle's rug over them, settled themselves comfortably on the cushions and a pile of hay in the one empty stall, with their backs turned to the empty manger, and set to work on their mangel-wurzels, making little windows in their sides with their pocket knives and scooping out places in the middle for the candles to stand. As they worked they sang, Peronelle beating time and leading them in a voice that had a blackbird's sweetness.

It was not until they had finished singing that they commented to each other upon the strangeness of the stable, and then only very tentatively, each afraid that the others would laugh at what they were all feeling.

"It's a nice old legend," said Michelle airily, "that all stables were changed and sacred on Christmas Eve, and that at midnight the animals knelt down and worshiped the manger."

This was an old belief on the island and had lasted for hundreds of years. The peasants still believed it, and the children.

"Wouldn't it be fun," said Colin, "to be here at midnight in our stable and see what happens. I say, you girls, let's get back from the carol-singing when midnight is striking and look."

"Ye-es." Michelle spoke doubtfully. "Perhaps just after midnight."

"Yes," decided Peronelle briskly. "After midnight. . . ."

"Very well," said Michelle airily. "Surely we've done enough lanterns now? It must be teatime. Come on. Where's Colette?"

Turning round they saw Colette behind them at the empty manger. She had filled it with fresh hay and decorated it all round the edge with herbs and Chinese lanterns and now she had climbed inside it and was pressing the hay with her fat hands and her dimpled knees to make a soft place in the middle.

"She's like a bird preparing to nest, isn't she?" whispered Michelle.

"She's like a little angel," said Peronelle softly.

But Colin had no such illusions.

"Teatime, Colette," he roared.

Colette rolled over the edge of the manger like a cherub falling from heaven, picked herself up and trundled eagerly toward the door. "Come on," she cried to the others, standing on tiptoe to lift the latch. "Come *on*."

It was moments such as this one, thought Rachel du Frocq, the mother of the children, as she lifted the old silver teapot in her beautiful hands, that made life worth while. Her eyes passed caressingly over the bright heads of the munching children and met those of André, her husband, opposite her at the old kitchen table, and he nodded, reading her thought.

They were an attractive couple: Rachel, beautiful, strong-willed, tall and proud, with dark hair coiled on her shapely head like a coronet and black eyes whose indomitable fire not sickness, sorrow nor hardship had ever been known to quench; and André, a dreamy idealist whose gentle unselfishness more than made up to his family for his complete lack of any practical ability whatsoever.

But silence never lasts long on a farm and this one was shattered by the sudden clattering entrance of Matthieu Torode, their milkman and mainstay on the farm, come to wish them good night before he tramped off to his lonely cottage.

"Good night, M'sieur, M'dame, Mamselles," he said.

"Good night!" they cried. "Merry Christmas, Matthieu."

"Merry Christmas!" he echoed, his dark eyes suddenly somber.

"So lonely in that cottage of his!" murmured Rachel compassionately. "That wretched girl!"

For two years ago Matthieu, so large and capable and seemingly full of common sense, had allowed himself to be made a fool of by a slip of a girl, Denise Marquand, the granddaughter of the eccentric savage old farmer who owned Blanchelande, the desolate farm upon a cliff-top not two miles from them. When Matthieu had triumphantly announced his betrothal to her Rachel shook her head in gloomy phophecy. She did not know Denise, who had only a few weeks before come from school in France to live with her grandfather, but the name Marquand was an ominous one.

The Marquand farm had for centuries been shunned by the islanders. The present owner, old Alexander Marquand, returned the compliment. He set his dogs upon any but his own laborers who ventured near. He was not even neighborly with the du Frocqs, though friendship between Bon Repos and Blanchelande was an old tradition. In business matters he had for years been rewarding André's fair play with doubledealing, and his friendly greetings with black looks. So no one from Bon Repos except Matthieu had ever set eyes on Denise when she eloped to France with some idle handsome holiday-making Frenchman whom she met down on the sands below her home. Strange stories were told of the old man's rage but no corroboration of them could ever be got out of Matthieu.

"He's not got over it," said Rachel to André, recalling Matthieu's sudden exit.

"Surely," said André. "It was two years ago."

"Two years," said Rachel, "though they may pass like two centuries, do not heal a wound."

"No," agreed André sadly.

398

It was when the children had gone and she and André sat one on each side of the glowing fire that the knock came at the front door. They went together to open it and together they stared in astonishment at the slim girl with her baby.

"Can you give me some food?" she demanded, her clear imperious voice in contrast to her beggar-maid clothes. She swept past them, across the hall and into the lighted kitchen.

"I've enough money left to pay for a night's lodging in the town," she said, "but I'd like food and a rest before I look for it. I'm tired. . . . I crossed from France today." The shawl had fallen back from her beautiful little head and showed her white face drawn with fatigue. "Oh, and could you lend me a needle and thread?" she went on. "My skirt's torn."

On one side it hung in jagged rents round her ankles and Rachel exclaimed. "You fell?" she asked.

"No," said the girl briefly. "At the place where I went some dogs were set on me," and brushing André's ejaculations of horror contemptuously aside she reached for the food he brought her.

"I chose this house to come to because I liked your children," she said. "I met them in the lane this afternoon. Nice children. The children of good parents."

"This baby," said Rachel rocking her knee, "has a good parent, I've never seen so clean a baby." She looked up, her eyes on the black clothes. "You are widowed?" she asked gently.

"Yes, Madame," replied the girl. "But that is not a matter for condolence."

The sudden hardness of her tone opened a door upon a blackness of sordid disillusion upon which one hated to look on Christmas Eve.

"That is past," André said hastily. "That is past."

"Thank God," said the girl.

It was when she was preparing for departure that André, with a flicker of his left eyelid, a half gesture of his head toward the chintz-covered day bed and a whole gesture of his right thumb toward the ceiling, suggested to Rachel that Colin should be put to sleep in the kitchen and his little room given to this mother and child.

But Rachel received these hints with no signs of enthusiasm. "They will give you a bed at a fisherman's cottage I know of at the hamlet of Breton Bay," she said kindly but with the utmost firmness. "The woman is an old servant of mine and I will write a note saying that I have sent you. Tomorrow I will come down and see you and you will tell me how I can help you.

"You will find the way quite easily," continued Rachel evenly. "Take the lane to the right at the crossroads and go straight on."

"I know the way," said the girl proudly.

André, beaten and sorrowful, turned and went out. As he slammed the front door behind him, a voice tolled over and over again in his brain, "There was no room for them in the inn."

Slowly he crossed the courtyard to the stable, for it was time he lit the oil stove that kept his beloved animals warm through the night.

Maximilian, running to him, kissed his hand and folded an affectionate black body round his leg and André suddenly remembered that he always did leave the house for the stable on Christmas Eve. Their dogs always had. . . . Odd.

Dismissing the oddness he fumbled for matches and bent to light the oil stove in the empty stall.

He started and came nearer, then stood gazing, not ashamed of a pricking behind his eyelids as he looked at Colette's Chinese lanterns like tapering flames about the manger.

Half in play and half in earnest he set to work to complete the preparations that she had begun. He tidied the stable, putting in a tidy pile the rug and cushions that the children had left in disarray and finally he lighted the lamp so that it swung like a star from the raftered ceiling. Then he went softly out into the courtyard and neglected to lock the door behind him.

Some hours later in the snowy lane the children stood together in a little group, palpitating with excitement. Everything had worked out according to plan. They had gone obediently to bed and then left the house by way of the back-door porch.

"Where are we going first?" asked Michelle.

"Blanchelande," replied Colin.

He expected an outcry from the girls, for the farm of Alexander Marquand was "out of bounds." But there was no outcry, only a quickly drawn breath of excitement.

The only dissentient voice was Peronelle's. "Won't it be too far for Colette?" she asked anxiously.

"If it is you girls can carry her."

"Carry her yourself," said the girls indignantly to Colin.

"Not going to be carried," lisped Colette indignantly between two yawns. "Colette walk."

"Come on, then," said Colin. "Step out. It's a goodish way."

Blanchelande was true to its name on a night like this. Between the white moonlight and the white snow its gaunt granite walls gleamed like white marble. There were no lights in the windows and no smoke rising from the chimney.

Resolutely the children made their way to the front of the house where a door of such strength and grimness that it seemed to defy all entry faced a littered courtyard.

"Now," said Peronelle. "Do we sing out here, or knock at the door and ask to go in?"

But no one answered her question for suddenly pandemonium broke out in such a fury of barking and baying and snarling as the children had never heard. They had forgotten the Blanchelande dogs. They came streaking out from behind the house.

"Steady, you chaps," said Peronelle's quiet courageous voice. "Stand together with Colette in the middle. Remember that dogs always like us and we like dogs."

Dogs? But were these dogs? The heart of each child turned to water within it.

"There are only four," said Peronelle counting. "Speak to them very politely and hold out your fists for them to smell."

"Good dogs," murmured the du Frocqs courageously. "A merry Christmas. Peace and good will. We're only carol-singers and we don't mean any harm," and they bravely held out their doubled fists to the snarling jaws.

The dogs lifted their inquiring noses to the fists and smelt them, they lowered them to the hems of the children's coats and smelt those, they cocked their ears to the children's voices and gazed with deep absorption at their boots. They were satisfied. Four pink tongues curled out to caress and four tails were raised in welcome.

"Hi! You get out of there!"

The door had been flung open and a harsh voice was shouting at them from the dark cavern within.

"We're carol-singers," explained Peronelle. "We're coming inside to sing to you."

"Oh, are you?" inquired the voice grimly. "Not if I know it. You get along home or I'll set the dogs on you."

"You can't," said Colin. "The dogs like us."

The voice materialized into a tall stooping figure that came out into the moonlight and confronted them, and for the first time the children looked up into the face of the hated Alexander Marquand. He was an old man, fierce-eyed, gray-bearded, with a lean weather-beaten face. Yet the children, who had never yet met cruelty in any form, felt no fear of him. They smiled engagingly.

"Let us in," they pleaded.

Hands in pockets he surveyed them, the moonlight and lantern light illuminating for him their glowing pink cheeks and bright eyes and delightfully bunchy figures, and the dogs standing round them with sterns a-quiver and eyes raised beseechingly to their master's face.

But it was Colette, tired out by the walk along the cliff, who

clinched the matter. Both her father and her grandfather had
gray beards and the very sight of one recalled to her mind strong
arms that in her babyhood had lifted her off her inadequate
legs—Colette's legs had never been equal to her weight—and
a personality from whom emanated all the good things of this
life. She ran to Monsieur Marquand, clasping him with her fat
hands imploring warmth, shelter and an opportunity of sitting
down. "My legs ache," she said.

Before he realized what he was doing he had picked her up
and carried her into his dark stone-floored kitchen, the dogs and
the other children following pell-mell at his heels, and set her
down before the dying fire, staring at them in comical bewilderment.

But the children knew quite well what to do. They pushed
Monsieur Marquand into his fireside chair and gave him Colette
to hold upon his knee; they flung wood upon the dying embers
and lit the oil lamp that hung from the rafters. They took
chestnuts from their pockets—chestnuts were a very important
part of Christmas fare on the island and every child's pocket
was full of them—and set them to roast upon the hearthstone,
and then sitting down crosslegged before the fire they sang.

The years rolled away from Alexander Marquand. All his
bitterness and hatred, his inheritance from a line of savage
forbears, fostered in him by years of misfortune and bereave-
ment, seemed to be going with the smoke up the chimney. Old
memories awoke; the figures of his childhood, the brothers and
sisters who more than a half century ago had sung these very
same French carols; his own dead children, his little granddaughter who used to sit upon his knee as Colette was sitting
now. . . . A bitter memory, this last one. His pride would never
forgive her for the disgrace she had brought upon his name.

"I think we ought to be going now," said one of the children
suddenly. "You see, we want to be home by midnight, so as to
look in the stable and see if the animals are still kneeling down."

Monsieur Marquand started and looked up. For how long

had he been sitting here, eating chestnuts, listening to carols, dreaming dreams and seeing visions? The child, he was astonished to find, was now asleep in his arms.

"I'll come with you," he said, "and carry the child."

The homeward journey was as magical as the outward one. None of them spoke until they were nearly home and saw three figures coming to meet them.

"Mother and Father and Matthieu Torode!" cried Michelle.

"They went up to fill our stockings and found us gone!" said Peronelle. "Idiots that we were not to think of that!"

"You naughty children!" cried Rachel, thoroughly exasperated now that her anxiety was relieved.

"You have made your mother very anxious," reproved André.

Suddenly Matthieu, who had been grinning jovially, saw who it was that carried Colette. "Monsieur Marquand!" he ejaculated, the smile wiped off his face.

"Monsieur Marquand?" asked André and Rachel, astonished.

Monsieur Marquand made a move as though to put Colette into her mother's arms. "May I restore your property to you, Madame," he said coldly, "and then bid you good night."

"No, Marquand!" said André sharply. "You have done us a service tonight and you will come home and have a drink with me."

Monsieur Marquand hesitated, then with a curt nod he yielded.

The first stroke of midnight rang out as the cavalcade entered the courtyard. The four Marquand dogs went like a streak of lightning across the snowy courtyard and the foremost one, making a little crying noise like an eager child, pushed his nose against the door and the four dogs went in.

The last stroke of midnight sounded from the last of the churches, there was a pause then, faint and far away, the Christmas bells rang out in silvery peals.

"Now," said Colin softly and with the now fully awakened Colette close at his heels he ran to the stable door and flung it open.

He was not surprised of course, and neither was Colette, but to all the others what they saw inside the stable had the quality of a blinding vision.

All the animals had gathered round in a semicircle; the horses, the cow, the little donkey, the five dogs and the golden cat. They were not kneeling down now, though Colin stoutly declared afterward that he had heard them get up from their knees when he opened the door. The dogs were lying with their noses on their paws and the other animals were standing quietly brooding, their wide dark eyes fixed on the baby who lay in the decorated manger, in the soft place that Colette's hands had pressed out. Each stalk of hay seemed a line of golden light and Colette's Chinese lanterns glowed like petals of flame. The deep stillness in which they watched lasted for a few more minutes.

It was these minutes that the children remembered ever afterward, and not the swift tumult of following events that seemed a dream. Yet a few details of the dream stuck in their memory; Matthieu's cry of "Denise! Denise!" Denise's face raised to him, white with her mute passion of penitence; old Monsieur Marquand unaccountably bursting into tears and Denise's clear voice, restored to her at last, saying over and over again, "Forgive me. Forgive me, Madame; I did not want to go down to Breton Bay and so I crept into the stable instead. Forgive me, Grandfather. Please, Matthieu, forgive me . . ." Monsieur Marquand asked no one to forgive him though, goodness knows, thought the children afterward, his behavior in setting the dogs on Denise when she tried to go back home had been atrocious enough, but then perhaps his tears, the first he had shed for sixty years, so he said later, were a rich ransom for his evil deeds.

So many things were ransomed by the events of that night; the ancient friendship between Bon Repos and Blanchelande; the old affection between Monsieur Marquand and his granddaughter; the old love between Matthieu and Denise that born again transformed her into Madame Torode, a rosy-cheeked matron who lived in the little cottage in the gorse-filled hollow on the cliffs, and watched her son grow to strength and vigor.

But to the children Denise and her baby were not to be identified with the mother and child they had seen in the stable. No. These were eternal unchanging figures. A mother who would never grow old and a child who would never grow up. The children would probably never see them again; but the animals would. Every Christmas Eve, when the church clocks of Saint Pierre struck midnight, the animals would kneel down and worship what they saw.